THE
MANOR
HOUSE
GOVERNESS

THE MANOR HOUSE GOVERNESS

A NOVEL

C. A. CASTLE

alcove
press

Copyright © 2023 by C. A. Castle

Published in the United States by Alcove Press, an imprint of The Quick Brown Fox & Company LLC.

Alcove Press and its logo are trademarks of The Quick Brown Fox & Company LLC.

Library of Congress Catalog-in-Publication data available upon request.

ISBN (hardcover): 978-1-63910-560-1
ISBN (ebook): 978-1-63910-561-8

Excerpt from *Orlando* by Virginia Woolf. Copyright © 1928 by Virginia Woolf. Copyright © renewed 1956 by Leonard Woolf. Used by permission of HarperCollins Publishers.

Cover design by Jaya Miceli
Illustrations by Tiff Lai

Printed in the United States.

www.alcovepress.com

Alcove Press
34 West 27th St., 10th Floor
New York, NY 10001

First Edition: November 2023

10 9 8 7 6 5 4 3 2 1

To those who've struggled to see themselves, and who struggle to see themselves still—I see you.

Prejudices, it is well known, are most difficult to eradicate from the heart whose soil has never been loosened or fertilised by education: they grow there, firm as weeds among stones.

—CHARLOTTE BRONTË, *Jane Eyre*

To put it in a nutshell, leaving the novelist to smooth out the crumpled silk and all its implications, he was . . . afflicted with a love of literature . . . It was the fatal nature of this disease to substitute a phantom for reality.

—VIRGINIA WOOLF, *Orlando*

PART I

1

TOMORROW THE BUSHES WOULD be stripped of their berries, but today they were abundant and blooming. From where Bron stood, naked at the window ledge of the dormitory's topmost story, he could spy on the gardener clipping away at the stems of a tree. He'd been observing the man's labored reach toward every branch—the length of his torso, the nod of his head with every snip—inadvertently mirroring this man's posture as his own fingers dug into the sill's grooves. Bron held himself out for one last glimpse of his surroundings: the woods on the left, the hills on the right, the pipes trailing the crumbling walls of the school's east court. All the while he was doing sums in his head.

Below, the gardener descended the ladder and raised his sleeves to gather the foliage that had fallen into a heap at the base of the trunk. But captured by birdsong, he looked up to the building's eaves. What did he see there? What did he make of the lone figure framed by the square lattice window, shoulders bare and pearlescent, with hair loose and coiling down sharp, rung-like collarbones, a flat chest exposed? An androgynous statue or a careless young woman trapped in an all-boys boarding school? A school teacher, perhaps, there through the holidays.

The gardener moved to get a better look, when—"Ah, Christ!"—he tripped on a branch, falling to his knees. Above this scene, Bron stepped back and drew the window shut, having finally decided.

Upon arriving in Cambridge, he would take a taxi from the train station to the address on the envelope, a certain Greenwood Manor, which sounded very grand. Google Maps estimated a near two-hour walk to the manor, marked by a red pinpoint, and the weather forecast threatened the usual early September drizzle, so there was no chance of walking. He couldn't show up to his new place of employment drenched and smelling of sweat. What would his employer and new pupil think of him, then? He had to make a good first impression.

The television flickered scenes from Merchant Ivory as he dressed. The boys with whom he used to share these quarters had long since returned home for the summer holidays and were due back in the coming days. The place stood barren, no trace of character or belongings left behind except his own, most of which had already been packed away. He could only carry so much, and the remaining boxes would come to him at a later date, set aside and taped as they were, in the furthermost corner of the room. Inside them were an assortment of clothes alongside his most prized possessions—sets of books by the Brontë sisters; a collection of Austen novels; those of Hardy, Forster, Woolf, and Shelley—all of them collected, over the course of his life, from the high-street's secondhand bookstore, accompanying him through his years like a friend. He opened them up again and again for comfort. He'd highlighted his favorite passages, written notes to himself in the margins, and learned to turn his favorite quotes (*"Reader, I married him"*) into a digital scrawl of black calligraphy which he and thousands of others would post and share across their social media channels. His most cherished book, a hardback edition of *Jane Eyre*, with foiled spine, lithograph illustrations, and a ribbon to mark his progress, was comfortably tucked away in the bag he'd be taking with him.

He fixed his hair, a bobby pin stuck between his teeth as he angled another in before applying a little bit of mascara and eyeliner. When it smudged, he wiped it away and applied it again with a steadier hand. But it was no use. He couldn't get the flick right. He stopped, shut the compact mirror, threw it into the open bag, and turned to watch the screen, comforted by its misty feel, the light it threw across the room, and the soundtrack muffled by aged speakers.

The film had played to his favorite part: a yellow-green poppy field pockmarked red, the display of wild barley and Italian countryside, and those two people who should not have been together by matter of convention, coming together almost in celebration, in tandem with Bron's defiance of what some might call "normal." For times had not changed: boundaries continued to exist, and a child born in possession of an external appendage, or lack thereof, must be either one thing or another.

As someone assigned male but who came to be fond of primarily feminine clothing in his early adolescence, this was not a truth Bron had been born into. It had been an otherwise uneventful Friday evening when Bron stumbled upon Judith Butler's theory of gender performativity on the internet, and such power did he find in those words, where *performance* was no longer a thing ascribed to the arts, but a behavior in which we are all complicit. This theory proved to be a major checkpoint in his life, and with a new mantra to follow, he immediately swapped the shapeless, faded trousers and dull patterned hand-me-down shirts for leggings and other much-loved articles procured from the local Oxfam: high-waisted jeans, frilly blouses, and oversized jumpers that fell just below his natural hipline. Apart from the silhouette sculpting him to appear shorter, he was pleased with this newfound style and would eventually get used to walking without the luxury of pockets at his side. On the weekends he'd haunt the local bookstore in a pinafore dress and trail the fields in a maxi skirt, enjoying the way it flapped in the wind, all the while shrinking at the back of the classroom, during the week, in his stiff collar and baggy school trousers, waiting, cyclically, for his snippet of freedom. It always came back to this claim: *It is the clothes that wear us, and not we them*, and the notion coiled around his mind like a tourniquet, limiting the flow of other thoughts. He was not performing. He was fashioning himself in an already established social structure. He knew the codes, and from there governed his own being.

Bron wasn't a woman—of that he was *fairly* certain—and yet there was no denying that something feminine lingered at the core of his character. He was always more conscious of himself and attuned to the differences between him and his male counterparts. For years he'd prescribed this as merely a gay tendency, very much aware of his attraction to the boys around him, always measuring their nearness. He could recall the summer where things clicked into place, when his dorm mate returned from the holidays quite changed, his voice broken, puppy fat gone from the neck to reveal a more definitive jaw, and a stronger smell about him after PE class. And then, cementing his love for boys, the arrival of his best friend, Harry Blackwater. But as his circle of peers grew into adolescence and the boys at St. Mary's developed that bisexual instinct that pervades such English institutions, he found himself existing outside those circles. And once Bron had graduated from student to teacher's assistant, still he was looked upon as something different. Not quite one of them. Not quite authority.

He turned off the television, after packing the last of his things, and gripped the wooden balustrade before descending the stairs. He would not miss this phase of his life: the regimented row of iron beds beneath the ceiling, slanted like an attic's; the plumed yellow mattresses, streaked like varicose veins; the distressed floorboards, which, though polished in anticipation of the boys' return, did little to mask the scent of rot. And yet he couldn't mistake the swelling of his heart, the stiffness of his neck, for something resembling sadness. This place was all he knew. St. Mary's had always been home. But a new servitude awaited him.

He scrolled to read the email once more. A much-needed boost of confidence.

RE: Application for Manor House Au Pair

Richard <r.edwards@greenwoodcambridge.com>   3:55 PM
to B.Ellis

Dear Brontë Ellis,

Thank you for taking the time to meet with me, via video call, regarding the live-in tutor position for my daughter, Ada, at our country-house residence. I very much enjoyed my consultation with you and was impressed by the more than satisfactory references provided, as well as your academic achievements and work experience so far. I particularly enjoyed your application by hand-written letter, a habit that has fallen quite out of practice. As it stands, I would like to offer you the position, and I would be delighted to welcome you into our home, should you still be interested.

With kindest regards,
Richard B. Edwards

And in the following chain of emails: Bron's acceptance of the role, the back-and-forth toward an agreed-on start date, and finally Mr. Edwards's personal contact number, should Bron need it on his journey.

He zoomed onto his employer's email signature with his forefinger, enjoying the almost clacking sound his nails made now they'd grown long: Greenwood Manor, Cambridgeshire. Cambridge, in truth, was a place Bron had only dreamed about, having experienced its centuries-old magnificence through celluloid depiction and literature—a place of towering spires reaching up to the heavens, of academics strolling about with black winged gowns and reading poetry and Latin aloud on punts.

Access to the University, of course, was not a thing that just *happened* to someone like him. After finishing his mandatory education at the age of eighteen, St. Mary's knew he had nowhere else to turn, and offered him a job as a teacher's assistant. Over these consecutive years he'd applied to the two Oxbridge universities, hoping that in this day and age his grade-A average and position as an orphaned, working-class, queer applicant might help him in his ambition, but *twice* he hadn't gotten in. Though his spirits dampened, all wasn't lost; by the age of twenty-one he'd saved enough of his wages to earn him his escape from the school, and now with a job to accompany him. This wasn't the route his dreams had tread, but still there was something powerful about the prospect of change in both his situation and his surroundings. A great academic he wasn't to be, but a great governess-like figure? Well, that was attainable, almost prophetic.

The journey to Cambridge was to last almost three hours. At the train's window he occupied himself by tracing the high and low folds of the green and yellow fields rolling past at high speed. He caught sight of old villages, followed the length of the marshes, picked out the square of each clock tower before locking onto a large estate in the middle of nowhere, with its large plot of land seen only by some longing passengers at a distance and zipping through the tracks. He was thinking, at that moment, of his beloved Jane Eyre delivering her letter, from Thornfield Hall all the way to Hay, on foot in the bitter cold, and wondered if he too would be tasked with such an errand, and who he might meet on his way.

After the inspector came to check his ticket, and once the train had passed through enough tunnels for him to lose Wi-Fi and his patience with loading reels, Bron opened up his book and spent the remainder of his journey sunk within it.

He'd brought himself up on anything Victorian, everything Georgian, and mourned like a loss his having not been born into one of these earlier times. This yearning for the past was a search for tradition, a lineage—anything to which he could attach himself. It had been easy to forget at St. Mary's, with the daily sermons, the supper eaten by dim light, that what he was seeing in real time versus reading or watching were not one and the same.

These forms of media all provided a soothing nostalgia for a life he'd never known, an escape from the loneliness of every day. And so he clutched at them tightly, pored over the words and shots of characters therein and lived vicariously through them, either by torchlight after dark, or a lit-up ghoul behind a gray-blue gleam of a screen.

The train pulled into his first stop. Bron closed the book and used the ticket as a bookmark—would make a point of holding onto it. This ticket served as a talisman, he thought. The very thing that had brought him to his future, linking him back to his past. A memento mori of sorts. Five syllables forming in the front of his mouth, though he didn't sound them. The old Bron, he'd decided, was dead—had perished the second he'd stepped onto the train. And like Jane's departure from Lowood School, he'd throw off the shackles of his past, and today he would be reborn! But what would that mean for him now, he thought, in that limbo space between Stevenage Station and Cambridge, where he turned outward of the platform, in search of his connecting Thameslink service? He'd need to think about that.

The Thameslink's train carriage was only half full. He dragged his luggage through the tight aisle, passing a suited man drinking from a Styrofoam cup, and a family who'd taken over a four-seater, the table strewn with mobile phones and the cardboard wrappings of a meal deal. He picked a seat at the back of the carriage and closest to a window.

Soon after departure, he spotted a woman sitting in the seat adjacent to him. Bron had no doubt she was staring at him. Her hair was scraped back and hidden under a purple bucket hat, her body devoured by a long black coat, dazzling with brooches. It was a shock to feel, each time he lifted his nose from his book, the brown-eyed glance from her lightly wrinkled face. She held her newspaper wide open, severing head from body and appearing to float. But she wasn't reading. It knotted his stomach, this stranger's judgment. Anger and sadness rose within him. He'd made such an effort to look presentable, professional, maybe even pretty. Put together for the first day of his new life. And for what? This stranger's stare to bring him down.

When the train drew into Hitchin Station, the woman stood as if to leave, but instead she placed a many-ringed finger on his shoulder, which startled him.

"Would you like some tea?" she asked, bending to offer him the flask from her bag. He shook his head, softly declining. Smelling strongly of peppermint, she settled into the seat opposite before pouring a cup for herself. "I had a child about your age. He liked pretty things too." She gestured to Bron's pearls, the pride flag pin he wore on his lapel, and then to her own accessories, as if to say his taste resembled her own. "I'm Ndidi Flanders."

By way of introduction, he told this woman, whom he addressed formally as Mrs. Flanders, all about his reasons for taking this train into Cambridge, about his new position at Greenwood Manor—"Do you know it?"—and his barely contained anticipation for exploring the city. He pointed to the suitcases he'd stowed above their heads.

"Do you always travel alone?"

"No. This is possibly my greatest venture," he said, and felt his mouth break into a smile. "I feel as though I'm stepping into a great novel." He waved his copy of his beloved Brontë book. The text that brought him the most comfort, that had the greatest effect on him—always prompting his thoughts like a ghost, telling him that he could be who he was, dress the way he wanted. The world as he knew it was wrecked—the sneers in the street whenever he walked past, the state of his country, the foul air he breathed—but the poor, obscure, plain, and little heroine got there in the end, and this was the start of his own story.

Mrs. Flanders congratulated him on his move and his starting up at the university: "It's so difficult to get into!" He chose not to correct her mistake and instead allowed her to think of him as some high achiever. This warmed his insides like a hot water bottle. Mrs. Flanders spoke for the remainder of their journey about her son "Emmanuel—El—Ellie," who she said had been a student at Oxford and who was "just like him." He noticed the way she looked at him, and then outside the window beyond, whenever she said her child's name. "But that was all such a long time ago."

When they'd reached their destination and exited the carriage, he appreciated the cold air biting his face. The rain beat down on the overhead structure, and after walking through the barriers, Mrs. Flanders linked herself onto his arm like a limpet, steering him to the bay from which she would catch her bus home. She insisted on his having her telephone number, and before he could ask her to input it into his mobile, she ripped a page from her notebook, held it close to her bag to save it from getting wet, and penciled down an address to which she insisted he pay a visit once he was settled. After helping her aboard the bus and waving goodbye as it pulled onto the road, he tapped her address and number into his phone.

Swallowing great gulps of air, he took in this new life. He'd thought perhaps someone related to his employer might have met him at the station and held up a card with his name, by the taxi rank. Looking anxiously around but finding nobody, he walked across the road to the pickup point and thought how gratuitous it was, his decision to splash out on the luxury of a taxi ride, for he was already soaked through; and by the time a car had come to collect him, the probability of making a good first impression had become all the more unlikely.

2

THE DRIVER DIDN'T HELP Bron with his bags. He'd allowed himself to bring only two: a wheeled travel case and a large vintage bag. It wasn't a fine suitcase of hard leather where initials would ascribe the possession to himself, but something more like a carpet bag.

The car turned the corner of Station Road. Siri was on loudspeaker, directing their switch onto Hills Road, where he saw the Church of Our Lady and the English Martyrs before the car twisted into Fen Causeway. The drive through Cambridge was only half the scenic, sprawling landscape he'd imagined it would be: no bustling students and only a few recognizably medieval landmarks so far this side of town. Over there were the long stretches of countryside, but where were the cows grazing the field, or the university spires said to dominate the sky? If he was honest, it didn't look that much different from the surroundings at St. Mary's. Less dingy, perhaps. Still, he took in the streets and welcomed this lingering yet unfamiliar environment, knowing it to be the perfect rite of passage for any classic literary figure, and he the protagonist.

While he'd been not so much left on a relative's doorstep at birth—no wicker basket and no cotton blanket to which he could cling in remembrance of a time unremembered—his life

had led him onto a similar path to those who had such beginnings. After the sudden death of his parents when he was three
(the details of which he'd never been explicitly told but which
he'd pieced together over the years, to involve "speeding" and
a "midnight jaunt"), his aunt, who'd been in no position to take
on another child, did so with resentment. She shunned him, his
cousins tolerated him, and it was in the pages of literary classics
that he found comfort, sneaking the books off his aunt's shelves.
Ashamed of the effeminacy that appeared more prominently as he
grew, he was sent off to St. Mary's at the earliest convenience—
aged seven—his small inheritance expended to cover the annual
fees. Little did his aunt know that she was merely depositing him
into an environment that would only accelerate his education in
the desires and practices she thought so unmanly.

For rumors abounded at St. Marys' school, of boys sneaking
out, the things they would get up to at night: in the woods; in
the broom cupboard at the end of the fourth floor; in the left-
wing bathroom stall behind the science lab, where the lightbulb
flickered after its being turned on; in beds pushed together when
the others feigned sleep. This lack of discretion was tolerated in
most circles, should they conform to the way of the world. But
come Monday morning, these same lads would enact their tried-
and-true method of averting attention away from themselves by
reverting to everybody's favorite topic: anything from the flower
that Bron adorned in his hair to the fact that he hid a wand
under his pillow to make his lashes longer. So while dirty gossip emerged from the woods beyond the school ground's north
lawn, it was he who was marked for being entirely of a different
kind. Whom one was attracted to was no longer vilified; it was
his femininity they reviled—that is, when they weren't trying to
court or coerce him into playing the girl's part in their nighttime
rendezvous, because they always called him pretty in the dark.

Now he looked at the rearview mirror, where he could see the
driver's puzzled reflection. Bron glanced away, focusing instead
on the large Edwardian houses hidden behind great gates and full

hedges, reading each of their names on the affixed plaques as the car pressed past. Soon, they turned into a side street—feeling the bumps of the cobblestones under the tires—and the tree-lined street darkened their path.

Then the engine stopped. *This couldn't be it.* No houses loomed behind the wall that stretched ahead of them, and the pathway didn't lead into any driveway. Had they broken down? Confused, Bron said to the driver, "Everything alright?"

The man turned his head to the back seat, nodded, and pointed for him to open the door. Bron stepped onto the empty street. The signal on his phone showed one bar. "But where are we?"

The man replied, "We are here."

When the engine revved, he feared the driver would thieve away with his things still inside. He tapped on the car's bonnet until it halted. Muttering something about paintwork, the driver jumped out of the car to finally assist him, lifting his cases out in a single swoop before setting them aside on the street.

Bron asked him which way he ought to go. The driver muttered, "That way," then slammed the door shut, made a U-turn in the narrow street, and sped away.

Bron started walking northward, in the general way of the driver's waving hand. The little arrow on his phone vaguely mapped a similar path, and when the mobile app told him to, he turned into an alley, where a row of plastic wheelie bins had been left disarrayed. He walked through a slightly rusted gate knocked off its hinge and into a grove-like expanse dense with trees, hyssop, and sage. He bent his head to avoid the low-hanging branches, and continued onward, hoping the path would wind into some adjacent street. Instead, the ground filtered into a graveled surface, and his route was barred by a wrought-iron gateway. A stone plaque was affixed beside the door; though choked by moss and worn by time, it read *"Greenwood."*

Before accepting the job, he'd searched Greenwood Manor's Wikipedia page to find it had quite a history, as country houses often do. Once described as a fortified medieval hall, it was sold to the duke and duchess of somewhere or other—he couldn't quite remember—in the early 1710s, when its new owner decided to pull and re-erect parts, in favor of a more glamorous style, before running out of money. After lying dormant for almost two centuries, the manor had been purchased by the Edwards family in 1948, after the war, originally as a plot of some thirty acres, before sections were inevitably divided and sold off. It had also been the shooting location for several BBC productions, including an Agatha Christie drama and an episode of *Britain's Historic Homes*.

Behind the gated wall stood a magnificent structure that to Bron seemed almost a natural part of the environment, to have grown there. The tresses of vine grew stories high, and the gray brick—from which castles were surely made—held twelve-paneled bay windows sweeping the length of its facades, reflecting the sea of green lawn that encircled it. Fields rolled along in the background, and a cobbled pathway, lined with cedar trees, led from the gate to the house and spread in tendrils around all sides of the building. A small fountain burbled in the middle of the manicured expanse, water spouting upward into the sky.

Bron rang the buzzer—unsure which button to press, he decided on the porter's lodge—and a crackling voice spitting from the wedge of the speaker asked for his name and whom he was here to see. He was let through easily enough, and approaching the first pillared porch, he lifted the horse-shaped knocker and waited two minutes before deciding to ring the doorbell.

It was a man who came to the door, in a silken blue dressing gown, who removed a pipe from his mouth and gave him the most quizzical look, eyebrows arched and white and wispy. "Yes?"

"I'm Brontë Ellis, sir. I'm looking for a Mr. Edwards, who should be expecting me?"

"House one," he said flatly, eyes trailing him up and down. "This is apartment five." He shut the door.

Bron made his way around the building, past coppery dahlias and a patch of bright blue delphinium and orange chrysanthemums, and climbed the stone steps that led onto yet another cobbled lane, another stretch of wall. A door signaled number four, and then apartment two—the Hansons, from where he heard another fountain playing, much louder than the first; and down the long, straight path like a brushstroke, a small black gate lay ahead.

Along the balustrades, a door was tucked beneath a stony alcove. He only needed to knock once before it started to edge open of its own accord. Bron didn't exactly leap backward, but was hesitant to step forward as the gap continued to widen, almost in stop-motion. A small pair of hands appeared at the edge of the frame, and soon emerged the form of a little girl, who pressed her body against the door to help it open.

"Sorry about that. This old thing always jams," she said, and offered a half-curtsy. "Bonjour!"

"Hello," he said back.

"Are you alright there? You look a little . . . scared."

"I'm fine," he said, darting his gaze away from the girl's incredulous stare.

"Are you sure?" she said, pointing at his hands, which he saw had reddened at the tightness of his grip.

He set his bag down before considering the girl, who he thought matched the description Mr. Edwards had related to him over the phone. Petite in size and reaching about four feet in height, she had messy locks that flowered into a bun piled atop her head, adding two inches and accentuating the bold features of her face. She wore an off-white tunic with bows at the shoulders, making her look almost like a ballerina.

"Are you Ada?"

"Oui, c'est moi. Are you Brontë? Vous êtes ma nouvelle tuteur? Papa m'a dit que vous vivrez avec nous et que vous allez m'enseigner beaucoup de choses."

"Yes, that's me—hello," he said rather animatedly, overwhelmed by the clarity of her French and how much he struggled

*Soon emerged the form of a little girl, who pressed her body against the
door to help it open.*

to piece together and translate the words. Curse his old ways: he should never have skipped over the foreign dialogues in books, and would download a language learning app immediately. "The cab dropped me off in the wrong place, and I just knocked on your neighbor's door. The guy who answered wasn't very nice and shut the door right in my face and . . ." He pointed behind him to the right, realizing quickly he'd come from the left, and that he was rambling. "Sorry, it's just I didn't know I had to parler français. I'm not very good at it."

"That was probably Mr. Graham, at number five. Don't mind him—he's the absolute worst. I swear I caught him picking his nose once and throwing it into the daffodils—really disgusting. Why don't you come through, and I'll call for Madame Clarence?"

Ada gestured for him to step further into the expanse of the hallway's entrance. She shut a second door behind him, cutting off the natural light, and his eyes adjusted to the darkness of the space. He was conscious of his muddy shoes and careful not to tread the Persian rugs as he followed Ada, who skipped through the hallway into a large open foyer, where a grand staircase trailed up one end of the room. A chandelier glistened in the center of the ceiling, and pillars lurked in every corner. The clean, tiled floor sparkled, and the wooden-paneled walls were etched with cursive shapes and embellished with flowering patterns. He hadn't noticed the woman, who'd been dusting the marble bust of some veiled figure—possibly the Virgin Mary—until Ada pointed her out. The woman perched the duster atop the bust, offering Mary a temporary hat, and brushed her hands on the fabric of her bosom, approaching then to shake his hand.

"Hello," he said, confident in his addressing her. It was she of course, the housekeeper, who would be his confidante throughout his stay here, who was there to guide him through the things he didn't know about the house, about the family. "It is very nice to meet you."

She might have uttered something, but he didn't catch it—she pointed to an armchair, where he eventually settled, in the corner of the room, before flitting away with his bags. When he looked through the open doors beyond the staircase, he couldn't quite tell if it led to another room or if the symmetry of everything was the work of mirrored glass. He was off the chair and back on his feet when he heard his name echoing through the foyer.

"Mr. Ellis?" said the voice. Bron struggled to locate the sound's origin, peering into each of the room's entrances, until he spotted the figure moving toward him. "Welcome, welcome."

"Thank you, sir," he said, presuming that this must be his employer, Mr. Edwards. "How are you, sir? That is . . . I mean, how do you do?"

"How do you do?" He chuckled, holding his hands to his large stomach, which strained against his intricately detailed waistcoat, dressed as he was in a two-piece tartan suit. "Did you hear that, Ada? 'How do you do?' I like him already. Some proper manners, here. What a gem."

Mr. Edwards moved forward and gripped his shoulders. Bron hesitated, unsure how to respond to that showcasing of male solidarity, when the little girl coughed. "Papa," she said, and shook her head. Mr. Edwards looked from him to Ada, back and forth, smiling as though he'd missed something.

"Ah, I'm so sorry, my boy," said Mr. Edwards, his grin depressing into a single line. Bron could smell the alcohol on his breath and felt a slow downward turn of dread in the pit of his stomach. Mr. Edwards gesticulated for a firm handshake instead. "My children tell me I am too forward with people, too excitable, too . . ."

"Embarrassing, Papa. Too embarrassing."

"Oh, hush now, hush. One can never say or do the right thing nowadays, no matter how hard one tries." Mr. Edwards motioned for them to follow him through the archways, through the many beautifully decorated rooms. "This way, this way. I dare say you'd like some tea after your travels, or some whisky? We should have brunch now—how does that sound? Some nice smoked salmon—oh, and you must be shown the house and meet the rest of our little family—where's that son of mine?" he called into the void, then turned to the housekeeper. "Clarence?"

She reappeared in the corner of the room, where she was now wiping down the bust of a Greek face, which Bron guessed could be Apollo. Maybe Zeus. He had no idea. "I don't know, sir," she said.

"He's gone to Marseille for the week. Have you forgotten, Papa?" Ada said. "He left last weekend."

"Ah, that boy," Mr. Edwards replied. "Always someplace or other, and such an extravagant life he leads at my expense. And always causing trouble! Very much a heartbreaker, my son is." Bron wasn't sure if Mr. Edwards winked at him or if it had actually been a twitch. "Don't worry, Ada—it'll be your turn to break hearts soon enough."

"I'm nine," she said.

"More than enough time to work on that particular skill! Worry not, Ada. Mr. Ellis is here to teach you all kinds of things. Then you'll be the smartest girl in all of England." He considered her a moment. "Or Cambridgeshire at the very least."

"The smartest girl?" she said, pondering this. "But not the smartest person?"

"Perhaps if you tried *really* hard," he said, to which Ada gave a little huff.

"Well, perhaps I'm not a girl at all." She smiled.

Mr. Edwards gave a pompous laugh. "Well, if that's what you decide . . . So open-minded, isn't she?" And he turned his head toward Bron, spotting his rainbow-pinned lapel. "Nice badge! That's exactly what we want here. To fit in with the times." Bron was, for the moment, conflicted; at once comforted by their outward demonstration and acceptance of who he was, and yet feeling as though he'd been thrown into the spotlight. "Well, Ada, what have you decided? Boy, girl, friend, foe?"

"Well, I haven't decided yet."

"Plenty of time then, plenty of time . . ." said Mr. Edwards, petering off. "Clarence, it'll be three for lunch. We need sandwiches, tea, salmon, eggs!"

Bron searched for a likeness in these two faces, compared Ada's harsh but pretty nose to Mr. Edwards's dome-shaped one—red, he guessed, from drink—and related her deep brown eyes to those of her father, which were a striking blue. Her complexion was a light honey tan, whereas Mr. Edwards's was fairer and slightly freckled. Finding no resemblance there, Bron deduced they couldn't be blood relations. Was Ada the ward of the house? How would she have come into their care?

"I do apologize," she whispered as they moved toward the sitting room. "I know he talks a lot of rubbish, but he really is the best. He's not like other daddies. He plays cards with me a lot and lets me do whatever I want. He's like a mummy and a daddy *and* a friend, all wrapped in one!"

Mr. Edwards stumbled into an armchair and reached for a glass readily filled with drink.

"It's just sometimes he gets really thirsty."

"I understand," Bron said.

A grand piano stood on the other side of the room, and Bron imagined the spirit of a lady, one of great importance, sitting at the stool and demonstrating her talents, fingers prodding, puffed sleeves beating, to the rhythm of the keys, beside the gramophone that glinted in the dark cabinet behind. He summoned two more women—they might have been three sisters, with varying levels of talent, battling to impress a certain somebody at a party . . . and this *was* the room for it. Atop the piano's belly rose a metallic, domed-shaped cage housing a white and blue budgie in its chest. It chirped, Disney-like, at the sight of Ada's approach, and with a swipe of her hand, she opened the little door. The bird took instant flight, encircling the room once, twice, three times, before perching on her outstretched finger.

"This is Birdie," she chortled. "Original, I know, but I felt I'd run out of options. Before her we had Sontag, named after the day he was brought here, isn't that right, Papa?"

"Right as always, my dear."

"I favored German as a language at the time. We suspect the old dog got a hold of him."

"Yes, we might've had a rather minor incident with Captain. Birdie was meant to be a sly replacement, but nothing gets past this little one."

"Well, first of all, Sontag was green," she said.

"A minor detail."

"And Birdie was brought on a Thursday—Donnerstag just doesn't have quite the same ring to it. She's been with us ever since." She placed Birdie back into her cage before scampering to the Chesterfield settee and coffee table, where a three-tiered stand had been set.

The housekeeper brought in the tea with the china, and Bron nodded in acceptance when she offered to pour it, reaching afterward for the little tongs and bowl of sugar cubes. He dropped two into his cup and stirred while eyeing up the stand that offered egg mayonnaise, plain cheddar, and—notoriously—cucumber sandwiches! He thought immediately of *The Importance of Being Earnest*, and of Mr. Jack Worthing—J. P., as he was known in the country.

"Excuse the lack of variety, but we've gone vegetarian for the week, haven't we, Papa?"

"Oh yes," he said, words spoken between chews, though he appeared to swallow one of the triangles whole. "I was wondering where the salmon had got to. It was vegan *and* gluten-free last month. Very bad. Couldn't cope. Almost died."

Ada tipped her cup, with its tiny print of blue hills, to her face, keeping her pinkie inward. Bron felt suddenly conscious of the way he sipped his tea, how he held the scalding cup not from its handle or saucer, but in the palm of his hand, fearful he would spill it. He set the cup down on the table before going in for one of the sandwiches.

Mr. Edwards soon produced a sheet from his blazer pocket and ran through his list of job responsibilities and the expectations that would be had of Bron, the specifications being much as he'd expected.

"It would be great if you could almost always be available between the hours of seven and eight in the evening, to wind Ada down for the night. Extra tuition can also be worked out between the two of you, around your own schedule, of course . . . you are welcome to a life outside this house." Mr. Edwards scanned the paper again, squinting as though it were a complicated recipe he couldn't understand. "Oh, and yes, discretion, of course . . . discretion. My word, why must it be in bold? Have we so much to hide?" He laughed. "The people we commission to write these things!"

He couldn't believe he was here. Finally in Cambridge. And living in a house like this. "Everything sounds perfect, Mr. Edwards."

"Splendid, that's exactly what I like to hear." Mr. Edwards downed the last of his tea before standing, and handed the paper to Bron. "Now, I will leave the two of you to better acquaint yourselves. Your room, Bron—may I call you Bron?—is ready for you. I'm sure Ada will be happy to escort you there. Ada?"

She mimicked Mr. Edwards by taking one last sip of her tea before jumping from the sofa to stand by his side—"Aye, aye, sir!"—and pulling at Bron's arm. "Alright, let's go."

Ada raced down the hall. Bron wanted to say thank you again to Mr. Edwards for offering him this position, for allowing him into their home, for trusting him and believing in him, for giving him this opportunity. He wouldn't let him down. Instead, he said nothing but left his own cup of tea to sit, undrunk and still steaming, on the low mahogany table, and hurried quickly after her.

Up the stairs she veered right and pointed to each door, identifying them as: "Guest bedroom, guest bedroom, guest bedroom with en suite, this one just a bathroom, guest bedroom again, and that there's the library," and before he had time to reach the end of the way, she spun round on her heels and ventured left, power-walking back. "Guest bedroom, a games room that's really just a room with a billiards table that no one ever goes in, guest bedroom again, and now see here? This is my bedroom"—which he might have guessed from the purple neon sign that hung on the door and read "Stay out"—"and way, way down there is Daddy's room."

"I see." He hesitated before asking, "And where will I be staying?"

"Oh yes, well, you're right here." She backtracked three steps and opened one of the doors she'd only a second ago claimed as a guest bedroom. Inside, the room was fragranced rose, and wallpapered aqua with a green and white flowered pattern. The big window overlooked a garden, offering a view from which the solution to the shrubbery labyrinth could be decoded, all the way to the black gate. When he touched the soft silk of the curtains, they dripped through his fingers like water. The four-poster bed and patterned eiderdown; the intricately detailed cornicing and ceiling rose from which a glassy pendant hung; the fluffy carpet and modern bedside table, where both the *LRB* and *The New Yorker* were open to specific pages for his perusal, it felt more akin to a hotel suite or boutique bed and breakfast than a bedroom. There, too, was a writing desk and a corner sofa cozied up to an emerald-tiled fireplace. Another door led to a brightly lit en suite. Certainly a change of scene from the damp walls and hard bedsprings of St. Mary's.

"So, do you like it?" Ada asked.

He held back from squealing out something overly flowery and sentimental. "Yes, very much so. I wasn't expecting this at all."

"So don't worry about making your bed. Clarence will do that every morning." With a thump, Ada hopped onto the mattress. She lay back, flapped her arms and legs three times like a snow angel, then stood back up to examine the barely there impression left on the taut sheets. "She's truly a wonderful lady. I don't know what we'd do without her. I hate making my bed. Isn't it just the worst?" She tottered to a lower cabinet and opened its doors. "In here you'll find all the different teas and a teacup or two, if you happen to break or lose one, as I always do."

She produced a little kettle, shaking it about in her hand as if to explain that this is how tea is made. "I don't really like Earl Grey—tastes too much like Parma violets. I do like to dip my Nice biscuits into English Breakfast, though. Nice—is that how you say it? It's something of a conflict in this house . . . But sorry, no coffee. We don't drink coffee. Well, except for Darcy. He's always espresso this and double macchiato that, and honestly"— she shook her entire body, as if ridding herself of the ick—"I'd rather drink dirt than coffee."

Darcy? Bron thought. *What a loaded name.* Already he found himself projecting an idea of what this man would be like, who he might become. Mr. Darcy, the almighty lover. *Arrogant. Handsome* (depending on personal taste and the actor who played him—Bron much preferred Colin Firth, though he wouldn't say no to Matthew Macfadyen, thank you very much). *Unapproachable.* "Is Darcy your brother?"

"That's right. His bedroom is way at the other end of the house—you don't have to worry about him. He's never around, even when we beg for him to be. Papa's awfully busy, and I'm quite the loner, or so they say. It's hard not being a loner when I've always been alone. Are you a loner too? Because if you are, maybe we could be loners together. Oh, I bet you had loads of friends at that old school of yours. Did you?"

He thought instantly of Harry, who had once been his friend. His one and only. Until everything came crashing down. Seeing Ada standing there, his mind cast back to the first time he'd met Harry, around the same age as she was now. A dull and wintry afternoon in February, chillier than it was today but with the same sense of electricity in the air, where at any moment something could come to tilt him off his axis.

He remembered the boys, a swarm of them, misting up the school windows with their breath as they looked down at the boy who, crossing the quad, appeared to Bron like a candlestick, with walnut skin glowing ember-like against the falling snow, his gangling arms dripping at the sides like melted wax. The scuffle and scrape of chairs as they all returned to their seats, and then the opening of the door. The headmaster and boy stepping through. The boy introduced himself with an American drawl, his name sounding like "Hairy"—the voice rang in Bron's ears even now, as clear as water. And a cacophony of sniggers, quickly quietened by the headmaster's authoritative stare, had him thinking that this new apparition was an outcast, just like him. Eventually, the boy would take the only available chair, that nearest to Bron.

The sudden burst of confidence he'd felt remained a mystery to this day. But the presence of a new body beside him had his innards burning. What was he to say to this boy who came from outside these walls, who smelled so strongly of the wet green earth? Was this what America smelled like? "Hi, I'm—" He'd used his old name. The one he'd been given at birth.

Harry was not interested in making friends; he tucked his pointed chin into the folds of his arms and all but ignored him. But, for whatever reason, this boy had been sent here, and Bron felt it in his bones—Harry was destined to be his friend, the very thing he'd been lacking at St. Mary's: the Helen to his Jane.

He'd drawn the boy's portrait as another attempt at winning his attention: his head, placed as it was upon his open palm; the furrowed brows, full and tight-knit; and the mount of his russet hair curling like a thousand scribbled doodles. He could still picture it. The hair that he'd amplified to a fully-fledged tendril of flames.

"Show me the drawing, then," the boy had said after shaking his hand. Bron handed it over tentatively. "Cool pic—it's like I have a super power or something."

"I was thinking of the burning bush from the book of Exodus," Bron explained.

"Cool, or like Medusa or something. Snakes!"

And then the two boys who'd come round to them: "Hey there, Harry was it? You don't wanna go mixing with boring

Brontë over there. Only thing he's interested in is that girly old orphan book."

"Or, you know," the other piped, grabbing for the book that'd always sat, perfectly angled, in the corner of Bron's desk, "looking at our bums." They both laughed.

Bron had snatched the book back, tucked it safely away in his rucksack.

"Bron," repeated Harry in that American voice that made the *o* sound like an outstretched *ah*. "That's a nice name."

And suddenly, what had been given to him by his schoolmates as a taunt through the years became the name he'd use as his own, liking the way it sounded in Harry's mouth, the warmth with which it was said. Brawn. Finally, after years of searching, he'd found his confidante.

Bron shook the memory away.

"Friends?" he said to Ada. "I don't know . . . maybe. I mean . . . not really."

"You know I petitioned to advertise for a substitute sister rather than an au pair? But Papa wouldn't allow it."

"I see."

"But would you be my brother or my sister?"

He blinked twice. "Excuse me?"

"I mean, are you a boy or a girl?"

"Oh," he said. This was it, his first lesson. How best to explain it to her? "Well, it's not always as simple as being a boy or a girl. Some people might identify as neither. Some might identify as both. There's a whole spectrum from which to draw. It's pretty wonderful, really, if you think about it."

"Yeah, I know, but what are your pronouns?"

"Oh well, I mean . . ." *He, she, they*—the list hovered on his lips but failed to hit the air. Trying each on for size, he imagined what it would be like to be referred to as *she*. And then she imagined what it would be like to be referred to as *he*. Finally, they imagined what it would be like to be referred to as neither, but concluded that making such a decision would be too much right now. What if he changed his mind?

"*He* is fine, thank you. But it isn't set in stone." Ada tucked her chin close to her chest, unable to meet his gaze. She was pulling at a loose seam in her dress. "Is that all a little confusing?"

"I don't think so," she said. "No, it isn't. He—nice and easy then. Oh . . ." She snapped her head up. "I mean *she* would be easy too, or . . . or so would *they*. I think. I guess I'm still learning."

"That's fine," he reassured her. This was the first time he'd ever been asked. "I'm still learning too. We all are."

"You're just like me, I suppose."

"I am?"

"Yes," she said, crouching to the floor and lying there like a plank of wood. She was reaching for something beneath the bed's grand base, inching in further and further until half of her had disappeared. Her voice emerged diffused. "You don't care what other people think as long as you get to be you. I was adopted, you see. Given up at birth. I have always known it—I've never even met my birth parents. But I still call Papa my father and Darcy my brother because it's what I know to be true. They might just be words, but they mean a lot to me too. Just like your pronouns, I guess. Ah—here it is!"

She dusted herself off and presented to him a matted thing resembling a sock puppet. It was stitched at the edges, though fibers burst through where the thread had come loose, and a yellow clump of string spiraled out the top as hair. Two mismatched buttons for eyes, one larger than the other, and in the middle of its chest was a red blot of paint that, given the pin struck through it, must have been its heart.

"I knew I'd forgotten something down there. Oh, don't look so shocked—it wasn't meant for you. It's just a trick I played on my last tutor, Molly. She was very superstitious of . . . well, everything. I don't suppose you are? But where was I? Oh yes. It's a constant battle, discovering who you are . . ."

3

A<small>T</small> S<small>T</small>. M<small>ARY</small>'<small>S</small> Bron had been accustomed to the sounds of creaking floorboards and bumbling students, but here his new bedroom was too silent, too warm; he missed the familiar smells of the St. Mary's boys, the acrid sweat, the cheesy socks. The snoring to which he'd fall asleep like a lullaby. In the night he battled to tear away the heavy eiderdown, wedged as it was into the bed frame, and in the morning he struggled to leave bed, so comfortable was he. When the alarm clock blared, he twisted to shut it off. The blackout blinds accomplished their task well, halting any stream of light from entering through the window. He pressed his face into the soft pillows, inhaled the clean smell of lavender and chamomile in the linen, and let out a yawn. His stretch was long and liberating, bones clicking.

To the left of him, the door stood ajar, and were it not for the quilted fluff of the carpet, he might have heard the footsteps of the child who now stood at the end of his mattress. He didn't scream—he was used to the sudden appearance of faces at his bed—but he was momentarily fazed into a parallel world where past bled into present, where he was both back at St. Mary's and there at Greenwood Manor.

"Morning," Ada chirped, making him sit up at once. He glanced around, slightly delirious from his not-yet-woken state but conscious of the fact he wasn't wearing any pajamas. He pulled the sheets closer to cover himself, arranging them to appear as though he were just about to get up. Ada didn't say anything more, and he took a second to really look at her, at her cheeks; her upturned lip formed into a perfect bow; her hair, worn much the same as yesterday, only the scrunchie today was yellow; and her eyes, which pierced into him. She was standing with fists balled at her side, ready to levitate into the air at any second.

Was she waiting for his reply?

He said, "Good morning, Ada."

"It's eight AM and breakfast is ready. Daddy insists we wait for you on your first morning, but I am hungry and I shall just *die* if I have to wait any longer."

"I'm sorry. I'll be right down."

"You better be," she said, shutting the door behind her.

There was no time to make use of the luxurious shower. He washed his face and armpits under cold running water in the sink basin and dressed quickly. On the landing, Ada's voice echoed down the hall. He followed it downstairs and into the breakfast room, where Mr. Edwards was pouring tea and Ada was biting her fingers.

"Ah, at last!" said Ada, spooning some beans from a bowl onto her plate. "We can eat."

He made his apologies again and said something to soften his lateness: that his phone had died in the night—he hadn't quite realized the time. He pulled out the chair closest to Ada and sat tentatively beside her.

"What about the alarm clock?" Ada said, now forking some scrambled eggs into her mouth.

"Hmm?" he managed. "Oh. I suppose it didn't go off."

"But I'd set it up for you, to go off at seven fifteen so that we could eat on time. Molly was a late riser too. We were always waiting on her. I just *knew* this would happen. It'll be disastrous, daddy."

At St. Mary's, he'd always been awoken at ridiculous hours, and a lie-in was but a dreamed-of luxury. He looked down at his empty plate.

"Perhaps the batteries need changing," piped Mr. Edwards from behind his open newspaper. "Clarence, could we see that Mr. Ellis gets a change of batteries for his, um . . . alarm clock."

"Yes, sir," said Clarence.

"You will soon know never to be late to breakfast, Bron. Ada is one hungry bunny."

"I'm a beast, and we shan't wait for you again," she warned. "I was on the brink of death."

"Ada, don't talk with your mouth full," said Mr. Edwards, setting aside the paper and sipping his drink before passing over the empty cafetiere. "You've no need of this, do you Bron? I brought it out just in case you were *that* way inclined."

Bron hoped to win some clout by explaining that he didn't drink coffee; he pounced to say he thought the taste to be too bitter, and reached for the teapot instead. He winked at Ada.

She nodded. "It's decided, you can stay."

"And please don't worry about ever going hungry. Clarence starts the day at five thirty every morning, so there should always be food aplenty when you wake. We love to eat!"

How overwhelmed he felt, at first by his being late to breakfast and then by the assortment of food available: the fresh bread in baskets, and on the sideboard behind him, a toaster where he could heat it. The assortment of cereals, granola, and milk options too: oat, soy, almond, and cows'. On the table in front of him, a tray of sliced cheese and deviled eggs, a bowl of scrambled; hash browns; mushrooms; pots of jam, honey, marmalade; butter in its dish; jars of chocolate and peanut spread. In the middle of the table and out of anyone's immediate reach, a bowl of sausages and rashers of bacon. It seemed odd to Bron, who for most of his life had dined on porridge or toast and a glass of orange juice, if he was lucky, that anyone could stomach such rich food so early in the morning. He stood to pour some oats into his bowl, choosing, at least for now, the option most familiar, and added a handful of granola for variety. When he felt no one was looking, he dolloped some chocolate spread on top.

"OH MY GOD!" Ada screamed, at which Bron's spoon went flying out of his hands. What had he done wrong? He spun around. *"Daddy, how could you?"*

Mr. Edwards was chewing on a meaty-looking sausage. They all looked down toward his plate at once: what remained of the sausage appearing massacred beside a generous pool of ketchup. Buried under the bread and eggs, too, was a rather unsuccessfully hidden slice of bacon.

"We're meant to be eating vegetarian!"

"But Clarence put out all this food, darling."

"I know! I asked her to put out some meat for us—it's called practicing self-restraint, Daddy!"

"Now that would be a waste, Ada, and goes against your slowly forming vegetarian principles."

"I'm *so* disappointed in you. Think of the pigs, Daddy. The poor, innocent pigs!"

Mr. Edwards finished the remainder of his sausage.

Bron's settling into Greenwood Manor was not the best of beginnings, though it certainly could've been worse, and he soon fell quite in love with it and all its associations.

Mr. Edwards, he quickly realized, would not be the articulation of gruff masculinity he'd expected from such a character: there was never a furrow upon the brow or a harsh tone used against him. If anything, he thought him more flamboyant than impenetrable, less a man of the manor, with all their domineering ways, and more a liberal-minded man of the gentry. On consecutive occasions did Mr. Edwards come through the door after work (though it wasn't entirely clear what his job was, or what it entailed) and, immediately changing out of his suit, move from room to room in his wine-and-green-tartan dressing gown, always with Ada at his side, and offer to read to her by the fireside or play tea parties before bed. In the evenings, he'd sink into the wing-backed armchair in the library and laugh at the pages of his book—action-leaning titles and memoirs—and would even make the effort to hold light conversation with Bron.

Further to Bron's expectations, the first week of his being there deviated from his initial determination of guiding Ada into her studies. As her governess (yes, he'd decided he liked the way it sounded), he was tasked with developing a bond with this overly precocious child, but she was easily distracted by the many excitements about the house, and while he tried his best to work with her, any attempt to sit still for more than half an hour was time well wasted. It was mostly play she was after: dressing her dolls, catch in the grounds, even hide-and-seek. On the third day, he'd lost her for almost two hours. Not that he could blame her—she breezed through the math worksheets he'd prepared, already understood the components of an atom, and could summarize to him a surprisingly good account of nearly every book on her reading list. She even had a fun fact to spout about each one: "Did you know that *Animal Farm* is actually about politics and not really about animals at all?" or "Did you know that Jekyll should be pronounced 'Jee-kull' as in *treacle*?"

Bron hadn't known that at all, would even go on to verify the fact online—and indeed, he learned that an MGM film adaptation of the novel from the 1940s cemented 'Jek-ul' into our cultural consciousness forevermore. She declared Dickens to be "the most horrible writer," and *A Christmas Carol* to be "the longest, most stupidest book in the whole wide world!"

"I didn't understand half the words I read, and I know a lot of words because I'm smart."

"You are very smart," said Mr. Edwards, flipping through paperwork at his desk.

"Now I know not to suggest *Bleak House*," Bron said.

"Is it bleaker than *A Christmas Carol*?"

"Much bleaker," he answered.

"The bleakest," said Mr. Edwards without looking up.

"And what does *bleak* mean, exactly?"

He thought about its meaning, wanting at once to say "depressing" but thinking it not quite right. "Well, I suppose it means something like barren or cold, like a gray sky—"

"Think of Aunt Rosie," Mr. Edwards supplied. "A mind-numbingly bleak woman."

"Okay. And is it true that Charles Dickens was paid for every word he wrote? Is that why his books are sooooo long and sooooo boring? Maybe he's just like Mr. Scrooge!"

"I think that's just a myth. He might have been paid per installment—"

"Can I read something by a girl next?"

Later, Bron searched the shelves for something appropriate and picked out Louisa May Alcott. He was ready to show Ada his selection, when he found her at the kitchen island, scribbling away at a drawing. He made himself a mug of tea before setting the book at her elbow, peering over her shoulder while the bag diffused. Half expecting to find a work of genius, he smiled at the stick figures.

"I've got something for you," she said, producing a little box from the plastic bag on the floor. "It's another alarm clock, to help you wake up in the mornings—oh, and batteries for the other one. Whichever you prefer."

"Thank you, that's just what I needed," he said, accepting them. "Hey, Ada? I've noticed that you know quite a lot of stuff. Much more than I did when I was nine. Why am I here if you know all these things already? What would you like to learn?"

"You're here for company, I guess. *Finished!*" she declared, smacking down the crayon so hard it almost snapped it half. "See here—that's me in pink, and there's you. I didn't want to use blue, so I thought how about a beautiful yellow? Like a daffodil or a sunflower."

She had drawn a figure on each side of the page. Her own pink figure was short, wore a triangular skirt, and had long brown lines for hair. The figure representing him was tall and drawn aslant. It wasn't clear if he was wearing trousers or a skirt;

the squarishness of the bottom half kept it vague, and he liked it all the more for it. Shapes that she declared were books circled their heads like halos.

"It's brilliant, Ada. Why don't you draw Mr. Edwards now?"

"No, I'm tired, and it's perfect as it is."

"Company," she'd said, but he didn't think his company was much of a necessity. Mr. Edwards had plenty of time for Ada, and she had plenty of time for him. Bron would often declare it bedtime, only for Mr. Edwards to counter his misplaced authority by suggesting it to be too early (despite his having been the one to set her routine in the first place) and request she stay up just a bit longer. Sometimes he'd dance with her on the tips of his toes, jump to the muffled scratchings of a vinyl on the record player (often Whitney Houston's "I Wanna Dance With Somebody" or ABBA's "Dancing Queen," at Ada's request), and through the nights Bron would sit, pretending to enjoy the spectacle while keeping an eye on the decanter of whisky on the drinks trolley, which drained and replenished itself at an impressive speed.

"Ada, don't you want to go to a real school and mix with people your own age?"

"Been there, done that," she said, sticking the drawing on the industrial-size fridge with a magnet, only to pull it down and scribble at it again, adding her signature and the date. "School's the worst. I was always getting in trouble with the other children, and it was awfully far away. All the way by the sea. Darcy liked it when I went away, but Papa never did."

"I'm sure that isn't true, Ada. I'm sure your brother loves having you around."

"Nuh-uh, you're wrong."

By the second week, the remainder of Bron's belongings had been delivered, and the boxes were unpacked. The clothes hung neatly in the vast cupboard space, and his books lined the shelves and empty windowsill. Three weeks in, and Greenwood had started to leave a somewhat marked impression upon him: a tendency to opt for his wine- or emerald-colored velvet blouses in the evenings, for these, his most opulent pieces (designer finds purchased at a bargain), complimented the wood-paneled walls most perfectly, and the Edwardses always dressed well for dinner. Through the day, he leaned toward swishier layers: a long skirt, frilly blouses with a lettuce-edged neck, and a cardigan. Simple clothing in drab colors—dark blues, gray, black—that gave him a sense of movement as he wandered the house's many rooms. Something a governess might wear in the twenty-first century. However, he was soon ready to make his excuses to get away, claiming the need to post a letter to a friend, though no one batted an eye at his departure. For his first outing, he chose an understated set of pieces, matched with a mustard shawl to keep his neck warm.

He ventured into town with great eagerness, allowing himself to haunt the cobbled streets and explore the courts and quadrangles of the University City. Here he was, wandering through a place he'd only seen depicted through media, architecture made true by a perfectly angled camera shot, or inked and printed into existence. He took a selfie on the King's Parade outside the big college, geotagged it "King's College, Cambridge," and uploaded it to his social media, where few people followed him.

No beadle barred his entry as he tailgated another student through the door cut into the larger wooden door, but he *was* surprised to find the big sandwich sign that stood outside it, detailing opening times and ticket prices. He was saddened, even disgruntled by this; he'd certainly never seen such signs depicted in the movies that were filmed here. Now the beadle was a faceless sign who made a profit off the tourists, who dotted the city with maps pressed to their faces, and who exchanged their tickets for entry into places they couldn't otherwise access. When he thought of the extortionate tuition fees it cost to study, and the lengths he'd had to go through to stand even a chance of his application being accepted, he concluded that perhaps being a student here was just a more embellished variety of a ticket. Adult (eighteen years or older) admission: nine pounds. Student tuition (excluding accommodation) home rate: nine thousand two hundred and fifty pounds a year. International . . . too much for his mind to wrap around.

But admittedly, the grand structures he'd envisioned had a hundred more spires than these did before him, and he struggled to find a high dome from which the old city could be encompassed. Afterward, he walked the length of the Huntingdon Road, eager to find that point where the crests of the rotundas would paint a hilly sprawl on the landscape, where the troughs were spiked by chapels of the oldest stone, and the pinnacle spire of the city would catch the rays of the sun as it dipped below the rim of the world at the end of a September day, whether in 1919 or now. But so far it hadn't mapped out as magnificently as he'd hoped, and he wondered if Greenwood's splendor played a part in his disappointment of the city, or if Oxbridge was only a reality of the imaginary. Truly a city of . . . what was the phrase? *Aquatint.*

When he reached Girton College, he was charmed by the immediate difference in the buildings' color; the Victorian red brick somehow more welcoming than the vastness of the grounds of St. John's, the creamy champagne of Peterhouse and Clare, or the gate that barred him from Gonville & Caius. He hadn't seen much of Girton before; the period dramas were not so fond of this place (maybe it was something about the way red brick caught on camera?), but it was precisely how he had imagined it to be upon first reading about this very Girton mentioned in the pages of Virginia Woolf's *A Room of One's Own.*

Standing outside the building, Bron felt a sudden surge of pride for the past, pride for women and the fiction they were able to produce. Women who, like him, defied their expected gender roles, usurped the patriarchal system. These were the footsteps he imagined himself walking in too: to not feel like a man, to not be a woman, to exist as a symbol of society's tensions.

Returning to the manor that afternoon, he walked straight into the library to find Ada draped across the carpeted floor with a large number of envelopes fanned out before her like a double rainbow. She brought each to her mouth and licked them shut while Mr. Edwards sat at his desk and cradled his phone between his head and shoulder.

"Who knew I liked the taste of envelope adhesive? Oh, there you are, Bron!"

Madame Clarence sat in the armchair, sewing, and paid particularly close attention to Bron, sizing him up. He pretended not to notice, but felt suddenly very conscious of his body movement.

"I need the most impressive balloons imaginable, ma'am," blared Mr. Edwards on the phone. "Five hundred of them. I'm throwing a ball, you see."

Bron crouched on the floor by Ada and helped her seal the thick manila envelopes, the house's crest stamped on the back. "What's going on?" he whispered between licks. "What ball?"

"Oh, we're throwing a party for Darcy's birthday. He's usually on holiday and difficult to get hold of. Never with us! Age is a sensitive subject with him, you see, so he likes to think he can escape it, doesn't he, Papa?" Ada threw her head back for confirmation, but Mr. Edwards was negotiating the parameters of inflating so many balloons. "Make it a thousand balloons, Papa— oh, and don't forget to ask about the ice sculpture. Anyway, Darcy will be twenty-nine soon, and he's coming back for it. We can't not do anything. Twenty-nine is basically thirty, right? And thirty is a big birthday. I texted him to make sure he was really coming, and he actually responded to say that he was! Quite late that evening, he said. Not to wait up. But we must do something special, and Papa let me decide, and so . . . it is . . . a ball!"

Bron had yet to meet this son and brother so often spoken about, and wondered if he would be invited to this ball. He really hoped he wouldn't be; what would *he* do at a party? And the last few weeks of getting to know Ada and Mr. Edwards had pretty much drained him of social interactions. Here was an opportunity to recharge, a night off.

"I hope you enjoy your ball, Ada. I'll be sure to peek out the bedroom door."

"You will not peek!" She stood up suddenly. "You are coming, aren't you? I mean, you are invited, you know. Of course you're invited. Anyone and everyone with a pulse is invited!"

A night off it wasn't to be. And he was suddenly conscious that he wouldn't have anything appropriate to wear. More than this, he wasn't sure what he'd be *expected* to wear. He felt the temperature rise within him.

"I wouldn't want to intrude."

"You won't be intruding. Darcy doesn't have many friends here, just like me and you! Papa and I wrote out all these invitations—most are to strangers. See? Like this one to Mr. Fortescue from Searle Street; he fixed our washing machine once. Or that horrible old man who sells those awful ceramic dishes from India—what's his name?"

"Hindes, dear. Christopher Hindes," said Mr. Edwards, having hung up the phone. "Not horrible, mind you, but a bit of a scammer. Duped me into buying bricks of Marlborough Gold years ago for almost double the price."

"See, they're all rotten—they'll just grab my cheeks and tell me to run along like a good little girl. But it's a night to have fun, an occasion to dress up, and Daddy, well . . ." She turned to her father. "He likes the food and drink. Daddy, please tell Bron to come. Please?"

Mr. Edwards was scribbling away at a piece of paper, his face so close to the table that Bron thought he could have been analyzing the properties of a speck of dust and writing down his findings.

"Bron, please attend my son's birthday party," he said.

"Say yes or I'll have you fired!" Ada said, leaping into his arms so suddenly he almost didn't catch her. They tumbled onto the floor.

"Alright, alright," he said, laughing and thinking how he'd gone from feeling so alone in the world to being so welcomed, almost manipulated into attending a stranger's birthday party. "Okay. You win. I'll come."

"Yes!" she screamed, pumping the air with her fist, a sign of victory.

On the morning of the party, the house was infiltrated by every service imaginable. The catering company were in the beginnings of building a sushi stand in the middle of the foyer, while the young man interning at the Botanic Garden had arrived to prune the shrubs, only to declare them cultivated enough, and so helped the gatekeeper erect a gazebo and marquees in the garden to extend the courtyard into the paths approaching the orchard. Men leaned from ladders, fitting a net to the ceiling to fill it with a multitude of inflated balloons. Bron found Ada perched on a stool in the kitchen, legs swinging as her face turned blue, blowing up yet more balloons. He helped her bring them to the foyer, where they passed them along to the men who held the net aloft. They made quite the assembly line, continuing until the net was filled with colorful blues and reds and yellows that shone when the spotlight switched on.

At midday, Bron was asked to pick up a few bits for the party that Ada declared had been overlooked: party poppers for the grand entrance, birthday candles, and the numerals two and nine to be added to the top of the cake. Once he'd obtained these, Bron spent the remaining hours navigating the city, the great flâneur (or flâneuse) that he was, lingering in the crannies of forgotten places where the limestone was a pallid pink, looking up at unlit gas lamps, black pillars that rose into the sky. He strolled past the café windows and the swivel racks of photographs, the Cambridge University jumpers, the fudge and the tea. Down the Senate House Passage, where a hundred years ago men rioted and threw eggs over the vote on women's' right to take degrees, and over the bridge where

Bron found signage—again!—barring his entry into Trinity College. Students, students everywhere! Four PM, and some already in gowns, ready for the college meal; others probably rushing toward one of their many societies; and the rowers in their rowing kits, pumped for another workout on the water. Bodies rushing toward the river, toward their colleges, the splendor and newness of the place forever wearing itself on their faces.

A group of them, having just emerged from the college, stood in a circle outside. The girls listened to one charismatic boy, and he too was captivated by his voice. It wasn't what he said, but the way he said it: with an intoxicating smile, glinting teeth, and a sweep of the hand through his buttery-blond hair. Words that rolled off the tongue, the poshest of accents, pressed and perfectly ironed out, like the branded fleece sweater he wore over his shirt, compelling his audience in the way he spoke of his gap year in Africa, which he'd spent riding elephants. The girls' responses varied: some of them were charmed, bodies angling toward him, though one girl's cigarette bounced in her mouth as she alerted him to the fact that elephants weren't actually good at bearing loads, that carrying humans every day leads to spinal injuries, and that it was a very poor way to spend his time. This caused him to change the route of the conversation, to asking what they all thought of their classes.

Edging toward the college entrance, Bron overheard two of the girls whispering and then laughing: "Doesn't he just *stink* of money?"

He hated all this. He hated it. Such a brandishing of class and access made him feel his worthlessness all the more. What was he but a thing existing in an in-between—here in the great academic city, and yet on the wrong side of town versus gown. Living in a great house, with a great family name, and yet not a part of it at all: not as lowly as a housekeeper, and yet there only on the grounds of employment. His social standing was ambiguous, undefined; "working class" felt like a jacket he wore that itched throughout the day.

"It's considered the greatest love story ever told, but she was only fourteen! What about consent? It's such an important part of feminism, and it barely came up in the discussion. If it happened now, Romeo would be considered predatory. Con-sent: it sounds somewhat like a gentleman's title," the boy said, emphasizing its two syllables. "Viscount Montague, Lord Apperol Spritz, Consent Beauregarde."

Bron approached the group hesitantly, asked if they might know how he could get in, he seemed to have lost his student card already, such a klutz he was.

"Here you go." The girl who'd spoken against the riding of elephants flashed her card to the chipped black box and held the door open for him. She rolled her eyes as the boy continued his chatter by launching into a tirade of buzzwords he thought might impress them. Bron thanked her, stepping through.

He walked along Trinity's Great Court, in the midst of which stood a gothic fountain encircled by pillars. The surrounding buildings were long and lean and imposing, their magnificence taunting him with each step he took, a porter saying he didn't belong there. But just like that, here he was, existing in the Cambridge he knew and longed to see. Was he an actor, playing his role by hurrying along the cobbled lane and cautiously avoiding the close-shaven, grassy-turfed square despite the temptation to walk across it? Or was he real, and the fictional world suddenly made real too, manifesting around him? He listened to the click-clack of his boot heels as he went. It gave him an extra confidence, the sound like that of a woman's stiletto, as he turned into Neville's Court.

It had quickly turned to dusk, and the blueish mist rolling up the grassy banks of the river and hovering made him think of chimney smoke and earlier centuries. Stragglers huddled, smoked in quilted shadows against the walls. Others emerged from the Wren Library, glided along the way in fluttering black gowns, carrying books close to their chests. Bron could have sworn that one of them threw him a disdainful glance. *They know, they know, they know.*

Exposed, and on show for this world to look down upon, he took out his phone as a distraction and—Oh gosh, he hadn't realized the time! He quickly turned to rush out of the square, blind to the man walking toward him—felt the slip beneath his feet and two cries ensued. He felt a hard knock against his shin and his yelp was met by a twin exclamation and a curse.

Somewhere in the quad, a bark stirred the air. He soon felt the nuzzle, the slobber at his face—no Gytrash was this, but a dog that he pushed away before clambering up from the floor and picking up the spilled contents of his bag. Everybody's eyes on him.

The gray dog continued to bark and bound toward the fallen man, reaching onto its hind legs and encircling its owner. The man, brushing at the arms of his coat, was swearing, shushing, and patting the dog at his side. "Calm down, Captain, calm down, boy, you stupid dog!" Captain continued to bark and scratch at the ground.

Bron was desperate to flee, embarrassed by the commotion he'd caused and for knocking this man down. Nervous and hot in the face, he reached out his hand to help. "Are you alright?"

Having ignored him, Bron watched in awe as the man, who he guessed might be in his mid-twenties, rubbed at the dog's snout till he had calmed, before going on to examine the cuff links on his sleeve. He was handsome, in a way that could only be described as fictional, unreal—with a dark but subtly fine air about him, looking as though he might have stepped out from the set of some modernly stylized Austen adaptation.

Noticing the cane at his side, Bron bent forward to pick it up. But the cane turned out to be a very elaborate umbrella. And with this stranger's belonging now in Bron's possession, he thought it best to ask his question again, fearing that the natural quiet of his voice hadn't been loud enough to hear. He repeated a variation of the question: "Are you hurt?" He needed to be useful, or at least appear to be useful. "Is there anything I can do to help?"

Nervous and hot in the face, he reached out his hand to help.

The man uttered a quick retort with such an energy it forced him upright from his slightly kneeled position: "No, you bloody well can't." Every word a plosive, he snatched the umbrella from Bron's grasp.

Bron backed away slowly, letting out an "oh" that was also a breath. The fictional moment vanished; the pointy chin, the slightly curling hair, painted to him an image of a man he would be best to avoid. He offered his apologies again and turned on his heel to leave.

"Hey," the man said, "would you mind retrieving my hat?" His voice was a little less venomous now. "It's rolled away."

Bron obliged and went for the abandoned hat, which had rolled, indeed, quite a way down the colonnade. Giving it a slight brush and noticing the hardness of the thing, he handed it back, surprised when the man thanked him.

"And would you help me up?" the man said. Bron gave him his hand, small and limp, compared to the man's, which looked far too big.

When they again faced each other, the look Bron received from him was one he couldn't at first understand, a mix of both interest and confusion. Bron understood this man—so heroic did he look in his hat and dark coat and with the kind of physiognomy that enabled him to defer a whole life from a single glance—to be judging him. Take his nose for example, with its aquiline arch . . . And from there he envisioned a moment. How many times had that nose upturned itself toward the likes of him, sniffed at those who worked essential jobs, meanwhile quaffing a rare expensive whisky at the Ritz? As he brushed himself off, the dog keeping to his heel, Bron paced back, to stand away.

"Do you live in one of the rooms here?" He gesticulated with his umbrella toward the buildings surrounding them. "I could walk you there as a sort of reparation, for my severeness just now."

The man was taller than Bron, rising to around six foot three, with a couple of inches added on by the towering hat. Bron's own face came to the height of his shoulders.

"No, I'm afraid I don't."

"Oh, my apologies. I'd thought these quarters were private." He gestured to the sign at the end of the way, the one that read, "College closed to visitors. Trinity members only."

"Sorry, I was—I was just cutting through—"

The man smiled at Bron's sudden fumbling. "Don't worry," he said, taking a step closer toward him. "Your secret is safe with me."

Not knowing what else to say or do, Bron thanked him.

"So which college *are* you based at, then?" the man pressed.

This was the second time he'd been mistaken for a student, a thing he'd wanted but failed to achieve, and felt it on his lips like a crack, the ease in which he could alter his reality, pretend to this stranger that he was indeed a Cambridge student, as he had with Mrs. Flanders on the train. It would be easy enough to purport for the duration of what was only to be a short conversation. But up at Greenwood, he was living a different sort of life, an impressive one, nonetheless, and it was bound to unfurl into something beautiful.

"I'm actually not a student at all. I live much further west of the city, in, well, in a mansion, really, on the outskirts of town. It's like . . . like something out of *Downton Abbey*." *Just like Thornfield Hall.* There was no need to overly embellish the grandness of the house, for grand it really was, and it was sure to impress this stranger. He felt a certain amount of prestige boasting about it, liked the way it tasted. "You really wouldn't think places like it existed anymore."

"Well, I wouldn't say that," the man said. "Highclere is beautiful around the Christmas season. But a Downton you say? And what is the name of this haven? I might well know it."

He hesitated giving this stranger the house's name, the address at which he lived. "I cannot remember."

"Ah, I see. So you're clumsy and forgetful?" He laughed, but the way he turned away from him, as though he could be dismissed at once, made the insult sting.

Bron couldn't control himself: "Greenwood."

The man halted in his tracks.

"Greenwood?" he heard him repeat.

"Yes. Do you know it?"

"Know it?" The man turned to face him again. A pause later, he said, "No, I don't know it. Not well enough, anyway. And how long have you been in Cambridge, did you say?"

He suspected this question, quick as it was to be asked, to be an absentminded gesture posed not with any desire of hearing an answer, but as one lobbed for the sake of enabling him to ask another. He kept his answer vague. "A couple of weeks, give or take."

"And how is it that you've come to reside in such a place?"

"I'm employed by the owner. Not like a housekeeper or anything. I tutor his child. Well, I'm sort of like a governess."

"A governess?" he said, lips curling upward into an almost smile, perhaps not because of the answer he'd given, but because of the seriousness of its delivery.

"Yes, but I'm not sure she needs much of my help." He offered this bit of information as a gesture of goodwill.

"Well, how *utterly* amusing." The man's face broke into a grin, his tongue furling over a neat set of white teeth. The way he tossed his head aside was surely an attempt to hide it. Bron felt suddenly like the biggest joke in the world. "Intriguing even . . . So what do you call this?" The man prodded his finger at him, into one of the holes of his patterned shawl. "It's awfully garish."

He was used to these sort of comments, had even expected it from this man—the nose told all—but still he felt a chill run through him as he took in this stranger's words, words which jammed in his sternum. This was the thing about people—they always had opinions to share, and when it came to him and his clothes, they felt all the more convinced of their right to air them. It is inherent to our species to comment on people's appearances, some going so far as to advise what one could or should not wear.

A trifle though it may seem, everybody, at some point, is interested in fabrics and plays the role of the tailor.

He flung the man's hand away. "I'd prefer it if you kept your thoughts to yourself."

"Well, I beg your pardon," the man said, shocked at the outburst. "I was only—"

"What? Did you think you were being polite?" He spoke with confidence; closed his remark with a breathy and sarcastically considerate *sir*.

"Oh, I have touched a nerve." The man paused, looked him up and down once more. "Perhaps it'd be best if we forget this little episode ever happened and say our goodbyes for now."

"Goodbye," Bron said, refusing to shake his outstretched hand. "I'm sorry to have tripped you over." And with a click of his heels, he walked away out of the college grounds, feeling the tears prick at his eyes, and cursed himself for ever having thought that a collision could result in a meet-cute. In reality, men continue to be assholes.

He would definitely be late getting back for the party now.

When he finally reached the house, he made his apologies to Madame Clarence, who had been waiting for him at the door. Mr. Edwards soon bellowed, "There you are, Bron!" and pulled him toward the kitchen for a quick chat, but it was Ada who noticed he'd been crying as he handed over the contents of his bag. He couldn't find the party poppers anywhere. "I'm afraid I must have dropped them," he said, quickly explaining that he had fallen, but withholding certain crucial details.

"No worries, no worries—it's time to get dressed!"

Bron climbed the stairs quickly to his room and shut the door behind him.

4

M R. Edwards walked into Bron's room without knocking, carrying several hangers draped in plastic, which he soon laid down onto the bed.

"Take your pick of suit, son, take your pick!"

Son. Bron rose from the ruffled bedspread to consider the suits and rested his palm on one of the plastic coverings, smiling at Mr. Edwards to show his appreciation. *Son* was not a word he could carry, nor was it a word he'd ever had to associate with. *Boy* he was used to. *Boy* was thrown around at St. Mary's all the time and could mean any number of things or could address any number of persons. But *son* . . . it was for other things entirely— shoved down his throat, a word sandwiched between words that meant nothing and everything. A daily ritual, said in the morning at assembly, between each lesson, and at night. In the name of the Father, and of the Son, and of the Holy Ghost. He was nobody's son, nobody's male anything, and certainly nobody's child. No one had ever called *him* son.

"Well, what do you think?" said Mr. Edwards, taking one from the hook and holding it up for him to inspect. "I rather like this one, myself."

Bron felt an overwhelming heat flush his cheek. "I thought I'd just wear my own clothes, sir." He looked over to his wardrobe, then peered down at the clothes he was wearing. He looped a finger into the knitted shawl, but it hung limp and ridiculous at his neck. "Is this not appropriate?"

"Well, I wouldn't wear it myself. Not to a party." Mr. Edwards led him with a kind hand toward the freestanding mirror and unzipped the bags from their hangers, passing the suits along one by one. Like a good son, Bron inspected the detail on each cuff, the fabric of each lapel. He recognized how expensive and delicate they were, these brands he'd never thought he'd wear. When he carefully set one aside, Mr. Edwards would bring it back again for reconsideration, scrutinizing and then pointing out the feature that made each piece unique.

"But where did they come from?" Bron finally asked.

"These are just a few of Darcy's old things—oh, do not fuss; he won't mind at all. He hasn't worn them in donkey's years."

Bron quickly searched the inside label for his escape route, suppressed an outward sigh of disappointment but felt internal relief. "I'm awfully sorry, sir, but these are just too big for me."

"Don't worry at all about the fit. Clarence has already seen to that."

"She's taken them in . . .? All of them?"

"One can never have too many blazers." Mr. Edwards handed them back in a loop that moved more quickly with each rotation. "Oh! Was that the doorbell?" said Mr. Edwards. "The guests must be arriving." He backed out of the room slowly, pointing and nodding and mouthing the words "that one" before closing the door.

They were all the same to Bron—blazer, shirt, tie, trousers, blazer, shirt, tie—uninspiring and everything he hated. He might as well slip back into his school uniform; at least there'd be familiarity in that prison. The suits were indeed perfectly tailored, some of the trousers appearing never to have been worn; they clasped about his waist so accurately he wondered how Madame Clarence had guessed his size. The shirt was a pristine white, and the embellished blazer a navy velvet. He panicked when it dawned on him that neither of his two pairs of shoes would match the Edwardses' expensive taste, but sure enough there was another tap on the door, and he opened it to find a pair of black suede loafers at the threshold, crossed as though a ballet dancer's feet were en pointe. He noticed they had quite a large heel to them, and appreciated Mr. Edwards's thoughtfulness. Mr. Edwards had only ever been kind to him, and the night wasn't about what Bron wanted, after all. Dressing the part would be expected of him. A shirt is a shirt is a shirt. A tie is a tie a tie. There was nothing more to it than that. He wanted to be a good "son," whatever that meant.

When he dressed, the mirror showed his doppelganger, the person he was supposed to be—he was particularly surprised by how handsome his reflection shone, and brushed another hand over the velvet tux, adopting the ballerina's position when he felt an itch on his ankle. *Just for a night,* he said to himself. *This doesn't change me.* But he would wear at least some items that were his— he swapped the tie for a set of pearls around his neck and finished the look with a metallic-gold headband scraped against his scalp. He liked the sensation—the tightening of the hairline, the comfort of the scrape. It was one of his favorites, with a cute bow on the side. He could at least *try* to feel confident. Then surely he could pass through the party and maybe, just maybe, have a good time? Follow a conversation or two in the hopes of forming an acquaintance. Who knew what could happen if he put himself forward? For as energized as Ada was, she was much too young to be his confidante. And Clarence, well, she hadn't warmed to his presence quite like he'd imagined, and a confidante, indeed, was necessary to his surviving here.

The manor's ground floor was almost unrecognizable. When he emerged from his bedroom, he could see from the height of the stairs that a segment of the foyer had been cordoned off and turned into a temporary kitchen of sorts: the chefs, with their

white bubble hats atop their heads, shaking their pans and driz-
zling alcohol onto shish kebabs—the flames erupting, charring
the food, and dying at their command. A wonderful performance,
magicians skilled in elemental magic. His eyes went bleary from
the flames; he jumped when Mr. Edwards bellowed his name
from the other end of the hall.

"There you are, dear boy. Almost didn't recognize you in
those clothes."

"Thank you, sir."

"You should dress like this more often, Bron. Really makes
you stand out, and for all the right reasons."

"Thank you, sir," he said again, holding back a grimace.

"Oh, 'thank you, sir, thank you sir'—come, come, there is
someone I'd like you to meet."

But they didn't get very far. With every few steps taken, Mr.
Edwards stopped to greet his guests, to laugh at welcoming banter
or lob back a joke of his own. Bron would stand and nod, wait to
be introduced, but he wasn't. With Mr. Edwards's arm still linked
with his, he couldn't make an escape. The guests looked at him,
and he would look back, produce an awkward smile. Sometimes he
would get one back. After the sixth pit-stop greeting, Ada could be
seen rushing toward them, speaking into her headset and announcing there to be "not enough napkins to go round!" She tapped
aggressively at her clipboard but soon appeased herself by shouting
"Uncle Gio!" to which Mr. Edwards squealed and let Bron loose.
They hurried over to the man who hovered by the doorway.

"It's been too long—far, far too long, my boy." Mr. Edwards
brought the man forward, introduced him as Mr. Vespa—
Giovanni, the man corrected—who was a very dear and very
beloved friend of the family, before correcting himself. "Friend of
the family—why do I use such formalities? You *are* family, aren't
you, old boy? But we must talk, we must! Thank you so much for
coming. There is so much still to discuss. What do you think of
my amendments? Of course, you both understand, don't you? It's
time we fix all this nonsense—life's too short, it can't keep on this

way." Clapping a hand on his back, Mr. Edwards steered Giovanni away through the hall, and Ada returned her attention to the clipboard, hurrying away and muttering into the mouthpiece some concern that the hors d'oeuvres had yet to go out. This left Bron alone with a group of guests who made light conversation of the weather, and commented upon the wonderful food being served, and of course the house is looking better than ever.

Words quickly turned to politics, which wasn't of any interest to him. Even if he had been interested, his conversational skills were not up to the task. Everyone around him made it look so easy, the art of dipping in and out of streams of dialogue, whereas he just stood there, waiting for his turn, which he never jumped onto, and watching as the moment grew distant the longer he worked himself up. Of course he *wanted* to talk, but something always stopped him. He'd close in like a flower, tuck himself into a corner of his mind and offer only clipped answers: "I'm fine," and always "Thank you," feeling ghostly and invisible, the maidservant of a Victorian novel, involved in life but never recognized. A governess at a party, who stood at the edge of it all.

Sure, life was going on around him, but *living* was something other people did. Sometimes he imagined another life unfolding nearby, with only a veil of air, as thin as a bubble, separating him from it, where he participated in society and said things like, "Yes, these are quite the times we are living in," or "No, I don't agree with the new prime minister." Because everything he knew about existing around the genteel was a self-taught construction, mimicked gestures learned from award-winning actors enacting their craft, like Keira Knightley's sprightly spirit: a pure artifice. Why couldn't he do the same with these people, who took note of his silence, sensed his awkwardness? They made the necessary steps to include him, and he tried to play the part, but when the woman asked him his name, and his one-word answer led her to say, "Oh goodness, like the sisters?" still he came up short.

"And who are you to the Edwardses?"

"Oh, well—"

For fifteen minutes he lingered there; Mr. Edwards continued to chatter away at the end of the hall, and the man called Giovanni cast several glances his way. Standing there with the tingle of eyes on him, Bron felt all the more singled out for it. Only this man's eyes were not that of confusion or disgust or the familiar burn he was used to feeling. No, these were inquisitive eyes.

Mr. Edwards and Giovanni soon disappeared into one of the house's many rooms, and Bron had almost forgotten about the woman, who was still awaiting an answer to one of her questions.

"Um . . . will you excuse me?"

Around the corner at the other end of the stairs, Ada sat with her head wedged between the railings, watching the splendor below. She'd discarded her clipboard and headset. Bron crouched beside her.

"It's all pretty great, huh?"

"Always the best for my brother, Darcy," she said, dispirited. "But it's all gone terribly wrong."

"You've done a wonderful job, Ada. What has possibly gone wrong?"

"The vegetarian platter was incorrectly labeled 'vegan,' and I heard poor Mrs. Fortescue exclaim how really like cheese the Emmental tasted! She couldn't tell the difference. Worst of all, we've no gluten-free options, and Daddy forgot to order the ice sculpture!"

"I'm sure an ice sculpture isn't necessary."

"It was meant to be the pivotal accent! To make the party memorable."

"Look around you—this is all memorable. And I'm sure your brother will love it and appreciate your efforts, no matter what."

"I haven't been able to find him yet. Do you think he wouldn't show up to his own party? He promised he would."

"I thought it was meant to be a surprise?"

"I might have told a few people."

"Well, did you tell *him*?"

"Well, of course I did. I *had* to. Otherwise how would he have known to show up?"

"There are a lot of people here, Ada. *If he's anything like me, he'd be on his way to Scotland right now or hiding away in a little den somewhere far away and——*" was what he wanted to say.

"Ada! There you are, you little rascal. I couldn't find anybody anywhere!"

Bron turned at the great boom of voice behind him. Ada pushed past, running straight ahead into the open arms of a gray-suited man who skipped up the steps toward her. He lifted her from the landing and twirled her into a wide three-sixty spin, the hem of her silver dress billowing into a circle as they turned, like the moon orbiting the earth tilted on its axis. They looked striking together, like a young father and daughter.

Bron would have hardly recognized the man he'd tripped over, in his tightly fitted suit, his frame slender and muscular—less bulbous than it had been under the coat—and his hair slicked back, if it hadn't been for his deeply affected voice.

Who *was* he? And what he was doing here? Another "friend of the family"? Bron unconsciously stepped back, and quickly strategized the quickest route away from here.

The man soon set Ada down. "Right, that's enough now." But Ada went in for another hug at his leg. He ruffled her hair, but peeled her off and looked up at Bron. "Now who's this?"

Ada pulled at his arm. "Don't you know? This is Bron, my tutor, and already a very dear friend. He's very smart and very creative, and teaches me things I didn't know I didn't know. Bron, this is my brother, Darcy."

"So," Darcy said, extending his arm. He put his hand in Bron's. "We meet again. It's nice to see you in something other than a shawl."

Bron relived the moment in flashes across his mind, his throat constricting, his stomach clenching. He felt this man take owner-ship of his body like a commodity once again.

"You two know each other?" Ada piped up.

Where Bron said "no," Darcy said "yes." Ada looked from Bron to her brother.

"Well, I suppose you could say we have met," Bron said, "but only for a moment."

"And quite the moment it was," Darcy said, looking him up and down and lingering at his head, making a point of his headband. "So, this is Bron—Ellis, is it? The boy wonder my father has been going on about for quite a week? I suppose you *are* a step up from the bitter old woman, Fräulein Malene, I had tutoring me. Father has mellowed in his age, and Ada is lucky to have . . . what did you call yourself? A modern-day governess?"

Bron tried to speak, but the words were glued to his throat. He was embarrassed that the man who had humiliated him was both his employer's son and also now there standing before him. His position in the house had turned into a farce before his very eyes.

Mr. Edwards broke into the trio, patted his son's back, and proceeded to make introductions again before Ada explained she'd already gone through the formalities.

"Good girl, I'm glad all that fuss is over. And now we dance!" Mr. Edwards took hold of Ada's little hand and led her down the stairs. Not wanting to be left alone with this man, Bron followed them into a less-clustered corner of the room. To his annoyance, Darcy trailed after him.

Resting against a wall, he watched as Ada and Mr. Edwards danced to "Electric Avenue"—Ada was flossing, Mr. Edwards did the robot—around the onlookers, who did little by way of dancing, sloshing their champagne flutes around with nodding heads and swaying hips. Darcy accepted a flute from one of the passing servers and knocked it back, swapping his empty flute for another drink at the first opportunity. Bron accepted one also, conscious of his arms, limp at his side, and grateful for something to hold. He watched as Darcy surveyed the room, glanced at his wrist, and then smiled at the guests who nodded at him. When they approached him with small talk, Darcy invited them in cordially, only to artfully dismiss them before the conversation had even started.

If Bron could've had it his way, he'd have marched back up the stairs and away from everybody there. But the house had many corners in which to dwell and take shelter, so he stood instead at the edge of the foyer, his presence pointless but somehow necessary. Were he to escape now, it would only result in Ada coming to fetch him from his room—or worse, one of the Edwardses' men, at her insistence, when he didn't comply. He accepted the canapes that came, not because he was hungry, but because he was eager for something to weigh him down, and took in the elegance in which the people around him lived . . . anything that kept him from looking at Mr. Edwards's son, who he knew was staring at him.

What must it be like to really be these people? The women, beautiful and rich and so well made up; and the men who stood beside them, broad, pruned, and ornate. When he looked at the women, he saw the smallness of their waists, the convex slope of their ribcages in their satin dresses, the peaking softness of their breasts; when he looked at the men, he saw the muscular fill to their arms, their necks, some with beer bellies and perfectly round arses, the thighs that plunged below them.

He held a grudge against everybody for the self-made categories people were forced to fit into. And tied to this, he supposed he should probably apologize to Mr. Edwards's son for his outburst earlier. Sooner or later he would have to make amends and forget everything that'd happened. That was the way the world worked: apologize before things escalated too far; otherwise, he was destined to lose.

He was sipping wine when Darcy approached, making him gulp and then choke on his drink.

"May I?" Darcy said at his side. He didn't look at him, but stared out into the crowd instead. Soon Darcy was pressing into his side, and Bron felt a tug of discomfort: here he was, existing outside the confines of his beloved novel, and he was unsure how to react. What would Jane do at this party?

"So I suppose I should ask what it is that made you want to uproot your life and come to work for my family? I can see it wasn't for the social gatherings."

·   "I guess I saw the ad online and thought . . ." Bron trailed off, shrugged.

Darcy seemed uncharacteristically interested in what he had to say. He was looking at him now. "You thought what?"

"I don't know. That I would be suited to such a position."

"And here you are." Bron kept his face forward. "Was further education not an option for you? Or does the student lifestyle not suit your . . . taste?"

"Not everybody can afford access to such an education."

"Aren't there bursaries for such situations as this?"

"Perhaps, but there is also the foundational education necessary to aid one's chances of entry in the first place."

"Aha!" Darcy jibed. "So you applied and didn't get in?"

Bron bit his tongue, forced himself to keep still. "Perhaps."

"But there are many other university options other than Cambridge."

"Can I not aspire to such heights?"

"Of course. But it is not all there is, you know. People have a very clear idea of what they think the city will be before ever stepping foot in it. I imagine it never quite meets the mark."

He didn't admit to Darcy that his words rang true, that the etchings of the cityscape paled in comparison to the years of his pining over Oxbridge via celluloid. Instead, he said, "I, for one, think Cambridge is beautiful."

"Beautiful, indeed. A place of historical prosperity and almost guaranteed future success . . . if you happen to be on the right side of it. So in an ideal world, you would have continued your studies at one of the colleges?"

"Yes, but the world is not ideal."

"Oh, I don't doubt it." Bron fixed his countenance on the liveliness of the room. Following his gaze, Darcy faced out to the crowd too.

"There is a right and a wrong way of reading a room," he said, so casually into the air that Bron wasn't entirely sure if it was him Darcy continued to address. "What you are doing now is the wrong way. No, don't move," he said when Bron finally turned toward him. "Keep looking as you have, and tell me what you see."

Bron pressed his lips together and made a point of looking. There wasn't anything he could do but oblige his host's son. "Um, okay. I see . . ." A crowd of people, some laughing in corners, others loitering to get the servers' attention and their hands on the canapes; smug-looking men looking complacent, and a woman who stood out in her hot-pink jumpsuit. Someone was tilting their head toward the ceiling's netted balloons. Bron wondered, then, when they would fall. "I guess I see what is right in front of me. I see a party."

Darcy huffed, unimpressed by the answer.

"Was that not good enough? Well, what do *you* see?"

"I see a lot of drunk people. Or people pretending to be drunk, and a lot of knockoff Chanel."

"An equally basic answer," Bron murmured.

"But the real question is, what do you propose they see? Other than you looking miserable."

He scowled. "I'm not miserable."

"Then why do you slouch?"

He righted his posture. "I don't."

"The best thing you can do is allow yourself to blend in, almost like a piece of furniture. You want to fit in with the landscape. Don't let the room read you."

Was that the best thing to do—to blend in? Bron gave it some serious thought. Certainly, life would be easier if he weren't so different, a sunflower amid a field of red poppies. But at what cost? He *did* notice that, on the whole, nobody strained to look at him tonight, nor did they offer him an odd look. Just because of the suit he was wearing? At that moment, Mr. Edwards advanced toward them and signaled with flapping arms for them to come forward.

"Come, Bron, come. I must have you dance."

"No, thank you, sir. I'm alright where I am."

"No, no, I insist," Mr. Edwards said, taking him by the hands. "And since I am dancing with the only beautiful girl in the room"—Ada continued to spin around behind him, frolicking to the music by herself—"I insist you dance with the next best thing." He turned to his son and grabbed him by the waistcoat.

"Father, don't."

And before he could protest, Mr. Edwards coaxed Bron into taking another step toward his son, and brought their hands together, insisting they step their feet this way, then that way.

Darcy stuffed his hands into his pockets, his eyes darting around in search of escape. After a few forced movements, he patted his father's back and walked away, leaving Bron to look intently at the floor. Rejected. He didn't want to dance either, but still the tears pricked at his eyes, and he looked over to Mr. Edwards, whose hands, now linked with Ada's, had formed a ring. Ada pulled him into their circle. It was hard to muster the liveliness and joy they experienced, dancing in a ring-around-the-rosy to a song he didn't recognize. He broke away before excusing himself.

Wading into the crowd, he crossed Darcy's path again, who was now surrounded by a group of women whose voices Bron could hear above the music.

"You've never been a dancing man, have you, Theodore?" said the woman in the jumpsuit, holding a glass high with one arm and patting Darcy's shoulder with the other. *Theodore?* "Do you remember all those years ago when I asked you to dance at the Trinity Formal, and you shut me down? Claimed you had a sprained ankle." She then linked arms with the other man who stood beside her. "Did you make that same claim now before running off like a little schoolboy?"

"I need do no such thing this time, Magda." Darcy laughed. He was sipping his flute when he caught Bron's eye.

"You've always been preoccupied with the way things appear. Why not be more carefree, like your father? He seems quite a changed man nowadays."

"Yes, quite. And yet here we are, still repressed."

"You repress yourself, dear. We can be anything we want to be. Our privilege sees to that," she laughed, and made to cheers the rest of the party. "And that poor boy in the sweet headband? I would have danced with him myself were I not already smitten." She pulled on her man, who stood rigid as a pillar.

Bron noticed Darcy's eyes flitting between him and the woman. "I'm glad you've finally found happiness, Maggie."

"Oh, you would be happier yourself if you just let loose. Tell me what was wrong with that boy?"

"Well, he is here to care for Ada."

"Is that all?"

"It is also rather strange, is it not, the way he lurks about like—"

Bron didn't catch the end of the sentence, for someone had walked past and broken his concentration. It was Maggie who was speaking now.

"—in any case, I think you're wrong. Times are changing. Are you saying you'd have been more open to the idea of his being Ada's tutor had he been a woman?"

"Definitely not. Ada seems to like him, and that's all that counts," Darcy said. "Ah, there I go again, assuming one's pronouns. Don't go telling me off."

"Announcing one's preferences will become normal etiquette soon enough."

The other man piped in. "People identify as 'queer', now, I do believe. Which I'll never get my head around. In my day it was something of an insult."

Despite the noise surrounding them, the words hung in Bron's ear like a curse, stinging like a needle. This mocking of a word he took pride in, as though they were being cast back to the 1980s. Queer was everything he had. Queer was specific, ambiguous, powerful.

"Hmm." Darcy nodded.

Bron hurried away through the dining room and up the staircase, unexpected shame encircling him like a ruff. People barred his way, standing in packs. He could no longer hear voices, only warped music and cackled laughter, and his bedroom stood too far out of reach, lest he push them out of his way. He doubled back to a corner of this mazelike house, feeling the rush-hour moments of St. Mary's in his legs, when all the boys on campus would hurry on the stairwell, running through the hallways and into their respective classrooms. He hurried into the last available room at the end of the landing, which was vacant. It was the library, and the music and screeching of voices diminished instantly, taken over by a heated silence. His arms pressed against the wooden door as if to hold out the intruders, and he hoped to lean there, feeling the warmth of the room on his back engulf him, press into him, and him into the walls—a furnaced refuge to the airiness of the hallway, where opinions flowed like a feather in the wind, landing wherever they may.

He had so hoped that things would be different here, that he wouldn't be subjected to the embarrassment he'd endured as a child. He'd been naive to think it was possible, that being an adult would fix things. His pain was as real as ever, a buildup that stretched the ribs and had his heart beating at the forefront of his chest. For now, though, he settled his breathing, took great gulps of it. Felt the strain in his neck as he lifted off the door, the weight of his head again his to carry. One suffering walk back through the crowd and to his bedroom, and he could sleep the night away and forget everything that had happened. But the knock of wood, or sound like the drop of a pencil, made him suddenly aware of the presence of another in the room.

A man stood behind the large mahogany desk, arms splayed out and bent over a mess of papers that, in the glow of the lamplight, made each individual paper look like a country in one large map of the world. He wore a dark turtleneck and even darker blazer, and emerging from behind the desk, silver-white trousers that stuck to his legs like paint. Oily, curling hair slicked back. He could have been missing a feather, this captain of the sea.

"I beg your pardon," the man said, shutting off his phone and tucking it into his jacket. "I did not mean to scare you."

Several words rushed to his throat but did not leave his mouth: *What are you doing in here? Why can't I get a moment alone? There are always people in this large fucking house.* He reassembled himself.

"Who are you?" He remembered this man, whom Mr. Edwards had abandoned him for atop the stairs. "What are you doing in here?"

"I am Giovanni," he said. "I would ask who you are, but I think I already know. Bran, no?"

He wasn't expecting the question to be turned back on him. Perhaps he was the one trespassing into a room when he shouldn't have.

"Bron," he corrected.

"Ah yes, Dickie's new project," he said. Bron was amused by the way his Italian accent almost separated the word into "pro" and "ject": *prowject*. "I am happy to meet you and sorry we were not introduced earlier. Dickie tends to . . ." He searched the air for words. "Board one train without getting off the other, if you know what I mean—e gli manca una rotella. He is a little bit crazy, missing a wheel."

Bron nodded in understanding, but curiosity stopped him from commenting. How did this man know the Edwardses, and what was his relation to them? Giovanni beat him to the next question.

"How long have you been living here?"

"About a month," Bron said, hoping the extra week might gain him more authority to have stumbled into this room. "It is very nice here. I had thought I'd be very happy just by being in this house."

"*Had* thought?" Giovanni countered. "Whatever could you mean?" And as if this man could read his mind, he said mockingly, "Has this to do with signore Darcy?"

"Darcy?" he echoed, his cheeks blushing red-hot. "I don't know whom you mean." Mr. Edwards's son had only appeared fleetingly over a single day of his life, and yet he couldn't deny the sudden power Darcy had over him. He gave Giovanni a knowing smile. "But it might have something to do with a man called Theodore."

"Pah, Theodore," Giovanni spat, lips curling into a smile.

Though they'd both voiced this new name, Bron couldn't picture Darcy by any other, and quickly inquired into the nickname's origin.

The explanation, overall, amounted to: "Theodore . . . Dorcy . . . Darcy."

"Well, that's quite a stretch."

"I believe it is what the little one called him as a baby, and it has somehow stuck."

"The little girl, Ada—she doesn't need me. Not really. Not like I thought she might. And now Darcy has shown up, and I . . . I can see I am not well suited here. I have no purpose." Saying the words out loud made him feel the impact of their truth. He sighed. "You know the family well?"

"I have been acquainted with the Edwardses for quite some years now. Dickie is a kind-hearted soul. He has a lot to offer the world. And the little girl is a great blessing to us all. But, if you'd forgive my forwardness, I cannot say the same for his son."

Bron was gripped, though slightly puzzled, by Giovanni's candid divulging of his thoughts. Mr. Edwards, the good guy; Darcy, the bad. Ada a gift to the world. But why? Who *was* this man, this family friend turned family? He had to know more.

"And why do you say that?"

"Dickie looks on me favorably, and I dare say Darcy has taken our attachment quite to heart. I think he might be more forgiving of me if his father liked me less."

Bron nodded, willing to learn more about the family he had come to live with, and finding comfort in another's dislike of Darcy. "And what is there to forgive?"

Giovanni hesitated before saying "Lots." He laughed a toothy grin, and Bron smiled alongside him. "And you? You do not like to dance?"

"Me?" Bron said. For Giovanni's smile belied the truth: that he had seen them in the foyer, and it had been clear that Darcy wanted nothing to do with him. "I do not find myself in the way of dancing enough to warrant a disliking of it. But what I can admit to is the unlikelihood of dancing again any time soon, or ever again for that matter."

"You sound displeased about it—but I say there are greater losses in life to be had, and you, my pretty thing, deserve much better than a man who talks of you behind your back."

He thought it a particular thing to say, and it was impossible for Giovanni to have eavesdropped on the same conversation. Hadn't he been tucked away in here, in this room full of books, the noise from the outside barely reaching their ears? Still, the pertinence of his description knotted his stomach.

It was then that the door burst open, and Darcy rushed hurriedly into the room, pressing himself against the door to hold it shut as Bron had so done before him. Bron didn't miss Darcy's face contorting into a snarl as he laid eyes on Giovanni, or the way Giovanni side-stepped away from the desk, his face drained a little of color, or the way his jaw set. They both stood rigid, and Bron's eyes darted from man to man: Darcy's hands flexing at his sides, Giovanni twisting the rings on his fingers and clearing his throat.

Aha, he thought, instantly processing the conversation just had and the subtle reactions of this encounter, to deduce that someone here played the character of the rival, and the other had been wronged by some unrepentant action. But what? Something was certainly alight between them, a fiery swell once snuffed but now reignited.

Giovanni leaned for Bron's hand and brought it to his lips. "Ciao, bella," he said before nodding in salutation to Darcy, who moved out of the way of the door as Giovanni left the room.

Darcy snorted before slamming the door shut, and rapped his knuckles on the wooden frame. This left the two of them alone: Bron rooted in place by the fireside, Darcy facing the wall. From the way Darcy's body shifted, it seemed he was hoping to avoid, perhaps even ignore Bron's presence altogether. When he finally acknowledged him, there was an unsettling silence. Darcy decanted some whisky at the drinks trolley, offering the glass to Bron with an outstretched hand. He declined, shaking his head. Darcy took a sip, then broke the quiet.

"I can't say I was expecting to find you in here," he said. "Either of you."

Bron allowed the words to linger, to dissipate into the crackling of the fire in the hearth, before replying, "I can't say I was expecting to be found in here either."

He crossed his arms, holding himself in, while Darcy slid his hand in and out of his trouser pocket. They moved to speak at the same time, freezing one another in the process, and as a result, said nothing. Darcy ran a hand through his hair, gestured as if to say, *"You speak,"* but when he didn't, they were again plunged into quiet.

"So I see you've met Giovanni?" He posed it like a question. "Christ."

"He seemed like a nice enough man. Nicer than most."

"Yes, I'm sure he gave off that impression," Darcy said. "And what were *you* doing in here when there is a perfectly good party happening downstairs?"

"As you might have already guessed, I'm not much fond of parties."

Darcy brought the tumbler to his lips, then lowered it. "Yes, that is something you and I have in common."

He didn't think he and this man could have anything in common. In fact, he knew they couldn't be more different. "You seemed quite in your element to me."

"I like to consider myself a wallflower."

"A wallflower?" Bron repeated. "I find that hard to believe."

"What is there not to believe? It is my lifelong goal to be a piece of furniture." Darcy smirked. "And I profess your judgment of character to be at least *slightly* off-kilter."

Bron thought then of all the times at St. Mary's when he'd confided in his peers: in Joseph Simcox, whom he'd once declared his love for in the sixth year and who never spoke to him again; in Bertie Barrett, who touched him in otherwise barren places, but who ignored him the rest of the time. Of Harry, who'd once made up his entire world, but who now barely acknowledged his existence. "You know, I wouldn't usually disagree with that assessment, but something tells me I'm slowly becoming better at it."

"And what makes you think that?"

He wracked his brain for an answer. Finding none, he took to looking into the fire.

"I see. Well, after all, isn't there something left unsaid? Something you've forgotten to say to me?"

He knew it would come to this, that Darcy would force him to apologize for his behavior outside the house, or threaten to dismiss him from his job at once. But he couldn't bring himself to apologize. Not for all the world. The truth was he'd been besieged by this man's need to offload his opinion, and he had no desire to hear it. He couldn't have helped his fight-or-flight response. Why should he apologize for defending himself? No, he wouldn't do it.

"If you insist on talking about it, then I cannot say I regret what happened between us, only that I wish it didn't happen at all. The way I choose to—" But his impassioned speech was quickly interrupted by Darcy's awful sniggering, the holding of his head in his hands.

"God."

"What?"

"I only meant that you'd forgotten to wish me a happy birth-day, Bron."

"Oh," he said quietly under his breath, wanting to die right there and then—*fuck my actual life*—before covering his mis-take with what he hoped was an assured "Oh, well then, happy birthday."

It was almost too much to bear, the constant silence that ensued. Darcy took to stirring the fire in the hearth. Threw in another piece of wood. But it was the sound of the mantel clock's ticking that filled the air. Bron could have swooned to the back and forth of the pendulum if he'd let himself.

"So how old are you now?" he asked, but regretted the ques-tion as soon as he'd voiced it.

Darcy raised an eyebrow. "Should a queen ever reveal their real age?"

"Um . . ." There was something very awkward about Darcy's referring to himself as a queen, the unnatural way it sounded in his voice, wrapped as it was in a playful tone.

"How old do you think I am?"

"I don't know." Ada had told him it was Darcy's twenty-ninth birthday, so he thought it only polite to shave off a couple of years. "Twenty-seven?"

"Hah, now that is treacherous. I look twenty-five at most?"

"I don't place much value on people's appearances. It has never served me well." He hadn't expected the accusatory inflec-tion of his voice.

"I see. Am I so unforgiveable for my moment of lapsed judg-ment after that little incident at college? Because I am quite sorry for it."

Bron appreciated this seemingly honest admission, thought it resembled something like remorse. Or was he being fooled? How best to arrange his next words. "Well, I suppose I could start thinking about forgiveness."

"And then I'm off the hook?" Darcy teased. "That would be most welcome. And as I have already shared my thoughts, perhaps I should extend the option to you . . . allow you to do the same? I suppose that would be reasonable."

"That what would be reasonable?"

"Go on, go on—don't be shy," Darcy quipped, settling into the armchair and tapping at his thighs like a schoolboy. "Tell me what you think of me."

Bron shook his head at the absurdity of this drunken request. Felt himself as though thrust on stage and made to perform a monologue he'd never even heard. "And what if I refuse?"

"Then I'll have you fired at once." Darcy crossed his legs, animated, but immediately uncrossed them. He was smiling an unruly smile, and his eyes were bright and alive, though for the first time Bron noticed one of Darcy's eyes seemed more red than the other. A little droopy. "No, think of it as a birthday present, I suppose. Please, I beg to know what you think of me."

"What I think of you?" Bron remained struck by the question, his being put on the spot like this. "I don't think anything of you—I don't know you."

"Well, what is your impression of me, then?" Darcy waved for an answer, decanted yet another drink. "Go on, the honest truth."

It had never been put to him so directly, a demand to offload his opinion. And opinions Bron surely had. Thousands of them, collected through the years. They spilled out of the contours of his being. Only up until then, he had learned to keep them carefully tucked away, hemmed in, cluttering his insides. A box of differently shaped toys. When Darcy took a sip from his glass and nodded for him to go on, Bron teetered at the edge of a precipice. And he was ready to jump. *The honest truth, he says? Well, then—*

"Honestly? I think you're rude and rather obnoxious—"

Darcy snorted his drink. "Rude? Obnoxious?"

"Yes, extremely so."

"'Rude' I'll own up to." He laughed. "But I simply draw the line at 'obnoxious'!"

"A hard line to draw when it's true. I suppose it can't be easy, listening to what other people might have to say of you."

"And you have a lot to say about me?" Darcy pointedly interrupted.

"Yes, indeed. You asked to hear it, and yet you won't let me finish—"

"So I'm the villain here, and somehow good old Giovanni's bagged himself yet another loyal follower?" Bron heard the hardness seep back into Darcy's voice.

"I don't quite know what you mean," Bron said. "I didn't say anything like that."

"You might as well have. I already know what you think."

"And what is it that I think?"

Darcy raised his hands in defense. "Nothing."

Bron cradled his arms to his chest. He was frustrated to have been snagged from his leap, of airing his truth. "No, please tell me, if we're sharing our honest opinions."

Darcy leaned forward in his chair. "I mean to say that one looks at me and thinks they know everything there is to know about me. Everyone else is allowed their freedoms, to say and do whatever it is they choose, and here I am, merely existing in a box that has been created for me. A cage. And how perfectly I fit, and yet you—and others like you—soar outside these confinements, free as a bird."

Bron's heart thrummed at the side of his neck. *Free as a bird?* "You think I'm free to do whatever I want? And that it is *you* who is confined to a box?"

"Well, aren't you?" Darcy said. "Free?"

"That is not quite the word I would choose."

"And what word *would* you choose?"

He didn't give it too much, though. "I don't know . . . obscure . . . lost."

"Oh, really? Well, let us take, for instance, the way you choose to dress. For truly it is up to you how you go about your day. But what if I said that as an employee in this house, you are representing us all outside these quarters, and that therefore we have something of a say as to how you choose to conduct yourself. How you should present. How would that make you feel then?"

Backed into this corner, Bron searched for a way out, deduced that the only way was to follow through in this game of whatever it was he was playing. "I . . . I suppose I would feel, as we said, rather confined. Controlled."

"Controlled! But look at you—so naturally handsome in that suit, and yet you paint makeup on your cheeks, color black around the eyes. With that little tiara on your head. One might ask what it is you gain by doing this, but that is not the point, is it?"

Bron felt the heat creep along his neck and flush into his cheeks. It took everything he had in him not to reach up and pull the headband away. This had been his life for years. There was nothing for him to gain, only the need to defend himself. He could never quite explain it, his yearning for a thing that brought him so much satisfaction at the consequence of so much ridicule. But he would not be forced into hiding, locked in an attic never to be let free.

He regretted this entire conversation. Would wait the question out or give Darcy room to ask another, one that would warrant a simpler response. A question he might have the answer to. But no such question came, and he felt immobilized. "No," Bron said. "It isn't."

"Exactly so. So isn't the point that you can, in fact, live your own life? That you might be, perhaps, the opposite of lost?"

Darcy's insinuating that Bron had an easier time of living was almost laughable, but he didn't expect anyone like Darcy to understand the difficulties that fed into his every day. Up there in the highest echelons of society, was there a cost to freedom?

Immediately he decided that there wasn't, that Darcy was for one reason or another trolling him. But if he'd allowed himself more time to ponder the question, he'd have concluded that whatever the price was to pay, Darcy could afford it. "You have a rather simplified view of what you think you know about me. Commenting on the surface level of things."

"The surface level of things? Well, I don't mean to offend you, Bron, but doesn't society struggle enough as it is to accept us as we are on the outside? Are we at a stage of letting anybody, truly, in?" and this Darcy said with an inkling of kindness. "I think living away from the eyes of enforced pressure affords one a certain freedom that some of us might lack."

He was certain he'd misunderstood him. *Us?* He let the word linger. "You mean you are . . ."

"Gay? Queer? Yes, and again, is it so hard to believe?" Darcy laughed. "Yet another thing we have in common."

Bron had quickly learned to expect that Darcy might say anything to him, but he hadn't expected to hear *that.* Darcy—gay? The two concepts didn't fit together. A man like him: alluring, confidently masculine, sartorially refined, the very embodiment of a perceived "Englishness." Flashy red trousers, a voice always pitched low. A man indistinguishable from the rest of his sort. Bron knew he had slipped into stereotypes here, but *how* could this be? Was he right? Were they the same? In their judgment of each other? And did their attraction to a specific gender make the two of them alike, of the same ilk? He didn't think so. His identity was a complicated thing, one that shifted and evolved. Darcy was not a part of it, but a different group altogether, where things like pronouns and bathroom bills were the epitome of the gender nonconforming struggle. *That* was the great fight. Not the constant debate of his existence in the right-wing press, not the scrutinizing of his body, nor the bouts of incredible loneliness and disconnect he felt at every glance in the mirror. It wasn't at all as serious as that. No, Darcy and the likes of him were at liberty to exist however they pleased, without any fear of mockery or violence every time they stepped outside. Bron had heard it, seen it more online now than ever before. That expression of a community broken and torn at the seams.

"I am my own person," Bron said, "as much as you are you. We struggle through life as best we can, and then we die. It is not okay for you to turn who we are into a comparative debate and make assumptions about my life. You say you feel confined to a box? Well, what a pretty box you live in. Some of us are not built to fit into any shape or size, and now that you are laughing at me—"

"I am not laughing." Darcy grinned.

"—I would rather you suppressed it, or at the very least had the courtesy of waiting for me to leave the room." This, he felt, was the perfect opportunity to stride toward the door and release himself from the situation. He flung it open.

"So I suppose there aren't to be any playful debates throughout your stay here? Between friends?"

Bron stopped. Friends. It was a gray word, like a rotting corpse. Fri-ends, like something whose conclusion was embedded into its very fabric, confirming its destiny before it'd even begun. They were not friends—he knew that much—and shielding his face away, he felt his heart break open, a safety pin yielding from strain. *Harry.* Harry had been his friend, there to support him when times were bad, when stony words were thrown at him. But where was he now, his friend?

"We are not friends." *And how I choose to live is not up for debate.*

"Ah, well then, that explains it!" Darcy stood to move toward him. Held out his arm in a way that barred him from leaving the room. "Now we understand each other a little better. You think me rude and obnoxious, and I need to be a little more understanding of who you are, you lost little thing. I've never been good at first impressions—but perhaps we may start again?"

Bron knew there was nothing left to be said, nothing else to be done. He nodded in agreement.

"Fine, but again starts tomorrow. In the meantime, will you please remove your arm? You are blocking my way."

With this, Darcy raised his arm, and Bron exited the room as tactfully as he could.

PART II

5

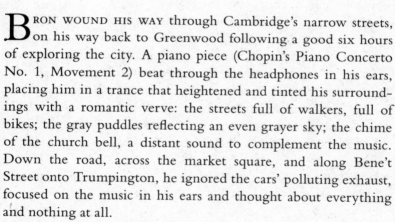

BRON WOUND HIS WAY through Cambridge's narrow streets, on his way back to Greenwood following a good six hours of exploring the city. A piano piece (Chopin's Piano Concerto No. 1, Movement 2) beat through the headphones in his ears, placing him in a trance that heightened and tinted his surroundings with a romantic verve: the streets full of walkers, full of bikes; the gray puddles reflecting an even grayer sky; the chime of the church bell, a distant sound to complement the music. Down the road, across the market square, and along Bene't Street onto Trumpington, he ignored the cars' polluting exhaust, focused on the music in his ears and thought about everything and nothing at all.

In town, he'd picked up a new eyeliner, a new notebook in which to plan his lessons, and a matching calendar for Ada to see what he'd planned for her learning a week in advance. Having earned his first paycheck, he'd also searched the racks for new clothes. But fast fashion never fit him well, clinging as each piece did to all the wrong places, so he'd hurried away from the high street, thinking how ridiculous it all was, the effort to find something that'd allow him to feel at home in his own skin. He stopped outside the robemaker's window display—"Ede and Ravenscroft, est. 1689"—and lost himself in the rigidity of a mannequin's black robe; the creaminess of the tuxedo; the bright yellow, green, and red of the folded cravats. He felt, as well as his gender, the reality of his class—yet more clothes he hadn't been born to wear.

As he continued down the road, two people, having emerged from one of the college's entrances, were heading straight toward him: a woman whose suitcase clanked beside her, and a man he was sure he recognized—oily, slicked-back hair; tanned skin. A man who was calling his name. He quickly pulled away his headphones.

"It is you?" Giovanni said. *New prowject*. He moved closer to his companion and said something Bron couldn't catch. He stepped back, pressed into the glass of the window. "Do you remember me? I am Giovanni, and this is my sister, Toni."

Bron shook her hand. The embarrassment of their first meeting kept him from meeting Giovanni's gaze, but the brother and sister spoke rapidly, earnestly flitting Italian words back and forth. Giovanni in particular seemed much freer and relaxed outside the rooms of the house, and explained to his sister how Bron was connected to the Edwardses. Toni was keen to inquire into the whereabouts of Darcy—whom she called Theo—and to ask after the health of that little girl of theirs.

"I don't trouble myself with his day-to-day activities," Bron said, "but Ada is very well."

"Bella Ada. But I see the man has got to you too?"

"He does have his opinions," he said.

"Yes," Toni piped. "He certainly does."

It was all talk of the Edwardses, whom they seemed to know a lot about, and beautiful, beautiful Italy: the carbonara; the pistachio gelato; and Giovanni's favorite Roman delicacy, cacio e pepe, which he craved so badly and which Toni teased him about. "Maybe you wouldn't miss it so much if you came to visit your sister more." Toni explained she was only here for a few weeks, catching up with old friends, and looking forward to a spa break in Edinburgh at the tail end of her holiday.

Giovanni quickly amended her narrative to suggest that she was being modest, that as an up-and-coming actress in Italy, she had been invited to do a photo shoot with a top-tier fashion photographer in London, and even had an audition coming up for a big-budget movie.

She laughed. "James Norton is rumored to co-star."

"I am so proud of you, Toni, after all you've been through. You deserve it all."

Toni quickly announced that she was running late for a meeting with one of her girlfriends. "We went to Newnham together for a time. Which college are you at, Bron?"

Giovanni quickly corrected her.

"Oh, you are with the Edwardses *full* time? How very brave." She said ciao to them both, with two kisses on the cheek, and disappeared down the street toward Pembroke.

Giovanni turned back to him as she disappeared from view. "So what brings you to town? I lecture at Corpus"—he waved in the general direction behind him—"so you can often find me here."

"Oh, is that Corpus Christie?" Bron asked. "You are a professor at the university?"

"A lecturer, and not a very good teacher. I do it for the research."

"I'm sure you're a great teacher."

"No, no, I'm not. I like to spend time with other people's opinions, then break them apart and form my own."

Bron was intrigued by what Giovanni had to say, how a researcher's time was spent reading, taking in information and countless arguments, only to come up with a new argument altogether, a new lens from which to view a book, a piece of media, the world. "So you don't care what other people think?"

Giovanni laughed. "You misunderstand me. I very much care what other people think, and at the same time I don't. It is the work of amalgamation, I suppose. A balance of many ideas. But it is hard to trust people, or share their views, when everybody thinks the same."

Bron was guilty of reading quickly fired threads on the internet and taking them as gospel. Opinions that he would hold and further distribute (if he agreed with them, of course). But were his thoughts, and the opinions he had of himself, his own or a diluted version of many similar think pieces?

"Well, that's right," Bron said, edging around a close to the conversation. He needed to get back to the house.

"And you are a teacher too, yes? You teach the little one."

"I suppose."

"Say, do you want to get a drink? Because we are here." Giovanni pointed to the café that sold bread and scones. In the window was a wonderful display of macarons and Chelsea buns. "You get us a table. I will order. Two espressos, okay?"

Ada would be expecting him back very soon, and the walk around town had tired him out. He was itching to say no. Equally, he was completely enraptured by this man's confidence. He also suspected he could learn more about the Edwardses from him. "Okay."

Most of the seats had already been taken, but he found a spot at the back of the café and grabbed the sugar tin from another table so that he could pour it into the coffee. He twiddled his thumbs, waiting for Giovanni, who casually leaned on the glass counter by the till, pointing to the pegged letter board behind the barista, then yanked a wallet from his back pocket. Bron thought Giovanni's black jeans to be particularly tight.

Giovanni approached and perched on the stool, his back and neck upright. *Why do you slouch?* Bron became suddenly conscious of his own posture. "I also ordered us two muffins."

"Grazie," he tried.

"Aha, prego!" replied Giovanni, enthused. Just like that night a few weeks prior, Giovanni's eyes were inquisitive. They made Bron's arm hair stand up.

Bron asked what he thought would be the obvious question: "So, what led you to teaching?" and it emerged that Giovanni had a passion for all kinds of things: causes relating to diversity and inclusion; HIV and AIDS awareness; Barthes, Foucault—always Foucault—and other theorists and their frameworks. Anything that debunked old ways of thinking. A lecturing post offered him a space in which to discuss all his interests, and in the classroom, an outlet through which to share his opinions without his being argued against . . . much.

"The ones that do—those students, they are the feisty ones, the ones I like. A teacher needs an open mind, to be led by their students, but I find that most of them are too wrapped up in the books themselves. They are less concerned with what we have to say about the literature, but focus on what the literature says verbatim."

"But isn't what the literature says verbatim our gateway into making it anew?"

Giovanni seemed piqued by his statement. "Go on."

"I . . . I don't know. I just think that perhaps we are allowed to enjoy what is there, on the page. That we don't necessarily need to say anything about it."

"But what about problematic representation? Outdated views? I am not suggesting we silence them, but shouldn't we critique them? Otherwise, how will we fill in the gaps? Many say that certain histories are 'lost,' but they weren't lost—they were stolen. From many, and certainly from us as queer people. How do we go about rectifying that?"

Something was made clear in that moment: Giovanni's words were inclined to overhaul any sense of difference between them. To make clear that they were on the same side. And that he was ready to put in the work in the face of social change. Such an outpouring of opinion and passion ultimately led to the question "And what do you like to read?" paving the way for much easier discussion. Bron spoke about *Jane Eyre* and all its film adaptations.

"And there's this one scene where it is announced that a woman has come to Thornfield Hall to tell the people's fortunes. Mr. Rochester, the master of the house, is nowhere to be seen. When Jane enters the library, the woman asks her so many questions, all in the hope of tricking her into talking about her master, only it turns out this woman is actually Mr. Rochester in disguise, in—well, drag! It's one of my favorite moments ever in all of literature. And yet no one talks about it. The films always work their way around it, either having a real woman play the part or discarding it all together. It's such a shame!"

"A shame. See, you are exactly like my students. Swept away in specific stories. And I can see the way your eyes light up. But what is it actually saying about the world today? Why do they omit it, do you think? Remember, we fill in the gaps."

Bron had never thought of it quite like that before.

Giovanni moved on to admit that he had more time for the early modern playwright over any Victorian novelist. An opinion Bron completely disagreed with.

"So why don't you study literature yourself?"

He admitted to Giovanni that he'd tried to get into the university, that they'd rejected him twice, and that there was no way he could afford to ever be a student here.

"What rubbish. You want to study literature? Then study it—every book's a lesson. Have you seen *Edward II*? It has Tilda Swinton. Great costume adaptation. Very queer!"

Bron sat up at this. "You like period dramas?"

"Definitely not," Giovanni said, laughing. Bron's heart sank a little. "But I like Jarman. The rest is all a little too pretty for me, all these Hollywood remakes. And the BBC. Netflix too. Makes everyone go wild for all the wrong reasons. Austenmania and Brontifications—it's a real thing, you know."

"You don't like any of them?"

"I tend to avoid anything adored by all, although I do think there is something to be said of Emily, not that we appreciate or even recognize her true merit."

"And what about Austen?" Bron pressed.

"Oh, I despise the woman," he said, and they both let out a loud laugh. "When I hear 'Darcy,' I run."

Bron felt his face split into a smile. "I cannot say I share your feelings, but I do think Charlotte might have said something similar. She didn't see much in Austen."

"I find the gender politics of the early modern stage to be far more appealing than any proto-feminist novel, and definitely any of their more recent filmic counterparts. Have you ever read Marlowe?"

Bron had never heard of Marlowe, who Giovanni explained had been a gay playwright-slash-heretic-slash-spy, who was murdered under mysterious circumstances—scholars couldn't quite agree upon how—and spurred by their discussion of drag, spoke of the male transvestism of the Jacobean stage. What was cross-dressing, Giovanni said, but a reassertion of the patriarchal construction of gender, or an incredible site through which to question the strictures of gender boundaries?

"Oh, I see." Bron had of course thought about all this, in his own way, but had never felt he had the language to express it. Giovanni made it sound so simple and yet so complicated.

But when offered, Bron declined another coffee, claiming the need to get back. Ada really would be wondering what had happened to him.

"But I can walk with you, yes?"

His brain hurt, but he was glad to be asked. He thought Giovanni to be a fascinating man, and still hadn't learned much more of his attachment to the Edwardses. "Yes."

The university buildings and cobbled center widened into Victorian townhouses repurposed into legal offices. The Trumpington Road led them all the way to the university's botanic garden, where Bron had shared he'd never been and where Giovanni insisted he must visit.

Giovanni angled himself toward him, knocked into his side as they walked. Bron tried to ease himself away at first, but found the light press of a bone against his side slightly comforting. He allowed Giovanni this pleasure and got wafts of his musky scent in the breeze: lemongrass and bergamot. He even thought, for a moment, that Giovanni might be flirting with him.

But Giovanni soon stopped them in the middle of the street.. "It was nice getting to know you, Bron. I liked our little chat. I live that way, so I best turn back now before I end up all the way at Greenwood. And neither of us would want that."

Bron took note of the way he looked up at the clouds as if in search of something. Noticed the sun hanging low.

"It was rather awkward after the party, wasn't it? Between you and Darcy?" Bron pressed.

"It was, but Dickie needs me, so I will continue to crop up every now and then."

"But you and Mr. Edwards—Darcy . . . you never said how you came to know the family?"

"We went to school together. Theo—I mean Darcy—and I. Same college. Trinity."

"I didn't know that."

"Why would you? I doubt he speaks of me much." Giovanni said this almost too quickly, and Bron heard something like sadness bend his voice. "But for now I am very, very hungry."

"Cacio e pepe?" Bron said.

"Cacio e pepe." Giovanni nodded. "But we will meet again?"

"Yes. I'll need someone to quiz me on my reading, after all." And Bron still wanted to know more about Giovanni's strained relationship with Darcy.

"Good," Giovanni said, and kissed him on each cheek before bidding him arrivederci.

6

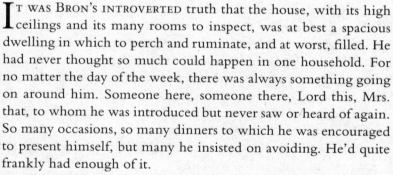

I T WAS BRON'S INTROVERTED truth that the house, with its high ceilings and its many rooms to inspect, was at best a spacious dwelling in which to perch and ruminate, and at worst, filled. He had never thought so much could happen in one household. For no matter the day of the week, there was always something going on around him. Someone here, someone there, Lord this, Mrs. that, to whom he was introduced but never saw or heard of again. So many occasions, so many dinners to which he was encouraged to present himself, but many he insisted on avoiding. He'd quite frankly had enough of it.

When he awoke in the early hours one Tuesday morning, to a moment of calm, he snuggled up in his bedsheets and scrolled through Facebook for something to do. He refreshed his timeline, the ads renewing themselves into previously searched skincare products he couldn't afford, and for a moment succumbed into the inevitable spiral of stalking an ex-classmate whom he had no real feeling toward but whose life updates brought a flicker of amusement to his morning. After a light release of endorphins, he opened his laptop to scroll the "Top Picks for You" category of Netflix. A favorite had recently been added to the list: *Pride and Prejudice*, 2005. *"Austenmania,"* Giovanni had said, but this particular period drama offered him not just a two-hour, nine-minute run of escapism, but a much deeper feeling of displacement.

He was familiar enough with the story, but it was the musical composition that brought it all to life, that settled him somewhere other; the sound of wind accompanying the protagonist's walk with book in hand, through fields of mildewed grass and filtered sunlight. This was home. Not the sound of a loving mother calling his name, nor the scent of roast dinner and gravy on a Sunday afternoon, but English mise-en-scène and set pieces, beautiful period-inspired fashion and the crescendo of song that transported his senses to a place on screen where he felt an undeniable kinship to these places and these actors. His wish to have been born in some other time and place fed by a multimillion-pound budget and actors toiling away on a cloudy day made sunny in a specified location hired out for the week. The ability to inhabit these lives had always been possible through reading, and he'd always been able to find a sliver of himself there—found the connection between himself and Jane at boarding school all encompassing—but while the great Victorian novel took up time, this adaptation, the first he'd seen of the sort, took up space, forcing what beforehand had only been illusion into reality, into the very fabric of his memory. If he could see it, he could remember it. And if he could remember it, he could relive it.

It had been Harry, the almighty tech whiz, who'd introduced him to these Americanized versions of Britain, where the glass of the screen worked as a mirror, reflecting to him that which existed only in his mind as absolutely possible.

He'd tried to get Harry to read the British classics, and at one point Harry had agreed to reading the book his friend had so adored. Ultimately, he claimed, it just wasn't to his taste.

"I thought it would be about dancing and marriage and other girly things like that. With that guy everyone seems to name their dog after?"

"You're thinking about Pride and Prejudice *by Jane Austen. This is* Jane Eyre, *by Charlotte Brontë."*

"Way too many Janes. Isn't it all kinda the same?"

"No. It's not. What did you think, really?"

"It's all a bit much, I think? A bit dull."

"Much? Dull?"

"Wordy. Depressing."

"No!" he'd retorted. "It's romantic—it's beautiful."

"Romantic? How? The main guy's a bit suss, isn't he? Like . . ."

They were sitting alone in Star of the Sea. Harry had just finished an afternoon game of rugby and was flicking through the pages of the book with cautious fingers. Bron had been marking up a diagram of a plant cell's structure, having already labeled the cell wall, the nucleus, the mitochondria, the cytoplasm, and the chloroplast. There was something still missing; he wasn't sure what.

"I don't know why you'd say that. It's the best book in the world."

"To you it's like it's the only book in the world. All I'm saying is, I don't get your obsession with it. It's always the same book, over and over again."

"That's not true!"

"Well, if it's ever something else, it's still something ancient written by dead people. Why not try something new?"

He remembered it like any fleeting moment, the impact it had on him: the snatching of the book from Harry's hands and his refusing to let him have it back, which only made Harry laugh. How Harry quickly came over to ruffle his hair, and told him his diagram was missing the ribosomes, how he'd dotted them in in pencil.

Harry had never been encouraged to finish reading *Jane Eyre*, but what he did do was teach Bron how to torrent the film versions of his favorite novels on the school computers, little digital files they kept stored on a memory stick or sometimes burned onto CDs. Harry enjoyed the illegality of downloading at the school's expense, and Bron was fascinated by what Harry explained to be a peer-to-peer network, a process where millions of people shared little bytes of the same file through the internet. How wonderful, he thought, for a group of people to be connected by the love of the same story, each offering up little bits of different pieces to create one and the same whole.

"*So every file is like Frankenstein's monster. Lots of different parts creating one and the same thing.*"

"*Uh, yeah, something like that. Why not?*"

And once, Harry had shared a Tumblr post suggesting a phase through which every adolescent would pass, a time where they would have to choose between being a "Brontë person" or an "Austen person," and that this life-defining choice would make up one's entire personality. Bron certainly considered himself a "Brontë person" through and through, would often cast himself in Jane Eyre's role like some readily available actor, see his face reflected at a window that could have been Thornfield Hall's, and read the *you* in "you strange––you almost unearthly thing" as a prophetic description of himself by some destined future lover. Jane was but a host, and he the parasite drawn from her blood and working its way into his bloodstream.

But then, Harry had said, "*It's obviously clear which you are. But what about me? Would that make me an Austen person?*"

"*I don't know.*"

And having declared that he would "*absolutely, under no circumstance, read any more of that trash,*" Harry downloaded *Pride and Prejudice* off the internet as the film that he would watch with Bron. "*Keira Knightley, now her I can look at. She's way too hot for this kind of movie.*"

Bron remembered that sudden shift in his perspective, how the book that he'd read became almost secondary to the film, how all the microelements together transported him to another place and made him, by some miracle, a bigger fan of the Austen narrative.

"*So what did you think?*" Harry had asked.

"*Well, it's not like the novel at all,*" he'd said. "*And yet it's so much more.*"

Now, here in Bron's room at Greenwood, the lovers' on-screen tension was breaking, their admission of love and their slow coming together in the blue-green-tinted darkness enrapturing him—the sunlight perfectly angled their chins and flooded between the two bodies, but he was stirred by a noise outside his bedroom. Hitting the space bar, the screen paused to a closed-eyed Keira Knightley and a featureless face that could have been any man. Bron opened the door into the hallway. Nobody there.

Aspects of the movie he had seen chinked against the layout of the house as he made his way downstairs through the almost silence—Birdie was twittering in her cage, the washing machine was lightly churning—and he glided gracefully and barefooted, as though he were living in a dream and roaming his own castle. Suddenly he wasn't himself, but a character, walking the hall with nowhere to go. Until he caught his foot on the upturned corner of a rug. In the kitchen, the flagstone floor was icy-cold and quickly stirred him from his light stupor, reminding him of the chilly floorboards at St. Mary's. He entered the breakfast room, suddenly hungry and wanting of some cereal. But a figure was sat at the table, holding a glass of juice and munching on toast. Flicking through a newspaper.

Madame Clarence immediately rose, knocking her chair back. "Sir, you startled me."

"Sorry, please, please," he said. "I didn't mean to disturb you, do continue. I was just—"

He backed out of the room, despite the housekeeper's plea for him to please sit, join her—"It's fine, I'm fine"—he scrambled back into the hallway. He dare not sit in there, alone with Madame Clarence and her keen-eyed stare. But then he heard the shuffle of feet, some gentle humming. Half expecting to find Mr. Edwards there, he turned to behold Darcy descending the stairs instead, wobbling and impish in baggy joggers and a blanket wrapped around his shoulders. A snail in his shell. He was holding what looked like a weightless purple dumbbell in his hand. It was strange to see him ungroomed and disheveled in this way, and in such mundane circumstances. Had he just finished a workout? Until now, Darcy had existed only in the most prominent situations, in chapters dog-eared as noteworthy, but here he was roaming the unseen footage of in-between scenes, the trimmings of the cutting room floor. Bron tried his best to make himself small, to fade into the walls, but Darcy, spotting him there, stopped his humming. He pulled the blanket away from his shoulders in one quick swoop, bundling it in his arms, ran a quick hand through his hair, hoisted up his joggers—all the while addressing him: "Ah, Bron. I see you're up early. Ada told me you liked to sleep in."

Bron scrambled for something to say. "I'm not—I mean, I do, usually like to sleep in. I was just looking for something . . . for some, er . . ." He could give any answer, really. "Some granola, actually." He twisted toward the breakfast room's closed door, as if to say, *The goods, the granola, is in there.*

"Granola?"

"Yes, it's one of the better cereals," he said to Darcy's puzzled face. He embellished it with "And I'm hungry," to demonstrate the truth of it. He rubbed at his stomach.

Darcy continued to look at him blankly. Bron wanted to die.

"Well, alright. And I see you're avoiding Clarence in there. Good idea—she likes to ask a lot of questions in the morning. But if it's cereal you're after, I know where the good lot is kept. Come with me." Darcy led Bron back toward the kitchen, where the cold floor stung his feet again. He placed his dumbbell onto the island. On closer inspection, it turned out to be one of those grotesquely large three-liter water bottles, with motivational messaging notched at timely intervals with statements like "Great start!" "You got this!" "You're halfway through!" "Almost there!"

Darcy opened the fridge, the light illuminating him to look almost vampiric. Affixed to the fridge door by a magnet was a yellow note in what must have been Clarence's hand, which read: cheddar (extra mature), ~~leg of lamb~~—which had been struck through—red onions, basil, parsley, painkillers. And then, in another scrawl that he recognized as Ada's: chocolate pots (white), cheese strings, tangerines (no pips), grapes (no seeds!).

Darcy placed a glass bottle onto the kitchen island—"It's milk," he said. "For your cereal"—and gestured toward the pantry, where, Bron guessed, the spare granola must be kept.

"Thank you." Bron stabbed at the inside light switch to illuminate the cupboard. Finding a wide variety of cereal boxes and a bowl in there too, he dispensed the granola as quietly as possible before bringing it to the island. Pouring the milk was its own kind of torture, the flow of its decanting a kind of ASMR that felt, in that moment, like something intimate.

He watched as Darcy filled the electric kettle with water, and was grateful when he returned it to its base and pressed its switch, the whirr helping to silence his own crunching as he brought another spoon to his mouth.

"I haven't seen you around lately. Been sneaking into any more colleges?" Darcy asked, reaching out to the island to grab his water bottle, where he refilled it at the tap.

Bron wasn't sure how to frame that he'd been very much around, that it was *Darcy* whose absence had been noted, who made himself scarce, and who Ada asked after every morning and through every evening. He was always on the lookout for him too, solely so that he could avoid him, of course.

He spoke to Darcy's back. "No, but I quite intend to. I just haven't had the time. It's been a task, keeping up with Ada."

"She's a tricky one, isn't she? Quite the handful."

"I suppose," he agreed, feeling bad for doing so. "Though 'tricky' isn't the word I'd use. But she's who I'm here for, anyway."

"Hmm" was Darcy's only reply, and he folded himself deeper into his blanket. With his coffee made, his bottle filled, he motioned to leave the kitchen. "If anyone asks, you haven't seen me."

Bron nodded.

"Right, good morning, Bron."

He watched him as he walked away. He was left alone with his cereal.

When he returned to his bedroom, he waited till seven thirty. Hearing the bark of the dog through the hall, and Ada rushing down too, he waded again downstairs. Ada and Mr. Edwards sat at the breakfast table, Clarence entering to pour the tea, and not looking his way. Instead, she went straight to Mr. Edwards's side and poured a cup especially for him. She didn't offer this to either Bron or Ada, and he noticed the tea's odd coloring in the cup, its murky, amber yellow. But his attention to the housekeeper's movements was quickly overridden by Mr. Edwards's casual announcement of another party, a second ball, in fact, which he quickly learned he wouldn't be able to escape.

"What, another one?"

Ada cheered for Halloween—"All Saints and All Souls," Clarence corrected—and when she caught his sigh, Ada ordered him to "just have fun. What else is there to do around here? It's a big old house. We might as well use it."

And have a repeat of the last time? He wanted to confess to his little companion the things he'd overheard her brother utter. But he couldn't—his duty to her overrode his feelings. "I've never been good with people. You—you're so good at talking. I wish I could be like that. I'm just so timid, and good at fading into the background."

"No, you're not," she said.

"I'm not? What do you mean?"

"You're not timid. And fading, well, you're actually *really* bad at that. In fact, everyone was looking at you last time, even though you were wearing boy clothes. I think it was the headband," she said. He itched to correct her, to say, *There's no such thing as boy clothes.* "But don't worry, I liked it."

"I did too, Bron," said Mr. Edwards without looking up.

"I just don't like people looking at me."

"Then you should probably stop dressing the way you do," Ada replied.

Bron felt the sting of her words, her easy assessment of him. He expected such sentiments to come from strangers, had heard as much from Darcy. But Ada? Is that what she thought of him? That he could turn off his authenticity as easily as a switch? Or that it was something that encouraged attention?

"Ada, I don't do it for attention. I dress the way I do because it's, well, it's me——"

"Anyway, it's a masquerade party, after all, so it wouldn't make a difference."

He would let her comment go. There was not much more he was comfortable saying here. Not in front of Mr. Edwards. He would be sure to teach his lesson at a later date. "Masquerade?"

Ada nodded. "Yes, I've decided it just now. With your help."

"That's a good idea," said Mr. Edwards.

"See?" said Ada. "And nobody will even know who you are."

He had to admit, there was an appeal to dressing up. Of becoming someone else in disguise. Costumes had once enabled him to experiment with clothing. At St. Mary's, many a bed sheet or scarf had crowned his head, sweeping the dirt along with him as he paced the dorm room alone. He thought himself a princess, like Rapunzel. His experimenting with makeup took an early form of jarring lipstick and eyeshadows, but the coloring in of his plain features blessed him with a reasonable androgyny. He'd escaped to the countryside whenever he could, in this newly put-together costume, away from the boys and the school, for he dare not let them see him. This was a place he could occupy safely, a place between man and woman. Under an oak tree he would sit, his back pressed against the ridges of the trunk, in a dress he hid under his mattress. When, at last, some passers-by would come, a dog ahead of them and sniffing away at the grass, they would smile at him, not a smile of liberal mindedness, but a polite English smile that said they were people of a certain je ne sais quoi, before they clocked him and hurried away. He would notice the stiffness he caused to their bodies, the way he brought them closer together, their leaning fit of whispers. Always, at least one of them would cast a cursory glance back.

"I just don't think I'm up to socializing."

"Well, you must. It's an order." Ada rose from her seat, and Bron felt her stare suddenly more piercing than usual. "Has anyone seen Darcy?"

"No."

"I need to tell him about the masquerade theme," she said, rushing out of the room.

"Ada, you haven't finished your food," Clarence called.

And Bron didn't feel up to running after her.

In the library later that afternoon, Ada refused to complete her homework. She wanted to show Bron the secret passageway hidden inside the room—it was about time he was let in on the secret—and poked at a button near one of the bookcases, which gave way and opened into a door. The hair on Bron's arms prickled at this, and though it only led to the other wing of the house, working as a shortcut of sorts, it was through here that they spent the rest of the afternoon, to-ing and fro-ing in and out the hall.

"So this is where you hide when I seek?"

"Oh, I forgot. I'm going to have to find a new hiding place."

Eventually Ada resumed the topic of masquerade, and after Bron made it clear he would not be joining the party, she returned with Mr. Edwards in tow, moaning about how difficult it was to convince Bron to come to her party. Mr. Edwards confirmed once again that it was important he be there.

"It is my dying wish, boy," he said. "And Ada's."

He couldn't argue with his employer.

"Will there be dancing, Father? Waltzing?"

"There will be only waltzing. We shall waltz the house down if that is what you'd like. Ada, play some music?"

Ada searched for an appropriate record on the vinyl player, and before the scratchings could develop into the melodic shushing of Björk's "It's Oh So Quiet," she'd already rushed back to her father's side and stepped onto his feet with hers. Arching her shoulders back, she held her arms erect. Allowed him to take them and lead them forward.

Bron watched in fascination as this scene unfolded, father and daughter pacing about the room as though it had been choreographed. When the music sped up and they with it, he suppressed a laugh, equal parts awkward and true fascination. Halfway through the song, Ada cut herself away and ran to the record to stop it.

She pulled Bron up from the chair. "Now you try."

"No, Ada, I couldn't possibly—"

"You must, you must! Daddy will show you. Here."

She guided him to Mr. Edwards, who stood smiling, eager to welcome him. "I never got to dance with my own son."

Ada fixed his limbs like a robot in need of oil. His palms were sweating in Mr. Edwards's hands, who quickly wiped away at his chest to dry them. Took his hands again.

"I really can't dance—"

The song started playing again. "Shh . . . shh . . ."

"You've got to move your left foot forward, right foot sideways—there you go."

"You're doing great, Bron," said Ada.

"I don't think I can do it—"

"Now step back," Mr. Edwards said. "Aha! See? Well done."

"You're doing it!" Ada cheered.

And they twirled and twirled, and Bron even felt himself smile at one point.

"Thank you, but I think I'd rather stop." Ada cut the music. "Okay Ada, I'll come to your party."

"Hurray!" She jumped into his arms, and he hugged her back. Mr. Edwards winked at him before grabbing for the tumbler of whisky on the side. "Thank you, son. I haven't had a moment's peace all morning."

Bron put forward the condition that Mr. Edwards was not to partake in any costume buying on his behalf: "Please," he said, "I'd like to pick something myself." And then he asked a question that'd been on his mind all afternoon: "Is Giovanni Vespa to be invited to this party?"

"Not if Darcy can help it," Mr. Edwards said. "But the invitations have already gone out, and he might have accidently gotten one."

So that was that. He'd been made to agree. He would be going to the party. And now he had to confront the most daunting task of all: finding something to wear. Black skinny jeans, a long black T-shirt that flared at the ends, a bit of red at the mouth, and a cape, if he could find one. A modest vampire—that would do the trick. Would be easy and the opposite of attention-drawing. But what did a Halloween ball mean to the Edwardses? Basing his imaginings off the last party, he translated it to include pumpkins and candles floating above their heads, with fire-breathers in the courtyard and circus gymnasts trailing down ropes from the ceiling. There would be no cheap spiderweb confetti festooned along the walls, or drab skeletal figurines creeping in the corners. Anything Mr. Edwards hosted would be affluent, anything Ada suggested would be agreed to, and he would need to think beyond daywear and tomato ketchup condiments at the mouth if he was to hold his own. Not that he planned on staying long— Ada and Mr. Edwards had only stipulated that he be present. He would escape to his room and be forgotten easily enough. He surveyed his closet, wrapped a spare sheet around his chest like a bath towel and then threw it over his head.

"Boo!" he said to himself in the mirror. "I'm a ghost." Wishing to disappear.

Halloween had never been much cause for celebration. It usually meant a day sitting in St. Mary's and listening to Brother Mark implore that Halloween wasn't a holiday for the religious, but for the wicked, that it was in fact a devil's day—only to sit up later in his dorm room and listen to the boys who compared what they might have dressed up as, what sweets they would have collected.

Over the next few days, Ada went through her shortlist of costumes: a fairy, a mermaid, an astronaut, a ballerina, a bumblebee, and then wrote a completely new list: a damsel in distress, a Viking, or a jack-in-the-box. Instead of conjugating verbs as per his instruction, she found some cardboard in the cupboard under the stairs and took to constructing a makeshift box from which she could pop out.

"What will you be going as?" she asked. When he couldn't come up with anything, she went silent, threw her cardboard aside, and picked up some paper. Then she handed over her work:

Teach, taught, taught,
Think, thought, thought,
Choose, chose, chosen,
Buy, bought, bought,
Dress, dressed, dressed

(as should be at) Present:
I dress
You dress
He/she/ it dresses
We dress
You dress
They dress

Present continuous:
I am dressing
You are dressing
He/she/ it is dressing
We are dressing
You are dressing
They are dressing

Optional imperative: Let's dress

And, alongside it, their Latin conjugation, which he did not understand and could not correct, but which he was told by Mr. Edwards she should be tasked with: Vestis, Oranuts, Habitus.

"Okay, okay, I get it," he said. "So you already know how to conjugate verbs."

And in the end, having finished her work quickly, he admitted to the struggle he was facing. He needed a suitable costume. "What do you think I should go as, since you're full of so many bright ideas?"

"Well, you said you hate being looked at, so maybe you should go as a ghost. Cover you up entirely. I have just the sheet for it."

"Already tried that. Any other ideas?"

"Hmm . . ." She brought the nub of the pencil to her lips and tapped it animatedly. "Well, I still think you should at least wear a mask. You'd think that at a masquerade ball, everyone would be wearing a mask, but Daddy actually only put 'costume party' on the invites, and, well, I just think it would be really cool if we were all in some sort of disguise. You know, like—"

At this he sat up; sparked by an idea that corseted his stomach and beat at his temples. "Ada, I have just the thing. Why, you're a genius."

"I know I am. But what's the thing?"

He had yet to spend much of his wages. Mr. Edwards even insisted on giving him a hundred pounds extra to help him with his costume, so he had a large enough sum to pull together a garment he could be proud of.

He skipped the cheap high-street costume shops that only came alive around the holiday season and picked out the white facade wedged between the champagne-bricked streets like a slip of paper. The dresses in the window, the silk, the chiffon, the lace, set his heart aflutter. A push of the emerald-green door, heavier than he suspected, and the sweet chime of a bell as it opened, alerted the woman behind the desk to his presence. She offered her assistance should he need it. He thanked the lady and appreciated her smile, but felt her eyes follow him as he made his way over to the rows of cream and ivory dresses hung together and displayed on elegant headless mannequins. He read their meaning: He should not be there.

The material felt soft in his hands, and he swooped, swooped through the hangers, knowing he'd never be daring enough to attend the Edwardses' party in such a lavishly civilized get-up. Not to mention the price. No, he was in need of something more modest, and quickly vacated the store. He moved along the street, to a vintage shop that offered boutique clothing for a more reasonable fee, and trimmings to accompany these selections. A quick rummage through and he found something he knew would bring his plan to life. Though crisp and in desperate need of an iron, the taffeta skirt was long and voluminous, designed to take up space. At forty-five quid, the silk and polyester piece seemed almost meant for him. A tenner for white powder and a couple of trinkets and bracelets.

This, he knew, would do the trick.

On the night of the party, Bron half hoped angels would descend from the heavens as he slept and guide the transformation, or that he could cross out the day from his life with a pen and find it securely behind him. But it wouldn't be as easy as that. He would not sleep for seven days only to wake up and find himself completely transformed like Tilda Swinton in *Orlando*. No. It wouldn't be as comfortable as that. He would have to rely on years of honing his skills with a brush, a good YouTube tutorial, and a tight enough corset to execute this right. After he'd shaved away the burgeoning hairs from his chin and neck—alleviating his body dysphoria, at least momentarily—and while he waited for the heavy makeup to set, he flicked through the pages of his favorite book, in the interest of rereading the chapter that had always arrested him every time he'd come upon it. A moment that had inspired his costume.

As Bron rose and stood before the mirror in his new garment, he felt all the more powerful. Just as Mr. Rochester had lowered his social ranking by transforming himself from a wealthy, educated man into a poor woman, so too had Bron transformed himself into something else. His waist wasn't as small as a woman's could be, but he reasoned it wasn't large either. His shoulders weren't broad—he'd never developed that mound of muscle that crests into the neck, and was confident in the peaklike folds of flesh and bone there—and he slipped into the bodice comfortably. His collarbones framed the neckline nicely. It wasn't quite Jekyll into Hyde—the effects of the alternation were not as great as that—but he was confident it would do the trick. The bones of his face did not change, his lineaments were naturally small, and the contour had the effect of lifting his cheeks. He did not stoop lower; if anything, his spine stood that bit more erect even before he'd slipped into the heels. He was not altogether another person. Instead, he lurked beneath the heightened feminine facade. The foundation gave him a peachier complexion, neutralizing the grayish, milklike tint of his skin. The stroke of powder had almost removed the leatheriness underneath, like a facemask, leaving him softer and a little more blushed with the rouge applied. He wore his hair, and the accompanying extensions, in an elegant braided up-do. This completed the guise.

He was still Bron underneath, but who was it that adorned him? How would he be seen tonight? This was not an urge to trick anyone into confession; he was not a figure come off the early modern stage, nor was he the lead performer in an impersonation act of Madonna's "Vogue." But he felt a thrill: Would he pass as a woman? Blend comfortably with the others in their hyper-feminine costumes, or hear cheers of *"Yaass! Queen! Werk!"*—words intended to bring him empowerment, but which only tripped him up. Because, like Mr. Rochester's guise, he was only accepted as performance, a fabrication. He thought of Darcy, of the shame he'd elicited in him, how men can get away with all sorts of trickery, and yet it is nonconforming people like himself that the world is taught to fear. He wrapped his mustard shawl around his costume and put on his pearls.

He hoped to impress Giovanni in particular, who had claimed to have no interest in the Victorians but had all the time for the early modern playwrights. *But look at me,* Bron thought. *A body through which I can be both.* The transvestism of the early modern stage existing at once with his beloved Jane Eyre. He'd never quite understood it before, that the problem with Mr. Rochester's cross-dressing was the trickery at play. So here he was, reclaiming what it meant. Giving Jane her power back, to be the one incognito at a party.

He hadn't felt such nerves in a long time, had bitten his thumbnail right down to the edge until it bled, tasting the metallic blood when he sucked its corner to alleviate the sting. The puffed sleeves made his shoulders feel both heavy and light, and the curls of his hair rested neatly on his collarbones. When he came into the hallway, he heard the music playing and the chatter of voices, the clinking of glasses. He wasn't expecting an announcement or for all the eyes in the room to turn on him as he descended the stairs like they did in the movies. But his cheeks burned as he held the banister. In fact, nobody was looking at him. Nobody at all.

He took off to the side of the foyer and tucked himself away beneath the left side staircase. Here he sat among the beautiful women who dripped in diamonds and floated in gowns fashioned from the night sky, strands of black and purple crafted into glossy fabric; or wore burgeoning gowns like downy clouds—the overpuffed skirts, the dramatic mermaid drops to the floor, the great white fur draped around the shoulders; and the men, who all looked the same in their three-piece suits, though he spotted the occasional superhero, a tennis player, and even one who claimed he was the scariest thing of all: a "stay-at-home dad." And still, no one batted an eye his way, but everyone smiled politely. He was delighted.

He enjoyed picking out his favorite trims: the lace, the fringe, and the Bertha collars, the bony shoulders and swanlike necks, the things people wore in their hair. He'd even seen what resembled a live raven perched on somebody's shoulder. What world had he stepped into? Where Halloween dress meant stumbling into a party for the rich and fashionable, where such luxuries were the norm, and people danced one moment to Strauss's "Blue Danube Waltz" and the next to some acoustic rendition of "Crazy For You."

He grabbed himself a drink and returned to the space under the stairs, inspected the vintage-style record player, the golden hornlike speaker. It produced no noise, was only there

*Look at me, Bron thought. A body through which
I can be both.*

for aesthetic appeal, but it had been hooked to a surround-sound system by a cord that trailed up the stairs. He followed it through the landing (which guests emerging from the bathroom continually tripped over) and into another room, then moved to the balcony overlooking the court at the front of the house. Watched as more of the guests arrived. They emerged from Lamborghinis, Porsches, an old Mercedes-Benz. He quietly expected to hear the clip-clopping of hooves on the cobbled pathway, the approach of a horse-drawn brougham or chariot, dependent on the number of such a party, with heavily curtained windows, a crack of a black whip in the hands of the coachman. He expected the coachman—or the butler at the front of the door—either would do—to drop the steps before opening the door, to offer his elbow to the white gloved hand belonging to the beautiful girl with golden ringlets, whose green silk dress would glint in the moonlight, who would take in the facade of the house and turn up her lips into a grin. Entitled, bold, she would make her way to the entrance, mask in one hand, dress held in the other. What would the night bring?

He sipped at his third glass of wine, even though he didn't much care for the taste, and left the balcony in search of an Italian voice. He thought he'd heard it, carefree and loud, but it was only the raised voices of the hired staff, demanding that the canapés be served at once! A young waitress, holding a tray of red wineglasses almost knocked him over as she passed. He took another from her tray and replaced it with his empty one. Tipsiness had reached his head, affected his joints to float. With the net of sobriety loosening its ensnarement, he moved, agile, through the chaos of the party, smiling at anyone who locked eyes with him, as if sharing in their secrets. He thought to look in the library—perhaps he'd find Giovanni alone in there again. But the room stood vacant. The fire was burning within, keeping it warm.

Ada occupied her usual space when it came to parties, crouched at the top of the stairs on the landing, her head between the buffed and polished beams. She was talking to a woman in a 1920s style dress who crouched beside her. Custom to Ada's desired theme of the night, a feathery mask obscured the woman's face entirely. *At least somebody got the memo* . . . He, too, was wearing a mask of sorts. One that allowed him to explore yet another part of himself. But Ada was quick to recognize him, and shouted his name as he approached. The woman, seemingly unimpressed, darted away.

"Don't give me away too easily. You promised to keep my secret." He hugged her. "How are you enjoying the party then, sailor?"

Ada's olive skin shone against the alabaster-white of her costume, a vintage sailor's outfit, with a dark necktie knotted around her chest and a hat atop her head. She reasoned that rather than wanting to be a mermaid, she wanted to catch a mermaid. She held a net in her hand, and a mask with a moustache was strung to her face.

"Positively boring. People are having way too much fun."

But by the way Ada examined his fabric, he believed her to be quite impressed with his choice of outfit, a nineteenth-century extravagance.

Mr. Edwards climbed the stairs toward them, wearing something akin to Highland dress. His tartan kilt was red and green, the bright white socks pulled up to his knees like a schoolboy's, and the sporran rocking at his waist. Slung behind his left shoulder was a set of bagpipes that swung to and fro as he wound his arm around Ada. She whispered in his ear, and Mr. Edwards looked his way, astonished. "My boy, I almost wouldn't have recognized you dressed like that!"

"That was rather the whole point, sir," he replied.

A sudden twitch from the periphery of his vision, and he saw a figure mounting the stairs. He was only privy to his profile, and the way the railings obscured his face meant he couldn't be sure it was him. But as he watched the figure ascend toward them and then look back out into the sea of people who danced below, he was certain it was him.

Darcy looked particularly handsome. He wore the same black hat that he'd worn in the courtyard at Trinity, and together with a crisp white shirt that frilled at the collar and dripped from his wrists, it looked all the more costume-like. From the stiff way he was walking, Bron thought his breeches might be too tight to be comfortable, and found himself staring at the way the fabric molded his behind. Perfectly rounded. Darcy's masquerade accessory was an eye patch, over the eye that slightly drooped.

"Father," Darcy acknowledged. "Ada, shouldn't you be in bed by now? It's getting rather late."

"Oh no, not yet, not yet!" she begged, and peered around her father's leg, looking down into the crowd. Bored as she claimed to be, she was captivated by the floating dresses, dazzled by the glamour. "Please?"

"To bed with you, little one," Darcy said.

"Father?" she begged.

"Darcy's right, Addie. We let you stay up the last time."

She turned to Bron in a last attempt, but her eyes already admitted defeat. "Bron?"

When she called his name, Darcy's visible eye flicked upward, taking in the whole of him, the copious hair, the mustard shawl. Darcy's face strained, and Bron felt his shaved arms prick. His clothes, which he'd felt comfortable in only moments ago, now felt like what they were seen to be: a costume.

Bron shrugged; he couldn't argue against the wishes of her family, and now she'd given him away, he was rather annoyed with her. Perhaps her bedtime wasn't a bad thing. It would help his escape.

"Come on, Ada. I'll take you to your room," he said.

"No you won't," said Mr. Edwards. "Enjoy the party. I'll see to it."

Darcy crouched, nodded his head against his sister's, and flicked her nose. "Off you go. And don't sulk."

Mr. Edwards took her by the hand, and they departed toward her bedroom. He could hear Ada gushing as they waddled away: "Didn't he look lovely, Daddy? You wouldn't have even recognized him!" And Mr. Edwards's agreement that yes, yes he did look quite lovely.

Left alone with Darcy, Bron felt himself move one step forward, and then one back, ready for the oncoming onslaught. Downed his glass of wine. The sudden movement made Darcy turn toward him. He smiled and offered a slight bow. The motion seemed oddly sincere, though comedic, and Bron brought both hands to his cheeks to conceal the blush that threatened to burn through the layers of powder. He was also conscious of the wide hem of his dress brushing the legs of Darcy's trousers. However stupid and wrong he was to think there'd been power in his disguise, he couldn't walk away now. He fondled the trimmings that crossed his shoulders, and filled the interval that stretched between them with a low, but short-lived growl.

"Argh." He curved his index finger, lifting it like a hook. Darcy furrowed his eyebrows and straightened his mouth into a line, considering his actions. Bron hadn't expected a blank response. "Aren't you, well . . . aren't you a pirate?"

Darcy closed his eye, and rocking on the balls of his feet, tucked his arms behind his back. "Well, no," he said, glancing around before leaning forward. "I was hoping to live up to my nickname. I'm dressed as Mr. Darcy, you see. But I suppose I'm not doing a very good job of it?"

He didn't think so at all, imagining at once Colin Firth emerging from a lake. Or was it a river? Who knew.

"Darcy playing Mr. Darcy. Alright . . . But why the eye patch?"

His stomach pulsed against the tight binding of his corset. Maybe he shouldn't have asked that.

"I thought it gave a particular Halloween flare."

"Oh, right," he said, his shoulders relaxing. "For a second there I thought I'd been insensitive. That you were partially blind or something."

"That would've been a good excuse for tripping me up."

"I'm sorry."

"I suppose that could have been the case. I once had a riding accident when I was younger. Fell off a horse that'd slipped on some ice, and that was that. A thorn scratched me up. I don't torture myself with the specifics. But I do have a scar to prove it, see?" He lifted the eye patch to reveal the tiniest of scars, silver, shaped like a moon, at the crinkle of his eye.

"I see," he said, thinking not of Mr. Darcy, but of Mr. Rochester, who, though blind at the end of the novel, regains his sight two years later. It's meant to symbolize something, of course, but he wasn't sure what. "I'm sorry."

"You said that already."

"I know."

Darcy looked down at his feet and clenched his fists, released them and looked up again. "You know, I must say I have never seen Ada behave as well as she has the past couple of weeks, or smile as much, for that matter. She is usually quite unhappy for such an accomplished little thing, and always playing tricks."

"Oh? What kind of tricks?"

"The usual childish things—claims of seeing ghosts, only to haunt the halls herself at night. I believe she planted a doll beneath the bed of our last hire and put a frog in one of her pockets. Truly beguiling childhood farce, but she's managed to scare off a fair few. But not you." Bron suddenly wished he had more wine, and pushed the empty glass to his mouth for dregs. Darcy sipped alongside him. "You are a good thing by her side. I dare say she's lucky to have you. I would've whisked her off to boarding school at the earliest moment if I'd had my way, but Father has other ideas." Darcy scratched at his nose.

"Lucky to have me?" he said. "I thought you disapproved of someone like me?"

"Someone like you?" Taking a step forward, he dipped lower to speak into his ear. "And who exactly is someone like you?"

A number of replies filled his mind. Someone whose existence was up for debate, someone reduced to a point of discussion. Someone like him, in certain circles, would even suggest a menace, an online troll hampering the progression of women's rights. But he knew who he was, as someone scared, courageous, authentic. Someone whose existence was, in fact, at the mercy of people in power. People like Darcy.

"In reality I am something so unnatural as to cause havoc unto the world," he said. "At least that's what I read in the press. Bathrooms are my haunt."

"Bathrooms?" Darcy questioned, and then blinked, realizing what he'd missed.

"Yes, particularly the ladies'. I cannot get enough of them."

"Ah, I see," he said, forcing a polite laugh and looking down at his glass. Darcy swirled the remains of his drink. "Well, I suppose we all have our stomping grounds."

"And where is your domain?"

Darcy's face suggested a deep consideration of the question. "I think I would have to say my bedroom, with the curtains fully shut and my head under the pillow. My own cocoon, where no one can bother me."

"I appreciate that. I would say that is all we want from our bathrooms too. To sit and pee in peace."

"You pee sitting down?"

He coughed away the question and made an "um" noise. Darcy, blushing too, made some sideward steps to place his glass on the console table, offering to take away Bron's glass too.

"Thank you," Bron said, handing it over, and Darcy placed it aside and rushed back.

"Now I think it's only fair I get a good look at you, after all the effort you've made. Away with that shawl at once! Always making its appearance."

Darcy inspected him, a sweep across his skin as he pulled the shawl away from his shoulders. Bron sucked in his stomach, righted his bad posture; held his neck higher and pulled his shoulders back.

"Spin," he demanded, and Bron spun a slow turn. "Hmm, I suppose a congratulations is in order. With the rest of the party you have managed well."

"But *you* see through my disguise?"

Darcy gave him no answer, held his gaze until he faltered. At this, Darcy took him by the wrist and brought him down the stairs. Bron didn't appreciate the tightness of the grip, and protested at the yank. But his voice came out silent, tinny.

"I believe we had something of a rough start," Darcy said, leading the way into the center of the crowd, where legs and arms swayed gracefully to the waltz. Darcy placed his hands on the small of his back, and he shivered away.

"What are you doing?"

"I'm asking you to dance, of course."

"Asked to dance? By a man who likes to insult me?" He snatched his arm away and peered in search of people's stares. Only he found none. "Is this a joke? Could you not ask any of the women here?"

"I am asking you," he said sternly, letting out a breath, "precisely because you are not a woman."

Bron felt his face drop into something like shock, or sadness, or both. He wasn't a woman, but that didn't mean the words didn't hurt. He didn't know who he was.

"Won't people think it odd? To see you dancing with me. What is it you said the last time? That we are representing this house?"

"I know what I said, and it was wrong of me to have done so," he was quick to respond, with a confidence seeped in truth. The way Darcy had a hold of his hand felt somehow electric, gentle. Willing and wanting.

But did he want to dance? He braced himself for mockery. "I don't know . . ."

"Just look at you. They aren't to know."

So that was it. The reason he could be seen with him. He wouldn't be an embarrassment. A spectacle.

"One moment I'm inappropriate. The next, befitting a dance.

Darcy leveled him with his gaze. "Will you dance with me or not? Was it merely your intention to cause a stir looking like that, if not to dance?"

"I don't understand why wearing a dress should cause such a stir. Look around the room. Isn't that what everyone else is doing here? Wearing some sort of dress?"

Darcy's gaze strayed from his for a moment and he fumbled for an answer. "In any case, they aren't to know." Bron had given him a chance to redeem himself, and thought it best to turn away, protect himself, and protest against the ludicrousness of this request. But before he could speak, Darcy continued: "Look, I'm sorry. I don't . . . I don't know what the right words are to say, to convince you. I can see it in your eyes. Every time I say the wrong thing. I'm trying here. I am." Hearing some truth in this, Bron immediately softened. Darcy paved over his quick moment of angst by picking some imaginary flint off his shoulder, before regaining his composure. "As host of this party, and the enormous amounts of money spent entertaining our guests, I should be allowed to dance with any person I choose. And I know who I'd like to choose."

There was no denying the statement to be saccharine and "try hard." But there was something about it that Bron liked. He bit the soft inside of his cheeks.

"Even if that person happens to be an epicene boy in a somewhat tacky garment."

He faked a laugh. "God, you almost had me there. I spent good money on this thing!" He gestured to the skirt.

"Bron, I will not force you. But would you like to dance?" Darcy took a hold of his palm and shuffled his feet in the square he designated his own. "With me?"

Bron was sure this man was pretending. Acting. Playing a part. Reciting words meant to be romantic but which rested on the cusp of cloying. Did Darcy think they would charm his victim into submission, with that look of sincerity now washed across his face? Was Bron as gullible as that? Yes, he was. And more so too.

His soft "okay" gave in to the full weight of Darcy's pull, and with Tchaikovsky's "Sleeping Beauty Waltz" playing in the background, Bron couldn't have predicted the night would take a turn like this.

Darcy said, "No, no, like this," and grabbed him tighter as they stepped about slowly, counting out one two three, one two three, as Darcy's father had done with Bron, until Darcy spun him in an unexpected twirl. Bron concentrated on the floor, his neck twisting left to right to ensure his feet stepped the right steps and followed Darcy's as they should. When they picked up the pace, Darcy spun him again as though he were a qualified dancer who could pull off such a routine. With each and every dip, Darcy brought him closer to his chest, his breath in his face, which smelled of wine, and the fragrance wafting off him a mix of leather and pepper and incense.

Bron risked a glance up at this man, who gripped at his waist and dropped his hands. He could feel the warmth and weight of them through his clothes, on the small of his back. It made Bron stop and pull away, conscious of the things it stirred in him. That there was perhaps too much drink in his own system, and Darcy's, to validate any of these feelings. Because while he was anxious and worried about others gawking at him with looks of confusion, he was also captivated by the unlocking of something like longing within him.

But settling into a slow rhythm, all those in his periphery melted away from view, a change of shot, but a continued sequence, until all he saw was this man leading him. Like all those women he'd seen on film, he felt as scandalous as Anna and Vronsky from *Anna Karenina*, as hypnotized as Natasha by Andrei in *War and Peace*—they were in a crowded room, surrounded by those who would scorn and sneer at him if they knew, but he danced alone in his own little world, with a man who didn't understand him but who, for one reason or another, charged a magnetic pull toward him. For a moment there was Darcy, and Bron was all at once Keira Knightley, Mia Wasikowska, Charlotte Gainsborough, Lily James. Of course it was an illusion, but for a moment he believed it to be entirely true.

He knew this was not how it went for people like him, and somewhere in the room he was sure to find the wizard behind a screen, directing their every move, shouting "CUT!" to end the take, so they would fall back into their normal selves.

"You must forgive me for my previous outbursts," Darcy said, again on his path of penitence. "There is something unnerving about the way you are, so comfortable in your own skin, and I shouldn't have made a mockery of it." He forced them to a halt, and Darcy seemed poised to say more, but then Bron felt a sharp contortion of Darcy's body—a quick tug away from his hand, a sudden stiffening.

Bron followed Darcy's gaze to that of a woman staring at them both, the same woman who'd been talking to Ada on the stairwell. Darcy brushed his lips against Bron's gloved fingertips in a quick motion, and bowed. All soft expression, the hint of what Bron could've sworn was genuine pleasure, melted away from his face, replaced by a formal, blanched look.

"Meet me in the library tonight when the party's over," Darcy whispered, close to Bron's ear. "But for now I must leave you."

Darcy left him feeling like a gutted fish, insides spilled out for all to see. He watched as Darcy ascended the stairs and walked toward the woman who looked at them. It made his heart beat faster, each step he climbed. And when Darcy glanced back over his shoulder, he felt himself closer than when they had been touching, a beam of light connecting his eyes to Darcy's. A floor apart, yes, but this was a vital moment in any story, where a glance of want is shared between two people. He felt it in his chest, how they'd ceased to be separate beings, how his heels pinched his toes, and how the music drowned his ears; how Darcy's glance back for him made him think he was somebody, not just some man in a dress, but someone whose life could be made into something. A glance that showed him where the old Darcy ended and a new one began.

Bron held out the hems of his dress and twirled around the foyer, through the halls where people gathered and spoke, between sips of champagne, about shambolic governmental policies, about trade deals or the monarchy. If one who had known him before could see him now, they would say that his face had transformed, that his skin emitted a glow, that his glide through the rooms allowed him to walk an inch above ground.

So, as instructed, he took himself into the library, where Darcy had said he would meet him.

———⟨§⟩———————————⟨§⟩———

7

B RON WAS DISORIENTED BY the ambiance of the library, the effects of the wine, and the dancing. The room was chaotic, a litter of objects fighting for his attention: the whisky bottles on the drinks trolley surrounded by crystal glasses and decanters, the gilded picture frames strewn along the mantelpiece, Ada's open books and paper scattered along the carpet at his feet. He found a tissue packet on the side table and wiped the makeup off his face. He'd never worn as much as this—scrubbed hard, and it chafed. Resorting to covering his face with his hands, he scattered back down the hall and into the bathroom, where he shrugged off the heavy accessories and wiped his face with micellar water and a towel before returning to the library.

His ears thrummed as he waited for the party to die down, loud voices still echoing through the house, the alcohol gone to his head. He lit the table lamp, the honey glow making a puddle on the floor. He climbed the decorative ladder that reached up to the shelved platform and grabbed for the book with the prettiest spine, the gold lettering: *The Hunchback of Notre Dame*. He read to himself, heard the words being voiced aloud but was unable to take in their meaning. The crackling of the embers in the fireplace, the ticking of the clock, this was all he heard. The silence spoke volumes.

He browsed the shelves some more. Great atlases the height of three books, and volumes with leathery spines and smelling like perfume, offered titles in Latin, Hebrew, Greek. There was a collection of Tudor Church sheet music, too delicate looking to touch. Large records in old cases, of Bach, Beethoven, Mozart, of Puccini and Schubert, Tchaikovsky and Wagner, and names he'd never heard of, but which sounded just as extravagant. His favorite find was the relatively modest set of books on the history of Hollywood cinema: the MGM story, the Paramount story, the Universal story, the Colombia story, the RKO story—such range!

And then he came across the Edwardses' story, or at least glimpses of it: a set of photo albums, all bound in an identical burgundy cloth. He selected the third at random and brought it to where he would sit in the armchair, feeling quaint and fragile as he sank back into the grandness of it, the large book open, displayed on his lap.

The photographs within weren't sepia toned, nor were they black and white, but the quality of these images had that archaic feeling to the modern eye, where they looked almost discolored. He leafed through the thin pages similar to Bible paper, the photographs amusing him at first, each with a little descriptor of the snapshot—the interspersed images of a younger Mr. Edwards with a baby in his arms, and a beguiling young woman at his side, who held this same baby in the images that followed. "Victoria & Theodore," they had been labeled. Mr. Edwards's late wife, Darcy's mother. And then a trio of photographs, two carefully set on each side, and one firmly in the middle of the row below.

The first image to the left was a display of the family: Mr. and Mrs. Edwards sat poised together with a toddler. Mrs. Edwards's center parting, so sharp and white in contrast to the darkness of her hair, a head that could crack at any moment; Mr. Edwards's smile beside her, indication enough that her plain features weren't of concern to him. The second image, of father and son, was a more entrancing vision: where Mr. Edwards wore black, the young boy wore white and was perched on his lap, demure, motionless, almost unhappy to be there, and looking away from the camera's lens. In the third photograph, the child sat on the stool alone, in an identical fashion, wearing the same expression as in the second photograph, so much so that it appeared to be the same picture, only altered, with Mr. Edwards somehow removed. Ada was nowhere to be seen within these pages; Darcy's growth from infant into adolescence took up most of the thick volume. In the latter pages of the album, he found an assortment of images which he hadn't expected to see.

The coarse, waved hair tied back, the warm brown skin. Giovanni. Pages and pages of photographs with the two of them— Darcy and Giovanni—together, clearly the best of friends, out in the city, together in a college dorm, in the rooms at Greenwood. The way they smiled, stood close to one another, hung onto each other's arms. Bron felt a pang of jealousy, of these two men so close together. The photographs took on a life of their own. In his mind, they flickered into movement like a motion-picture, where he first imagined them meeting at the university.

Darcy's eyes would have found him across a function room in one of the many colleges; they were attending an after-hours lecture on who knows what? Pamphleteers and the upside-down world of the Interregnum. Yes, something sophisticated and Oxbridge-sounding like that. And at the drinks reception they'd introduce themselves, bond instantly over their love of coffee, or red wine, the distaste they shared for the cheap pinot on offer. Still, they downed it by the bottle, made their way back to Darcy's dorm at Trinity to escape the rest of the cohort. What happened next? He could see it in his mind's eye: the vacant way their intoxicated eyes would wander. When they reached the dorm, Giovanni would retch at the threshold, in the in-between of the doorframe, and Darcy would immediately rush through to the en-suite bathroom to alleviate himself of the alcohol that thrashed around his own stomach, their dual puke-parade a bonding of friendship they'd never experienced before then. Though certainly, Bron knew, it would come to leave a dark mark on their lives, as Giovanni's vomit had on the wooden floorboards of some Trinity dormitory.

Bron blinked, in awe of his findings, and flicked to another page to find an even more captivating photograph: a rowing boat idle in the water behind two figures. Darcy, who was thin and wearing his rowing kit, perhaps having just won a race? And beside him, Giovanni, sitting with downcast eyes on the edge of the River Cam, one arm outstretched and only just touching Darcy's thigh, the other brushing at an oar. He was wearing a bowler hat, was smartly dressed—it must have been hot that summer's day, for his jacket had been tossed aside. What had gone on there? Was Giovanni not keen on the prospect of rowing, but still supportive of his companion? Had he agreed to run along the river and cheer on as his friend oared the murky waters? Afterward, with Darcy's muscles aching from the strokes and Giovanni's legs aching from the run, did they come to rest at the place in the photograph, where they sat by the river to talk about . . . what? Poetry? Their contrasting upbringings? Did they speak until the breeze grew cold and the night bloomed dark? The river's lip their haven. And on the days where night descended on them with words still left to share, did they linger at Scudamore's quayside and shuffle into the empty boats with a bottle of chardonnay, to watch the moon and listen to the lapping of water around their silent chuckles? The gentle jangle of the boats' sides against each other. A sound to settle these two lovers.

Beneath the page was written, in curled inky letters: *MICHAELMAS TERM, FIRST YEAR.*

Bron closed the book, returned it to the shelves, and stared aimlessly into the fire, thinking back to the way Darcy had reacted upon finding Giovanni in this very room with him, and Mr. Edwards's friendliness toward Giovanni. When had Darcy first chosen to bring him to Greenwood? Had Mr. Edwards taken as easily to Giovanni as a sponge to water? Certainly by the way Mr. Edwards's eyes sparked at the sight of him on the evening of the last party, it wasn't difficult to see that Giovanni had somehow become a part of the family, that there might be some truth to Bron's imaginings. But where had Giovanni been tonight? He'd almost forgotten that it was partly for him that he'd gone to the effort of dressing.

He'd almost given in to the drift of sleep, when somebody walked in and shut the door. Darcy. "Aren't you missing a pair of wings? Or something of a laurel crown?"

Bron shook himself awake, eyelids heavy. *What did he just say?* This mode in which he began, this riddled dialogue of an opening statement, had him grasping for meaning.

Resting his head in his palm, Bron wiped the drool onto his clothes.

"Only you look like the creature off Dürer's engraving," Darcy continued matter-of-factly, though his voice sounded heavy, annoyed. "Pensive and dejected, drowning in the folds of your own frock. What's the matter?"

"Nothing's the matter." He cleared his throat and glanced at the clock. "I'm perfectly well. Actually, I've been waiting for you, as you so kindly asked me to, but I see it is now past two, and I'm tired." He heard the irritation in his own voice, but really he was elated. Darcy had come. Just like he'd said. But the fantasy was over, and though he'd soared the skies like an angel only hours before, the oncoming sobriety had him tumbling back down to earth to have landed . . . where? In this armchair. A crash landing.

He both wanted and feared Darcy, standing there before him, and whose every remark was inflected with insult. Hanging onto the belief that he would be taunted, he rose. "I should probably take myself to bed."

"Wait," Darcy said, words slurring and slow from drink. "Just a moment. I know I asked you to come here, and that you have waited up for me."

"I think that you forget that I am employed by your father to look after your sister. I imagine such a task extends to his son should he request something of me, as you did tonight."

Darcy's face fell into a look of disappointment. Had Bron been too harsh? He wished he could take his words back.

"Are you saying that you waited for me here out of loyalty to a job description?"

"I—I waited here because you asked me to wait here."

"And you did."

"So?"

"Ah yes." Darcy sighed, as if he had forgotten the reason to their meeting, so late it was early again.

The house had quietened by now, and Bron wondered how many guests still drank downstairs, or if they had all said their goodbyes. Darcy gestured for him to sit back down in the chair, and when he did, he leaned against the desk. "I wanted to ask about a new acquaintance of yours, formed in the walls of this room." He paused, his fingers creating loops in the air. "Giovanni. In case you had forgotten."

"I hadn't forgotten," Bron said. "What about him?"

"He didn't happen to mention what he was doing here the other week?" he asked. "Or say anything to you that I should know about?"

"Not that I recall," he said, the image of Darcy and Giovanni by the River Cam still at the forefront of his mind. "You are not much of a friend to him anymore?"

"Hah, well." Darcy puffed, whisking a hand through his hair and looking only into the firelight. He peeled the eye patch away from his face, spun it around on his forefinger by its band. "No, I am not." The weight behind his words was heavy, a palimpsest that carried a history.

"Who was that woman who you met at the stairs? Who was looking at us?"

"Nobody to trouble yourself with."

He was not in the mood for evasive answers. Bron stood. "Right, well, if that is all you needed of me, I should probably get going to bed." He retrieved the clutter of his things before moving toward the open door. There was a part of him that expected—wanted—Darcy to stop him a second time, to invite him to sit down again and acknowledge the moment they'd shared together that evening, if he had felt something between them . . . or at the very least, reveal all that had occurred between him and Giovanni.

But Darcy let out only a breath before sinking into the armchair himself, decanting a whisky and then saying, "I admit I have enjoyed myself tonight more than words can express, both earlier on the dance floor, and even now in here with you."

Bron latched onto every word, felt himself pivoting toward him.

"But you're probably right. It is late. Take yourself to bed." Bron felt his chest deflate. "Goodnight, Bron."

"Goodnight," he managed, carrying himself through the door and leaving him there. When he glanced back, and he did so only once, it was to find him reaching for the poker and stabbing at the fire, and then twiddling with his eye patch in perfect silhouette. With a glass tipped to his lips, Darcy was a pirate docked in a pub after years at sea, huddling to the edge of the hearth for warmth, and Bron was a mermaid, slithering away beyond the bounds of his reach and his capture.

Bron loosened the laces of his corset, and his chest caved outward; he slipped out of the skirt and into a deep sleep as soon as his head hit the pillow.

He was soon dreaming of a moment that could've almost been true, though removed from himself, he a spirit hovering above and watching as it unfurled. There they were in Cambridge in a college dorm. At first the two figures were Darcy and Giovanni, but as he settled deeper into sleep, he came to realize it wasn't them at all. It was himself, another version of himself, who sat by the single mattress and who was comforting the boy who'd been crying.

"*Bron.*" It was Harry's voice, croaky, like parchment paper, a voice that had finally broken. "*I don't understand how you can live like this and just be okay with it all.*"

"*I . . . I don't know,*" he'd said. "*Perhaps I'll leave one day.*"

The setting was not a Cambridge dorm at all. It was a school. Yes, it was St. Mary's! The peeling wallpaper. The rickety springs of the bed. The drip drip drip of the pipework that filled the bucket nearest the windowsill. And he, as much a feature of the place as the floorboards. "*I guess it's just . . . my life right now.*"

"*Yes, your life. Your life to do whatever you want with.*" Bron knew the real reason Harry had been sent there—that his parents, who were always jetting off on a holiday guised as a business trip, had Harry's life already planned out for him. He was to focus on his education and eventually study medicine at Corpus Christie College, Cambridge, just like his father had before him. And *his* father before him. That's all they really cared about.

Was there a chance that Harry could really be there in Cambridge, in the same place Bron was now?

"*My life is all planned out for me, but not yours. You're free. I just hate it here.*"

"*I know.*"

"*Bron, I need you to help me. Will you help me?*"

"*Yes, yes, I'll help you.*"

"*Will you follow me? Follow me anywhere I go?*"

"*Yes, I'll follow you.*"

"*I need you to——*"

Harry's mouth went slack, gaped open, a face resembling a young boy's and then a man's and then neither. It whimpered, called his name, a throaty sound, again and again until it reached a scream.

"*Bron! Bron! Help!*"

Then Harry's face was Darcy's face, now Giovanni's, and then a child's face again. Harry's. Everything spinning around him, turning the world upside down.

"Bron."

"Bron, Bron, help!" it screamed.

Nails bit into his shoulder blades, and he was shaken awake. The shrieking face morphed before his eyes into a little girl who shook him in his bed. Ada was screaming and tugging at his arms. He hadn't any idea what was happening, but the urgency with which she pulled at him made him run after her. He was reeling from delirium.

His nose was clogged, and as she dragged him through the hallway, the smell of char and burning wood hit him. He threw open the door to the library, coughed on the smoke-thick air, the flames trailing up the curtains and eating away at the books.

"I couldn't sleep, I couldn't sleep!" Ada sobbed. "But I heard something and—my books—my books were in there, so I went to get them—" She slammed into him.

"Ada, please stay calm." He shook her shoulders. "We need to get your father now."

"Papa! Papa—he's not there. I went to his room, but he's not there!"

"Ada! Your brother then. Whoever you can find. Clarence!" he screamed, relieved to see her suddenly appear.

"I heard all the screaming. Ada, come now, quickly, quickly."

Their feet pounded the carpet. The flames inside the room licked up the mahogany desk like a coffin on a pyre. He ran to his room, the closest to the library, and grabbed for his phone, dialing for the fire brigade, then raced back to the library. Ada should have gone to the others first. Had wasted precious time coming to him. What could *he* do?

The room was red and orange and smoke. He spotted a hint of crystal glass rolling on the floor, a tumbler from which Darcy had been drinking. Darcy, who'd been left alone in the room, drunk, in the early hours of the night.

Ada's loud scream downstairs sounded like demonic laughter echoing through the halls. He turned away from the room. He should leave—leave and join them safely downstairs. Instead, he peered further into the flames, to the winged-back armchair, spotted the hem of a robe, the glint of a jacket—and was that an arm—a hand? Bron knew instinctively that it was Darcy.

Thinking not of his safety, and going against his instincts and everything he'd learned from years of fire drills, he pushed into the room, the smoke choking him and stinging his eyes. He shut them, thrust himself forward, and felt his way through, blinded.

"Darcy!" he called out, but coughed on it. He made it to the chair: empty but for the robe that had been left there. What had looked like a body within was no body—a trick of the eye, a moment of panic.

A hand pulled at his shoulder sharply, dragging him away from the flames and tossing him out of the room and onto the floor. He felt a dull pain at the back of his head as it struck against the door. Bleary-eyed, he saw Darcy towering before him in loose clothes, a white linen shirt, meaty thighs at his eye level. He threw a bucketful of water, knocking over one of the decanters in the meantime, which sent the flames into a more ferocious frenzy. The wallpaper melted away like unfurling scrolls. Bron peeled himself from the floor.

"Stay back," Darcy ordered.

He cowered at the doorway, and inside a window shattered, glass shards falling into the room like rain. They needed to get out of there.

"Come away," Bron said, gripping his shoulders, but Darcy only knocked him off. Ada's continued scream howled across the hall.

"It's lost, it's lost, it's gone," Darcy wailed, a wounded man, and sirens began to blare outside. The firefighters were quick coming through the doors, and Clarence urged them up the stairs, holding Ada close to her chest. Darcy hollered, asking the brigade if they had anybody manning the courtyard. "You can get to the window from there. And we must alert the Hansons!"

Darcy's chest heaved heavily through his shirt. The air was hazy with smoke, breathlike, as if it were Darcy releasing it into the cold night.

"Sir, you must both vacate the building immediately."

"I can't believe this," Darcy cried, his face, his hair dripping with sweat. Bron reached out to him, his chest prickling from gooseflesh. The sweat from Darcy's face dripped onto his; he pressed his forehead into it.

"*Now*, sir," the fireman repeated, pulling them away.

"I thought you were inside," Bron said.

Darcy allowed the fireman to maneuver them downstairs. Bron gripping onto his forearms.

When they'd reached the outside, Ada clung to them both. The fireman urged them farther away from the house, but Darcy broke away, ignoring the pleas for him to step aside, and took a hold of a hose. A firewoman took over, her face hidden beneath the dip of her glaring yellow helmet. She led Bron and Ada by the arms and guided them to the courtyard, where they looked up to the now windowless hole in the building, the flames continuing their dance as water fought to quench them.

"Captain! Where's Captain?" Ada said, screaming that the dog was still inside. The firefighters ran to the rescue—"Birdie! Birdie too!"—and they emerged with a quivering dog and a caged bird.

An elderly couple, who must have been the Hansons, stood in matching nightwear, the woman's hair a tendril of silver along her back, her blue and white hands clasped to her mouth as the ivy burned before them. Even the trellis outside the window had caught, although they'd managed to put it out before any real damage had been done to the borders beneath. Bron stroked the curls of Ada's hair and watched as the cursive smoke dissipated into the sky. They listened to the gushing of the water from hoses, the hooting of the owls in the trees, and the sirens still blaring.

"I'm cold," Ada said.

"Yes," he said, shivering now as the adrenaline drained from his blood. "I'm cold too."

An engine roared through the gates, and the car's headlights flooded their bodies. Mr. Edwards climbed out of the vehicle and rushed toward them.

"What is going on? Is everyone okay? Is everybody safe? What has happened? What has happened?"

They huddled together for warmth and inhaled the air that smelled like a bonfire.

8

BRON AND ADA HAD been bundled into a taxi before the fire had ceased and taken to the nearest hotel for the night.

When Mr. Edwards arrived that morning, slightly after ten, his eyes were heavy from exhaustion. Still, he insisted on joining them for a late breakfast in the hotel lobby, though Darcy, entering a couple of minutes behind him, went straight to his room for sleep.

Mr. Edwards explained that it had taken the firefighters a couple of hours to extinguish the outbreak in the library. There wasn't much they could salvage: a glass vase that had been tucked away into one of the wooden cupboards closest to the door, and a couple of picture frames holding photographs that were only slightly tarnished. Mr. Edwards also muttered something about smoke particles lingering in parts of the house, even though the fire had been contained to the one room.

"Smoke particles?" said Ada. "In the air? What does that mean?"

"It means that we'll have to spend a few days here until everything is deemed safe for our return."

Mr. Edwards spent the afternoon answering phone calls from many of the guests who'd been in attendance at the party, who called to say they'd heard what had happened, what a shock it was! What a shame for the community. Could they do anything to help?

"Did they say what caused it?" Bron asked eventually.

"Yes, did they?" asked Ada.

Darcy was the one to answer the question later that evening—he explained that he'd lit a candle while in the room that night, but was certain he'd extinguished it before leaving. He had shown the firefighters where it had stood, on the chance he'd been too far gone to snuff it, but whatever the case, they insisted the candle wouldn't have been the cause of the fire. It might have been an electrical short-circuiting, a faulty wire in the antique lamplight that lived on the mahogany desk, which might've sparked to set the drapes alight, and the blaze would've trailed to the bookcases. *"Paper feeds fire."* Though, nonetheless, they couldn't be certain.

They were given the all-clear a week later. Nobody slept that first night back in the house. Mr. Edwards could be heard pacing around downstairs, frantic and on the phone to anyone who'd answer it. Darcy shut himself away in his bedroom, wanting to be left alone. Little Ada curled up with Bron in her bedroom, the eiderdown pulled up to their chins—a week of sharing the hotel's connecting suite had brought them all the closer. They drifted in and out of sleep until the alarm went off that morning.

The atmosphere was considerably changed. The library had been gutted, a carcass of a room. The smell of smoke and burnt paper permeated the hall into the week that followed. At breakfast, Darcy flicked through the morning paper. Somehow, it was still being reported in the local, the headline reading: *"Grade II listed building, Greenwood Manor Fire: Library engulfed by blaze, family unharmed and set to return, no signs of foul play."* Ada tried to spark conversation, but only Bron acknowledged her. She took to buttering her toast loudly.

From the breakfast room window, he could see the cars that stalled outside the gates, onlookers peeking through to get a glimpse of the wreckage. But Bron didn't think there was all that much to see. When the doorbell rang, Mr. Edwards stood up from the table and excused himself from the room. Ada scuttled along behind him, leaving Bron and Darcy alone together. He was grateful for this moment. Since the night of the fire, there hadn't been much of an opportunity for the two of them to speak—about what had happened between them on the dance floor or of whatever it was he'd felt being pulled from the burning room. Had Darcy felt it too?

Darcy didn't look up at him, but sipped at his orange juice and coffee, took a single bite of jam toast. Sitting upright in his chair, Bron was poised to slice through the silence. Instead, he lingered over his food, and struggling to eat another morsel, placed the silverware onto his plate, knife and fork carefully in the middle, to strike a perfect midnight. He pushed for the words to leave his throat, but before they could, Darcy stood, knocking the table as he did, to shut the curtains.

"Why isn't there any bloody privacy around here, for God's sake?" he spat. Bron thought about answering but bypassed that for a statement to acknowledge and simply nod his head to.

Darcy folded up the paper, taking a last sip of drink, and hurried out of the room. Bron felt breathless. Was that all Darcy had to say to him after everything that had happened? The dance, the fire—had he imagined it all, the connection he'd felt between them? No, he couldn't have. It was real, as real as the tea that burned his tongue as he sipped it.

He heard Madame Clarence's French before he saw her. She entered the room, speaking loudly into her phone before stopping at his presence. "Excusez-moi," she said, though it wasn't clear if this was directed at him or into the phone. "I thought breakfast was over."

Through the remainder of that week, Mr. Edwards occupied himself by turning off all the lights and power sockets, inspecting every room for burning candles each night before for bed, and soon there were electricians testing the voltage of every appliance in the house. Ada developed an interest in fire safety and started using words like *oxidation* and *combustible material.*

"We really should have a blanket or extinguisher in every room of the house," she said, and explained the different types that were available: carbon dioxide, water, foam, and dry powder.

It seemed she was coping the best of them all, though Bron noticed the way she pressed herself against one side of the banister when climbing the stairs, so as to stay as far out of reach from the right wing of the house as she could. Every morning as he emerged from his bedroom, he too was shocked to see the vacancy of the library at the other end of the landing, the rectangular wooden framing and the bare limestone walls scorched black, the remains of ornaments, books, and other miscellanea burnt to a roughage of ash. It was like looking into an alternate reality. The library, once so snug and warm, now dank and lifeless.

Worst of all, Darcy was nowhere to be seen. Over the coming days, Bron couldn't stop thinking of him, suited and bowing and twirling him around one minute, disheveled and sweating in nothing but a white linen shirt the next. He wished to see his face, to hear his deep, gruff way of talking. When Mr. Edwards casually enquired as to his son's whereabouts, Clarence explained that Master Edwards had gone out, that there was no message left, only that he would be back later. Bron tried to hide the look of disappointment on his face, but Clarence must have seen something in it, prompting her to continue. "Around eight or nine. That's usually the time he comes through the door, just as I'm leaving."

As dusk closed and dawn approached, still he didn't appear. Bron made the effort to push thoughts of him out of his mind. To pretend nothing had changed between them.

Ada and Mr. Edwards, used to his comings and goings, simply developed a game for it: "Where do you think he's gone off to this time?"

Situated as the house was in close proximity to three airbases, it was not uncommon to find a plane flying overhead. Whenever they heard as much as a hint of plane traffic, Ada and Mr. Edwards would rush to one of the windows, open the latch, and play their round.

"There, there," Ada screamed. "Darcy must be on that plane, and he's on his way to . . . Germany!"

"No, no, silly," Mr. Edwards would reply. "That's not where that plane is going. He's actually on his way to Guatemala."

"You're wrong, Daddy. You're wrong, he's on his way to . . . Greece!" And on and on till they ran out of places beginning with G. When Ada said *Genovia*, nobody corrected her.

In the mornings, Bron took to ambling the gardens after breakfast, to breathe in the cool fresh air, reciting again and again to himself that what he was feeling, this eagerness to see and speak to Darcy, was ridiculous. *He owes you nothing, why are you thinking of him, he's older than you, and also such an asshole. Don't forget that.* And afterward, he returned to the house to do some algebra with Ada, go over Pythagoras's theorem or, more often than not these days, sketch a drawing or two, always demonstrating to Ada how he did it when she asked (and she *always* asked). With the library gone, they took their lessons in the downstairs living room, where he showed her how to draw a line with a steady hand, how to map out the skeleton and placement of a drawing before going in with any particular features. Ada's artistic skills ranged from limited to nonexistent, and the stick figures she produced were somehow more accomplished than her attempts at landscape. Keen to offer Ada a distraction from math (for he, quite frankly, hated math), he went back to the basics, purchasing a coloring book to help her color inside the lines, which she didn't.

He ran a bath in the evenings and watched *Howard's End* and other such films he could stream at night. This did little to slow his racing mind, but the waft of horse chestnut that seeped from the bubbles into his hair was effective at calming his nerves and distracted him a little.

But waiting as he did, day in and day out, for Darcy to appear, for something to progress, was mind-numbing. He couldn't just wait for things to happen. Neither Ada nor Mr. Edwards could answer any of his questions. But he knew someone who just might.

He made his way into the city and ambled down the road to Corpus Christi College, bypassing the sign that signaled it was for "Students only," and followed the arrows therein upon the walls that outlined professors' names and their office numbers. Hymn song spilled from the chapel ahead into the open square, and he moved slowly through the collapsing archway and into a back garden, where sunflowers and roses crept up the walls and along the black pipes. All the students surrounding him, walking to their dorms, rushing to their classes . . . could one of them be Harry, living out the life his parents had planned for him? He kept an eye out just in case, then turned into a building to skip up a tight spiral staircase, past an open bathroom currently being cleaned and smelling heavily of lemon disinfectant, and finally reached the landing.

A student was resting against the office's doorframe and nodding to the voice that spoke from inside the room. The young man was laughing, the books he clutched to his chest bouncing as he did. Bron twisted his head to read one of the spines— *Archaeology of Knowledge*, Michel Foucault. The young man spotted him standing there, and took a step away from the room: "I best be off now—your two o'clock is here."

"I don't have a two o'clock," the voice said jovially. Leaning out to take a look, Giovanni spotted him. "Ah."

Giovanni looked surprised to see him, but greeted him with a smile. Bron mimicked the gesture. Giovanni took the young man's hands and shook them vigorously. "Do not stress, Frank. This chapter is coming along marvelously." And he planted a quick businesslike kiss on his cheek.

Bron made himself as small as possible as the man named Frank squeezed past him in the stairwell. He apologized for being in the way and felt at once that it had been a mistake to come here. As though he were doing something wrong. Once Frank had moved far enough down the stairs, Bron turned toward the stairs and said, "I didn't mean to intrude. I can come back another time."

"No, no, no," Giovanni insisted, stepping out of the room. "Now is good. Please do come in."

He was guided into a room that was barer than he'd expected: painted a chamomile yellow, a green Chesterfield sofa rested on one side, and close beside it, a wooden-framed armchair with tattered cushions. The shelves lining the wall were full of books that spilled onto the floor, but apart from that, it seemed to him more like a room for counseling.

"Please sit," Giovanni said, and because he took the armchair, Bron unquestioningly took to the sofa. "How are you?"

"I'm okay," he replied, obedient and following through with the necessary small talk. "The past couple of weeks have been interesting, to say the least."

"I bet. Dickie told me what happened. I'm sorry not to have spoken to you sooner. I've been swamped with dissertation corrections and deadlines. But you are all good? All okay?"

"Yes, I'm fine."

"And the others, they are good, too? Dickie tells me they are. Theo and the little one? Nobody was hurt."

Everybody was fine, he said, although deeply shocked and still feeling the impact.

"I see, I see. And how can I help you today?"

He knew his reason for being here. To prod Giovanni into saying more about the relationship he suspected he'd had with Darcy. But now he was sitting before him, he didn't know what to ask. Or rather, how to ask it. He felt suddenly like he was going behind Darcy's back.

"You know, I was quite disappointed not to see you at the party that night," Bron began.

Giovanni shifted in his seat. "Yes, I . . . In the end I realized my presence would have caused more upset than good. I know Dickie wanted me there."

THE MANOR HOUSE GOVERNESS   133

The truth, of course, was that it wasn't just Mr. Edwards who had wanted Giovanni to attend. Bron had searched for him, had expected to find him. "I had gone through quite the effort with my costume in the hope to impress you." Bron's words were calculated.

"You impress me now, piccolino."

"Thanks." Bron gave him a rushed summary of his costume, about how their conversation about his favorite novel had inspired him to invert the situation and in the process explore a part of himself through his disguise.

"A Brontification of the Edwardses' Halloween ball, if you will?"

"Well, yes." Bron smiled.

"You thought critically about the piece and had something to say about it. Living, breathing performance art. Full marks—well done! I wish I could have seen it."

Bron cast his gaze to the floor in an embarrassment he couldn't quite place. A symptom of always wanting to perform well at school. "And the reason you didn't come . . . it's because of Darcy isn't it? The two of you—I mean, you were friends, weren't you? I've gathered that much."

Giovanni fell back into his chair with a slump, took in a breath before saying, "Yes. We were friends."

Bron looked up again and noticed the dark, almost purple circles under Giovanni's eyes. The sadness that glazed over them. The photographs of them together, edged beside the river, swam back into his mind. Giovanni seemed almost wolfish now, compared to his teenage years. "It doesn't make sense to me. The way you are in each other's presence. The rest of the family love you. I'm not sure I understand the friction. What happened?"

Giovanni shook his head; it was not his place to share such information. But Bron needed to know more. It was why he had come here, and something at the back of his mind needed to know if the animated life he'd given the image had any truth to it. He was rather attuned to seeing things that weren't always visible, like a sixth sense. At St. Mary's he could predict when the tempest outside would worsen and the damage it would cause to the already leaky ceilings. He'd place pots by his bed in anticipation, and come morning, they'd be full to the brim with water. He was good at identifying which of the boys was due to leave them weeks before it happened, and eventually he'd announce his parents were pulling him out or that he was transferring to another school. Together they would hustle around and bid their goodbyes. A quick glance at the face of the departing figure, and his eyes—which locked onto one of the boys who stood slightly away from all the rest—would confirm to him another invisible truth: which of them would be missed the most.

Bron didn't push Giovanni for an answer, but he must have read the disappointment on his face. "I suppose I could tell you about one time in France . . . The Edwardses, they keep a farmhouse there, a little building in the middle of Toulouse." He paused, and Bron thought that this was as much as he would get. "Theo used to love going there—he said it was something about the rooms being scantily dressed, that it allowed for a sense of freedom and expansion—his words, not mine—and that the views of the hills opened onto a land that stretched green and yellow. I understood what he meant. It reminded me of my hometown in Italy. But I remember he used to say how much he hated Greenwood, and every other English country house that seemed to him to produce quite the opposite effect. Claustrophobic, he said, where the rooms, though large, are oppressive; where the parks, though green, are manicured and at the mercy of the clipper, sheared into shape should they dare to grow outside the bounds of what's been deemed appropriate. Such a garden your Darcy claims England to be, and he the budding rosebush who's learned to hide his thorns. As had I, of course. I wasn't always this open about myself, but such natural inclinations are impossible to impede, and if forced under restraint will only emerge under another disguise. So yes, you could say that we were friends."

This was it. This was what he'd come to hear. But still he hadn't heard it exactly. "But you were more than friends?" he pushed. "You were . . ." *Lovers.* He let the pause linger.

Giovanni stood, shrugged into his coat silently. "Follow me."

Bron asked where they were going, but Giovanni gave nothing away. They descended the cramped stairs together, but instead of going back through the archway from which he'd come, Giovanni diverted, through another door and down a hallway that echoed with the cacophony of voices and the clatter of dishes. They entered a dining hall. Though it was quite past lunch, a few students loitered. For the most part the room was empty. Giovanni walked along the wood-paneled walls, the sunlight, filtering through the great hall's windows, bringing out the red undertones of the wood and making the golden chandeliers shimmer.

They stopped beneath a painting, one which depicted the portrait of a boy—or a man, he couldn't be sure—which hung for all to see. The portrait looked out with an androgynous face, and Bron felt immediately taken in by it.

The figure wore a black jacket with a white, almost fairy-wing-like collar—which Giovanni described as a doublet. He explained that the fabric was "probably velvet," and pointed out its leafy patterns exposing color underneath. It was pockmarked with gold studs for buttons. The boy looked rich, expensive, and confident.

"He was twenty-one years old and, I like to think, very, very coy, but still transgressive. Effeminate. Beautiful." The words "Quod me nutrit me detruit" were burnished on the wood beneath. Bron spoke the Latin aloud, butchering the pronunciation.

"It is said like this." Giovanni repeated it back to him: "Quod me nutrit me detruit. It means, 'That which nourishes me also destroys me.' Brilliant, no?"

"Who is it?" he asked.

"It is you," he said. "It is you, it is me, and it is nobody. Maybe it is Shakespeare. Who knows? But they say it is Christopher Marlowe."

"The gay spy?"

"That's one of his possibly identities. But he was also a great mind who made transgressive claims and met a violent end. He was brilliant, and so famous in his time, and yet now—who is he? You don't know. But we all know Shakespeare. Why is that?"

Bron was ruffled by Giovanni's riddles. Found them to be intense and scholarly. He was desperate for answers, and they made him feel stupid. He said the first thing that came to mind. "You think Marlowe is better than Shakespeare?"

"I think Shakespeare and his heteronormative mass appeal have had their time, don't you? But Marlowe . . ." Giovanni paused.

Bron tried his best to keep up. "You think that Marlowe's not as popular as Shakespeare because he loved men?"

"I hear a lot of people say, 'We live in the twenty-first century,' as if to say so demands and expects necessary tolerance in the world, but I've never understood what they mean by it. Twenty-first century—so what? We have always existed. Why now? History is afraid of Marlowe because of how he chose to live. Not just gay, but queer—I mean always against the norms. He lived boldly and passionately. Marlowe, he is something else entirely, fights the fight we all fight today as queer people. I am glad to share a college with him."

I don't understand any of this, Bron thought. "Why are you showing me this?"

"You wanted to know about me and Theo."

"What does this painting have to do with you and . . .?" *Darcy.*

"Nothing and everything. Theo and I, we are the same, and yet we are not. But why all this intrigue from you? Theo, he is a mighty catch, but a repressed spirit. I suggest you don't go falling for him—unless you already have?"

"I haven't," he said quickly.

"Hmm," said Giovanni. "I'll say I believe you. But there is something in your eyes that tells me otherwise. You have been hurt by something, by someone. I know it. I said the same thing to myself once—sometimes I still do—and I don't know if even I believe it. Look at the painting again."

He looked once more at the words inscribed there and tried to extrapolate their meaning.

Quod me nutrit me detruit.

"That which nourishes me also destroys me."

Bron concluded that someone here must have been the wronged lover. Then Giovanni said, "It's the things we cherish the most that can be our downfall."

Outside it was a gray, frosty morning. Mr. Edwards had departed in the early hours, skipping breakfast for an appointment in town, and Ada, after announcing that she didn't want to do any of her studies today, took to browsing the internet for information on aquatic sea life, reading out WikiNotes on each of her favorite sea critters. "Did you know that octopuses have three hearts—or is it octopi? And that the color of their blood is blue, like the royals? And that sharks don't have any bones?" She pulled the skin of her arm upward, the elasticity creating a fleshy mountain peak. "I wish I didn't have any bones."

Bron pulled on his boots at the bottommost step of the foyer, listening with feigned interest to the recited list of facts. "That's so interesting." He zipped up his coat, eager to get out into the early morning dew.

"If you were a sea creature, I think you'd be a seahorse."

"Why's that?"

"Because male seahorses carry their babies. Did you know that? Would that make them nonbinary or gender fluid?"

"I don't know," he said, because he didn't. "And what would you be?"

"A crab—no, actually, a tortoise. Wait, I've got it! A starfish," she said. "And Daddy would be a dolphin."

"And what about Darcy?"

"Hmm." She thought for a moment. "A shark. No bones."

Outside he took in the air, and his breath plumed around him. He strolled the cobbled path, his body tense and hunched in a fight to hold in some warmth. The house had many pockets of garden about it, and his favorite was a little walk away, where a bench at the end of the stretch overlooked the fields. Here he would sit and drift along, detached from his body and purging thoughts into the wind. Today the meadow, which had flooded with the week's rainfall, was like marshland, and the bench was cast in the tree's shadow. The twigs cracked under his boots. He had not expected to find the bench occupied by a man in a large black coat. Like a deer turning its head at the hunter, the man twisted to look at him. But it was no stranger.

"What are you doing here?" Bron heard himself ask.

Darcy was tossing stones into the flood; they didn't so much skid, but rather sank into the waterlogged grass. He looked pale and ungainly, bent like a branch off the tree itself. Darcy clumsily waved him over, sat up straighter, but Bron was slow to move as their eyes interlocked for an infinite second.

"Bron, I hadn't seen you coming—although I'm glad to see you."

He shrugged, mimicking Darcy's punctuated way of talking. "Glad . . . to see me?"

"Yes," he said. "Of course."

"I wouldn't have guessed that seeing me would cause such a feeling as gladness, let alone it being a matter of certainty."

"Don't tease me, Bron," Darcy said. "It's frankly annoying, if not despairing."

They had fallen into the rhythm of this. Again. He felt it prick as though he'd been scolded.

"Well, if that's all you have to say . . ." *Stop it, stop.* The walls were going up, his mode of defense ruining the moment. The last time he'd waited for something romantic to happen, with Harry, it had all gone wrong. And now that Darcy was here, this wasn't the way he wanted it to go. But he couldn't help himself. It was easier to take himself out of the situation than take part in this indefinite banter. "I'll be on my way."

"You are allowed to be annoyed at me, you know. I know you are. I shouldn't have disappeared for so long, but there were a few things I needed to sort out in my head, and I thought it best to keep myself to myself. I'm sure you understand?"

"Of course I do."

"I knew you would." Darcy dropped a couple of pebbles into his hand, and they chucked them into the water together, the splashy splodge bringing him unexpected delight. Afterward, Darcy brushed his hands on his coat and asked if he'd like to walk with him around the grounds: "Though I'll understand if you've done enough walking for the morning."

No, not at all—he'd love to take a stroll, and they did so in circles, around the house and its gardens and then in a loop again, always ensuring he kept enough distance and didn't tread too closely. Darcy skimmed the side of him every few minutes, a slant to his walk. Bron slowed his pace to keep one step behind.

All through the week, his mind had been plagued with agonizing questions: *Where did Darcy go? Why did he go? Was it because of me? Darcy, left alone in that room, and now he's gone. And what caused the fire?* But the questions remained unanswered, and with this came the realization that while he had been thinking so much of Darcy through his absence, it was unlikely that Darcy had been thinking of him at all.

He was stuck in this reverie when Darcy said, "Why did you do it?"

"Why did I do what?"

They stopped walking. "You went into the library during the fire. You knew you shouldn't have done that. What a stupid thing to do. Why did you go inside?"

What was he supposed to say? That he'd just had a tingling feeling that somebody would be inside the burning room, all because he thought he'd seen his hand? It felt so stupid now, but in the moment it was in his blood—that Darcy was in there, that he needed to wake him up, save him.

"Were you looking for something?"

"I wasn't looking for anything."

"Are you sure?" Darcy pressed. "You can tell me."

"I thought—" He wanted to be truthful. "I thought you might have still been in there. I thought I saw you lying in the chair among the flames."

Darcy held his gaze a beat longer. "You thought I was in there? You went in there to save my life?"

"Yes."

He threw his head back. Laughed. "Oh, I see. Who knew we had a hero among us?"

Bron's lips almost trembled. Was he just a fool to him? "I wish I hadn't said anything."

"I'm joking, Bron. You know I am quite capable of making them."

"Well, maybe you should stop," he said, more harshly than he meant to.

"I'm sorry," Darcy said, but he seemed somehow pleased by Bron's unexpected severity. His lips tipped upward. "I didn't mean to upset you. Go on."

"It's just—I couldn't help but think you were in the room because of me. And if anything had happened—"

"It wasn't your fault," Darcy said. "You know that. It was all completely accidental. Something to do with the electricity."

He heard Darcy's wounded cry as the flames engulfed the room, recalled the way he'd dragged him away from the fire so forcefully, how he'd held tightly onto him. A bruise had bloomed on his shoulder.

"I suppose you're right," he said. "Nothing more to it than that."

"You sound unsure—almost displeased about it," Darcy countered. "What is it? Not exciting enough for you? Electricity being the cause? How about something from one of your fictions instead, to keep things interesting? Ada tells me you like to read. Were you imagining something sinister, like someone had come to kill me in the night?"

He dared himself to think it: *Was it really an accident, or could it have been something planned? An act of violence from one of the guests in the house? Did someone wish the family harm?*

"Absolutely not," he said, hiding his face away.

Darcy's lips tipped up again. "Because what would they do that for? Am I really that despised? I'd be quite annoyed if it was arson—Father made me dispose of my candle collection, just to be on the safe side, and I'm really rather upset about that, but it's probably for the best."

Bron explained how he liked to go to stores like TK Maxx and spend an hour in the candle aisle taking in all the different scents. Darcy teased him for this, said there was a delicate balance to be found between natural smelling and overly perfumed. Where Bron enjoyed the sweet-smelling vanilla cheesecakes, pumpkin spice, and cookies and cream, Darcy preferred the more sophisticated brands that sold the likes of Pomegranate Noir, Essence of Oud, and perfumes scented with incense, myrrh, and bergamot.

And it was nice, laughing together as they did. When a bird twittered in the tree above, Bron lifted his head, and incongruous to the days and morning that passed, the clouds had moved over to reveal a blue sky the color of forget-me-nots, and the sun shone so brightly they could see the frost misting before them. It was a perfect backdrop, and Bron felt himself content. If he was being truthful to himself, he might have even said happy.

"Master Darcy." It was Clarence who approached, who broke the spell.

Bron noticed the furtive glance she gave, that questioned his being there alone with the young master of the house, a look that made him shift uncomfortably. Noticing this, Darcy pressed a thumb into his shoulder, as if to say *"Brush it off,"* and met her with a certain level of indifference.

"What is it, Clarence?"

"I 'ave found one of little Ada's things outside on the ground when cleaning up the glass." She showed them both a necklace and then pointed to the broken window and to the patch of grass below it. "She must have dropped it in the night?" she said, though it peaked like a question.

"The glass still hasn't been cleared? Well, what have we been waiting for?"

"I'm sorry, sir, but Mr. Edwards said—"

"I don't care what Father said. Please do ensure the glass is cleared by the end of the day, Clarence," Darcy said, reaching out for the necklace, which Bron knew, indeed, belonged to Ada. He'd seen her wear it every day. "Thank you, Clarence. I'll see this is returned to her."

"Thank you, sir."

"Bonne journée, Clarence."

Darcy, holding the necklace in his palm, glanced back over to Clarence, who'd quickly returned to clearing the glass beneath the window. Darcy shook his head, bewildered, before handing it to him. "Would you mind giving this back to Ada? She'll be relieved to have it returned before realizing it was missing. It is very dear to her."

Bron agreed, took it delicately in his hands, and pocketed it. "Of course."

Ada continued to be uninterested in her studies through the afternoon—or rather, was only interested in learning more about the rules and regulations pertaining to fire safety, or watching a wildlife documentary on animal behaviors throughout the planet's oceans. Wearing a flamboyant orange vest, she scrolled through her iPad and was scribbling onto a paper stuck to her clipboard. He wondered if this was meant to imitate a hi-vis jacket.

"Did you know that Christmas trees are one of seven very common reasons a house fire can start?"

"I didn't know that, no."

"It's rather concerning," she said. "We'll have to go without one this year. Which is sad because I do love a Christmas tree. We always get a great big one, twelve feet high, from a little farm in Warboys. I guess we'll have to make up for it with even more presents!"

She began to compile a list of present ideas, one for her father and one for Santa, and then worried about how he would get to them. "We used to keep the tree in the library. And that's one of the few chimneys that isn't closed up. We don't want him entering the house from there. What a horrid impression he'll have of us! What would you like for Christmas this year, Bron?"

"I don't know, Ada. I hadn't given it much thought."

"Don't worry about asking me," she said. "I'll write you a list."

He stared out the window; the setting sun cast a brilliant orange light into the room. Birdie chirped in her cage, and Ada topped up the feeder with seeds. He was hugging himself when he felt the hard lump in his left pocket, remembered the little necklace that was in there.

"Oh, I'd almost forgotten," he said, digging into his trousers and fumbling around for the onyx gem. As his fingers brushed the roundness of the stone, his eyes fixed on the chain wrapped around Ada's little neck, the locket that already hung there as she reached to shut the cage's door.

She waited, poised on her tiptoes to hear what he had to say. When he didn't answer, she waved her hand in front of his face for dramatic effect. Something stopped him from pulling it out, from admitting that Darcy had asked him to return this necklace to her. But it would not yield from his hand. There had been a mistake.

"Are there some presents you'd like me to put on your list? Is that it? Don't be shy. Daddy will get you everything you want."

"No—it's not that. It's just that I forgot to tell you that . . ." He searched the nooks of his brain for something, anything.

"Actually, now you mention it, I would rather like a new book, if you wouldn't mind."

"Okay. Not another copy of *Jane Eyre*, right?" she said, pretending to scribble a note.

"Well, what if it is? What's so bad about that?"

"Oh, I don't know—maybe because you have, like, a bazillion copies."

"You've been going through my stuff again, haven't you?"

"No, I haven't! I've just seen you reading it over and over, all the time really. And it's always a different copy."

"Well, I like having all the different editions."

"Why?" she asked. "It's a bit weird."

"No, it's not. Anyway, speaking of books, I was thinking we could stop looking at *Frankenstein* and move onto something else. I think you've grasped quite well what Mary Shelley was trying to accomplish with the text."

"Oh, that's good, I guess," she said. "I was getting bored of it anyway. Too much sitting around describing things. Not enough monsters."

Ada began to tidy away her books and set the clipboard and iPad down onto the dining table. "Maybe we can read *Jane Eyre* together next?"

"Maybe," he said quickly. "Though I don't think you'll much like it. There's a lot of sitting around too. And definitely no monsters. Oh, and Fire Marshal Ada?" This immediately had her beaming. "I've been meaning to ask you something. That necklace"—she clutched at her neck instinctively—"where did it come from? Who gave it to you?"

"Oh," she said, and dipped the volume of her voice, ready to admit a secret. "Well, I've always had it, really. For as long as I can remember."

"But do you have another?" he asked, wanting at once to discard the simplest of solutions. "Of the same likeness, I mean?"

"No," she said; and then in a questioning tone, "Why would I have another?"

He shook his head. "No reason. Of course you wouldn't."

"Darcy has one just like it, though. Brother and sister—we both do."

So there are two of the same. And this one must belong to Darcy. "He does?"

"Yes, I've seen it in his room before. Would you like to see mine?" She unclasped it from her neck, and held it in her palms so delicately he was convinced it was worth more than all the world. And of course, to her, it was. Worth enough that she'd wear it every day, and would have sought it out immediately had she dropped it in the dirt at night. She pressed the side of it, and the stone clicked open. The locket held a diamond ring inside, which she picked up, bringing it close to his eye to show him the inscription on the band. The letter **A**.

"A for Ada," she said. "Obviously."

He complimented its design, and she placed it back into the locket, snapping it shut. Declaring herself hungry, she left the room, leaving Bron with yet more questions on his lips that would go unanswered.

When he checked the hall to see she had moved far enough away, he turned back into the room. The iPad was still alight, the face of which offered rows of red and blue squares, which, on close inspection, showed rather grotesque images, the search for "dead dolphins" having brought up a gallery of the slaughtered creatures. He swiped the screen away, thinking there should really be a parental filter on that thing, and brought the necklace that looked like a stone out of his pocket. He clicked the side of it, just as Ada had, but nothing seemed to happen. Feeling only a hint of discouragement, he clicked it again, and this time to behold that this, too, was a locket, which also held a ring inside. He picked it out carefully, the dark purple amethyst a surprise when he'd just seen the diamond in the locket Ada carried. And as this was allegedly Darcy's necklace, he searched for the expected D, or maybe even T for Theodore, to be etched into the band. Instead, he found three letters engraved there, three letters he was not expecting to find.

ADA.

Ada? He scrunched up his face in confusion, did a little one-eighty spin to check the door again to ensure nobody found him holding the locket. He held up the ring to the light; there was nothing else inscribed inside the band. ADA. He'd been certain Darcy's name would be found there, so this twist in expectation seemed almost unreasonable. His heart thrummed in his temples, and he strained to make sense of it all. This had to be a clue to something. But to what? He ran through circumstances in his head and came up short.

Whatever it was, he had to know.

9

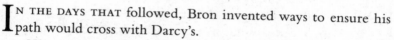

IN THE DAYS THAT followed, Bron invented ways to ensure his path would cross with Darcy's.

His growing desire to be near to him at all times, wherever possible, had developed into an ache that had him rubbing at his chest through the day, an indigestion that would not pass. And every morning, his first task of the day was to open his bedside drawer and click the sides of the locket with its hidden ring, to inspect any new names or words that might've formed upon it through the night. On one inspection, he'd been convinced it had, in fact, changed, reading now as ∀Ɔ∀—only to feel stupid for his absurdity.

A part of him wanted to do away with the thing, and such a reason it would be to strike up a conversation with Darcy, to find him in one of the many rooms and say, *"Remember that necklace you handed me a few days ago? Well, funny story . . ."* and that he'd been mistaken, that it was his own that had been found. And Bron would be the one to return it; this could only win him favors. But he held back from saying anything, sensing with a fluster that the locket could be useful to him at a later date, a clue in the manor's slowly unfurling mystery. For it was inevitable that in every great house there was a family, and in every great family there was a secret, and only time would reveal it.

Instead, he waited inside his bedroom, leaving the door intentionally ajar and listening out for footsteps on the landing. At the promise of a sound, he'd emerge from the room completely coincidentally—more often than not it was a false alarm, just Ada scampering by or Mr. Edwards's heavy-footed trot. But sometimes he'd hear Captain's low, excited whine and find Darcy there on the landing. He'd offer him a "Good morning."

"Good morning, Bron," Darcy would reply, barely looking up from the paper he held in his hands. And while this was not the dialogue he'd mapped and prepared for as he waited behind the door, it was enough to keep him going for an hour or two.

Through the afternoons he'd sit with Ada in the living room, who rested on the carpet at his feet and leafed through the work he'd compiled for her. Once Ada and Mr. Edwards had gone to bed, and the noises around the house settled into oblivion, he'd dawdle on with a book on his lap, often with the words swimming and meaningless, and the hot drink to his mouth scalding his tongue, thinking always that this was ridiculous, that he must have missed Darcy coming in. He'd close the book, finish the drink, rise to leave. Only to sit down again and wait another minute or two. Just in case. The keys would rattle in the door— he'd open the book again, to any page, bring the empty mug to his lips.

"You're up late," Darcy would say, shutting the door behind him.

"Oh, really?" He'd shoot his eyes to the clock. "I didn't realize the time. I should probably get to bed." Set down the mug, shut the book.

"Oh, that's a shame. I haven't seen you today. But I won't keep you if you're tired. Goodnight."

"Goodnight," he'd reply, cursing under his breath, watching as Darcy hung his coat and ascended the stairs. Could he shout out, say he'd changed his mind, that he wasn't that tired and would be staying up a little longer? No, of course he couldn't. With Darcy gone, he would rise from the chair and take himself upstairs with little to do but inspect the locket some more before going to sleep.

Some days went quicker than others. Once or twice he visited the city in search of . . . well, anything to do outside the house, and these days glided past, clouds on a windy day. Others were occupied mostly with Ada's homework, which she drove through quickly (or not at all) to give way for more childish endeavors, and these passed like the sun dipping below the horizon line: gradually when waiting for it, hastily the second he glanced away. It was those moments of calm that lingered the longest, where he sat and avoided Ada's interrogation into his wandering thoughts, with one ear listening out for tires on the gravel, for the opening of the front door. All through the week, he yearned to be close to Darcy, visited the bench at the end of the walk with a conversation starter at the ready in the hopes of finding him there, only he never was. He'd return to his bedroom and collapse onto his bed unfulfilled.

On most days he would touch himself, run his fingers down his torso or around his nipples and pretend that they were someone else's fingers. Sometimes they were a stranger's; often they were Darcy's. Or Harry's. He'd take a steaming bath and lie in it until the water went tepid and his fingers pruned, then climb onto his bed on his hands and knees, arch his back, ready to be taken. He groaned and brought out a pair of boxers that didn't belong to him, having lifted them from the washing basket, that infinite gold mine, after Clarence had extracted the washing from Darcy's bedroom. He inhaled it, took in the scent of him, and cried, exclaiming profanities into his pillow.

And yet when his wish was somehow granted, and Darcy stood outside his bedroom on the landing, or sipped at his coffee a little longer in the breakfast room, or when he came into the living room at night to talk to him, Bron would seek immediate deliverance from the encounter; the state of self-doubt, where he was kidding himself, was only being humored with this attention. Darcy laughed about him behind his back. He knew it. He was a bother. A plaything.

He was stirred from his nap one Sunday afternoon by the rev of an engine outside. His book had fallen to the side of him as he slept. Pulling on a T-shirt, he stumbled to the window. It was raining. A taxi had pulled into the driveway path, and an umbrella sputtered to life from the opening door, concealing the head and chest of the passenger who leaped from the backseat. A firm, ringed hand closed the car door and tapped the top of the car bonnet, before a man turned toward the house. He took swift, heavy strides to avoid the puddle that had formed on the gravel, and bounded up the stone stairs. Darcy looked up at his window.

Bron shut the curtains quickly. Heard the slam of the front door and Captain's muffled bark, threw himself onto the mattress. *Stupid. Idiot. He saw you looking.*

A knock on the door made his head snap up, cut short his languishing.

"Knock, knock," Darcy said through the door, before tapping again. "I know you're in there."

This was ridiculous. What could he want? Bron looked at himself in the mirror, scraped at his hair and rubbed the sleep from his eyes. All he could wish for now was some understanding that it was his day off . . . whatever that meant. This would have to do. He pulled the door open.

"Hey," he said, aware of the force in his voice to sound natural. "Can I help you?"

Up and down, Darcy's eyes glided over him, in his T-shirt and too-short shorts. It was cold, and the hairs on his legs bristled like a dandelion, his skin turning to gooseflesh. Darcy gave a little laugh. "What have you been up to in there?"

"Nothing," he said. "What would I be up to?"

"Oh, nothing, nothing." Darcy made a little humming noise. "I hope I didn't . . . wake you?"

"Not at all," he said, following his gaze to the unmade sheets, the mountainous duvet. "I was just"—he spotted his book lying there, the discarded laptop on the carpet—"er, watching a film."

"Ah yes, of course. Anything I might've seen? Or something you'd recommend?"

"No."

Darcy didn't say anything else, and the silence swelled between them like a balloon. Who would be the first to burst it?

"So . . ." Bron quirked a smile because he didn't know what else to do with himself. He nestled against the door, which leaned slightly inward.

"So." Darcy laughed, holding out his palm to keep it open. "I was rather hoping you would join me today for a little outing?"

"An outing?" he said, looking out the window. "As in outside?"

"Yes, outside."

"Isn't it a little cold?"

"Then I recommend you wear a coat."

"But it's wet."

"We've umbrellas to spare," Darcy said simply.

Bron nodded. Did he want to go, now that the offer had presented himself? Or would he say something stupid, make a fool of himself? Darcy was so suave, standing there in his room's doorframe and looking more handsome than ever. And he was, for Christ's sake, in a pair of shorts that had a hole at the crotch and a T-shirt he'd designed himself that said "Bookish & Queer" across the chest. Bron blinked to gain himself some time. Looked again out the window to assess the extremity of the weather. Either way, he knew he *wanted* to go. But the question was, should he?

"Alright," he agreed, and asked for ten minutes so that he could dress.

"Fine," Darcy said, breaking into another grin. "But do wear my favorite shawl."

"Shut up." Bron closed the door in his face, forgetting himself in the moment. Quickly he opened it up again to say he was sorry, he didn't mean—

"Nine minutes fifty-six seconds, nine minutes fifty-five . . ." Darcy said, to which they both laughed, and Bron rushed to the en suite, where he slabbed toothpaste onto a brush and scrubbed deftly to ensure the annihilation of morning breath, drove a comb through his hair before tying it into a bun, and picked out a blouse with ruffles at the end, and a cute, A-line skirt. Ready to go, he dabbed a spritz of whatever product he could find in the under-sink cupboard—rose-scented room spray, great—and dashed down the stairs to where Darcy was waiting, with Ada standing beside him.

"Please can I come?" he heard her ask. She turned to Bron with glistening eyes. "Please?"

"I said no, Ada. You need to learn to obey. Come on, Bron." Darcy handed him an umbrella, and Captain started to bark, wanting to follow them outside too. "You get in the car. I'll be with you in a moment." He did as he was told and left Ada clinging to the dog and watching him go.

Inside the car it smelled of orange freshener and a harder, more masculine smell, like a worn basketball. Leather. When the passenger door opened, Darcy sidled in beside him, apologized for Ada's silliness, and told the driver to drive.

"She wasn't being silly," Bron said, instinctively feeling the need to defend her and disappointed by Darcy's retreat into an uncomfortable mood. "You forget she is a little girl and vies for your attention."

"Little girl or not, she can't always get her own way." He looked amused as he said this. "Besides, I want to spend some time alone." His heart beat. "With you."

Another beat. Darcy leaned into him.

"Can I say that? Is that allowed?" Gently, he reached out his hand to Bron's, brushed his littlest finger with his own.

"Yes," Bron murmured, losing himself. It was so easy to forget all of Darcy's faults in the otherly confines of the car. "Yes, that's allowed."

"Good. I was rather hoping you would say that."

Bron looked to the green fields, dotted with cows and sheep, as they drove down the St. Neot's Road. He felt a little carsick, his tummy fizzing, and asked the driver if he could please roll down the window a crack. The sky was a tumultuous gray, and the swaying of the windscreen wipers helped to calm him. Darcy continued to hold his hand. Bron closed his eyes. The traffic grew congested as they crept closer to the city center. He wasn't sure if the slow movement was helping or if it made his sickness worse. Noticing his discomfort, and his sweating hands, Darcy lightly brushed his thigh.

"We should quite like to stop along the Queen's Road, if you please, driver. Whenever you find an opening."

The driver slowed, and the indicator clicked. When the car stalled, Bron stumbled out, which helped to sober him and settle his stomach. When Darcy came around to him, he declined his help.

"I'm fine," he said. "I'm fine. Just give me a minute."

How ridiculous he felt, how weak, like a sickly child in need of comfort. The trees were an avenue of bare spindles, and as they walked the muddy path, his shoes got caked in a brown sludge of mud and leaves. But the freshness of the air worked its wonder.

"Better?" Darcy asked.

"Yes, better."

He could see the backs of Trinity Hall, of Clare College. When they turned into King's, Darcy showed the porter his alumni card, and the gate clanged open. The lamplit pavement, aglow and speckled with the afternoon's rain, took them over a bridge, where the river was dotted with punts, and adventurous tourists sat in plastic ponchos, photographing their families coursing along the water.

The great college chapel loomed ahead like the tallest building in the world. Bron imagined what it would be like to run across its roof in the high heavens, look down the pillared spires, the great buttresses holding it aloft. It was this building, Darcy said, that they were visiting. They curved along past the chapel's face and the wooden door, which he assumed would be the entrance, and instead turned a corner to enter from another side.

Within the building, the outside world no longer existed. This was heaven, and heaven was quiet, with carved winged creatures guarding every door. He looked up at the stained glass windows, bringing to life stories of the Old and New Testaments, at the lofty pillars that rose vertically, soaring upward like a latticed spiderweb into fan vaulted ceilings. Each branch looked like a vein, and each vein broke into capillaries. Ten thousand cells. Weightless bone. A living entity. It looked, to him, like honeycomb, the inside of a beehive.

"It's beautiful," Darcy stated. And it was. But Bron was meant to say something in return, something equally as admiring.

"It's magnificent."

"I like to come here to think, to disappear for a while. It is rather fit for a king," Darcy said. "Or five. It took five kings to build this."

"But you are not here to disappear today," Bron said, commanding an answer from him now. "You wanted me to come with you."

"Yes," Darcy said placidly. "I did."

"Well, I was just wondering why?"

Darcy ambled toward a door, disappeared into a room. Bron thought he might have upset him, and stood back, dazed. Darcy remerged almost as quickly as he'd gone. "I have been feeling rather alone these past few days, and very much lost in my own head. My father, well, he is a nuisance at times, and Ada but a nuisance too, only she is harder to get rid of, like a flea." He took a deep breath, itched at his skin in jest. This made Bron want to itch too. "I have been trying to get you alone, to talk to you, for days now. But the moment never seemed to present itself."

Together they looked at the carvings on the walls. Darcy pointed at the symbols of the crowned Tudor Rose, the Beaufort Portcullis. At the organ, the wooden partition that divided the space, Darcy showed him The H's and A's for Henry VIII and Anne Boleyn. At one point, a priest made his way across the aisle, the altar boys in their white gowns gliding behind him. Darcy admitted to a time years ago when he thought he'd commit fully to his religious beliefs and join the priesthood.

"How awful would that have been? A life without—" Bron stopped, the words tumbling out without his thinking. Darcy looked at him curiously, his face amused. He was laughing. "I'm sorry. I don't know why I said that."

"I never know what you're about to say, Bron. It's part of your charm."

He tried to save himself, deflecting with another question. "Do you think you could have done it?"

"It's a tough one, but I think so."

"Then why didn't you?"

They exchanged a look. "I'm just not a fan of purple," Darcy replied, and glided down into one of the chambers off the main hall, where they found themselves alone. "And you're right, I would have missed a life without . . ." Chains impeded the small room from being fully entered. Above the mini altar was a statue of the crucifixion. Darcy stepped as close to the altar as he could get. "You know, I was married once."

Bron looked away from the altar and up at him. "What? To a woman?"

"Yes, to a woman. Oh, don't look so surprised."

Bron pulled what he hoped was a neutral face. "I'm not surprised."

Darcy quickly continued. "I knew I had wronged her, but I have atoned for my deceit. We are happily divorced now. Or at least I am."

"What was there to atone for? It couldn't have been easy for either of you." He wasn't sure why Darcy was admitting all this to him here, and why now, but he was grateful for it. He asked what he thought was the most important question: "Did you love her?"

"In a way, maybe—I don't know." said Darcy, clenching his jaw. "But I have never been much good at love." Love—Bron thought he knew what love was. Would have described it as something heavy, weighing on the chest like a brick, or a chamber full of water, drowning him from the inside and filling him up until he'd burst. He thought he'd felt it once. Sometimes felt it still. A wound. "Now, may I ask you something?"

"That would depend on what you wanted to ask me." Bron shifted in his stance.

Darcy stepped away from him, his back turned, and spoke into the air in an inflated tone. "Do you think me handsome, Bron?" Setting Bron's heart instantly aflutter.

No, he thought defensively, the word almost slipping from his tongue. Not because he didn't think Darcy handsome. On the contrary, he thought him extremely handsome. Sexy in fact. Had imagined so many precious moments where Darcy had come to him in the night and moaned, *"God, you're beautiful,"* to which he'd reply that nobody had ever said that to him before. That he considered himself to be freakish-looking. That it was Darcy who was beautiful, handsome. Who everyone wanted. A manly man. Dating apps told him this much: *no femmes.* Or they wanted more than he had to offer: *Trans. Smooth. No CD.* Not some in-between distorted thing like him. So handsome? No. Darcy was much more than that. The crème de la crème of handsome. Someone who wouldn't usually give him the time of day. And to admit it would be to expose himself. To stand naked in front of him. And he would be laughed at.

"Handsome? And why should my opinion matter to you?"

"I know, I know—you've said it before. Looks don't matter—I get it. But I'm just curious, that's all."

"Curious," Bron repeated. "Alright."

"Well?" he said, his voice mocking impatience. He stood in a gentlemanly pose, his umbrella used like a mighty cane, a prop. He coughed an amused cough. "What is your verdict? What do you make of me?"

"Hmm." Bron took steady steps and circled him for effect, scrutinized his nose, the jut of his chin just so, his muscular arms, toned waist; rested a moment too long on his arse, which Darcy was kind enough to pretend to have missed. Bron couldn't meet his eye after that. "I suppose you are," he petered off.

"Well, what is it to be? Handsome or not handsome?"

"Well, I'm not sure," Bron said loftily.

"I am hideous, then!" Darcy declared.

"Indeed, very hideous. Extremely."

"This is a blow. And here I was hoping for some kind of affirmation. That my looks would be pleasing to you?"

"Alright then, if you insist on my lying to you. I think you *are* handsome."

"Aha! I knew it."

If Bron had processed Darcy's beaming face correctly, then he thought he was doing a pretty good job of it all. Of getting closer to him. Of flirting. Because that's what was happening here, right? Darcy was flirting with him, and he was flirting back. Perhaps Bron was a little out of his depth, but he seemed to be doing okay. "I'm glad I could provide you with the answer you were hoping for."

Darcy poked him in the arm. Bron wanted to poke back, but didn't. It was all childish, really, but it seemed to be working.

"Hey!—but now it is my turn to ask you a question."

"It is? Well, I suppose that's only fair." They were standing face to face now. Darcy brushed at a strand of hair that had come loose from Bron's bun, twirled it between his fingers. Bron deftly weaved it back in. When he brought down his arms, Darcy placed a hand on his shoulder. "But on one condition."

"And what might that be?"

"You must kiss me first."

Bron's breath caught. Had he heard him right? Bron was frozen and a little unsure. He could not understand if Darcy's bobbing shoulders and silent chuckle were a symptom of nerves or an indication of mockery. "You're toying with me."

Darcy's expression turned serious. "No, no, no toying going on here. I just really, really want to kiss you. Like, right now."

"Oh . . . oh, okay. Well—"

But before he could say anything. Darcy had his hands on his face and brought his lips to his. Bron fell back on his heels and gripped onto Darcy's shoulders to keep himself from falling. He laughed awkwardly into his open mouth in a way that was anything but sexy. Darcy pulled away and shook his head in disbelief, but moved in again. And this time, Bron waited for Darcy's lips to push up into his before he opened his mouth, just a little bit. After a moment, he allowed himself to lean in more.

Bron was kissing Darcy. In a chapel, of all places.

When they broke apart, Darcy swiped at his mouth, and Bron was suddenly fearful that his kissing was altogether too wet, too sloppy. That he had drooled on him and that Darcy would never want to kiss him again.

But Darcy was smiling. "Well, that was . . . that was something." Bron felt the heat rise in his neck. "A good something I mean—a very good something." He sounded almost in awe. "You've certainly earned your question."

"My question? Oh—right." It didn't feel right to ask it now. But what if this was his only opportunity? He considered his words carefully. "I wanted to ask about you—and Giovanni."

Darcy's face instantly dropped "Vani? I wasn't expecting that. Well, what about him?" His voice was altogether changed, deeper.

"What happened between the two of you? Something must have."

"You wish to squander your question on this? You only get one."

Something like a stone rose in Bron's throat. Darcy's shoulders tensed, and the air was suddenly sucked from the room, into the breaths they both held.

Bron accepted his question to be prying, perhaps even callous, coming after a moment of such tenderness. But he nodded, and Darcy sighed, indignant. Cleared his throat.

"I'm sorry to disappoint you, but I cannot put it more simply than this: Some things just don't go the way one wants them to."

"But you were friends," he pushed. "More than friends?"

"You have brought this up before. What makes you so sure?"

"I just want to understand what's going on," he said, almost pleading. "I want to understand where all this is coming from. I've seen the way you two act when you're around each other, like sworn enemies . . . and the way you were—"

"And what did you read in our discomfort, hmm? That we wish to be friends again? To patch things up?"

"No, no, I just—"

Darcy paced back and forth in frustration. "Why can't anyone understand that we don't wish to have anything more to do with one another? That the past is the past, and I'd like to keep it that way." Darcy's irritation was apparent and quickly spreading—his cheeks strained upward, and his brows furrowed his forehead into lines. His lips tipped into a scowl.

Bron was frustrated too; he felt that Darcy's affection and interest in him was something to be turned on and off whenever he fancied it. Why couldn't they just talk openly about things— about serious things—without the need for their constant rebuttal, their sparring of words, or Darcy's temperament that was quick to change?

He knew what he had seen. Giovanni had all but said they had been together. Why couldn't he just admit it? What was there to hide? Was it really such a manly thing, to keep everything bottled in?

"But I saw the two of you—in the photographs, and I—"

"Wait." When Darcy finally looked at him again, his countenance said something different. A different language altogether. For a moment Darcy didn't say anything, just stared blankly, nostrils flaring, as though his head had taken him somewhere else entirely. But then he took a step toward him. Bron felt himself take one back. Thought Darcy might grab him. He pressed into himself.

"What do you mean?" Darcy said curtly.

"The night of the fire, when I waited for you in the library. I was flicking through the shelves, and I came across an album, and I saw the two of you, by the river. You and Giovanni. You looked . . ."

"Christ," he spat, patting the back of his head. "Christ!" The sibilance echoed through the chapel. Bron's breath stopped short. "Are you telling me that it was you? You were the one looking through the photo albums?"

Something told Bron that he had overstepped here, crossed some unknown boundary in a terrain he wasn't all too familiar with. That he should have stayed on a safer path and kept his thoughts to himself. "Yes, but I—"

"What else did you see? Tell me, what else? Was it just you?"

"Nothing, nothing, that was all—"

Bron couldn't bring himself to look up from the floor. He felt exactly as he had as a child being scolded. There was a heavy silence between them, dissipating into the airiness of the chapel into something resembling peace, tension leaching from the walls. But Darcy let out a breath. And Bron held his in.

"Were you not taught at that school of yours not to go prying through someone else's things? And am I wrong to want to keep my own life private? That I do not wish to air my problems with the fucking world?"

It took all he had within him not to break. He forced himself to nod, a dam blocking the sea of tears that threatened. "I'm sorry."

"I think we should head back now, don't you? It's getting late."

He watched Darcy pull the phone from his pocket and dial a number. After three rings, Darcy spoke into it and ordered two cabs, each to pick them up immediately from outside King's Parade, on the corner of the Corpus clock. When he hung up, he walked past Bron, a stranger. Bron spoke out his name, quietly, desperately, but Darcy wasn't ready to hear it.

"Just . . . I'm sorry. I need some space," he said, and left him standing below at the altar, alone.

When the car dropped Bron back at the house, he ran straight to his bedroom, flung himself face-first onto the mattress, his nose stinging from the impact, and yelled into his pillow until his eyes were raw and his throat sore. His insides stirred, full of want and anger. He had miscalculated, and this was the end, the end of whatever it was that had been building between them. The dance, the kiss—it all meant nothing now.

He'd jeopardized his professionalism too, his tact. The very things that had helped to get him this placement at Greenwood in the first place. When they were alone together, he often forgot the true relationship between them, the difference in their position. But the distance between him and Darcy was now greater than ever, a giant fissure. Hierarchies still reigned, and he needed to learn his place. Who was he to pry into Darcy's life, to ask such questions? Darcy could say whatever it was he wanted, make a mockery of him any time he liked—he'd been naive to think he could talk to his employer's son in such a way. That was the way of the world. It was just that, for a moment, he'd forgotten.

Was Darcy talking to Mr. Edwards that very instant, discussing his impropriety? Were the next three words he'd hear would be *"Pack your bags,"* terminating his employment? Who would be the one to deliver it? Not Mr. Edwards, surely? He'd always been so kind to him. And where would he live? He had nowhere else to go.

Oh, how wretched. How cruel. He gasped, feeling the terror of his life—that he was destined to be alone—clinging to his upper belly, that weightless space below the ribs, like a suction. Because, finally, he'd been happy. He could admit that, now that all was lost. It had never occurred to him that this place had slowly started to feel like home, a concept he hadn't understood until he'd experienced the comfort of these walls. Here he had come to escape the moroseness of his past, where he cared for a little girl almost like a sibling, could look up to a fatherly figure through Mr. Edwards. He had earned this world after having gone so long without. Yes, sometimes he hated it here, and sometimes he thought about what it would've been like to have stayed on at St. Mary's, or to have successfully gained entry to the university, but now he didn't want to leave. Here he had made a life for himself.

Perhaps if he could only explain himself, maybe he could rectify some of the damage he'd caused. Though, Darcy's reaction to the photographs only confirmed his suspicions. He was convinced that Darcy and Giovanni had been lovers, and something had gone terribly wrong between them. He dragged himself to the writing desk, grabbed a piece of paper, and mindlessly scribbled down his thoughts, finding the process of handwriting cleansing, an erasure of reality through the creation of something material. But feeling no comfort or relief in this, he threw open his bedside drawer and brought out the locket. The stupid thing which he knew had to mean something—he just hadn't quite worked out what.

A knock at the door made his heart lurch. Here it was. The moment everything came crashing down. He stashed the locket away. Swiped the tears from his eyes. Took a deep breath. Opened the door.

"Oh, Ada, it's you."

"Yes, it's me. Hello. Oh, have you been crying?"

"No," he said, but the tears were there, rising to the surface again. He looked away.

"Don't worry—it's okay to cry, you know. It's good for the soul."

"What do you want, Ada?" he said harshly. She didn't respond. "I'm sorry. I'm just a bit tired."

"I was just hoping for some company. Could you read me a bedtime story, maybe?"

What he wanted to do was close the door, climb back under the safety of the duvet, his own little tortoise shell, and cry the night away. He would face the consequences tomorrow. But if this was to be her last request, her last demand of him, he would oblige her. "Yes, that would be nice."

She smiled and ran into the room, headed straight for the shelves to grab a copy of *Jane Eyre*.

"Ada, what are you doing?"

"I thought you could read me this—"

"No." He snatched it from her hands, maybe even too quickly, thinking at once of Harry's dislike of the book. He'd rather keep it to himself. "You won't like it."

"Of course I would. Why wouldn't I?"

"I just said no, okay? Can't you pick something else?"

"Pleeeeease?"

"Ada," he said, snapping the book shut and placing it back on the shelf, "let's go to your room now. Come on, I'll read you something before bed."

"Fine." She took him by the arm and led her into her bedroom. He sat in the fluffy desk chair, swiveling round to face her as she climbed into bed. Immediately she said, "Come up here," and tapped the space beside her. This he took as a sign, a last moment of companionship between the two of them. He didn't climb in, but as Ada sank further beneath the covers to snuggle her bedfellow—a teddy, in pinstriped pajamas, named Terence—he made a point of tucking her in before moving to the bookshelf.

"Would you read me some stories from the Bible?"

He plucked the large hardback from the shelf and flipped through its gilded pages. Daniel In the Lion's Den, David and Goliath; they were all here, and up there among his favorites. He remembered doting on the Good Samaritan, on Jonah and the Whale, which merged in his mind with the animated Pinocchio and Geppetto in the whale's belly. At St. Mary's he'd been taught to believe that these words, in this very book, were the true word of God, of history. A documented fact. His own Bible had been hefty and battered, a copy that took him through from childhood into early adolescence.

It was the Bible, after all, that had taught him who he was today. He had always wished to understand if he was more like Adam or if he was really intended to be an Eve. He'd always enjoyed the advantages that came with being a man, and particularly enjoyed Adam's task of naming the fowl of the air, the beast of the field. He also understood Adam's feeling of loneliness, but was much more interested in the contemptible Eve. Having scanned the pages of Genesis, he was shocked to learn that Eve's birth could be summarized in a single line: *"Bone of my bone, flesh of my flesh."* When he'd asked Brother Mark where the rest of the creation story was, the clattering of rosary beads against the classroom's chipped desks punctuated his answer: "Man came first, then woman," Brother Mark explained, an elucidation worthy of documenting the whole creation of mankind. "The rest is history."

As Bron witnessed the development of his own body, the wiry strands at his chin, the sprout at his navel like a weed, evolving just the same as those boys around him, he finally accepted that he could not be a woman, the rib taken from Adam without consent. Now there was David Bowie, Miley Cyrus, Billy Porter, Sam Smith, but back then it had been Genesis he read for clues, and he'd longed to revert back into a rib or a speck of dust, the ground from which man was made, and acquire a new form altogether. Something less distinct, less fixed. Having only two ways in which to exist was too restrictive. Not at all a viable way of living. Not for him. Adam, Eve—Adam, Eve; he couldn't choose.

Then, he had that Eureka moment, that spasm of knowledge. The forbidden apple had fallen from the tree. He was not Adam, he was not Eve, but a variation on the universal human, who at one time had been neither, had been both. This is what the words in the Bible taught him. Man, woman: it was not grown from the earth itself, but established in the manmade walls of schools, churches, homes. It pressed itself like mildew upon panes of glass, and today he was able to feel amused by the cartoonish pictures that accompanied the abridged words of Ada's gift-edition Bible.

"Let's go with this one!" she said when he'd flicked back to the contents page.

"The Parable of the Lost Son?" he said, remembering it from his edition as the parable of the prodigal son.

"Yes, yes. It's Daddy's favorite. He's always calling Darcy his prodigal son."

"Why?"

"Because of all the time he spends away, I guess."

He began to read, and was instantly captured by the story of a father and his two sons. He related to the child, who wanted to leave his former life behind, but felt compassion for the father, who was hopeful for his son's return. When he turned the page, the cartoon laid out the big house atop the hill; the son returning, his head cast down; the father, with his long beard and headpiece, running down the lane, arms wide open to greet him.

This was not how he'd pictured the tale at all. The pages here were much too colorful, cheery. When he read, he tried to remove any bleakness from his oration.

"'My son. You are always with me, and everything I have is yours. But we must be glad because your brother has returned to us alive and well. Once he was lost, but now he is found.' Ada"—he stopped reading—"are you crying? What's wrong? What is it?"

"I'm not crying," she squeaked, only to prove that she was.

"You know it's good for the soul," he repeated.

"It's just that—" She took in a deep breath and sighed. "Darcy. He won't speak to me. He won't even look at me. All he does is try his best to get rid of me, just like he did this morning. Haven't you noticed?"

He *had* noticed—the way Ada would address him at the breakfast table, only for him to grunt a response and ignore her, how he would get up and leave any time she entered the room.

"I'm sure he's just got a lot on his mind."

"He does hate me. I so wanted to come with you this morning. He's been ignoring me ever since that night because he knows—he knows I did it!"

"What do you mean?" Bron said, soothing her when she covered her face under the sheets. "Did what, Ada?"

"It was me," she said, her voice muffled by the duvet. "I started the fire in the library."

"Of course you didn't, silly. Why on earth would you think that?"

"I did, I did!" she screamed, emerging from the sheets. "But it was an accident, a complete and total accident. Please don't tell Daddy, please! And Darcy—now he'll hate me forever. I know he will, and they'll send me off to boarding school as soon as they can."

"Calm down, Ada," he pleaded. Her face was panicked. He swiped away the tears that rolled down her cheeks, the mention of boarding school worming its way into his heart. He tried to settle her. "Of course I won't say anything to your father, but he wouldn't dream of sending you away. He loves you. Explain to me why you're saying all this?"

"I heard them talking about it. At the party. Daddy and Uncle Gio—they were talking about me, and boarding school. I know that's what Darcy wants, he's always said so, and Daddy's getting tired of me too. I can tell. Everybody's always out of the house, away from me, and they say I can't join them. Now even Daddy's going off without me."

"Did you say Uncle Gio? Giovanni was there? At the party?"

"Yes. You had been looking for him just before."

He'd almost believed her for a moment, had forgotten she made things up sometimes, played tricks. "You are mistaken, Ada. Giovanni couldn't make it to the party. He wasn't there."

"No he was, he was there." She sniffed. "Daddy had already put me to bed, and I really, *really* wasn't tired at all. The music was so loud, I could hear it from my bedroom. So I got up and went back into the party. I tried to hide so that nobody would see me and send me back to my room—I hid from you, Daddy, and especially Darcy. But I needed to know more."

He tried his best to process it all. Why was she lying about this? What was the point?

"You know, Ada, when I was younger I used to like to go around looking for things too, and—"

"You think I'm lying."

"No, no, I don't think you're lying, it's just . . ." He scrambled for an answer. "I don't see how this makes any sense. What else did you hear?"

"I know it sounds crazy, but I found them all together in that room with the random billiard table that no one ever goes in. And they were talking about me and . . . No, I cannot say. You'll think I'm making it all up. But they were, they were talking about me and that it was about time I knew the truth."

He was oddly suspicious of this. "What truth?"

"Well, the actual truth—you know! But I must have made a noise or something, because Uncle Gio saw me, and then he told Daddy, and Darcy—Darcy got very angry and told me to get back to bed at once. Uncle Gio said that they should talk about these matters somewhere more private, that anyone could just walk in, and that must be why they all went away that night. To talk somewhere more private. Uncle Gio, Darcy, and that lady."

Lady? "What lady?"

"I don't know. Some lady who was there, she was arguing with them too. I didn't see her face—she was wearing a feathery mask thing. She'd spoken to me earlier, though. Before you came along."

He remembered, vaguely, this mysterious woman. The same woman Darcy had rushed away with that night. "Even if you're right, Ada, and I'm not saying you are, what does this have to do with you causing the fire?"

"I really couldn't get to sleep that night. There was so much on my mind. I waited for everybody to go to bed, including you—Darcy must have come back, but the two of you were up so late in the library, and I waited to go inside to find things out for myself. The things I heard them talking about. I lit a candle because I didn't want to turn on the lights and have anybody find me. I was sitting behind the armchair and looking through the album when I found them—the pictures. It was true what they were saying—I couldn't believe it. I was just staring and staring. But then I heard a noise, someone coming from the other door—the secret passageway, remember? The one that looks like a bookcase? So I ran out quickly, hoping he wouldn't see me."

"Hoping who wouldn't see you?" Bron had been sucked into this tale. Was even on the brink of believing it to be true. "Who came into the room?"

"Well, Darcy! I saw him, from the end of the hall. He started throwing things around—I heard something break, and then he came out looking angry. *So angry.* The album was in his hands, and oh, you should have seen his face. I think he was crying he was so angry."

The photo album. "Did he see you?"

"No! But he knew because then I saw him coming toward me, so I shut myself in my room and pretended I was asleep. I know he was standing there. I could feel him outside the door. But he didn't come in. He must have gone straight to his room."

"So then what did you do?"

"Nothing at first. I was so scared I'd get into trouble. But then I smelled something funny and remembered I'd left a candle burning behind the armchair. I went back to make sure it was out, and then I saw the room. On fire! That's when I ran to you for help. But Darcy knows I was in there—he knows it was me who left the candle burning, and now he'll hate me forever."

The photo album. Somehow, Bron connected the dots in his mind. Ada, who had leafed through its pages, had seen something in there she shouldn't have. And Darcy, who originally thought it had been Ada, was now under the impression that it was *he* who'd looked through the album, because he'd directly told him that he had.

Something still didn't make sense. What would make Darcy so angry? Was Darcy now under the impression he'd caused the fire too, and regretful for treating Ada with so little patience all this time, blaming her for something she hadn't done?

"What was it you saw in the photo album, Ada?" he asked.
"Was it a picture of Darcy and Giovanni—Uncle Gio?"

"No, no! It wasn't that at all."

"Well, what was it then?"

"It was . . . it was . . . my mother."

"Your mother?"

"Yes, yes. They said they thought it was time I knew the truth about my parentage. That I should meet my mother! I've always known I was adopted, but I don't know who my birth mother is, I don't even know her name. But Darcy and Daddy and Uncle Gio, they all know!"

"Ada, slow down. I can't keep up. So you know who your mother is?"

"Yes—I mean no. I mean, Daddy said to Darcy that everything was in there, in the photo album, for safekeeping. And I just had to look! And there was a photo in there, with me as a baby, and my mother. Holding me in the hospital! It said *Ada, born 2:15 p.m.* I never ever knew that!"

"Your mother, are you sure it was her? Not somebody else holding you?"

"Yes, yes!"

"But I don't understand."

"I don't know, I don't know!"

Back and forth, back and forth until Ada worked herself up into an inconsolable state of anxiety, leaping out of bed and begging to be taken outside for fresh air. They looked up at the stars together for some time and settled back into her bedroom when the sky clouded over. It had taken him a few hours to finally get her to contemplate the idea of sleep. It was back to the Bible, and some parables he read twice, once for the story itself and once for the lull of his voice.

"I like all the dips and troughs you do," Ada said, and so he made a point of accentuating these moments, rolling the singsong question of *"Where have you lain him?"* and deepening his intonation when announcing for Lazarus to *"come forth!"*

At some point, he must have fallen asleep too. He shifted uncomfortably and blinked his eyes open. Ada nestled into his side, and Terence the teddy was wedged between them. He was hot and sticky with the heat on full blast and with no window open. He climbed off the bed, careful not to wake her, and smoothed the covers over her limp frame before turning off the lamplight and shutting the door. It was the early hours of the morning. The air outside the room was chilly, and he was grateful for it. He tiptoed his way through the hall and back toward his bedroom.

When he stepped inside, he heard a rustle beneath his feet. He shut the door, turned on the light. A single sheet of paper had been slipped beneath the door, half folded. Lifting it, he read its contents. A single word, so small he could've easily missed it. His heart quivered. Five letters, the length not longer than that of a thumb. It read at once hasty and overly thought-out, insincere and yet from the heart. He was shocked, confused, and unprepared to see it.

Sorry.

10

B RON CLAMBERED THE STREETS of Grantchester, a village not too far from Greenwood and southward of the city's meadows, where the centuries did indeed blend and blur, as he remembered reading in a poem once: the windy roads, the thatched cottages, the old brick. What would it have been like to spend his summer days here, to laze in the grass by the River Cam under the gauzy shade of a willow tree? Walking along Broadway Road as his phone instructed him to, he felt anything but the reality of these thoughts. The cold wind was blustery and had him shaking under his coat.

Mrs. Flanders's residence was a charming Victorian terrace ten minutes' walk from the long church, with the shrubs in its front porch appearing manicured at first, especially if you were to only brush down the street, but when passing through the wrought iron gate, one could see how untamed it was, how the flowers curled into the ivy and wreaked havoc along the walls.

He had written to her the previous Monday, a modest message that apologized for his delay in writing to her, that he'd been very busy with his job but that he'd settled in well and was getting to grips with the ebb and flow of Cambridgeshire life. When he pressed "Send," the wall of text, first green and then blue, seemed an appropriate length to be writing after so long a wait.

Perhaps she wouldn't remember him after all, the random person she'd spoken to on a train once to pass the time. He was sure their interaction would have faded from her memory.

She responded almost immediately.

> Lvly 2 hear from u. R u free nxt week? Come rnd 4 tea?

She double-messaged, providing her address again, even though he had it saved in his phone already. In a third message, she wrote:

> C U then x

And now he rang the doorbell. The smile that lifted Mrs. Flanders's face as she greeted him, the way she opened conversation by asking how his journey had been, made him feel as though no time had passed at all between him and this lady he barely knew. The journey was fine, he said, and how are you? Stepping through the front door, he was hit by a foreign smell that he thought he recognized—a blend of sage and onion and hot bread.

She ushered him down the compact hall and through a door that opened into a living area, where plates and framed photographs hung over every bit of wallpaper. She gestured for him to sit in the armchair by the electric fire, an eighties installation. Across the room she'd dressed the small table with a white tablecloth, a three-tiered stand full of sandwiches, and delicate pink china cups upturned on their saucers. A whole pot of tea had been brewed, and she carried this over to him slowly.

"I am so glad you could make it," she said while pouring. "It's not often I'm greeted with company, you know. An old lady like me."

"The pleasure is all mine—that's enough, thanks."

For someone not met with many guests, Mrs. Flanders kept her house spotlessly clean; tidy and organized in that homely grandmotherly way he could only guess at, but chaotic and clustered with knickknacks. *What else is there to do when one is old and lonely? Tidy up and gather things, and tidy up again.* He imagined a glimpse of his future, the unlikeliness of having his own home, the inevitability of his ending up alone.

She wobbled about, the limp to her walk more evident than he'd remembered, and fussed over his gorgeous good looks, the smallness of his size. Asked if he was eating enough. She brought over the tier of sandwiches, and he took a little triangle in his hand. She insisted he take more, and when he took a second, she pressed him to have a third.

"Eat, eat, it is good for you. It will keep you strong."

He was grateful for her hospitality, if not a little self-conscious by the way she watched him eat the sandwich until he made a start on the other. He slowed down his chewing. Mrs. Flanders reached out to the coffee table to push the tier of sandwiches closer toward him.

"It's very kind of you to have gone through all this trouble."

"It is no trouble, dear. No trouble at all. You remind me of my son," she said matter-of-factly. "He liked to eat and was small like you."

"I remember you saying you have a son—"

"Yes, he went away to Oxford many years ago. He was so fragile and curious. My little boy."

"Where is he now?" he asked between mouthfuls.

"He is gone."

He lurched when she said this. How stupid he was to have asked. "I'm sorry," he said, there being nothing else to say.

She nodded her head and chewed her bottom lip. "Almost twenty years ago. He is Ellie now. But he will always be my little boy."

Wait. He backtracked. Must have misunderstood. So they weren't dead after all. "Ellie?"

"Yes, he's, ah, I don't know what they say these days . . . just like you."

She rose from the armchair and brought over two photographs. The first was framed by black cardboard: Ellie stood in academic dress, holding a makeshift scroll for their graduation snapshot. Their dark skin without a blemish, teeth bright and straight, and their full Afro springing from their head in a luxurious halo. The shirt, buttoned up to the neck, was tucked into high-waisted trousers.

Emmanuel Awolowo Flanders, Keble College

In the second, Ellie stood beneath the Radcliffe Camera, black gown caught in the wind, but they were missing the square hat. They leaned against the spindles of the black fence, looking straight into the lens. A bicycle was chained up beside them.

"That's my Emmanuel—he was so full of life."

It would've been the later noughties, an unbridled time after the hardship of Thatcherite Britain, a nation that had lived through an epidemic and had also lost a princess. What was it like to be Black, femme, and male presenting back then, or even now? All these things at once. Trans, but without today's discourse. Now a tick box in the equal opportunities form, a 0.01 percent increment in the still low Oxbridge proportions, Ellie's minority presence at the university would have been questioned by their peers. White authors were read, white teachers would teach, and exams would be taken on white sheets of paper. But Ellie was an anomaly, wasn't meant to exist in that space. Had anything changed, really?

Mrs. Flanders clutched at her bosom, and he focused on the thinness of her fingers, the sagging skin, and the threads of vein that wriggled as she caressed the necklace around her neck like hands playing a chord on a harp. "He gave this to me before he left."

"Where did they go after university?"

"America."

America. The word was a ghost in his ears.

"And they never came back?"

"Never came back," she repeated. "I don't know if he's still there. It's all my fault. I didn't understand it. I said, Emmanuel, you are being ridiculous. Why are you doing these things to me? Whenever I found him wearing my shoes, or with my gel on his head. He used to say to me, 'Ma, I'm just like you. I am a woman.' And I would say, 'No, no, you are not, Emmanuel. You are not a woman, you are a man.' And Emmanuel, he said he will live how he chooses to live. And one day he was gone, never came back. But it was different back then. I didn't understand, and now I have lost my son."

He wanted to console Mrs. Flanders, grieving as she was for her child, and yet she still referred to Ellie in a manner that didn't see them at all. Who they really were. He thought about explaining it to her.

"Mrs. Flanders . . ."

"Please, call me Ndidi. That is my name."

"Okay, Ndidi," he said, though it didn't feel right in his mouth. Nor did it feel right to explain to her the correct usage of her child's pronouns, especially because he wasn't certain what pronouns Ellie used. Instead, he took it upon himself to respect Ellie's wishes in the hope she'd catch on. "Have you tried reaching out to them? To Ellie, I mean? I'm sure they will forgive you, will want to hear from you."

"I have tried. But I don't know where El lives."

"Have you tried looking on the internet?"

"Yes, yes, but it is no use."

He didn't push it further, conscious of potentially winding down the wrong path. He sipped his cup of tea as she continued to speak of all the things Ellie used to do, all the while hanging onto the necklace. How familiar were those fingers with the shape and curve of its intricate design? He imagined her once youthful hands, caressing it, pulling at it, and then sagging, aging in five fluid seconds as she suffered through life without her child. He thought suddenly of Ada—of the necklace that her fingers mindlessly held through the day, as Mrs. Flanders here latched for her child—and then the locket he kept hidden at the bottom of his drawer. Ada was pining for details of her mother, yearned for something she didn't have and sought comfort in the solace of an accessory, one that rooted her to a family.

And then there it was, that nervous feeling, one of both fear and excitement. He couldn't explain it, the sudden shift in his thinking, but this is what he knew: there was a little girl searching for answers, a family that hid secrets from her as well as from him, and a locket without its owner; a son who'd erupted into inexplicable anger at the mention of some photographs and what was to be seen there, and who was seen just before the fire broke out, holding onto the photo album that hosted these same images; and finally, a man who surely had a part to play in all this, who'd claimed not to be in attendance at the Edwardses' Halloween party, only to have been seen by a girl in a sailor's costume.

Bron had an inkling that the locket held the key to the Edwardses' family secret, and in the safety of another house, outside the bounds of Greenwood, he thought a particular thought: that there was something about these events that didn't add up (or perhaps added up all too well).

And what if maybe, just maybe, the fire hadn't been an accident at all?

When he returned to the house, he'd planned to head straight to his bedroom and inspect the locket again, but he'd barely made it through the door before Ada pulled at his arm and slammed the door shut behind him.

"Don't keep any doors open." She was shifting from foot to foot, peering around the foyer and looking up at the ceiling as though a ghost were creeping along and haunting the place. She was gripping onto a fishnet.

"Ada, what's going on?"

"It's Birdie—she's gone,"

"What do you mean she's gone?"

"*Shh,*" she silenced him, and then whispered, "I'm listening out for her wings." She opened and closed every door as they passed through them, eventually pulling him into the utility room. "Oh, I bet it was that wretched old dog again. Nasty Captain, naughty boy."

It was a large though narrow room behind the length of the kitchen. The washing machine was spinning with a hum, and the birdcage sat empty atop the tumble dryer. The cage's hatch door was swung right open, and he instinctively looked to the ceiling for any sign of the bird, a perch of feet. Along the wall ran a line of bells on a plaque, each labeled with room names that no longer existed within the house: the billiard room, south-facing hall, pink dressing room. He itched to find the disused cord connecting to these, to pull and activate the bells to ring—how awesome would that be? But he'd never seen such a cord through his time here, and noticed that the plaque was disconnected from the wire. It was only left here for show, as rusty as a disused railway sign, an emblem of bygone years. Something an estate agent might describe as quirky and characterful.

"What are you looking at?" said Ada.

"I was just searching the ceilings. But don't worry—she couldn't have gone far."

"Will you help me look for her?"

They engineered a plan. Ada would check all the rooms on the upstairs floor, and he would continue the search downstairs. Then, they would reconvene and assess the situation based on their findings or non-findings. If they still hadn't found Birdie, they would swap floors and start the search all over again.

"Actually, I think *you* should continue your search down here, and I will go upstairs," he said. "You've already covered so much ground, we don't want to double up until we've searched everywhere at least once."

"Hmm, I suppose that does make sense."

When they parted ways, he marched up the stairs to his bedroom, first because it was an easy room to tick off the list as "searched," but also because he needed a moment to catch his breath. He sat on his bed for a minute, opened the drawer, and then pocketed the locket before rising again to properly begin his search. Yes, he'd keep to his word, would help find the little bird, but he was looking for something more, still.

He searched the hallway, the spare bedrooms, and the games room in quick succession, opened the door to the library and peeked his head in. The shell-like walls were still in ruin, seemed almost glossy in their limestone sheen now that the soot and char had been scrubbed away; the floor was still being replaced, and the exposed beams stuck out like piano keys through the floor. Beyond, the windows were still empty, toothless gums. A room exposed to the elements save for a sheet of plastic used as a barrier. The wind outside was light, but he felt the breeze on his face; it sounded like the ancient walls were wheezing. If the bird had flown in here at all, well, he reckoned she was long gone. Free.

It was hard to imagine the room now as it had been in its once so opulent way. The fire had eaten away at everything. But not the photo album. That had been safely carried away. Ada had seen Darcy carry it out of the room. He wasn't sure why, but Bron was almost certain he'd find a clue as to the locket's importance inside the album itself. If only he could get his hands on it again.

Along the hall once more he swooped into Ada's bedroom, where everything was still and as it always was: her toys neatly put away, her books lining the shelves. In the built-in wardrobe he found the little matted sock puppet that Ada had pulled from beneath his bed when he'd first moved in. He searched the remaining spare bedrooms, giving them a quick once-over, all the while guessing where the photo album would be. In Darcy's bedroom.

He had yet to venture this far down the hall. Had never had a reason to. Now he was drawn not only to the prospect of finding further clues within the album, but by the curiosity of surrounding himself with a treasure trove of Darcy's things: his clothes, his aftershave, his everyday utilities. To inhale the air in which Darcy slept, existed, and festered. The intimacy of standing among his possessions. But it was still daylight, and the undertaking was risky. He couldn't possibly go in alone. If anyone were to catch him, what would he say? That he was looking for a bird? He could *almost* get away with it.

He turned away, disappointed, and found Ada in the kitchen downstairs, lifting the lid to a pot and making a clatter of everything she touched. He explained to her that he'd searched all the other rooms, top to bottom, but that he needed her to go with him if he were to step into Darcy's bedroom, or even her father's.

"Oh, Papa won't mind."

"I actually think he would, Ada. Why don't we look together?"

"Okay then, I'll do it myself. And you can keep looking down here." She handed him the pot.

"But I'd like to come with you."

"Hmm," she said. "It would be more fun searching together."

"Exactly."

"But like you said, we'd cover more ground if we do it separately. Search down here first, why don't you? We've more chance of finding Birdie quickly then," she said before trotting away.

Dammit. What now?

He scanned the kitchen's surfaces, checked the store cupboard, thinking how best he could get into Darcy's room to find the album without it seeming suspicious. He could just walk up in search of Ada. But was that too clumsy? With a sigh, and growing bored of the search, he went back into the hall, where a whine and little scratchings at a door alerted him to Captain's being locked inside the broom cupboard—*Ada.* He let him out, led him instead into the more spacious kitchen, and closed the door behind him.

In the living room he searched everything again—the ceilings, the curtain poles and their finials, and even behind the curtains. Shut the latch to the window that was still slightly ajar. Lowering to his knees, he stuck his head beneath the drinks cabinet, the armchair, the two sofas . . . nothing.

"Bron, what on earth are you doing?" It was Darcy's voice, making him bang his head.

The first thing he thought was, *My ass is in the air. He's looking at my ass.* He threw himself back, used the sofa's wooden arm to hoist himself up, and dusted off his knees. Darcy stood at the door, a cup of tea held from the saucer, and a newspaper tucked into his armpit.

"I'm just—I'm just looking for something."

"Oh?" he said, coming into the room and setting his tea down. "Don't tell me Ada's got you looking for that bloody bird?"

"Ah, well . . ." He shrugged, gave a defeated look.

"She's up there tearing through my things like a bulldozer. Kicked me out of my own room. Sometimes I think she lets the thing free just so she can have a good snoop."

Hadn't that been his plan exactly? He heard it almost as an accusation.

"Yes, well, the bird's cage was empty, and so here I am, looking for it." He felt a twinge in his stomach being alone again with Darcy. He wasn't sure if he was pleased to see him or if he wanted desperately to get away. This was the first time seeing him since their little excursion gone wrong. He felt uneasy and screwed his eyes shut, readying himself to wince through an apology, until Darcy said:

"In which case, I ought to help you look." He took a swig from his tea and set it down with a light clank.

"Oh no, please don't. There's no need—"

"Have you found it already?"

"No, but—"

"Well then, let me help, Bron—I want to," he said before Bron could protest any further. Darcy quickly began opening cupboard doors and lifting pillows from the sofa.

He wondered what had changed between them. Whether Darcy had chosen to forgive him. Had he thought it best to forget the episode altogether? Otherwise, what was it that induced him to help find this bloody bird? Bron looked impatiently at his searching companion, and with an effort that seemed impossible to keep up, started searching behind the pillows too.

They inched closer together through their search. At one point Darcy lowered to his knees, explored the same spot that Bron had already searched under the sofa. Bron took this juncture to stare at him, hunkered down on all fours.

"I don't think the bird is under there."

"I know," Darcy said, arching his spine and stretching his back out. "I just thought it was worth another look. You know, just to be *absolutely* sure." Bron stared at the firmness of his buttocks, at his underwear's band slung at his waist now that the shirt had come loose. "Oh, bloody hell."

Bron looked away, startled, as Darcy lifted back. Almost like a twerk. "What?"

"I think . . ." he started, standing up and righting himself, "I think I found the bird."

"What?" Bron repeated, following Darcy's line of vision. "Where?"

Darcy took five strides toward the TV stand and leaned over to brush the curtains away, lifting them from their tiebacks. "Um, here."

"Oh God, is it dead?" he said before he had even seen the thing.

"I think it's a bit more than dead. Executed more like."

Oh no. Oh no oh no oh no.

He skirted away before forcing himself to move into the corner where, almost as though it had been hastily stuffed under the TV stand, was a bloody, feathery carcass.

"I can't even look at it," he said, a hand over his mouth to stop from gagging. "I wonder how long it's been there for."

"It couldn't have been long. It hasn't started to smell. Don't worry, I'll take care of it. Stupid dog."

"What are you going to do with it?" Bron risked another look, then actually gagged.

"I don't know. Throw it in the bin or something."

"You can't—Ada—she'll find it."

"Alright, alright. Well, I'll bury it in the ground somewhere, a nice spot outside—

"You can't do that either. Can't we just tell her the truth? Sit her down—"

"*Bron!*" Ada's voice, calling his name. "*Bron, where are you?*"

"Shit." They glanced at each other, jumping quickly into a position that hid the bird from view. They stood together, arms touching.

"Ah, there you are," she said, coming into the room. "Oh, Darcy, what are you doing in here?"

"Nothing, nothing," he said. "I was just . . . helping."

"Helping? With what? Were you helping Bron find Birdie?"

"Yes, yes, he was," Bron said, and Darcy tapped twice on his shoulders as if giving reassurance.

"Oh, that's just brilliant. Brilliant. Ah, okay. Well . . ." She looked at their two faces, smiling so widely her own face could have broken in two. "You two keep looking and—well, I'm sure together we'll be able to find her. Oh, this is so exciting. I'll keep looking in the other rooms since you've got in here covered. Let's share notes in about . . . fifteen minutes? We can tick off the rooms searched as being all-clear. What a fun game this has turned out to be! *Birdie, where are you?*" she screamed, running out of the room and back up the stairs.

They waited a moment before pulling apart.

"Right, well," Bron said. "Do you want to be the one to tell her, or should I?"

"I really don't think we should tell her.

"Why not, it's always best, telling the tru—"

Darcy held up the decapitated body. Brought it closer to him.

"Oh my God, stop. That's disgusting!"

"You really think we ought to explain . . . this?"

"Okay, okay, I get it. Just get it away from me."

Darcy placed the thing back on the floor and muttered under his breath, "Poor little murdered bird. I think it was Miss Scarlett, in the living room, with the—"

"Stop it." Bron slapped him on the shoulder. "If we're not going to tell her, we have to make sure she doesn't see this. Seriously."

"Okay, okay. She won't see it."

"Good." Bron moved to guard the room's entry. "Okay, I'll tell you when the coast is clear."

It only took them a few minutes to clear up the evidence. Darcy grabbed a wad of paper towels from the kitchen and rolled what was left of the body into it—"This is truly vile, bits of it keep flaking off"—and used surface spray to wipe away the blood that had yet to leave a stain on the wooden floor.

"Hurry up!" Bron urged.

Darcy snuck through the front door while Bron stayed put in the living room. He watched through the window as Darcy walked the perimeter of the house, stopped to point at him, and held out his hand to signal—*You. Outside. Five minutes*—before trudging away.

Once he was sure Ada remained upstairs and all the evidence downstairs was gone, he, too, crept out of the house to find Darcy where he knew he would be, at the bench overlooking the fields. He'd dug a little hole under the tree, where the mummified bird drenched red would now be laid to rest.

"Well, I guess that's that."

"Do you think we should—?"

"No."

"—say a few words?"

"Absolutely not. Bron."

"I think we should. Ada would."

"I draw the line here," Darcy said, wiping his soil-brown hands onto his jeans before walking back toward the house. "I'll see you inside."

Bron hovered back to say a quick prayer himself—*"and lead us not into temptation, but deliver us from all evil, amen"*—then used his shoe to repave the hole with soil. He found two sticks on the ground and placed them at the top of the heap, in the shape of a cross.

Back in the kitchen, Darcy was rinsing his hands under the running tap. Captain was barking at his feet. Bron swirled through a list of possible things he could say to Ada. Should he really keep this from her? He could say that they had found the bird—and then what? Poof, into thin air? No . . . Perhaps he could distract her, have Darcy drive somewhere and purchase a quick replacement budgie. A Birdie 2.0—although wasn't that what Birdie had been in the first place? Shit.

Darcy looked at him. "I suppose this would be a bad time to ask if you'd gotten my note?"

"Yes," he said.

"Yes, it'd be a bad time?"

"Yes, but I also got your note."

"I wanted to apologize to you in person. I shouldn't have snapped at you like that."

Bron shrugged as if to say *"no biggie,"* but Darcy reached out to him. Tipped up his chin so that he'd meet his eyes. "Hey, I mean it. I'm sorry. It was genuinely very wrong of me."

Bron exhaled in relief, though if anything he felt himself too hot. Embarrassed by Darcy's apology. He shrugged again and blinked to clear away the tears that threatened to form. "Thank you for saying that." Bron allowed Darcy to caress his cheek, to stroke the back of his ear. It was his turn to say something now. "I'm sorry too. I . . . I shouldn't have pried."

But when Ada came in, they righted themselves, Darcy quickly returning to the kitchen sink. Bron prepared himself for whatever emotions she was to bring up at having not yet found Birdie.

"Good news, team." She pulled herself up onto a stool near the island and grabbed quickly for a pencil. Producing a sheet of paper, she crossed out the last line on her list and held it up for all to see. "That's Papa's bedroom clear. That means all the rooms have finally been searched."

Darcy shut off the tap and ambled toward the door. Bron side-stepped to block him from leaving.

"Well," Bron said. "Are you . . . are you sure we've checked absolutely everywhere? I could check my room again. Or maybe Darcy's."

"Hell no," Darcy said.

"Oh, we don't need to do any more searching," Ada said. "I found Birdie ages ago."

"You—you did?" they said in unison.

"Yeah. Flying about in the breakfast room and perched on the little ledge. She was staring out the window so beautifully. Of course I went to grab her, but then I thought, 'Hey, she's a bird. She's meant to be out there, flying free.' And so I opened the window. And she took off. It was wonderful to see."

Bron paused before stumbling over whatever words tried to come out of his mouth, and then looked up to Darcy, who looked equally baffled.

"Well, that sorts that then," Darcy said. He sidled up to Bron's shoulder, gave his arm a little squeeze, then whispered into his ear, "The little liar."

Bron brought his hands to his mouth to cover his smile.

"Wait," Ada said, jumping to her feet. "Darcy, where are you going?"

"Out. Some urgent business."

"Alright. Bron? Will you come upstairs and read to me?"

"I—"

"No, he can't. Sorry, Ada, I'm afraid I need to ask a little favor of our Bron. This business of mine, it's very urgent. Very urgent, indeed. I'm in need of his expert hands."

"What expert hands?"

"Run along now, Addie," Darcy said, and guided Bron from the small of his back out into the hall. From there, he pulled him into the breakfast room and secured the door shut. "That girl. She's bound to be a politician, the way she can lie so easily through her teeth like that."

"Maybe she wasn't lying."

"What? You think that while one bird flew loose through the house, another identical bird just *happened* to swoop in and just *happened* to land in the jaws of my whippet?"

"It's possible?" Bron started, but his entertaining of this non-fact had Darcy clutching at his stomach, and soon they were both laughing.

"I suppose it's better off this way. That in some revised version of the world, the blasted thing made it out alive."

Bron ran a finger through his hair and looked to the sash window, the pane securely shut and much too high for Ada's reach. He felt Darcy, the height of him, press against his back. He could let himself fall into him, if he wanted, rest his back onto the hardness of his chest, curve into the pit of his stomach, and linger there a while.

"What are you looking at?" Darcy asked quietly.

When Darcy rubbed his shoulders, as if to release the tension from them, he inadvertently let out a sigh. He dropped his head back and pretended, for a moment, like this was completely normal behavior between the two of them. That there were no ghosts in the closet to be revealed. No strain in the way they just *were* when they were together. The different worlds they occupied. "Nothing. I was just thinking that I should probably go upstairs. Plan a lesson for Ada or . . . or something."

"Must you really go?" Darcy swiped Bron's hair away from his neck, caressed him there with his fingers. He worried—no, that wasn't the right word—he was quite certain that if he let this go on any longer, Darcy would kiss him again. He could feel his breath on his neck already. He could give into it. He could.

He stepped away quickly, putting some distance between their bodies by walking the length of the breakfast table. He made some slight reply, spinning on his heel. Because though Darcy looked blameless in the way he now pouted his lip or the way he gripped the chair to stop himself from reaching out, he couldn't bear the uncertainty that existed between them, never sure which version of Darcy he might get at any time.

"Well, alright, if you so wish."

Bron nodded and made a dash for the door. Darcy made a point of brushing his hand against him as he passed. Bron unbolted the door, giving a simple, yet effective "Goodbye." In the hall, he stopped at the staircase, wrapped his arms around the marble pillar, and waited for Darcy to follow after him. When he didn't, he climbed the stairs two at a time, and it was to the safety of his own room that he fled.

11

ALL WAS SERENE FOR a time, and merry too. The streets were silenced by a coating of frost, and the manor was made alive by carols playing on a loop through Classic FM and the smell of citrus, oranges having been placed in baskets throughout the rooms, and eaten for breakfast and lunch every morning and afternoon. Mr. Edwards, a connoisseur of the spicy mulled wine, drank copious amounts of the drink, which Darcy mixed in batches in the kitchen; and Ada, who sipped it at Mr. Edwards's allowance, declared it to be the sweetest thing in all of the world.

Stockings hung from the fireplace's mantel, a trio of *ADA, DARCY, and BRON* scrawled on each in Ada's handcrafted glitter. Wreaths and garlands draped the walls, knotted with ribbons of gold, scarlet, and green. Ada would creep up to them and pluck the red and pink berries with fumbling fingers and later, Bron would sit with her and weave them along string, fashion them into a necklace she wouldn't take off until the skins broke and the juices stained either her mouth, clothes, or more often both. All worries surrounding the fire in the library had all but dissipated by this time, though the air felt considerably altered, colder. Any attempt at getting his hands on the photo album was foiled by the house's many eyes, the joyous weeks of welcoming guests into parties and gatherings.

At Ada's insistence, they'd all agreed upon a little potted fern, instead of a Christmas tree, from which hung a couple of baubles and a rhinestone ornament of a hot air balloon. Of course, it was still all about the presents, and though it wasn't quite Christmas Day yet, Ada's begging for something to open started from as early as mid-December. Mr. Edwards insisted on her waiting till at least Christmas Eve, but after they'd all parted for bed, and Bron remained in the living room with his book, it was only to find Ada sneaking up to the potted fern, where she'd sit and sulk, her white nightdress spreading around her legs like a snowflake. Ada had never seen him watching her, and he had never made his presence known, for it was never longer than a minute that she'd linger, by which point she must have grown cold, and with a huff of revival took herself to bed. How strange it was to watch her return night after night to that same spot, a sleepwalker stuck on the same loop and always meeting the same disappointing end. She was a specter, her pale legs and bare feet standing in the middle of the dark hall, her hair blacker than it was in the daylight, and dripping from her nighttime bath. And as she crept back up the staircase, he saw her, and then sometimes himself—a younger version of himself—haunting the stairs, running up and down them, as he'd so done through the winter holidays at St. Mary's.

For the majority of the boys would always return home for the holiday, and for the unfortunate few who'd been left behind, a group to which he had always been part, there was nothing to do but wait for the others to return, a different kind of loop in which to exist. There was one year, he remembered it clearly, when a distraught Harry had been left to stay behind too. It was no news to him that Harry hated St. Mary's—they all hated St. Mary's—but for Bron, it was the most perfect gift he could have received. More time with his friend, more time with Harry. They played snake on his old Nokia phone, told ghost stories at night, and more often than not, they roamed the school halls with the lightest of footsteps, hiking up the legs of their striped pajama bottoms and tiptoeing barefoot despite the bitter chill. Their shins exposed to the damp air, they'd hunch through the hall like hags, past the teachers' quarters, past the dorms of Our Lady of Sorrows and Our Lady of Mount Carmel, and into whichever rooms they fancied. Always in search of adventure.

Harry at the sash window, pushing his weight against the frame. Bron standing there motionless until it came unstuck.

"Hold it there, just like that," Harry had said until he'd got one leg through and then his waist; and then, after ducking like a swan, he helped Bron through the window too, outside into the cold.

"Remember, if you hear anyone coming, we say we were sleepwalking. Understood?"

They'd waddled along the ledge, hands tracing the wall. One foot forward, then another. Hands gripping the pipes, then pushing at another window, into another room, through another door. Up they climbed, round and round the spiral staircase, hands swiping away at the cobwebs, the dust tickling their noses, itching their eyes. Hands stretched outward in the dark, feeling for the scratch of the hatch, fumbling for the handle. Out they'd come onto the school's secluded roof tower, the cold wind enveloping them and the long stretch of black above. That was what they came to see the menagerie of glittering stars, the freedom of the world above, just within their reach.

"See, look over there," Harry had explained. *"That's Jupiter and Saturn. They're always hanging out together, even though they're like a gazillion miles apart—and do you see that line that curves slightly upward? That's Andromeda, who was said to be more beautiful than all the Nereids—that means sea nymphs, the fifty daughters of Poseidon— and look. See there! Do you see that square?"*

Harry had pointed and traced the stars with his hands until Bron nodded and said *"Yes, yes, I can see it now."* He couldn't really.

"That's Pegasus, the winged horse. He's my favorite because it looks like he's fallen over in the sky and can't get up, so maybe he's just floating there forever and ever, which I think would be really cool, don't you?"

"Yes," he'd agreed. But today he would give a different answer. He'd say that floating forever and ever in a sea of black with no one to ask for help would be frightening. Lonely.

Harry had taken his hand, then. *"You're my best friend in the whole world. You know that, right?"*

Out there in the impressive cold, it was an unspoken promise: that they would never leave each other.

"I know." And in that moment, he believed it to be true. Truer than anything else he knew.

I know. I know. I know.

When he looked out the window now in Greenwood, and up at the moon and stars, he saw in the windowpane's reflection his own waning face, and then beside it, Harry's, murky like a puddle and enticing Bron to roam the halls with him yet again. He touched his hand to the window. The question remained: Had Harry ever made it to Cambridge? What if he opened the latch— would Harry be there, outside and roaming the city, cruising down a punt or drinking himself silly in a bar? When he pulled his hand away from the window, he looked at the smudge of condensation left by his palm, and then suddenly, a face. Not Harry's face, but a different one entirely.

"Are you alright there?" It was Darcy, from the other end of the room. Standing with a mug steaming in his hands, mingling with the moonlight, appearing to evaporate.

"Yes," he said, shutting his book and rising to stand. "I was just finishing up, going to bed."

"Oh were you?" Darcy said, looking at him for a moment. "I was hoping we could talk. You know, about . . . well, everything, really. But are you sure you're alright? You look a little depressed."

"I'm not depressed. I was just . . ." He sat back down. "Thinking."

"Ah, thinking. That awful process. It troubles me too." Darcy wandered over to the sofa, sat on the edge of armchair opposite him. "May I ask what you were thinking about?" He took a sip from his mug and placed it on the coaster, waiting patiently for a response whenever Bron was ready.

"It's just, you know, I was thinking about somebody I used to know, somebody I lost touch with and haven't heard from for years."

"Friends drifting apart?" he said. "It happens to the best of us."

They locked eyes with each other then. "Yes, I suppose it was bound to happen at some point or another."

"But this friend was special to you."

"Yes, he was very special."

"You know, sometimes it takes losing someone pretty special for us to really appreciate what's right there in front of us. What's really important to us. And sometimes somebody's loss is another's gain." Darcy cocked his head slightly, offered him a knowing look. Confiding. "I don't just *pretend* to know what I'm talking about here."

"And what have you gained?" Bron asked, almost too quickly. "Through your loss."

"Well, I . . ." Darcy contorted his face into a serious pause before letting out a deep sigh. "I suppose I've gained an awareness of who I was before my loss, and in doing so it has informed the person I've become after it. It's not always easy." Darcy held his jaw in his hands, rubbed at it like an ache, and Bron looked to the floor, felt the heaviness of his chin and lids cast down. "Trust me, I've lost a fair few friends along the way, and more than that too."

Darcy rose to leave the room, a movement that, as he shuffled away, made a scratching noise on the wooden floor like a mouse burrowing through.

"Thank you," Bron said. "For saying all that."

Darcy yanked at the sleeve of his dressing gown, twisting to face him. "I haven't said anything you didn't already know," he said before ascending the stairs and disappearing into the dark.

On Christmas morning, Bron had woken to find a box, wrapped in silver paper, outside his bedroom door. It read his name in a miniature hand, and within the comfort of his rooms, he lifted the lid. Inside was a netting of tulle and gauzy paper that looked like a wedding veil, and beneath it were two neatly folded items: a cozy, maroon-colored jumper that read "*It was not the thorn*

bending to the honeysuckles, but the honeysuckles embracing the thorn," and underneath it, a garment of gray cashmere. The softest thing he'd ever held. Lifting and fanning it out, he realized it was a shawl. He read the note accompanying the box:

> To keep you warm in case you fancied a change from the yellow, though you continue to be a thorn in my side. A quote possibly from the wrong sister, but the sentiment stands.
> —Darcy.

This gift had touched him, made him truly, properly cry. The shawl offered to him a sense of finally being seen by a man he so desperately wanted approval from. And the jumper, well, he continued to think about that deep into the night.

But Christmas Day came and went, and with it another year had passed. It was safely, securely January, and he was watching Netflix on his Sunday off, again alone in his bedroom, all the while struggling to fully immerse himself into the folds of English countryside, into the strained love affair that was happening on screen. He had found the repetitive string of festive days unsettling, considered the way the house came to life to be a burden. At each gathering, Darcy nodded his head in acknowledgment of his presence—a conspiratorial nod, but he wished every time for Darcy to take a step further. To envelop him in his arms, there in the room, for all to see; to ask him if he had received his present, what he thought of it. Bron would say that he understood the sentiment perfectly, though he wasn't really sure about the whole thorn thing.

So Bron grew bored of the movie, closed the streaming service's tab to open another, and tried to occupy himself through other means. Inspired by Birdie's departure (whichever version of it was taken), he ripped a page out of one of his many books and, borrowing Ada's new art supplies, ballooned the quote *"I am no bird; and no net ensnares me"* into its center in a steady calligraphy. Once dry, he'd frame it, take pics of it in good lighting, and in the interest of working toward his New Year New Me goals of being more business minded and professional, he'd upload it onto some online marketplace and wait for someone to buy it. Afterward, he tingled for something else to do: opened up several apps on his phone to key variations of the name *Ellie Awolowo Flanders*—*Eleanor, Eleanora, Eloise* into Instagram, Twitter, and even LinkedIn, but with no luck. He swiped away the different interfaces but dwelled on the last, backspacing Ellie's name and slowly typing in another, hesitant to hit "Enter" on the search.

Harry Blackwater's name loomed at him like it always did, and then the countless older men he'd come across who shared the same name, the blank profile that had once been active, and the wall of unanswered text messages he'd sent to it:

> Hope you've been well . . .

> It's been far too long x

> Any chance you'd want to chat?.

> Hey, I was just wondering if you wanted to talk?

> I've tried contacting you on here for the longest time, but I'm not sure if you're seeing any of this. Could you write me back?

He swiped the last screen away, blacking out his phone. There was a double rap on the door, a twist of the handle, wedging as if locked. This gave him enough time to pull the sheets closer to his chest. The handle rattled again, and Madame Clarence walked in.

"There you are, Bron," she said. His eyes flicked from her to the screen, as hers did from the screen to him. It was a verbal conversation only on her part, but his silence urged her to go on. "Mr. Edwards would like to see you downstairs in the drawing room." She was mid-retreat when she stepped back into the room and said, "The door was not locked?"

"No," he said. "It wasn't."

"We will 'ave someone come to oil it."

He quickly changed out of his slacker clothes and made his way downstairs. He walked past the library's open doors, the room erected with scaffolding, and into the drawing room, where Darcy and Ada stood by Mr. Edwards at his desk, looking not unlike two misbehaving schoolchildren who'd been sent to the headmaster's office. Bron joined them in the line. Mr. Edwards poised over his ledgers like an office clerk or a merchant. While most of his things had been lost in the fire, the drawing room had become Mr. Edwards's new domain for office work. Bron thought of the room as a redesigned set piece, a filming location on budget with all the typical supplies there to be found: the tower of folders, the hole punch, the stapler. Mr. Edwards dipped his pen into an inkpot. With one hand, he stroked Captain behind the ears, and with his other hand concluded his letter writing with a flourish. Darcy called the dog's name, startling both pet and master.

"Oh, good heavens, you three," he said. Rising from the desk chair, he asked them to sit on the couches, rustling Ada's hair as he did so and patting his son on the back. To Bron, he offered a light brush on his shoulder. The dog trotted away to his bed by the fireplace.

Bron waited for Darcy to sit first before dropping onto the opposite couch.

"So, do I have some exciting news for you all? Ah, there you are, Clarence, with my tea."

Clarence strode into the room and handed him a steaming cup. She stood waiting for him to take a sip. When he did, she smiled, and leaned forward to rearrange his tie.

"Th-thank you Clarence."

"You're welcome, sir." Bron had noticed this before, the way Clarence's face rearranged itself around her employer, morphing into something less uptight, something gentler. At first he'd taken it as a nervous fret, but now he wasn't so sure.

Mr. Edwards's eyes lingered on her as she left the room. They were all waiting for something to happen.

Ada finally squeaked, "Papa?"

"Oh yes, yes. The news, the news—exciting news. The very best. Well, it turns out that the house fire has spread a little further than first suspected."

"I knew it," said Ada. "It's the smoke particles in the air."

"Yes, yes! I mean no, Ada. Not the smoke particles. The fire has spread from the library out into the entire county! It seems that the gentlefolk out there really do seem to love our little place and are wanting to hold a charity fair to raise some money to help restore our dear library."

Ada squealed. Darcy muttered something like "Oh God, Father," and Bron remained silent.

"We'll be offering an open house, so Ada, please ensure your room is tidy!"

Her squeal turned into a groan.

"Why do you feel the need to invite everyone into our home?" Darcy asked. "All that need out there, and this is what they want to donate to? A crumbling old manor house?"

"You are right, son. Of course you are. Absolutely right. A fair, of all things. I couldn't possibly let that happen." Mr. Edwards turned to the desk, plucked a newspaper from underneath his ledger, and handed the open paper to his son. "Take a look for yourself." Mr. Edwards urged him to read it aloud.

"*'Following the fire at Greenwood Manor, and the humble decision on behalf of the conservation society and the local community to host a county fair in a bid to raise money for repairs, estate owner Mr. Edwards and family have decided to open up their private residence to the charitable public and host a cricket match between house and village, to raise money for Cambridgeshire Fire Services and their excellent company, who managed to quell the fire and deliver the rest of the house and its inhabitants from harm.'* A cricket game, Father?"

Bron watched Darcy closely, his eyes displeased and taking in more of the paper before they finally glanced over to him.

"What better sport than a good ol' game of cricket!"

What was it about sports that caused such total uproar among people?

Bron had always disregarded sports as something entirely separate from his abilities or interest. At St. Mary's, he'd watched as the boys grew more athletic around him: the dreaded bleep test, propelling the other boys forward in a lively sort of competition, confirmed only that he'd not been created to run at great speeds or for very long; the curved rubber discus on the edge of his fingertips, weighing like the earth flattened in his palm, flew as easily as a Frisbee when the others threw it, but not for him; the length of the javelin pole, which unfurled his shoulders to a breadth more typically reserved, would never fly very far, though the others sent it hurling like a rocket ship. Through these solitary affairs he could stand at the back of the line, go unmissed, but this was not a privilege that extended to team-based games.

Typically, he'd have stood at the far end of the pitch, T-shirt mud-splattered, socks stretched as far up his leg as they could go. The PE teacher would force him into the huddle, and he would always obey, stumbling to the boys' sides—heads between legs and close enough to smell sweat—conscious, always conscious, of where his arms and hands landed, where his eyes were looking. The boys would study him; he'd suffer for it afterward. Performing the appropriate side-step was always his focus as the boys crashed into each other, in case they should choose to shame him for such contact later. But he remembered that one time when the ball had somehow found itself cradled in his arms. He'd leaped into a circular run, dodged one boy and then another before tossing it away into the arms of the opposing team, who ran forward and scored at the goal line. The abuse that ensued.

"For fuck's sake!"

"You sabotaged us with that girl throw. Running like a little sissy."

"You're gonna lose us the game, aren't ya, ya little bender."

The whistle again. An order for them to regroup, and each of the boys racing back into the huddle, his being shoved at the shoulder as they ran past. He'd stumbled away, afraid of getting any closer to them. But then, the *"Hey,"* and the light touch at his shaking arm. *"Don't listen to them."* Harry, always the portrait of kindness, his shield and sword. Harry, covered in a mixture of mud and grass. *"Come on, then,"* he said, eyebrows raised and teeth white like popcorn, doing a backward jog. Harry rejoining the huddle with swaths of patting at his back, his shoulders, at his dense and sprawling Afro hair. The way Harry looked back for him, tipped his head forward as if to say, again, *"Get in here."*

The boys grunted as they pushed further into one another, a giant spider body pushing along the pitch. Somehow, the ball ended up in Bron's hands again, and he ran until the cold breath of air felt like fire in his lungs. He was tackled to the ground, his eyes stinging as they climbed off him. The game continued, and no one paid him any notice, but Harry, always Harry, was there to offer his hand.

"You gotta run faster than that, Bron. At least pretend to try. Don't give them a reason to hate you."

He struggled to his feet, shook the sludge off his shins, wiped the dirt from his face, and looked across the field at the opposing team, Harry's team, who had scored again. Harry, doing a little whoop in the air with his fists.

"You wanna shift that one and thank him now do ya, Blackwater?" A shout from across the pitch. *"Practically handed you the game he has."*

"What's your problem, O'Brian?"

"He is. The little faggot."

"Don't call him that."

But it was only said again. Then names were shouted in turn. The teacher, liking nothing more than the opportunity to allow his boys to let off steam, as boys were wont to do, turned the other way.

"I'll say whatever I want to say."

The gaggle regrouped around them. Chanted their names. Harry threw the first punch. The chants turned to cheers. The next punch gave an audible crunch, a splatter of blood. Bron remembered how he'd screamed, how he was pushed and pulled away from them when he tried to intervene.

And though Greenwood was no school playground, it was with some disdain that the day of the cricket game approached. The match wasn't to start before noon, but before he knew it, the clock had struck eleven, and vehicles were parking outside the gates behind the hedge, were even allowed into the driveway. The grounds populated with people. From the window, he and Ada marked out the differences between those who were here to play and those who were merely spectating: men who walked to and fro with their staple cricket jumper and its colored V-neck, geared for the game. Those who treated the weather as though it were a summer's day: the men in their khaki shorts or chinos, the women in their summer dresses and espadrilles, the large sunglasses, the occasional straw hat, though it was barely eleven degrees centigrade.

The green had morphed into a pitch: white lines chalked into the grass, the wickets secured into the ground. Chairs and pews were laid out for people to sit, and bunting festooned along the way. A long table had been set up under the cream marquee: a buffet luncheon for the crowd who accumulated there. When Bron entered the tent, he smelled the pungency of roast beef and lamb, of buttery potatoes in their big serving dishes. There were pies and finger sandwiches and crudités, and he heard the sound of the carving knife being sharpened, and a multitude of "Good day, sir" and "Capital weather we're having for such a day in February" spoken about the garden.

"One must feed them before one beats them." Mr. Edwards laughed, spooning a second (third) helping of prawn cocktail into a crystal bowl. Bron felt the sense of urgency, the excitement radiating off Mr. Edwards as he picked his way further down the table, leaned forward for the curved knife and its glinting handle that stuck out from the wheel of cheese like a sword in the stone. He cut off a wedge, popped it into his mouth.

"I can't wait. I can't wait. It's been far too long—far too long since I last played. A child in school, I think! Those days at Eton. Ah, Hanson. There you are at last." He rushed away. The women came round with their baskets and their smiles, collecting the monies that would go toward the fire services.

Bron allowed himself one sandwich to settle his stomach, and then scanned the sky, the unexpected cloudless blue, thinking that maybe he would find some enjoyment in watching all these men in their flattering white flannels, until Mr. Edwards pulled him from his thoughts to announce that Bron would be filling a vacancy in the home team for the Greenwood versus Village rivalry.

Fuck. How would he get out of this one?

"Me? Whatever for? I mean, why not anyone else?"

"Well, Darcy has outright refused to take part, and you're the only one left to ask!"

"Are you sure? There's nobody else who could do it?"

Darcy emerged from the crowd of sandwich eaters, and having overheard their conversation, was quick to add his own two cents' worth. "My guess, Father, is that Bron would share a similar distaste for the game as I." Which, in part, was true. Bron hated sports. Hated everything about them. But he also thought that cricket wasn't rugby, football, or some violent showmanship of machismo, and there was a part of him, however slight, that had always wanted to play this genteel game. It was a staple of the period drama. "Isn't that right?"

"Oh, you two! Never time for fun and games. Why must you dampen our spirits? No, I'm putting my foot down. I insist you both play."

Darcy agreed to volunteer for the position of twelfth man for the Greenwood team, as a substitute player on the off chance someone was to be injured, which satisfied both himself and his father immensely. That left Bron to fill the gap.

"But I haven't got a kit to wear," Bron argued, to which Mr. Edwards walked about in search of anyone with a spare kit. Finding none, he was hopeful of his not having to partake in the game after all. Until:

"I'm sure I could find an old T-shirt and white shorts lying about somewhere, if Bron was open to it?" said Darcy.

"Yes, yes, good idea, son," said Mr. Edwards. "Bron?"

He gave Darcy the side-eye. "Of course."

And with no argument left to be made against it, he was made to agree.

In baggy shorts falling to just under his knee, and a clean but yellow-stained T-shirt on his person, he was ready to absolutely *not* make a fool of himself. His fate was inevitable. And with no time to read up on the rules of the game, he quickly skimmed the internet on his phone to learn that there were figures called batsmen and bowlers, and fielders too, although their role seemed to be rather less important, or less appealing anyway, to the crowd. The practicalities of how the team would work had already been determined: Greenwood was made up of Mr. Edwards and his friends, occasional staff at the house, the neighbors—faces he recalled from their coming in and out of the house. The other team would be made up of volunteers from the village council. All in white flannels, the class distinction was less seen here. It wasn't about where people came from or the families they were born into; it was more about the game itself. Love for the game. Love for what it represented. *"The way things used to be,"* he heard people say a lot. As he looked around, he questioned his own thinking: What *did* it represent? The men's wives, dressed as though attending a game at Ascot, perched by the table to labor as spectators.

He scarfed down a tuna and cucumber sandwich while the hierarchies of the world, village versus estate, rich versus poor, commoner versus those who controlled the world, were paved over by the white clothing. Bron knew that the women had not been asked to play, and felt acutely that he was on the wrong team, himself a poor, gender-fluid commoner. Something about his testosterone levels allowed him this access. And that felt deeply unfair. To the women. To him for being in this mess.

One of the men at the table spun to him, forking the last of the deviled eggs first onto his plate and then into his mouth. "Looks like we're going to need a refill before the game's even begun." This was said between bites, and in a way that completely implied his expecting Bron to refill the platter.

Ada trotted up to them and tugged at his side, to explain that she was outrageously bored and that it was very clear from the setup that no girls were going to be allowed to play.

"It's deeply unfair," she said.

"I was just thinking the same thing."

She pulled him away from the buffet table and schemed to steal a bat and ball that'd been discarded on the ground. Successful in their plight (nobody was paying attention), they settled a while away from the rest of the cricketers, and she demanded he help her bat.

"Give me your best shot."

Bron threw the ball her way. Ada's bat barely scraped it. He tried again, and on that second time it made impact—a small one.

"It's no use," she said, tossing the bat to the ground. "I'm beyond rubbish."

"No you're not," he said, stepping toward her and lifting the bat from the grass. She took it back from him. "Don't give up yet. You've barely even tried."

"I *have* tried," she said.

He gripped the ball hard, ready to throw, but Ada pointed behind him, and Darcy's voice intercepted them.

"That's no way to hold a bat," he said, shielding his eyes from the sun. "Your stance is all wrong." Darcy approached her and lowered her elbows from her face to her chest, held her wrists into position. "You need to be able to see the ball coming when he throws. Ready?"

"Yeah, ready."

Bron released the ball, and in one big swoop she sent the ball rolling off toward the buffet table.

"I did it, I did it! See—did you see?"

"Of course you did," said Darcy, ruffling her hair. "You can do anything if you put your mind to it. Now go over there and practice your throw. You want to arch your wrist as you do it."

Ada took the ball from his hand and ran away of her own volition. Darcy looked at him intently, but it was Bron, eyeing up the cream, but not the whiteness, of Darcy's clothing, his jumper with its black and yellow stripes, who was first to speak.

"It is a real shame you won't be playing. I think Mr. Edwards really wanted you to."

"As I said before, Bron, I rather detest the game."

"Detest? That's quite assured."

Darcy looked out toward the marquee, toward the pitch. "I wouldn't dare to be seen playing cricket. It symbolizes everything I hate about this country. A portrait of propriety, a natural social order, a myth upheld by the village green."

Yet more symbols for this quaint, idyllic game—but he wanted to counter Darcy, to say that everything he'd just described was the very thing that Darcy exuded. But then again, he thought about what it meant to exist within a space once inaccessible. The team he was playing on. He could feel it acutely, his time on the rugby pitch at St. Mary's, the discomfort of being there among the other boys. Felt it even now, embedded into his core. He was their baggage, a weight they'd rather have done without. And yet here he was, invited to play on yet another field. As one of them. Cricket was kind of dance, performed by men, to each other, across the field. A love affair (kind of gay—a sentiment he'd also felt when watching his schoolmates play rugby).

When Mr. Edwards jogged toward them, already in his gear, he began to stretch, first each of his arms and then his legs, dipping into lunges. The rest of the players gathered onto the makeshift pitch for gameplay. None of the men looked particularly athletic—they did not resemble the St. Mary's rugby team, with their large biceps and agile way of moving even as teenagers. Instead, these were middle-aged men whose hobby it was to play sports on the weekends. Which was to say, they looked exactly like themselves. Just clad in white. The necessary paraphernalia appeared. The batsmen were handed their bats; cricket pads were unfolded and strapped on; shin pads ornately shone, having been polished for the occasion. The fielders took their places, scattered about.

Bron asked one of the players for a round-up of the rules. He still didn't understand some of the terms he heard being thrown about, though he nodded and said he did when the player explained them to him again. He decided there was no use in trying. Like a language, one had to grow up with it to be truly fluent, to understand it fully with all its nuances: there were too many rules, too many players, too many things going on at once. It seemed to him like a game of baseball, a game he was familiar with, having heard enough about it from Harry. But that was the extent of it. When he vocalized this comparison, he was met with a flout of tutting.

The umpire was at the ready. Ada, who had elected herself assistant umpire, was tasked with watching the match closely and to enforce the rules and settle any matters which might arise; she was as well assistant scorer, whose job was to note of each team's number of runs. She brought out the usual paper and clipboard, gripped hard at the pencil. Wore a whistle around her neck.

The village team was to play the first innings. This was the division of the game where each side was to take their turn at batting. In gameplay, he watched men huff and roll about as he stood beside a wicket, practically a bystander. So far, so good. Unscathed. Village had won the toss, and soon they had scored three. Balls were flying every which way, and at an interval after the first inning, they were brought back to the buffet table to a grating of knives and forks against plates, and an undignified amount of chewing. Mr. Edwards resumed spooning food into his bowl when Clarence approached with a cup of yellow tea, different from any of the options in the caddy. Mr. Edwards swiped the sweat off his brow as he drank, wincing at the taste. "I seem to be out of practice, Clarence."

"It's okay, sir. It's okay. Drink, to replenish you."

The sky grew overcast, and Clarence fetched blankets from the house to drape over the spectators.

The game resumed. Bron followed Mr. Edwards, who at the wicket continued to fan his reddened face. It was his turn to bat. Readying himself for a swing, Mr. Edwards lurched forward, dropping the bat suddenly and running four meters away to puke into the grass, out of the way of the players. Bron would have approached him if Darcy hadn't sprung from his chair and gone to him in seconds. Mr. Edwards waved Darcy away, but when the retching didn't stop and he turned ghostly pale, he allowed Darcy to stir him away from the pitch and plant him into a chair under the awning.

The spectators whispered through this commotion, and the game stalled for a few minutes. Mr. Edwards insisted they go on. Darcy walked to the center of the ground with a grace that, had Bron not heard of his aversion for the game, might have pronounced a naturalness to the setting. A perfect scene to be shot. Knowing of this reluctance hardened the soft glow of his vision.

Darcy stopped at the wicket, called out, "Too many prawns, I suspect," then gestured toward Mr. Edwards, who made a sign with his hands that was quite in agreement and had the crowd laughing. Darcy picked up the bat, taking his father's place.

It was nearing the end of the game, and the village team was up by twenty. It was all on Darcy to win the game for Greenwood. On his first swing, he hit one four, and then another four, and slowly the gap between the scores inched closer. Clearly he'd played before and was even rather good at it. Of course he was.

Now it was Bron's turn to bat. He rolled his shoulders, and his eyes met Darcy's, which froze him into place. Darcy nodded at him, a kind movement.

"You need to see the ball coming," Darcy had said to Ada. He imagined Darcy saying it to him as he focused intently at the bowler, poising his legs, his arms, ready to launch his swing. This blurred with a recollection of what Harry used to say to him on the rugby pitch. *"You don't want to be afraid of the ball. The ball is your friend. If you look scared, they'll know it, and you'll lose. You want to outmaneuver them, anticipate their throw. You can do it, Bron. Don't listen to them."*

He would listen to Harry, would listen to Darcy.

The ball was thrown. The first time he hit, the ball was lost. On the second throw, the bat made contact. Into the air it rose, and he ran backward, backward, backward, reaching his arms into the sky and jumping up in a way that any other person on the ground might have described as running like a girl. He saw the ball being passed back, back between the fielders. Despite what they thought of him, he could and would succeed. He wasn't an addition, an anomaly, or a small percentage of the population to be overlooked. He was no longer a schoolboy, forced onto the pitch at risk of detention. He was as real as the rest of them—those playing, those sitting down, those from his past. He was knocked by impact, but it was his feet that threw him into the air.

He had batted and scored the required number. Mr. Edwards roared from the sidelines, and Ada ran up to him and helped him back to his feet. The teams shook hands, and Darcy tipped up his head in approval. Behind them all, sitting among the spectators, he saw a boy who looked like Harry, smiling that smile he used to know so well, and hearing echoes of that cheeky laugh he doted on. Harry would have been proud.

He may have run like a girl, but he'd won them the game.

12

MR. EDWARDS HAD YET to overcome the bout of illness that had taken him from the cricket match, and kept to his bedroom as much as was possible, with Ada taking on the part of nurse wherever she could.

Bron and Ada made meals together in the kitchen: a mac and cheese, her favorite food, whenever she fancied it (revealing a secret once shared with him by one of the chefs at St. Mary's—that a dollop of English mustard could go a long way in giving the cheese sauce a much richer taste than the powdered granules and hot water alone would allow), and later, when Ada declared her father to be in need of soup, they sautéed onion, garlic, and celery on the stove, and softened the carrots and potatoes in a pot, before pouring in the water. Mixing it all together, they ladled the concoction into a bowl. Ada insisted Bron be the first to taste it. He took a sip and hid his grimace as he swallowed.

Ada tasted it next. "Mmm, delicious."

"Ada, we forgot to add the stock."

"Don't worry. He won't notice."

She carried it on a tray, and he trailed beside her up the stairs to steady her trembling hands. They knocked on the door and Clarence opened it from within. Mr. Edwards sat, jovial, in his pinstriped pajamas. He was watching the Discovery channel.

"Be careful—it's still hot," Ada said, and he blew it thrice before bringing it to his mouth.

Bron only hoped he could stomach it. Or that his illness had ridden him of his sense of taste.

"Mmm, it's wonderful, Ada—truly scrumptious. We'll make a chef of you yet!"

Ada cheered, and hurried quickly to fetch some water at his request.

"Clarence," he said, once Ada was out of the room. "Would you be a dear and bring me the salt? It is quite an emergency."

"Of course, sir."

"Don't go telling Ada now." Mr. Edwards winked at him.

Over the next few days he seemed to get better, and then worsen, only to appear better again. The family doctor, Mr. Braddon, paid his visit between the hours of three and four, every Tuesday and Thursday, but offered little in the way of illuminating Mr. Edwards's ailment. With each visit he would touch the wooden stick to Mr. Edwards's yellowing tongue, which made him gag, and measured his breathing with a cold touch of the stethoscope to his back, which made him flinch. Mr. Edwards assured the household that everything was fine and as it should be, but it had become clearer to all that it wasn't simply a batch of bad prawns that had cast him to his bed.

Bron felt a change in the air, like a mounting pressure. He wasn't sure what exactly had changed, if anything at all, only that the buildup inside him amounted to a nervous fretting that left him constantly on edge. He feared the thought that ate away inside him: knowing, beyond reason, how this would go. Mysterious illnesses—they led to sudden death.

Was Mr. Edwards going to die? On some days he thought he might. When Ada brought his tea to bed, they often found him asleep. When he wasn't, he could hear the shortness of his breath, could sense the way that Mr. Edwards's nodding and smiling at Ada's attempt to soothe him was a suffering through pain in silence, an attempt to mask discomfort. His lymph nodes inflamed. He would barely touch his dinner, and the weight loss was quick to take effect, and most evident in his face. He called Bron by the wrong name more than once.

Bron wanted to take Darcy aside and alert him to his worries. Could it be tuberculosis? The profuse night sweats, the high temperature, the weight loss and fatigue. All the symptoms were there! Had Darcy spoken to the doctor directly? What, exactly, did they say was wrong? But then, Mr. Edwards seemed suddenly himself, laughing and cracking jokes, inviting Ada to hop onto the bed. Madame Clarence would bring in his medicine and his yellow tea and order him to sip it. At his gentle protest, she'd launch into a spiel of French, to which Mr. Edwards responded back. Bron had never heard him speak the language, but it seemed he was quite fluent. Without Ada there to translate, the conversation was lost on him. Once the medicine had been taken, Clarence brought him a plate of beef lasagna, his favorite meal, but his appetite had never been fully restored.

There was one evening, when the moon lingered silver like a broach on a cloaked sky, when Ada and Mr. Edwards fell asleep together early, at eight o'clock. Bron took to walking along the paths outside, to take in the air that smelled heavily of burning wood. At the edge of the lane, he saw the chiaroscuro of Darcy's outline against the moonlight. He knew what he wanted to do before he did it: like a physical reaction, he wound his way to Darcy's side. Didn't think too hard about it, just brushed his hand against his. Darcy always brushed back.

They filled the silences with whatever it was they could: Darcy's enjoyment of the spring season, the way the rhododendrons were in bloom. They spoke of Ada's commitment to the caring role and how wonderfully she'd behaved through all this. Bron shared how Ada took to turning off all the sockets and electricals before bed. That she had become quite the busy bee. In fact, she hadn't sat with her schoolwork in days and had become more demanding of him in the evenings, often needing his presence in order to sleep. This was something they ought to discuss when Mr. Edwards was better.

The discussion of Ada's bedtime stories prompted him to ask, "Why does Mr. Edwards call you his prodigal son? Ada mentioned it once, and I couldn't help but think about it."

"You know the parable? You didn't strike me as the Bible-reading kind."

"Going to a religious boarding school for more than ten years makes you the Bible-reading kind even if you aren't the Bible-reading kind." Bron laughed.

When Darcy relayed a summary of the parable back to him, he didn't stop him. Instead, he listened to the lull of his voice, the natural way of his oration.

"Years ago, when I left my family, when I left England, I admit I may have dipped into my father's pocket more than once. I just bought a flight to wherever it would take me. Ordered the most extravagant champagnes and alcohols for myself and anyone who wanted them. Quite the bachelor's dream. But it couldn't go on for long, and my father, well, you wouldn't have guessed what he was like back then. Or what he thought of me. I was loathsome."

"Mr. Edwards?" he said. "I can't imagine him disliking anyone, let alone his own son."

"Well, imagine it. I was twenty and already on the path to ruining my life—I'd dropped out of university months before graduating, separated myself from those I cared about the most, and drunk myself into oblivion. When I finally had the courage to answer one of his many calls, he demanded to know where I was, and I threatened never to return. Theatrical, I know—I had to inherit at least some quality from him—but at that moment, I couldn't have said anything more truthful. I never wanted to come back. I detested my life here. My life and everyone in it. Everything that happened—it was all too much."

"What did happen, Darcy?" Bron asked, thinking of Giovanni and of the woman Darcy had been married to. He interlaced his fingers with Darcy's. "You can tell me. It's okay."

And to his slight astonishment, Darcy did tell him. Told him everything that had happened between him and Giovanni and how awfully it had ended. Bron's suspicions had been correct— they had been close. They'd enjoyed times together in France, developed an intimacy through their years at university. At one point, they'd even considered themselves boyfriends.

"Boyfriends?"

"Indeed, and all in secret, of course. As necessary."

"But why the secret? Your father—"

"—has not always been the man you know today, Bron. He didn't always understand. You see him now as this carefree man, and quite the caricature of it, with a penchant for drink, but he wasn't always like that. Well, I guess the drink always was there, but he was much more *traditional*," Darcy stressed in a way that imbued meaning. "Once upon a time he was quite fixated on what a family of our standing ought and ought not to be, what my future would look like, and—well, I didn't fit the bill."

Bron couldn't imagine the joyous, benevolent man who'd taken him in and welcomed him into their home as being anyone other than the person he was today. Completely accepting of who Bron was, a father proud of his children. But people, they were capable of change. He thought, then, of Mrs. Flanders, who years after admitting her mistake, still vied for her child.

"I'm sorry you had to go through that. But he is a different person now and only wants to do good by you. He loves you for who you are. You and Ada both—I'm sure of it." When Darcy added nothing to this, he hastened to say, "And if it makes you feel any better, I absolutely cannot imagine *anyone* fitting the bill of pompous straight-acting twat more than you."

Darcy pursed his lips and thrust forward, grabbing Bron under his arms. He tickled him lightly and ordered him, "Take it back—"

"No!" Bron squealed, but Darcy allowed him to wiggle free with relative ease. Their laughter permeated the breeze.

"So I wear my disguise well, then?"

"Very well." He giggled, still leaning away from him. "So well, indeed, that I can say with the utmost confidence that you pass for . . ."

Darcy narrowed his eyes.

". . . a genteel man of the highest arrogance."

"I do, do I?"

"Yes, one hundred percent."

Darcy took this assessment of his character gracefully, even declared he liked the sound of it all the more when coming from Bron's lips. "But suppose my arrogance were a ruse, a facade? An attempt to make one look elsewhere?"

Bron had his response at the ready, could be quick to retort that perhaps he shouldn't be so good at playing the part of such an arrogant and temperamental character. But Darcy's tone had resumed a lilt of seriousness, so he stayed quiet. "Going about hiding . . . it got a bit much, for everyone. Especially for Giovanni. He wanted more, hated the sneaking around. Demanded we tell everyone we were together, and slowly we became less cautious, relaxed in each other's company. We almost got caught a few times too. And then, partway through our third and final year at the university, he started telling people—random classmates to begin with, then my friend Magda. But I couldn't face it."

Bron soothed him, sympathetic. "So what did you do?"

"I told him to stop. That I wasn't ready. But he couldn't understand it. He said that I was ashamed of him and that if I didn't come out now, then I never would. Of course that wasn't true, I just needed time. But he said my time was up and continued to tell more of our cohort despite my begging him not to. So I broke it off. Quickly. Skipped classes to avoid seeing him, banned him from coming to the house. My work suffered, and friends called me up, asking if the rumors were true. I denied them. Claimed Giovanni had mistaken our friendship for something more and that he was bitter when I didn't share in his feelings. That really riled him up."

Bron hooked onto each word with great sympathy. He, of all people, understood what it was like to navigate people's opinions. What they had to say of him. He had never had a coming-out moment himself. Not really. They'd told *him* who he was, what he was, before he'd truly vocalized it himself, and then he'd simply slipped into that identity already hailed as his, and from there crafted it into his own. For Darcy, the world had come to know his secret before he'd accepted it himself. Before he understood it. The burden of it all.

Maybe they had more in common than Bron had once thought. He said what he believed Darcy needed him to say. Acknowledged his feelings. Said that what Giovanni did to him was wrong. "So Giovanni went behind your back and outed you? You know that was wrong, no matter how he felt."

"I just wanted things to stay as they were, hated everyone prying into my life. Turning into gossip. To do that, I needed him out of my life. But then I . . . I started seeing someone—to prove to myself that I could be different, straight, which just made everything worse. Gio told my father everything that happened. And Father, he saw me as the bad guy. The one messing with people's lives. Giovanni told him I'd broken his heart. And I guess I had."

Bron knew how it felt to be wronged by someone one had trusted with all their being. Darcy may have broken Giovanni's heart, but Giovanni had broken Darcy's trust beyond repair. What had been his motivation for outing Darcy? As an attempt to . . . what? Claim him? Hurt someone closeted for validation that what Giovanni felt was true? Not just a fantasy or a nothing cloaked in empty promises.

"You cannot take back what you did to one another; you can only move on. Giovanni crossed the line. Nobody should be forced into doing anything they aren't ready to do."

"What it did was force me into a marriage I didn't want. Father couldn't understand the situation at all. I insisted Gio was lying, but Father considered my sexuality something I could just turn on and off. And if I could be with a woman, then it was all the more important I do right by her, what was right for the family."

"Right by her?" Bron repeated, confused. "How is marrying a woman as a gay man doing right by anyone?"

Darcy shifted in discomfort, his demeanor making it clear to Bron that this was a question he wasn't ready to answer. He asserted: "I needed to prove to myself and those around me that I was straight, that I was not who he said I was. But then . . ." Darcy stopped, wouldn't look at him. "I just had to get away. I'd done so much wrong, and there was a whole world out there full of possibilities. I was stuck here, hating the person I'd become. So I left."

"And where did you go?"

Darcy described places Bron had only dreamed of, and it exhilarated him in a way nothing had before. He told him of the pilgrimages he'd taken in Morocco; the alcohol and drugs he'd done in Berlin; the provincial villages in the south of France, where he'd swum in lakes frequented only by locals; and finally, his excursion across North America. He spoke of the great California hills, and when doing so, re-created the slopes in the air with his hands: "They were gold, tinged red and brown," he said. "One color and three all at once." He spoke of the vastness of Virginia, the sprawling landscape of New York City.

"When I close my eyes, I imagine I'm still there. I can see the stretch of Los Angeles as I stand atop the Griffith, the city and stars just there at my fingertips. I can smell the air wafting off the New York's East River, or still feel as though I'm at the edge of a broken world when standing beneath the Brooklyn Bridge and looking over at Manhattan. Such places that made me feel finally alive. Free."

Bron talked comparatively little, just shut his own eyes and tried to imagine himself to be there with him. But he couldn't. Darcy and America—the two entities didn't fit. He belonged here in England, walking along the cobbled streets and medieval colleges of the city. Darcy in jodhpurs and a hat atop his head, in cricket whites leaning against the column of a pavilion, or chasing dogs along the Cornwall coasts in muddy boots.

"England can be such a suffocating place," Darcy continued, gesturing to the dark fields beyond. "The longer I stay here, the closer I am to accepting this life, this false promise. The most successful and ugliest lie told in all of history. Although given the view of the English green, you wouldn't think so, would you? Such things that appear one way aren't always so."

"Things appear as one intends them to appear," Bron countered. "There's always so much more below the surface, and a facade is never there by chance. It's crafted and calculated, as you know."

"We both wear our fair share of masks."

"But if our insides were to overshadow our disguises, the world would be a more honest place."

Darcy was enlivened by this; he reached out to him and spoke with a subdued earnestness. "Bron, the way you speak. It's like you've experience of the world."

"Don't I have experience of the world? I speak from a place of pain. I speak like somebody who has been hurt, just as you have."

"But you've still so much to the learn," Darcy said, his hand brushing the top of Bron's shoulders, the sensation lingering moments after he'd snatched it away. "So much to see. I'll take you to these places one day, if you'd like." Darcy searched his eyes for an answer, tilted his head in anticipation of his response.

"One day," he agreed, but he'd heard this once before and knew that such a day would never come.

For the rest of that week, he'd use any spare moment he found to return to this suddenly sprung Eden. There were some days when Darcy was already out there waiting for him, and other days where Bron would be out there first, unsure if Darcy

"Looking at you, I feel there is nothing more right in this world."

would appear. But he always did. At times there was nothing to say. They lingered in each other's presence and shared awkward glances; flicked, tapped lightly at each other's flesh to provoke some sound—Bron's gentle giggle, Darcy's loud guffaw. Darcy remained irritable, preoccupied with thoughts he wouldn't share, and taken over by a dark mood that only lightened when he stood that much closer to Bron's body. When their fingers entwined.

At one point, Bron readied himself to be kissed again, the light wind flustering his heart, feelings he'd buried deep within him blossoming like newly grown roses. But no kiss came.

Bron always managed to coax him out of his mood by repeating some of the terribly awful jokes that Ada had relayed to him that day: "What did the farmer say to the cow? It's pasture bedtime!" But often enough, the conversation flowed as pure and smoothly as a river's current, and the scented garden stained Bron's cheeks red with every exhalation, with every rise and fall of his chest.

"Do you remember that feeling of being tormented by your own desires?" Darcy asked. "The demands one sets oneself to suppress them and the agonizing questions that follow?" Bron appreciated how he'd become Darcy's ear. His confidante. He need no longer pry. Darcy shared his feelings willingly—when he was ready to. "I remember it all so clearly, and even now with such times past, when I am sitting alone, those thoughts—they creep in, demanding to take hold, and cast me back to a time and place I never wanted to be a part of. Sometimes I wonder if I'll ever be free of it. But looking at you, I feel there is nothing more right in this world. You, Bron, are so otherworldly, so authentic. Other people's opinions don't alter you. You just are."

This he could not listen to, felt deep inside his consciousness that he had been somehow overlooked. Pasted over with some other version of himself. He corrected him. "You have such a sentimental view of who I am, and you're wrong to think it. Other people's opinions—they do alter me. They alter me immensely. Who I am is conditioned by what other people think I should or should not be. Those torments you speak of? I know them. And those questions you asked yourself—I ask them still. I'm not brave, or anything of the sort. I'm as brave as the leopard that walks out into the world with its spots proudly on display—just doing what is necessary in order to survive, and incapable of enduring the pain that comes with being anybody else." It was a relief, saying this out loud. He felt himself about to cry and pulled away.

"I've upset you," Darcy said, stepping back. "I said the wrong thing. I didn't mean to suggest—"

"No, you haven't upset me. It's just a lot. People see me as some walking experiment of true authenticity. A political thing. But I am not a statement. I'm just here, living my life. Just as you are living yours. When people see me, they think they know me. But for so long I've heard those things they know. And how wrong they are."

"When you see me," said Darcy, "I know what you see. That I get to walk about this world with a buffer. Passing as straight, as male, the most powerful in the pecking order. But there is a flaw in your thinking too. Wait—" he said, for Bron was about to stop him, to oppose him. Let me finish. That while I am out to the world now, still I get to choose who I share aspects of myself with, and where and when I get to share it. But it is at the expense of walking with this extra baggage all the time, Bron. This unnatural second self I've always cause to wear. People make their assumptions about me, too. It's exhausting, having to correct them. Or stay quiet, and let them think they know me.

Bron gave this some thought and wondered in his own mind if a reassessment of certain privileges was in order. "The world, the dresser; and you, their mannequin?" he chimed.

Darcy gave a sad sort of smile. "Precisely."

Bron raised an eyebrow. "Sounds a lot like the times you've proposed to tell me how I should exist."

"I am a fool, Bron. A stupid fool. Like that great Emperor Nero, I thought it would've been easier to have made of you like Sporus, suppress you into my fixed idea of what I thought was right." These details were lost to him—he made a mental note to google these figures Nero and Sporus, but he could see the anguish simmering in Darcy's eyes underneath that filmy water that he was always so good at blinking away. "I suppose I am a little jealous."

"Jealous? What—of me?" Bron understood the framework they were working in, the wanting to be honest, the need to feel truth—only this felt absurd.

"You are the most perfect thing," Darcy said.

Bron would not let him believe such a mistake. "I am not perfect. Far from it. What is it that you think makes things so difficult for you? You are not without power. You can be anything, whoever you want to be."

"That's easy for you to say—" The words quivered as they left Darcy's lips.

"And what's *that* supposed to mean?" He pushed him for an explanation when, again, his words faltered. "Why is it easier for me? *You* enter the world everyday as you please, and yet its toxicity continues to have you keeling at the thought of what other people see." He continued on like this, batting Darcy's arguments away until they fell to pieces. "You say you are jealous? Well, I am jealous of you. Had I been as privileged as you, I might have developed the skin to take on such comparisons."

When he turned from him, Darcy grabbed his arm and pulled him so close that he felt his own body stammer, a bird fluttering in some shaking grip, powerless and easily crushed. He wouldn't just nurse away Darcy's discomfort. But to separate himself from him now was impossible. If he latched on, everything would be right in the world. It had to be. He would push the iron bar that weighed on Darcy's heart until it gave way. The closed off valves, which prevented him from seeing, truly, who he was, would fill his veins with blood in the place of lead.

He imagined what he could look like through Darcy's eyes: a pathetic, small thing alone in his bedroom, undressing and exposing himself to the mirror, in which he'd look upon the curving of his hips, the lankiness of his body with something of a yearning. The same mirror which he himself would look into, the same body he'd take in with much unkinder eyes. Was it the boyishness that Darcy adored of his figure or was it the truth of his spirit, his androgynous style? The feminization of his entire persona that had captivated Darcy on the dance floor. What version of him did Darcy desire?

"For years I have struggled to admit to myself the very things that seem to have formed you," Darcy confessed. "For months I have struggled with the feelings that arise within me whenever I step outside the very doors of this house, always looking up to the window in the hope of getting even a glimpse of you. You must know how I feel for you, Bron."

"I do know," he admitted, and was shocked to hear the ease with which he revealed this. "At least I think I do." In his heart he knew Darcy's pull toward him. But the tangles Bron spun in his head were as fine and delicate as gossamer, prone to come apart with every other thought. And yet, he hadn't always got it right—he'd also thought he knew how Harry had felt.

Bron reached out to him, delicately, knowingly, and he felt Darcy's body resist him, tensing. Bron stopped, thinking he had gone too far, and turned his head away.

But Darcy gripped him by the arm. "Wait." Touched him tentatively with the other, knuckles brushing at his cheeks. He took breaths that made his core shake. "My own little governess." He laughed. "Please, let me reassure you of your feelings by expressing to you my own."

Darcy pulled him in closer, and Bron felt the firmness of his muscle, his nose against Darcy's, and the downward sweep of Darcy's lids, close, as the lashes tickled his cheek. Darcy smelled strongly of leather and myrrh. His lips, when they touched Bron's, were soft, but soon they were wet with need. The evening light had turned to dusk, and under the shadows of the trees, Bron could make out little more than his outline.

When they pulled apart, Bron brought his head to Darcy's chest—so tall he stood suddenly!—where he could hear the beatings of his heart. They leaned against the stony balustrade and held each other for what seemed like both minutes and like hours. His insides unfurled into a pulsating rhythm that beat for him to move even closer to this man, who was both his fear and his desire, his shame and his pride. And in the light evening's gloom, he would accept that whatever was happening could not be real, occurring only in the seams and slips of space and time.

They kissed again, fiercely now, the heat Darcy invoked in him burning down his throat, an unquenchable thirst that singed a hole. It spread to his arms—his fingers flexing to grab Darcy closer—into his loins, clogging his veins, feeding the itch of longing he endured throughout the day, a discomfort that forced him into the fetal position at night but which, at that moment, made him curve around Darcy like a leaf bending toward the sun.

Darcy pulled away to take in a deep breath, and Bron thought he'd lost him forever. But Darcy guided his head again to his shoulder, and they settled into the quiet. The quiet which brought them closer together, a gap in time that allowed them to just be. While Darcy contemplated their surroundings, Bron considered the weight of his head, how long it would be until he'd have to pull away again.

"Do you see that chestnut tree far back over there, behind the fence and overhanging the stream? They say a servant stabbed herself there in the early nineteenth century. She'd made the journey on foot, all the way from Hertfordshire to that spot you see just there, returning to her lover, the master of this house. She learned quite quickly of his true feelings, that he didn't want her anymore. She begged in agony for him to love her, just as he had before she'd left him."

Darcy's voice dipped into a bass as he reproduced the imagined voice. "'The fervor of my flesh is strong,' he replied, 'but my will is stronger still. I will not surrender to such degradation.' And with this unbearable proclamation, she ripped off her muddied petticoat and stockings, drew out a knife, and plunging it into her own heart, bled until the grass turned red. Flowers no longer bloom there."

"What a horrid story. Did you make that up?"

"Maybe. I shall call it the Garden of Gethsemane."

"Well, before hearing that, I'd rather considered us to be living in an Eden."

"Then an Eden it shall be. A new Eden! Where we are free to be ourselves without the trickeries of a snake."

"And what's the snake a metaphor for here, exactly?" Bron asked, but Darcy didn't answer—he kissed Bron again, holding him so close Bron could feel him harden beside his waist.

Bron poured his consciousness into those parts of his body that Darcy touched: Darcy's lips on his lips, his hand on his back, and his leg between his own legs, like a third; his blood ran through him like a river's current, forking into lands that surpassed the boundaries of his body. But when Darcy looked at him—and he often did this, as though he was worried Bron would disappear at any moment—Bron could read the nervousness in his eyes, was guided to his chest again. He could feel the tightness in his stance, in his arms and chest, like a rope frayed to its last thread.

"Something's wrong," Bron said then. "What is it? You're not happy—"

"Quite the contrary, Bron. It's rather that I feel we should stop because I am worried of getting carried away, if you understand me." Darcy smiled, looking down and back up again. In that smile, Bron sensed something he hadn't sensed before, that there was a yet unexplored innocence to Darcy, a shameless adolescence, something on the brink of rebellion. "At least not here."

Darcy leaned in again to steal another kiss, when Bron saw a flickering from the periphery of his eye. He pushed Darcy away, pointed behind his shoulders. It was Clarence, watching them from the window, and she quickly shut the drapes.

"C-Christ," Darcy stammered. "What is she still doing here so late?"

"I don't think she saw us," he said reassuringly, for Darcy or for himself he did not know. How would it appear, to Clarence, and to Mr. Edwards even, his cozying up to his employer's son? Was he breaking some code of conduct? "It's dark. We're hidden."

"Yes, you're right, it is fine," Darcy said, eyes flicking back to the window. "But for now we should go our separate ways. Me and the governess . . . not a good look." He smiled.

Bron smiled back. "Okay. That's okay. I will go to my bedroom, and you will go to yours."

"Alright, I mean unless . . . unless you were to go to your bedroom, and I were to join you there?" Bron sensed shyness in his eyes. A boyishness that Darcy wore well. "I mean, only if you wanted me to."

Several thoughts raced through Bron's mind, but there was one that shone out like a beacon, dimming all the others. Darcy sniffed through the interval of waiting for an answer.

"I want you to."

Darcy laughed. "Are you sure?"

"Yes, I'm sure."

"Alright, then."

"Alright, then," Bron agreed. "But Darcy, may I ask you something?"

"Yes, you must—ask away. Always with your questions. But Clarence is quite the curtain twitcher. I'll go now, then join you soon, in thirty minutes, once Ada has gone to bed."

"Okay."

They said their goodbyes, Darcy going one way, through the back of the house, and Bron, taking a moment to digest what'd happened, going through the other. Inside, the entrance hall was quiet, though there was a noise—Clarence playing about with her keys, suggesting she was about to leave. She gave him a keen-eyed stare, confirming to him what she'd seen. He looked back at her intently, and she shuffled away without a word.

When he reached his bedroom, he didn't flick on the lights, but climbed straight onto the bed in the dark and counted down the thirty minutes in his mind. He gave up after five and brushed his teeth and washed his armpits instead. He returned to his bed, and here he waited for Darcy to come to him. He'd hear the footsteps outside the door and listen keenly for the knock. Darcy would climb into the room, and he would emerge from the bed fully dressed, as if to say, here I am, all wrapped up and ready for you to open, like a present. But a panic arose in his chest, and he rose to pull the curtains from their tiebacks, shrouding the room in yet further darkness. What if his body wasn't good enough? What if it failed to meet the contours of Darcy's desires? When the knock came, he lunged for the door, hesitated before opening. The doorknob shook in his hands, and he yanked at it when it stuck.

"Hello," Darcy whispered, leaning against the frame and rubbing at his neck. He cast a glance down the hall, to ensure nobody had seen him. His sleeves had been rolled up to his elbows, revealing deep blue veins and muscles straining at the arm. He gave an awkward grin and shuffled his feet, making him appear, to Bron, that much softer, cordial, and all the more pleasing. He was the only thing Bron wanted right now.

"Hi." They were both whispering now.

"M-may I come in?"

Bron stepped out of the way. "Yes, of course." Closed the door. It was strange, seeing Darcy existing in the middle of his room, among all his things.

"So," he said quickly.

"So . . ." Darcy mimicked, shoving his hands into his pockets. "Here I am, as promised."

"So I see."

"And a nice place you've got here," Darcy joked, surveying the room in mock admiration. "It's very . . . neat."

"Well, thank you." Bron cleared his throat. "I like to keep a tidy room."

"And this here is your bed? The very bed in which you sleep?" Bron shrugged.

"And what else do you get up to in this bed of yours?"

He was teasing him, and Bron wasn't sure if he should tease back. "I don't know . . ." He tried to be flirty. Coquettish. "Lots of stuff."

Darcy reached out to Bron's chest and rubbed him there in circular motions. He didn't utter a word.

"Do you like it when I do that?" he asked.

"Uh-huh."

"And this?" he said. And Darcy's lips were on his cheeks, his eyelids, and then his lips, moving toward his neck and lulling him into a state of intoxication. "And this?"

Bron sighed. "I like that very much."

Soon Darcy's hands were on his ribs, then crawling down to his waist to pick at the tight band of his skinny jeans. Bron lifted his arms, and Darcy swiped his top over his head, tossing it away. Bron instinctively covered his chest with his arms, but Darcy quickly removed his own shirt, and they pressed their bare torsos together.

"Mmm, that's nice."

"You're very hot," Bron said. "Temperature-wise, I mean."

Darcy lifted an eyebrow. "Just temperature-wise?"

"N-no. Not just temperature-wise."

Enveloped in the middle of the room, Bron rocked on the balls of his feet in a bid to stand tall and still. He thought he might topple over. Clung unsteadily onto Darcy's shoulders.

"Should we move to the bed? To make things slightly easier?"

A pause.

"Okay."

He went to the bed and hustled to one side of it, where the sheet was cold on his back. He took a sip of water from the glass on the table, and Darcy watched as he drank it. Sitting on the edge of the mattress, Darcy turned on the bedside lamp before lifting his legs and twisting sideways to face him.

Bron thought there to be something miraculous about that moment, the two of them lying on their sides and facing each other, suppressing the awkwardness and hesitancy to reach out for each other through cautious, silent laughter. Their closeness, two bodies scooped up in the dark, made him think back to his schooldays, but Darcy soon leaned out to hold the hard ball of his hipbone, and closed the gap between them. They began to kiss again. Bron slipped his fingers in between Darcy's, and suddenly he wanted to bring them to his lips, slide them all the way into his mouth.

He rubbed at Darcy's trousers, pushed his body against his. When Darcy climbed on top, Bron guided his hands gently down his muscles, strayed to the square patch of soft hair at the small of his back before descending into his underwear and squeezing him. Darcy whimpered, and Bron's own breath came out in spurts. He couldn't stop the thoughts encircling his brain: *Why has it taken so long for us to do this when it feels so good and so right?*

He loved the musky smell of Darcy's sweat, the worn-off scent of his cologne. The way he pressed his weight into him as though he couldn't bear for them to be two separate bodies any longer.

"You okay, Bron?"

He nodded, no longer feeling the need to use words, super-fluous words that said nothing other than surface-level niceties. Words—they were best left in fiction. This here was reality. He communicated with his body, willed it to say a number of things, that yes, he was okay, more than okay, but also *"Take me, I'm yours, devour me, shatter me."*

"Bron, I haven't . . . I haven't done this in a while."

"Me neither."

Darcy touched him through his trousers. "I want to, though."

"You do?"

"Yes, I do, very much. I get this strange feeling, whenever you are near, that at any moment you could disappear, ghostlike, into somewhere unreachable. Sometimes I think I've completely imagined you, lurking about as you do." He continued to rub him, tease him at the band of his underwear. "But if you were to disappear now I . . . I don't know how I'd—"

"I'm here," Bron said, grabbing Darcy's hand and placing it on his chest. Kissing him all over. "And here and here and here. And you say you want me?"

"I do," Darcy repeated.

"How much?" Bron said, steering him through limits they had yet to cross. "Show me."

Darcy parodied a stern voice. "Unbutton your trousers."

Bron did as he was told, and Darcy knelt at his head to kiss his collarbones, then down to his nipples, and eventually to his stomach. He streamed back up to Bron's lips after spitting into his palm, and slid his hand into Bron's underwear, holding the length of him.

"Is that nice?" Darcy asked.

A nod, a constancy of them.

"I want you to say that it's nice."

"Yes, that's nice," Bron whispered. "It's really nice."

"I think I should like to see you now, all of you."

"Okay," Bron said, sitting up. He shimmied his trousers down his hips, his legs, until they got stuck. Soon he was yanking at them and conscious of Darcy's laughing.

"Could you . . . I mean . . . maybe stop laughing and help me?" Bron was laughing too, so loudly he worried his voice might carry.

Darcy pulled them until he was freed. "That's better." He brought his hands to Bron's mouth to suppress his laughter, almost suffocating him.

"And now you?"

"If you insist." Darcy unbuckled his belt, undid his zipper. Bron sat up to kiss his stomach and helped him lower his trousers. He nestled his head in Darcy's lap, ready to take him.

But Darcy pushed him onto the bed and climbed on top of him. From there, he nuzzled his head into his neck and lingered there a while. Before they knew it, they were completely naked, Darcy gripping onto his hips and Bron holding onto his back, grinding into each other. He dropped his hands lower. Squeezed.

Bron's tongue in Darcy's mouth, their faces wet, the groans in his throat, then out of Darcy's, an animalistic moan. A cry met with another, one of equals, of need.

"God, I want you, Bron."

Bron. Bron. Bron. When Darcy called his name, he claimed him. And Bron responded: *Take me, take me, I'm all yours.*

"Oh, the things I am going to do to you—"

Tap, tap, tap.

Three little knocks on the door, which, in that moment, sounded like a bang. Darcy pulled hurriedly away from him, hitting into the side of the bedpost.

"Bron, Bron, are you awake?" Ada's little squeak from behind the door.

"Don't you dare answer her," Darcy whispered, stumbling onto the floor to search for his shirt, fumbling to drag up his trousers. In a frenzy, he searched for a place to hide. Bron looked from him to the door, and back again.

Three more little knocks.

"It's Papa—and Darcy. They won't answer their doors to me. Have they gone somewhere?"

He, too, was on his feet now, and yanking on his dressing gown that hung on the back of the ensuite door. "N-no, I don't think so, Ada."

"Oh, you *are* awake. May I come in?"

He widened his eyes, knowing well what Darcy would see in them: *Fuck, fuck, what do we do?*

He didn't have time to answer before the doorknob slowly turned. Darcy lunged to the floor on the opposite side of the bed, successfully hiding himself from view.

When Ada stepped in, she clung to the door and poked her face into the room, as if to scrutinize the scene. He made as though he were just emerging from the bathroom, tying the loop of his belt.

"What, what is it, Ada?"

"I had a bad dream."

"Is that all? Don't worry, you know that's just what they are—dreams, not real."

"I know, I know, but it was really scary."

"A nightmare, then. Come on." He motioned toward the door, as if to escort her out.. "Let's get you back to bed now."

"I can go alone," she said. "I might just check on Papa again."

"Your papa's not too well right now, Ada. He needs all the sleep he can get. Maybe Darcy will come and check on you, how does that sound?"

She pondered that for a moment. Through the silence, he could've sworn he heard a cough emanating from under the bed, and felt his ears burn red. He was shaking under the folds of his toweled gown.

"Well, alright. Good luck trying to get him to bother with *me*."

"You're not a bother, Ada. You know that. I'll rouse him from his slumber if I must. I promise he'll be with you soon."

"Alright then, goodnight."

"Goodnight."

When he shut the door, Darcy rose from the floor, started brushing at his person. "Well, that was a close one."

Bron went immediately to his side and encircled him. "You could have hidden in there, you know." He gestured to the bathroom door, mimicked the turning of a key. "And closed the door?"

"Alright, smart arse. Now I'll know for next time."

"Next time. Oh really?"

"Yes, now, where were we?" Darcy grabbed him by the face and kissed him, but Bron pulled away.

"Didn't you hear any of that? You need to go to Ada; she's waiting for you."

"Christ in heaven, why?" Darcy whined.

He poked him in the chest. "Stop. Moaning. It's the right thing to do."

"Fine," he agreed, as Bron helped him to do up the buttons of his shirt. "You're right. I'll go."

"And I'll be right here waiting for you when you get back . . . to undo these again."

"I'm sure you will, my—" he stopped, smirked, kissed him on the cheek, and rushed out of the door in a movement that said, *"I'll be back quickly."*

Bron sat with his legs crossed in the middle of his bed and noted the time on the clock. Nine PM. He smiled at himself, having never felt such happiness. He stood again to tug at the bedspread that Clarence always tucked too tightly, so that when Darcy came back, the bed would be easily accessible. They would climb under the covers, and he'd allow himself to be undressed again. Their figures would touch, and he would feel Darcy's warmth on his skin, on his body, which yearned, yearned to be filled. He flicked on the bedside light in anticipation, then turned it off again, preferring to wait in the darkness.

But soon nine turned to ten, ten to eleven. *What's happened? Why hasn't he come back?* He curled himself up into a ball, paced his bedroom up and down, only to curl back up again and wait. *Did I say something wrong? Do something wrong? Have I fucked it up again?* Like a ghost haunting the corner of a room, his thoughts, digesting the intimacy he'd just encountered, dissolved into memories of another. Of Harry, whom he missed so much. It didn't matter where he was, or how much Darcy set his heart aflutter, Harry was always on his mind. Memories of Harry danced across his eyelids. And as he waited for Darcy to return, he remembered the moment that had changed his relationship with Harry forever.

They had gone upstairs to Star of the Sea. Neither of them had been very much interested in talking about anything, not even the movie, *Maurice*, which they'd just seen. It was something about the way it made them feel that kept them silent. He remembered the stir of inspiration, how his mind was full of romance: stolen glances and transgressions. And Harry—well, there was something off-ish about Harry, about the way he stared into the shadow of black space like a lifeless entity, or the way his chest rose and fell like a vessel.

He'd had been careful to read the signs, was sure that what he was feeling at that moment was tension. A buildup of tension.

Years of it. The way Harry would occasionally brush his hand against Bron's and then smile; the complete casualness with which Harry would remove his clothes in front of him, where all the other boys would keep a strict eye on him. The way he said things like *"You know, you're the best thing in the whole wide world, don't you, Bron?"* and *"You know I couldn't cope without you, right?"* At his most vulnerable, Harry would curl up into a ball and cry into his open lap. He would say, *"I hate it here, I just hate it here,"* and Bron would gently shush him and run his fingers through his hair, telling him it was *"Okay, you'll be okay,"* as he curled his hair around his fingers and lightly brushed at his nose.

Sitting beside his best friend, he knew something was bound to happen. One of them just had to do it. He'd always imagined himself as the female protagonist, had waited patiently for things to unfold, but at no point did Harry's wrist twitch or flex in a yearning for him, or his hand hover over Bron's in a way that suggested the moment had finally come. But they'd just seen for themselves the way two boys could kiss on screen, and if one of them would just lean in and do it, then that would confirm everything. He'd practiced kissing the crook of his elbow many times, or his own reflection in the dirty mirror. But for him to do it would be like stepping across a threshold and into a house that should be entered with caution. One that goaded him with signs to "Keep Out." But still, it tempted him, called him in.

So he'd leaned into his friend and kissed him. A peck at first, but when Harry looked back at him, startled, he leaned in again, and more determined this time. He could still taste the mint of Harry's toothpaste. Feel the rolling of his tongue like a wave and the little whiskers of hair at Harry's upper lip tickle his own. The pecks and movements improving the longer that they did it. No one in the world had kissed him like that before or held him like that. He touched his hand to his lips.

"Bron," Harry had said, gently pulling away. He was holding Bron's hands in his and he was looking into his eyes. It was the most perfect moment Bron had ever lived through.

"Yes?" This was it, the moment he had been waiting for. Harry was about to say that he loved him.

"I think we should stop."

Stop. The tenderness that had swept through his body left him. The hairs that had risen still stood, but guarding themselves from the onslaught of shame as it rippled across him. His buckling as he pulled farther away.

"What's wrong? Did I do something wrong?"

"No, no you haven't, it's just . . ." His memory was a blur, the words that Harry uttered that day ranging through a multitude of narratives that changed with every recollection, though he could still envision Harry's hand wiping across his wet mouth, a cleansing of the kisses he had given him.

"I think we should just forget about this, alright? I think that's probably best."

"Forget it? Why forget it? I don't want to forget. What's happened?"

"Nothing. Nothing's happened."

"Did you . . . did you not like it? I thought you would. I hoped you would."

"I don't—I don't know. I don't think so. I'm not gay, Bron. I'm not . . . like that. I'm not like you."

"Oh." The rejection. It lived on in his body. A memory. More than a sting, more than an ache. I'm not like you.

I'm not like you.

I'm not like you.

In the darkness of the room now, he felt as though he had two hearts, one that still longed for Harry and one that burst with an immediate need for Darcy. He imagined them as two separate organs, one blue, one purple. His blue heart ached with a coldness that frosted over, and all it took was a warming thought to thaw the icicles away. But no, no. Frozen it was to remain. He'd make sure of that. And the purple heart . . . well, that was a muscle that hardened over time, darkened through its lack of use, swelling and knotting like the veins of a bruise. But slowly, the purple heart was turning to red, pumping blood, and working. Letting something like oxygen in.

He saw the shadow eclipse the slit at the base of the door before he heard the shuffling outside. His heart leaped, and he snatched his teasing hands away from his body. *He has come back. He wants to unravel me, know me from the inside out.* The intense breathing, almost like a stifled cry, carried from outside. The notion of Darcy's body behind the wooden frame burned like a furnace, and he willed him to open it.

Darcy didn't knock this time. He pulled open the door with a silent scrape. The point of no return. Stepping into the room, he was a great mass of shadow seeping across the expanse. The curtains, though, were soon flung open, and the moonlight casting through the window lit him up like a phantom. Bron wondered whether he should feign sleep, remain motionless and pretend to wake when Darcy came to touch his body, or should he slowly stir, sit right up and say, *"I'm here, right where you left me, ready for the taking?"* He'd almost made his decision when Darcy gripped him by the shoulders, shook him, and said his name, first at a whisper, then more loudly.

He simulated drowsiness, worked up a smile that would make him look surprised, doe-eyed, but also desirable as he fluttered his eyes open. Darcy's face contorted, and there was a strain to his voice that he hadn't heard before. He leaned in to kiss him, touched the wetness of his cheeks.

"Bron," he managed.

"What's wrong?" Bron's vision blurred briefly; Darcy's cheek and neck burning hot. "What is it? What's happened?"

"It's my father, Bron. He's . . . he's dead."

PART III

13

DAYS ELAPSED, DURING WHICH there was little to account for. The household was still, having falling into a gentle hush that made every uttered word reverberate, as an exchange would in the middle of a sermon. The air was heavy, stale. Bron burnt incense in his room to ease the ongoing headaches; only sometimes that made them worse, and in his sleep he dreamed of smoke and red glows under locked doors.

Madame Clarence busied herself with the constant cooking of meals and continued to arrange the dinner table with utmost precision, tinkering the cutlery left and right as if her employment depended on it. When visitors arrived at the door with food parcels and flowers, she welcomed them and their excessive displays of grief with open arms. Suddenly everyone had known Mr. Edwards, loved him like a sibling, and the house took more visitors than even the most populated parties had. An aunt and uncle from Cumbria, and another pair who'd made the trek back from their country abode in Aberdeenshire, were here to check on Ada and Darcy and stressed their availability should they need anything through this troubling time. Family must stick together, after all; otherwise, what else have we got? Bron watched them take in the fineries of the house, walking through as if it had already come into their ownership, commenting on the rooms

that Mr. Edwards had let go to disrepair. Their light murmur-
ings suggested they would, in fact, one day own the place, men-
tions of "the incident" and "being underage" reaching his ears.
"Who else would he trust if not his own brother?" And neighbors, friends—men with bulbous noses—were all here to lament
"how Dickie used to laugh" and "what a bonkers man he was,
our Richard."

And how had Mr. Edwards died? Well, that Bron still didn't
know. Nobody had told him much, and he didn't dare ask. The
body had been quickly taken that same night, and a death certif-
icate issued. Darcy broke the news to Ada and Madame Clarence
first thing that morning. Since then, Ada had taken to crying in
her bedroom, and Darcy was nowhere to be seen. While everybody had known of Mr. Edwards's sudden illness, there had
been no communicating, at any point, that it was anything very
serious.

In his favorite memory of Mr. Edwards, from shortly after the
fire, Bron recalled him marching into the breakfast room with a
grin on his face—he was always mischievous with his smiles—
and with his hands about his neck, failing to tie the specific knot
he desired, requesting Ada's assistance.

"I want it the way Darcy does it—you know the one, not that
silly cravat he sometimes wears, but the one with the—the—oh,
what's it bloody called?"

"The Trinity Knot," Ada had said.

"That's the one, yes, right."

"Let me just finish buttering my toast, Papa."

"Yes, fine, butter away! Stick one in the toaster for me too,
would you now, son?" he'd asked of Bron as he rose to toast a
slice for himself. He picked up another. "There's a good lad. Yes,
there's a good idea—make that two."

"Certainly, sir."

"Sir, sir, certainly, sir! When will you learn to call me
Dickie?" Bron couldn't bring himself to admit that this name
made him uncomfortable.

"Where's Darcy? I dare say he's never around anymore."

"He caught the eight o'clock train into London for a matinee performance of *The Phantom of the Opera*," Ada said, who'd moved on to work on his necktie.

"*The Phantom of the Opera*? Without us? Where's the fun in that?"

"He didn't go alone, Daddy. He went with that Magdalena woman."

"Oh fie, how I dislike that girl. Nothing against her, mind you—she just isn't right for my Darcy. Always teasing him, she is. You know, Bron," he'd continued, "I brought you here for his sake as well as Ada's—perhaps even more so! Reckon you can help the boy see sense?"

"I can only try, sir." He'd handed him a plate with two slices of toast on it, heated just so. Barely toasted, just as Mr. Edwards liked it. His smile said more than his "Good, thank you" did, but his eyes were narrowed, stern but kind for having called him sir.

A week had passed. Day to day, Madame Clarence ensured the drapes were opened at dawn and closed at dusk: to allow light into the manor was very important, she explained, for the darkness of mourning was tangible throughout the halls and filled the gaps between the furniture in the rooms. Only light could drive it out, light and time. To close the drapes every night was to put the past to rest and hide away the cruelness of the world. But this way of talking only brought out the worst in Ada, who didn't understand why she needed to keep eating and why she needed to get dressed every morning. A sob continued to leak from the rim of her bedroom door whenever Bron walked past, and she threw shouting fits and tantrums whenever Clarence stirred her from her stupor. He checked on her discreetly through the day too, and in the evenings would often find her calm and snoring. This only guided her into staying up long into the night, her back pressed against pillows set up to support her little body, her face curtained by drooping hair and pointed at the television screen with eyes unseeing. The way she sank into the duvet, the white plumes gathering around her nightdress, made her look dangerously like a sick angel. Occasionally, with a slight nod, she'd allow him to sit with her until she fell asleep.

No one knew where Darcy was through all this, or what he was doing. Already gone before anyone had awoken. Always returning deep into the night. Ada felt his absence like a double loss. She needed him now more than ever, and when she cried for her father, she cried also for her brother. Only Bron could stifle her tears by bringing tea to her bedroom in her favorite mug, shaped like a bunny. When Darcy was eventually seen, he plunged past without uttering a word, shutting himself away and refusing to talk.

Walking from the kitchen and past the drawing room, Bron hovered at the mahogany desk, tentative not to disturb anything scattered there, as though Mr. Edwards might walk into the room at any moment and sit on the grand chair to tend to his papers. But it was a different sort of mess here—not Mr. Edwards's chaotic but still organized pile, but an upturned, rifled-through scatter.

In his bedroom, he scribbled a few lines, crossed them out, and began writing onto yet another page. But nothing seemed right.

I miss you.

Please talk to me.

I'm here if you need me. But it was all too despairing and self-involved. What comfort could he bring? It was he who needed Darcy, not the other way around.

I'm here. And Ada needs you.

He slipped the note beneath Darcy's bedroom door.

Bron peered into the library, its shelves devoid of books, and the room of its furnishings, still. Its vacancy sent a chill down his spine in the cold hour of that afternoon, as both a space of interest, now that it had been restored and repainted, and a room from which he was repelled. He found, to his horror, a little figure atop the ladder near the empty shelves. His overheated imagination worked to bring a scream to his throat at the sight of the ghoul, the library finally revealing its haunt. Only it was Ada who stood atop the ladder and who fell at his scream, but recovered herself by latching onto a rung, knocking her knees.

"You scared me!" she yelped, the only ghost here the memory of overflowing shelves and, later, the purpling bruise that surfaced on her knee.

One night, when he came to offer her favorite nighttime tea with marshmallow root and fennel, he overheard Ada praying by her bedside, whispering faintly between gasps of breath to bring him back to her. *Him.* He wasn't sure what Ada wished her God to do—to bring back her father from the dead, like Lazarus, or her brother Darcy back from his desertion? Darcy's absence and then avoidance of them was felt so profoundly. His return seemed as impossible and unlikely as the other's.

But the next morning it seemed as if such a thing as God existed. Ada was sitting in her bedroom's window seat, a book cast to the side as she stared out the barred frame and into the graying clouds. Bron had been keeping her company, spread out as he was on her bed and texting with Mrs. Flanders, who'd expressed her condolences and wished to attend the funeral and offer her support to him as best she could, should she be welcome.

With a cry that shook the phone out of his hands, Ada, who'd seen something outside, jumped up and was gone from the room in seconds. He knew not whether to follow her, but observed from the window a coated figure approaching the front of the house, hand clutching the brim of his hat to conceal his face, and hurrying to the door in the heavy rainfall. His heart jumped in his chest as he, too, raced down the stairs, eager to get a glimpse of Darcy before he could shut himself away. How he longed to hold his hand, touch his face, feel his lips on his own again, but from the top of the landing he was met with the loud patter of rain on the cobbled stones outside, and Ada's little frame appearing littler as she ran toward the door. When she opened it, it was not Darcy's face that emerged from the man's shrugging off of his hat, nor was it the body Bron longed to be held by.

"He's not here," Ada said. "He comes and he goes, and he locks himself away. That's all. He won't talk to anybody, especially to you, Uncle Gio."

Bron met Giovanni's eye across the way. He held it for a second before Giovanni frowned down at Ada, his face softening as he crouched to meet her height.

"And why do you say that, sweet one?"

"I'm not an idiot, you know. You both hate each other."

Giovanni hesitated, reached out to tuck a loose strand of hair behind her ear. "We do not hate each other, Ada."

"Yes you do. You were all fighting last time. I saw you!"

"Don't worry, little one. It'll all be okay. Come here." Ada allowed him to envelop her, buried her face in his shoulder. He rubbed her lightly on the back. "When you see him, can you please tell him I came by? It's very urgent." He pulled away and rose to his feet. Looking at both of them, he said, "I'm so sorry for your loss," and nodded his head before turning back into the rain.

Ada slumped against the door behind him. "I wonder what he wants with Darcy."

Bron had shared a similar thought and wondered what it would look like if he ran into the rain and asked Giovanni what he wanted with Darcy. Why he had come to him at this time. There was something Ada said that puzzled him further too. When had Ada seen them in an argument?

Bron's phone buzzed in his hand. He read the notification bubble that came up on his screen.

Mrs. Flanders:

Y dn't u come 4 tea? Bring the little 1, poor thing.

He looked at Ada again, at the way she carried her shoulders, how she dragged herself to the staircase's bottommost step and sat there, waiting. But for what? Despite the open curtains, darkness still surrounded them. And the house, with all its things, felt empty, steeped in the deepest loss, holding them in its grip. He needed to be the adult here, look after his charge as best he could. That's what he was here to do. That's what Mr. Edwards would have wanted.

He sat on the step beside her and gently nudged her shoulders. "Hey, what do you think about getting out of here for a bit? Going somewhere nice?"

"No thanks." She was twisting a thread on her dress, come loose.

"Are you sure? The fresh air will do you good."

"I know what you're trying to do."

"You do? Go on, tell me."

"You're trying to get me out to take my mind off everything. Because you think that'll help or something."

"My God, you genius," he said. "That's exactly what I'm trying to do. What d'ya say? You, me, some fudge from one of those tourist shops in town . . . a little food. I have a friend who's just *dying* to meet you."

He quickly shut his mouth, hearing the words he'd just spoken. *Shit.* Ada didn't notice.

"*You* have a friend?"

"Don't act so surprised. Of course I do."

"Huh. I didn't know that. Well, okay. But if I get bored or sad, I want to come home."

"Deal."

"And I want gelato, not fudge."

"Double deal."

"Alright."

Mrs. Flanders spoiled them. Her small sitting-room coffee table was a labyrinth of trays filled with biscuits, bowls of crisps, and anything else she could find in her cupboards.

"How lovely to see you—how lovely!" she said, embracing them in a hug. "And you must be little Ada?" Mrs. Flanders immediately took to her, complimenting her pretty dress, her beautiful thick hair. Ada seemed elated by this and did a little curtsy at the door before accepting the lollipop and sherbet Mrs. Flanders offered her.

"This is your friend?" Ada whispered as they sat on the cracked leather sofa while Mrs. Flanders moved to the kitchen to bring through more tea. "Bron, I didn't realize she'd be *old*. Like, older than Clarence old."

"Be nice," he whispered, poking her.

The snacks were quickly eaten, though Ada proclaimed they weren't at all necessary, that they had only come into town for the sake of gelato. The conversation progressed from the inevitable talk of miserable weather to a short offering of condolences. Ada quickly bypassed the latter, chose instead to talk about all the things Bron had taught her, from the books to the math, to the fact that she could now draw.

"I've still got a lot of practicing to do, but I'm much better than I used to be, wouldn't you say so?" She looked up to Bron, who nodded. "I'm so glad you taught me. You're just my best friend in the whole world. I don't know what I'd do without you."

Bron's heart sank a little at her heartfelt speech. Mrs. Flanders interrupted to sing the same tune as she had done upon his last visit, saying, much like before, how he reminded her of her own child. She brought out the same photographs again, said how proud she was of her son's going to Oxford, that she missed him dearly, hadn't heard from him in years. "I wonder what he is up to these days. If he is safe."

"He?" Ada turned to Bron with a quizzical look. "I thought Ellie was a girl now. Isn't that what you said, Bron? In the taxi here?"

"Yes," he said. "I did say that."

She looked back at Mrs. Flanders. "But you just called her a 'he.' She's not a 'he,' right?"

"Yes." Mrs. Flanders nodded. "But Ellie will always be my son."

"Oh, okay. But maybe that's why she left?"

His palms quivered as he sipped his tea, embarrassment clinging to him as the leaves did to his mug. What was he to say? He knew exactly what she meant, would in any other circumstance have been proud of her—*was* proud of her—but the pressure to be polite, and the look on Mrs. Flanders's face as it dropped, pulled at him.

"I don't know why he left, little one."

"See, you just called her 'he' again." Ada looked up at him for reassurance, and then back at Mrs. Flanders.

"It's not as simple as that," said Mrs. Flanders.

"Yes it is—"

"That's enough now, Ada," he said, thinking it best to end the conversation here. She looked up at him again. "We are guests— let's not be so impolite. Say you're sorry to Mrs. Flanders."

"Why should I?" she spat, standing up.

"Hey, come on, Ada."

"No!" she shouted, stamping her foot and screaming at once that she wanted to go home.

Bron was dismayed by the ferocity in her voice, by the way she ran from the room, and after following her, he found her crying in a corner of the hallway, arms crossed against her face and leaning against the door. When she turned around and wrapped herself around his waist, he saw the grief in her eyes, felt it in the way she clutched at him. This little person, who'd endured so much, had lost her only parent.

"I'm so sorry about that," he said softly to Mrs. Flanders once they'd gathered their things. "We've had a difficult few days. I'm sure you understand."

"No," Mrs. Flanders said, "the little girl is right." Unsteadily, she crouched to her knees. Ada tucked herself away and hung on his leg. "I am always looking at what was, ignoring what is right there in front of me." She pulled a five-pound note from her purse and folded it into Ada's coat pocket. "For your gelato."

They were standing at the junction of Bene't Street and Trumpington, on the corner of the Corpus Christi clock. Ada, having settled her crying in the taxi ride, was eating her cookie-dough gelato, and Bron was admiring the clock of twenty-four-carat gold and the locust's metal sculpture that arched upon it. The chamber glowed pink in the twilight.

He'd passed the clock many times before, but had never really stopped to look at it, to admire the way it functioned. It didn't appear to tell the time at all, not accurately at least, or in any way he could make sense of. The pendulum would stick in place for a second and then start up again at speed, trying to catch up, and the blue LED lights would dance around in a circle of its own ring. The locust climbed, open-mouthed, every thirty seconds.

"It's eating time," he heard a tour guide explain to a group who huddled to take photos of it. "The time-eater is a symbol that reminds us that once time has passed, it is eaten, it is gone, and something we can never have again. The clock's inaccuracy is a symbol of life's irregularity, that time plays tricks on us."

This, inevitably, led Bron to thinking about time and what a construct it was. It didn't matter if the pendulum stopped or if it ticked along accurately. No matter how time was measured, still he would be standing there, for however long he would. Whether it be a second, a minute, or even an hour in length, it was the moment itself that counted.

Time is eaten, it is gone. He thought he disagreed with this statement. As he watched the locust open its mouth to eat the thirty seconds, close its mouth upon the minute only to open itself again, he thought instead how time is consumed, how it doesn't just pass or disappear. That the past lives on inside us, forms the way we speak, think, and feel. That Mrs. Flanders loved her daughter, loved her son, and continued to battle and learn from her mistakes. That our past never leaves us. We are always evolving into better people, into our truest forms.

He looked at Ada, his youngest ally, who would grow up to change the world, make it an easier and safer place for people like him. And then, at himself: he was not just a person standing on a street corner; he was a person with twenty-two years of moments—and more than that too. He was the lives of countless others he had brought with him. He was a nineteenth-century governess and a twenty-first-century au pair. He was gender queer, gender fluid, nonbinary to some, a cross-dresser, a kink, to others. A period drama set in 1800 but watched today was both a vision of the past and the present: he couldn't help but bring his own twenty-first-century life to these nostalgic views of the world, and equally he was unable to emerge from the film untouched, bringing this nostalgic lens of life into the outside world today.

And then, almost as if he were in a time-induced stupor, he saw *him*. Or at least, he thought he did.

The sky behind the rim of the building blocks was a deep inky blue. His eyes panned along the cobbled street and fixed onto a man's hunched back, fussing with the bike attached to the railing, slipping a helmet onto his head.

He didn't really think about it before he called out—

"Harry!" He was completely certain it was him, and then at once not so certain. "Harry?" The man did not turn.

The street was white noise in his ears, but still he heard the unchaining of the bike's lock, the man's laugh as he reached for another man's outstretched hand, and pulled him into a kiss. "See ya," he said in an American voice, like the one Bron heard in his dreams.

These two men who fit together so well, who looked almost *too* natural together. *It is him, it is him, it is him,* and then again *It is not, it is not, it is not. It cannot be.*

He's free of you. He never needed you. Stop it. Stop. You're making it up.

His heart was beating in his temples, and his legs were about to buckle beneath him. He felt his face heat up, and very quickly he shed his coat. He could see Ada talking, her mouth forming the shape of words, but he couldn't make sense of their meaning. The pain at his side and the clenching of his stomach made him think suddenly that he would faint. His eyes stung chlorine sharp, and he held onto the wall to steady himself. *Why can't I let it go?* he thought. *Why can't I let him go?*

One man crossed the trafficked road, the other mounted his bike. Cycled away. He could hardly believe himself anymore—his heart that was telling him that the man across from him was Harry, his eyes that were telling him it was not.

He looked at the pavement with its cobbles, and the many feet that trudged past. His mind spun, playing tricks on him, made him think he could see only what he wanted to see. Over there, at the corner of the clock, where time was meaningless.

14

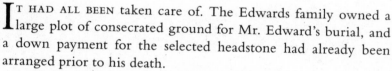

I T HAD ALL BEEN taken care of. The Edwards family owned a large plot of consecrated ground for Mr. Edward's burial, and a down payment for the selected headstone had already been arranged prior to his death.

The sky was a clear and azure blue, the late spring sun beating down and the smell of green hanging in the air. The party curved along the winding path toward the quaint, gothic mortuary chapel, the headstones and monuments encircling them as they walked. Bron advanced slowly behind, looking at his feet. The shoes had never been worn and pinched. His suit was one of Darcy's many hand-me-downs that hung in his closet, the one Mr. Edwards had professed to be his favorite. Despite his own wants and discomforts, he thought it appropriate to wear for the occasion.

Ada went ahead of him in a neat black dress, arm in arm with Clarence, who was fussing with her purse like a bouquet and whose sunglasses masked her face almost completely. They followed behind the pallbearers, one step at a time. Darcy carried the casket alongside the others—Mr. Edwards's brothers who'd come down from Cumbria and Aberdeen, and some other friends of the family. Bron focused on the strain of Darcy's neck muscles, his head dipped to the ground. He wished he could carry some of the burden.

Inside, the chapel was cramped and echoed with their footsteps, but the air felt still, the space vacuous. The pillars stood so close together he feared the aisle too narrow for the coffin to pass through, but onward toward the dais, alit with hundreds of candles, they laid it to rest. They searched for a seat at the front beside the dark-wooded confession boxes, with its heavy red drapes and intricately detailed fretwork. Ada latched onto Bron's hand before he could move to one of the back rows, and brought him to sit on the pew between her and Darcy. Slowly the chapel filled with faces he recognized and faces he didn't, who dropped flowers at the altar and murmured words to the Edwards children. Ada suppressed her little weeps, and Darcy thanked them for their presence.

Mrs. Flanders, true to her promise, made her way toward him with the aid of her stick, and brushed a light hand under his chin. A stranger to Darcy, she patted him too, and finally the little girl, before moving to take a seat at the back. Bron bowed his head in silence, longing for the service to be over before it had even began. The club-shaped windows cast blues and reds upon them all, and through the priest's sermon, Bron was transfixed by the imposing crucifix, the pained Christ, and the four letters above him: *INRI*. He'd never learned their meaning, and suddenly he needed to know.

The crowd was asked to rise. This, so far, had been the only time Darcy looked up from the floor, and slowly he also stood. When they again sat down, Bron felt Darcy grip his thigh, a piercing sting that made his leg go numb. Carefully, he reached out to hold his hand, but Darcy snatched it away and instead reached into his blazer pocket to take a swig from the flask he'd hidden there, using Bron's body to conceal the action. Someone rose to the pulpit and offered their Biblical reading. When it was Darcy's turn to participate in the Liturgy of the Word, he stood mightily, the strain gone from his face. He delivered a short reading, introducing it as from the letter of St. Paul to the Romans:

"It is not easy to die, even for a good man—though of course for someone really worthy, a man might be prepared to die—but what proves that God loves us is that Christ died for us while we were still sinners."

Afterward, the celebrant explored the ways in which Mr. Edwards lived his life as a good, dedicated Christian man, and opened up the floor to allow for the mourners to share their own memories of the departed. These were mostly stories they'd already heard from visitors to the house that week, their practice run. A couple were refreshing anecdotes that brought further tears to his and Ada's eyes; even Darcy peaked his head, just a little, to listen.

The gifts were taken to the altar through a hymn played in a low key: Ada offered the water, Bron declined the invitation to carry the wine. And after the transubstantiation, the taking of communion and the closing prayer, there developed a muted chatter below the sound of the organ. Darcy returned to his position as pallbearer, this time leading ahead.

The sun was blinding as they emerged to the fresh and pollinated air. The walk to the grave wasn't far, the flowers growing wilder and the ground less flat as they passed the churchyard and moved farther into the cemetery. He saw the mound, a pile of heaped dirt masked by a green blanket like a little hill, before he saw the hole in the ground. They stopped in little clusters at the opening. He struggled to look, feeling the emptiness of his stomach, as they lowered the coffin down with rope. He averted his gaze, instead stared emptily at the inscription on the back of an old white gravestone, reading but not reading it as people shuffled him toward the coffin. Blessed with holy water, the first handful of earth was thrown. Then the next and the next. On his turn, he scooped the soil, less like grains of sand and more like a lump of dirt, feeling its moistness. Thud. A splatter of paint on canvas, a spreading that bid a final goodbye.

When he looked up from the coffin, Darcy nodded his head in a trance, chewing on his lip. Behind him and the mass of

The walk to the grave wasn't far, the flowers growing wilder and the ground less flat as they passed the churchyard.

people, Bron saw two figures, hand in hand, rushing up the cobbled lane. He stepped forward, forgetting to say amen, and went
quickly to Darcy's side. Ada, following his line of vision, and
hearing the click-clack of the woman's heels, turned around too.

"Listen to me," Bron said, forgetting himself, where they
were, and the people around him. He touched Darcy's shirt.

"Hmm?"

When he pulled his hand away, it left a smear of mud on his
chest. "Behind you, coming up the lane." Darcy remained puzzled, still, a statue with ferocity in the brows. He didn't turn at
the warning, and Bron explained further. "Giovanni."

He stepped aside, the service continued.

Giovanni and his sister—Toni, he remembered—stopped at
the edge of the party, to face them. Neat and primed, Giovanni
gave a little nod, acknowledging them both. Bron dipped his
head in return. Giovanni offered his arm to his sister, whose
gloved hand slipped through the crook of his elbow. She stood
taller, cinched in a tailored black dress, with heels glinting in the
sun and her hair cascading down her back like a horse's tail. If
he didn't know any better, Bron would've mistaken them for the
most beautiful couple in the world, and she a Hollywood star.
Toni was looking at him too.

The crowd started to disperse, departing down the lane and
back toward the church and the row of taxis that could be seen
on the periphery, behind the gates and trees. Darcy twisted in the
other direction, toward the late arrivals.

Bron followed alongside him, spotted the fists that balled at
his waist, and quickly whispered at him to calm down. Darcy
stopped about a meter away, facing Giovanni and Toni.

"The nerve you have, showing your faces here."

Giovanni immediately raised his hands. "Come on, Theo.
We're only here to pay our respects."

"And what respect is this toward me? Toward my family?"

"Dickie would have wanted us to be present."

"I deign to think it. And here you both are, late as ever."

"Boys, vi prego, non fare scenate." Toni stepped forward and lowered Giovanni's hands. "Come on? Not today. Let's forget, today."

"How can I forget?" Darcy demanded. "When this man stole *years* from me and my father. And you, Toni? Don't you have some movie to be preparing for? Some terribly important audition somewhere? Why do you both insist on being around today? Is today not for me to mourn?"

"He would've wanted us to be civil," said Giovanni.

"Do not tell me what my father would or wouldn't have wanted."

"I think we are more considerate of your father's wishes than you are, Darcy."

"Gio," Toni warned. "Piantala."

"Che cosa? Let's not pretend we don't know who is and who isn't the bad guy here." Giovanni's eyes flicked over quickly to Bron and then back to Darcy.

"Oh yes, poor Giovanni, always the victim, never the problem," said Darcy. "Might I suggest you keep your opinions to yourself and stop leeching off me and my family?"

"Leeching? You accuse *me* of that? And your family, are they? When you'd so happily abandon them for traveling and drink—"

"Watch it, Gio," Darcy snapped.

"Where were you for your family when Dickie begged you to take responsibility for your actions? Where were you when Ada was growing up? Nowhere. You left them for all those years—"

"It is because of *you* that I left!"

"You do not give a *shit* about me," Giovanni retorted.

"Boys, stop this, please!"

"I'm warning you, Gio."

"Warning me, are you? Aha, e alora? Like when you dumped me like a piece of shit and fucked up my entire family? Look at yourself. Not even your own father could trust you with his life. He'd rather come to us than his own son—"

Darcy was the first to throw a punch. It all happened so quickly. Bron heard the crunch, saw the blood splatter from Giovanni's nose and speck their shirts. The screams, from Ada, from Toni.

"Teo, Gio, smettetela!"

And, he realized, from himself. "What are you doing! Stop!"

Ada wailed, and Bron dragged her away; Toni, too, launched into pulling her away from the men in hustle, though she kept looking back.

"Stop it, both of you! What's wrong with you? Mostrate un po' di dignità, ah?"

Farther away, the priest was pointing and hoisting up his Bible. A man unknown to Bron ran toward them both to break up the fight. Giovanni's nose was noticeably bent. Darcy had a slash up the side of his face. The crowd, meters away now, were looking on. Bron rushed to them, asked for any tissues they could spare.

It was Mrs. Flanders who supplied them to him, delicately brushing his chin again. "Be careful."

"I will," he said, thanking her. "I'll see you soon."

He handed them to Darcy, who snatched them and quickly walked away, one hand on his hip and the other dabbing at his face. Giovanni, delicately accepting the remaining one on offer, thanked him.

Toni came to hold the tissue to her brother's nose and helped him sit up, tipping his head forward. Bron looked on, wanting to follow Darcy, but he thought it necessary to give him his space and stay by Ada's side. Ada, who was staring intensely at Giovanni and Toni, with a stricken face.

Clarence soon came rushing up the lane and shouted, "What's all this? What is this?" taking hold of Ada by the wrist and shielding her away from them all. "Shame on you—all of you." She looked at Bron as if he'd been the one to cause the fight.

Toni looked up and said something to Clarence in Italian. Clarence responded in the same tongue, and Toni's eyes darted from Clarence to the retreating Darcy, who was quite a way off now.

"Go, go—I'm fine," Giovanni said to her.

Toni waved for Bron to move closer to her side, told him to substitute her hands for his. He crouched down reluctantly, holding the tissue in her place. Giovanni's head felt heavy in his hands.

"Don't let him get up until the bleeding stops," she said, and left them there as she rushed up the lane.

"I'm taking Ada home," said Clarence.

"No, no, I want to stay!" said Ada.

Bron and Giovanni both said it would be best for her to go home.

"I'll be back as soon as I can," Bron reassured her through her protest, and hugged her with one arm. His addition of an "I promise" brought some ease, and he let go of Giovanni's head to fully accept her hug before Clarence could drag her away. They hurried away quickly, and all the while Ada flicked her head to look back at him and the retreating figures of Toni and Darcy farther ahead.

"What a mess this all is," Giovanni said, and Bron detected a hint of laughter in his speech. Giovanni moved to spit in the grass beside him. "Will you help me up?"

Bron took hold of his head again, resisted as he pushed it forward. "I think it's best you don't."

"Let me rest beside that tree." He moved to stand. Bron had no choice but to help him, one arm slung across his shoulders, bearing the weight of his body.

"You shouldn't have come, you know," he said, easing him down the trunk of the tree. Though he'd been kind to him in the past, he felt somehow wronged by Giovanni, on Darcy's behalf. Yes, he felt sorry for him, knew what it meant to feel rejected and have your heart broken, but Giovanni shouldn't have outed Darcy to his entire family. Giovanni was the one who had brought Darcy pain, turned his life inside out, and then affixed himself so close to his father's side, like a substitute son. How else could Darcy feel? Bron was also wary of Giovanni's lie, in which he'd claimed to have not attended the party all those months ago. While Bron had questioned Ada's sincerity at first, there was nothing to suggest she'd fabricated Giovanni's presence. Bron trusted her through and through. Who knew what else Giovanni was hiding. "What did you expect?"

Giovanni pulled his hand away, but Bron persisted at holding the wad to his nose. Giovanni looked at him sideways. "Do not judge me, Bron. You don't know a thing about anything."

"For what reason then, did you come, if not to provoke him?" The pause was inevitable, the glance furtive but direct. "You know what you did was wrong, no matter how much he hurt you."

Giovanni swiped Bron's hand away and gave him an incredulous look. "Don't tell me you are in love with him."

Bron let go of him to stand. "I'm not."

"You are. I know it."

Giovanni lifted his head, his hair mottled with spit and blood. The priest appeared then with a cloth and an ice pack, which he handed over to him. Giovanni moved closer again and clenched his jaw. "I am telling you, Bron. You don't want to get mixed up with all that. He'll eat you up like a ravenous boar, all the while believing he's entitled to it."

"I know you were together. I know you were in love with him too." Bron wanted to go a step further. *I know you still are.*

"Ah, I see," Giovanni said, mockingly. "So he's told you everything?"

"Yes," he said. "He has."

"And you know that he is already married?"

There it was, an attempt to unbalance him. A piece of information meant to worm its way into his mind, start the questions, the guessing, and cause mischief. He let the statement go, though the length of it jabbed at his nerves. He had the upper hand now. Darcy had trusted him with that, and he felt the absence of Darcy's touch, the presence of Giovanni there like an envious lover.

Had Darcy touched Giovanni the way he'd touched him? He almost couldn't bear it.

"Yes, I know he was married. What were you hoping to gain by telling me?"

"I see. You know that he is married to my sister?"

Bron went rigid, his momentary hold of power leaching away as the words washed from his mouth. Suddenly he looked up, in the direction in which Darcy and Toni had taken off, searched the margins of the cemetery through the glaring sun to find two little specks in the distance. He saw a knife-sharp flash of Darcy hurrying away from him on the dance floor, toward a woman who stood at the top of the stairs, waiting. Somewhere in the tree above, a bird twittered.

"Your sister?"

"I knew he wouldn't have told you everything."

Bron couldn't fully hide his surprise but hoped he could deflect from the tinge of sadness by coming to Darcy's defense. So he hadn't told him the entire truth. So what? There must be an explanation for it. "He did tell me, actually. That they were married years ago. And so what? They are divorced."

"Is that what he tells you? And I suppose that he has also told you that that girl they present as their ward is not a ward at all? Ada is Darcy and Toni's daughter, my niece."

His words were like poison. This couldn't be the truth. *What?* "You're lying."

"No lies. Dickie knew; that is why he kept me around. Toni around. For Ada's sake."

Bron recalled Darcy's words: *"It was all the more important I marry and do right by her, what was right for the family."*

Ada's face swam into his vision. Ada, who looked unlike either Mr. Edwards or even Darcy, with her honey-toned skin and dark eyes. She looked just like the Vespas. Like her mother.

"You're only here to cause trouble," Bron said. "And I would prefer it if you didn't say anything else to me. I'll leave it to Darcy to be honest."

"Darcy, honest?" Giovanni retorted. "You couldn't find any-one more dishonest. He was never a truthful friend nor a loyal son. You are better off searching like a vagabond if honesty is what you seek."

Bron closed his ears to these words and felt suddenly the need to be alone. A jab at his side, a spear to the ribs. His heart went out to Ada, whom he loved like a sister, who had the most to lose. She was the pawn and wasn't being considered at all in this game. What would happen to her now Mr. Edwards was gone? Ada was being lied to, and that was all that mattered.

He needed to get home to her at once.

15

THE FAMILY HAD BECOME suddenly unknown to him. Every-thing was darker, the corners of the manor shadowed in ink. From outside, its walls seemed much grayer, and the surrounding trees decrepit; the vines, the wisteria creeping along the walls were knotted and devoid of green and flower; the windows, with their large once shining panes, took on an oppressive glare, a lan-guage in itself that said: *"This house, it harbors secrets."*

He couldn't fathom why they would have lied to Ada about her parentage. What was there to be gained? And why had Darcy withheld the truth from him? When he got back to the house, he climbed the stairs, every creak a threat, and went straight to Ada's bedroom, where she was flicking through the pages of her illustrated Bible.

"Are you alright?" He knocked quickly on the door before entering.

Ada nodded her head and snuggled up to him when he sat beside her, the still oncoming tears marking a patch on his shirt.

"I'm tired. Bron, tell me the truth. Has Daddy really gone to heaven?"

"Yes, Ada, of course he has." He didn't much believe in heaven. Hadn't for years. "Where else would he be?"

"I don't know. Will I go to heaven too?"

"Yes, but not for a long, long time."

He should tell her what he knew, about her mother, about Darcy. But it was complicated; how would he explain all this to a child? Should he? She was fragile, and he didn't want to hurt her any more than she was already hurting. But what else could they be hiding? From her *and* from him? What else went on behind these walls when their eyes were closed?

"Bron, I need to tell you something. It's . . . it's about Birdie."

He looked at her, unsure. "Alright."

"I was the one who opened her cage."

He hadn't expected that. "You did?"

"Yes. And the truth is, I never really did find her. I said I'd let her go, that I set her free. But that wasn't true at all."

"Then why did you say that you did?"

She took a big sigh and looked into her lap as she spoke, mumbling through most of it. "Everyone was too busy for me. Darcy, Papa, and you too. And I just thought, if Birdie was flying about, then someone would have to help me find her. But then you and Darcy were both helping me, and it was so much fun. But to tell you the truth, I wanted to see those pictures again. Of my mother. In the photo album. And there they were, in Darcy's room. And I just thought, while you two were looking for Birdie downstairs, I could take another look at them. But I guess Birdie must have really flown out because I couldn't find her afterward, and I didn't know what to do. When I really thought about it, I was happy because, well, she's a bird, she's meant to be free. But then you all went back to doing your own things. And then Birdie was gone and now Papa, and I just . . . I don't know what I'm going to do without them."

"Hey, it's alright. You've got me."

"Bron, was that lady at Daddy's funeral . . . the one with Uncle Gio . . . my mother?"

He couldn't bring himself to conceal things from her. Not now. But he shouldn't be the one to reveal the truth to her. "I don't know, little one. Maybe."

"But she's the same woman I saw in the pictures. I'm sure of it. And that night, when they were all fighting in the games room."

"I think it's best you wait for Darcy to explain everything to you when he's back."

"He won't," she said, finally.

It didn't take them long to fall asleep. He awoke beside his little companion in the middle of the night, with sweat on his brow and his throat dry and scratchy. He sipped at the water glass by Ada's bed, the shape of his dreams dissipating from the black of his mind like water churning down a plug hole, but his brain was stained, dregs clinging to a basin sink.

They were strange, his dreams, and stranger still that they remained with him as he woke. This led him into thinking about the convenience of it all, that nobody had questioned the household's lately occurring tragedies. The scenes were there, each neatly wrapped up as little snippets of a whole story, and the questions asked themselves: Was it merely coincidental that two incidents, a death and a fire, had affected the same family within a single year? These suspicions spiraled, and his mind took him to places that warped the people he'd come to know and love. Was it really faulty electrics or negligence that had caused the fire in the library, or was it something far less accidental? There was no madwoman in the attic to set the place aflame here, but there was a set of characters that could be substituted in her place: Giovanni and Toni, two lovers wronged; Darcy, the misunderstood son; Ada and the lies she'd been told. And how Mr. Edwards had died so unexpectedly, but of what? He'd never been told. How many lives had his employer touched—surely someone was to gain from his death?

Then there was Darcy's unexplained anger toward the photo album and what Ada had seen there: her mother, Toni, he now knew. The explanation came suddenly to his head, as though it were obvious: Darcy had found, or thought he had found, Ada flicking through the album, and knew that if she'd seen the photographs of her mother, then she might start to ask questions. This was what had made him so angry.

But what about Ada's locket, Bron thought, found on the ground beneath the library's broken window after the fire, which turned out not to be Ada's locket at all? Darcy had thought it was Ada's and Ada had said it was Darcy's, that "brother" and "sister" had one and the same likeness. He looked at her now, at her resting figure: she continued to wear it around her neck. There was something in this, he was sure.

Bron's task now was to thread together these singular events, fill in the gaps to reach a conclusion. Nothing happened in isolation—there was a point to everything. The more he dwelled on it, the more he convinced himself it was up to him to untangle these events, for him to get to the bottom of. As he drifted in and out of sleep, the characters in his life merged with violent and heinous visions, shadows of moments and characters that already took residence in his mind. It was far easier to discern something from what he knew rather than what he didn't, and this seeking of answers wreaked havoc upon the household.

In the first of his fantasies it was the taciturn housekeeper. Her apparition, black gowned, white aproned, keys jingling in her hand as she glided through the dark hallway, incognito. Drawing back the gallery curtains to let in the morning light, Clarence progressed to the kitchen, where she ate breakfast at the island after hours or sat with tea in the breakfast room, neglectful of her work. She took slow bites of her toast and sipped apricot juice between swallows, her eyes poring over the newspaper. What words did she read? Black dots swirling around the page, a mess of spilled ink, a colony of ants. Her eyes were filled, not with the black and white of the print, but the map of the house as she plotted her scheme—the long corridor, the library to the right, Mr. Edwards's bedroom far along to the left. She had accounted for their whereabouts, Bron's own too, and would wait on after her duties were complete into the late hours of the night, where she would lock herself into a discrete room in the farthest corner of the house, a room to which only she held the key.

How long did she wait for them all to take themselves to bed? Then, when the house was still, did she tread with muffled feet down the stretched hallway, guided by candlelight, and into the vacant library, where she set fire to the very drapes she'd drawn open that same morning. She *had* been there after hours, at the scene of the crime—just as Bron and Ada needed her the most. And then—he thought! A couple of weeks later, it was she who had picked the locket off the ground outside the library's window and handed it to Darcy, claiming it was Ada's. Darcy mustn't have thought anything of it himself, having given it quickly over to him. Was the locket really the central clue in all this? If so, what did it mean? Or was it in fact some kind of decoy? Did Clarence know what he knew, that Ada had in fact been inside the library that night before the fire? Had she seen her on her way in, and therefore performed stumbling upon the misplaced locket in the hope of removing herself as a suspect in the night's dealings?

And months later, she would enact another of her schemes. Was it drops of poison she let fall into Mr. Edwards's yellow tea, her special brew, bringing his life to a slow but calculated end? Very possibly—that was often what was used. But what of the motive? What would drive Clarence to such actions? Perhaps she and Mr. Edwards had once been lovers, engaging in an affair that Mr. Edwards ended prior or maybe even after the death of his beloved wife, and failing to commit himself to her thereafter, she sought revenge to heal her broken heart. All those years of loyalty, of pining . . . If she couldn't be with him, nobody could.

Was this plausible? Bron had noticed the way Clarence lingered close to Mr. Edwards, how she'd clean the already sparkling vase that stood beside him and blush whenever he requested something from her. There was one time, in the middle of the afternoon, when he'd seen Mr. Edwards slip an envelope into her hands before quickly exiting the house. This he'd seen her open—a wad of notes, bright as anything, which she thrust into her pocket before rushing away. What was he paying her off for? What secret?

No, it couldn't be. Why would it all have happened now? Would a lover be able to endure so many years of unrequited love? *Or* had they continued their affair in secret? Had it been going on under their very noses? Clarence, the avatar, the unlikely suspect, seeking her revenge at the most opportune moment, who'd looked at the photograph of Victoria Edwards in the photo album that night and in a fit of rage set the room alight with the very candle Ada had left burning behind the armchair.

The housekeeper did it. The housekeeper did it? Was it that simple? But what if she hadn't done it?

In his mind's eye, Clarence grew slimmer and shorter, wore a face more youthful and olive toned, one framed by pigtails that slithered down each side of her face. Now it was Ada who propped into his mind, a smart little girl who was far more capable of things than anyone gave her credit for.

If it wasn't Clarence, then what about Ada? Ada, who'd kneeled at the rugs behind the wing-backed armchair and tossed aside her playthings, the schoolbooks she'd left in the library that night. Slowly, carefully, setting the room aflame—but why? What else would she have seen in those photographs to make her want to burn the place? What secret could she not share with him, her confidante?

He pressed the thought further. Ada had confessed to him that she believed she had set the library on fire, although it had been a mistake. But why let him in on that knowledge? Had it already been there for the taking, she thinking Darcy had indeed seen her? And therefore was it a distraction—a successful deflection to make him think her admission a childish whim? Who knew what went on behind those glossy eyes of hers? Did she begrudge Mr. Edwards and Darcy for their actions, for hiding the truth of who her mother was, and in some impulsive fervor, had she smashed the pillow over Mr. Edwards's face, suffocating him under the guise of a caregiver? The same hands that set Birdie free and into the mouth of a hungry dog.

Was she capable of that—Ada who snuggled up to Terence the teddy and who cried herself to sleep? In his half-awake state, he saw her face cast in moonlight, the tears dried as white specks on her cheeks. No, she was not capable of that.

This was what he feared most, his mind taking him to the darkest places, fabricating fantasies he couldn't unsee. He was a fool for even thinking it. This little girl, she was just like him. Lonely and in need of a friend. He pinched himself, having slandered his image of her. But like a serpent eating its own tail, his thoughts were fed and fueled, developing into thoughts that kept him tossing and turning.

He slipped out of Ada's bedroom and into his own, trying to get back to sleep. But he was guided through the night and the early hours of the morning by the single pressing thought: none of it could've been an accident.

So what of the most obvious culprits? Darcy, Giovanni, and Toni? The unbreakable trio, with so many secrets between them.

He imagined them now, on their escape to France. The furnishings of their minds where each was concerned with the desire to take hold of another's hand on their walks. Darcy's eyes would linger on the brownness of Giovanni's skin at the lake, which darkened in the sun whilst he sought protection away from it, hiding in the shade of the closest tree. Darcy would have tried to look away in Toni's presence, and Giovanni would have given him the pleasure of pretending not to notice, both desperately wanting to feel the wetness of one another's skin after swinging from the rope that hung off the tree over the river. Over time, they would take more risks—swim naked in the waters, rub cream into each other's backs. At college, they would kiss in the shade of their dorm room, hide away in the walls of the university. And finally, one day they'd speak of their days beyond, what would happen once their undergraduate years came to an end.

"You will go back to Italy," Darcy said. *"What else is there to do?"*

"No, no, I want to stay. Can't I stay here, with you? Tell me you'd consider it?"

"Hmm . . ."

"Darcy, please? I cannot be without you."

"Bene," he said. *"Come una famiglia."*

"Sempre."

But slowly, over the next year, what would change? What alteration did Darcy witness in his lover? In the finery of his clothes through their second year at university and into their third, in the quality of the food he'd order, in his lack of complaints about the bourgeoisie and the kind of people Cambridge attracted. Maybe Darcy offered to always pay for dinner. But maybe Giovanni wanted more, to really be as well-to-do as his companion.

Bron allowed this to play out, pushed Giovanni into telling one person, now two, about his secret relationship. Darcy being outed. And then, when would have Darcy brought an end to all that? And when would he have first laid eyes on Giovanni's sister? Of course he would've known of her. Certainly Mr. Edwards would've enquired as to who was the beautiful girl who stood beside Giovanni in every family photograph, who had the same beauty as him: the dark locks, tan skin, the brown eyes that held you captive the moment you caught them. She had also started at the university, Giovanni would explain, a year after them, with big dreams of one day being a movie star. When Darcy and Mr. Edwards finally witnessed the siblings together in the flesh, they would have experienced the same intelligence and wild laugh through two different bodies, nearer in nearness than ever he'd thought brother and sister could be. It was something about the way they looked at each other, an unspoken language understood with the bat of an eyelid, the slightest of gestures, which made the other move in fluid response. There was no doubt Giovanni would have told his sister, his confidante, about his lover. Unless he hadn't . . .

For one day, one evening in autumn, she turned up to her brother's dorm room, and he refused to admit her entry. His voice was strained—he was a wreck, but he wouldn't explain why.

"What is wrong, Gio tell me?" she said.

"Just go, go!"

She combed through countless thoughts that might explain her brother's wave of sudden grief, but she couldn't think of anything. Unsure what to do, how to help, she'd gone to the Edwardses—alone, in the hope of gaining answers. She apologized for her brother's absence. Work had caught up with him, she said, and she hoped they wouldn't mind her attending alone; she needed an escape from the workload herself. Mr. Edwards, delighted, took her under his wing, and complimented the grace with which she held herself, the way she fit the glass of wine to her lips. She was glad to feel a semblance of normalcy. She also rather fancied the son, and finally they'd have some time alone.

But of course Darcy's mind was elsewhere. He had just broken his boyfriend's heart, and in doing so, his own. Why was Giovanni's sister here? Had she been sent there on her brother's behalf? Did she have something she wanted to say to him? He'd bite his fingers with worry, but as the night wore on, he'd catch onto her light attempts at flirtation. He'd play along because it was easier to do so than not. And he needed to prove that he could.

Then, later that night, after her departure:

"Son," Mr. Edwards said to Darcy once the moon had risen, pouring himself a cognac by the fireside, "she is perfetto. Just like Giovanni. What do you think?"

"Think?"

"Of her."

"I think she is pleasant and nice and definitely beautiful."

But what then? Had Darcy latched onto this idea of dating a woman, trying to suppress his attraction to men and prove the contrary to whomever Giovanni had outed him to? Why

Giovanni's sister, of all people? Was this all the more of a draw, finding a similarity to his ex-lover in her? Would they have dated behind people's backs? Swapped one secret for another. How far had he taken things? For how long? Surely Giovanni would have admitted everything to his sister eventually, and she in turn would have shared her dating life with him?

Eventually, the deed was done, and afterward, Toni, unaware of everything that had gone on, would grip to him, thinking that if she were to let go, they would be severed from each other forever. And what would Darcy have felt? Trapped and as though he were losing control of his life. Throwing on his clothes he would have rushed out the door, and left her to think she'd made a mistake. What else was she supposed to think of a man who deserted her so quickly after? Who used her and refused to see her for weeks, who wouldn't answer her calls? She needed to speak to someone . . . herself a foolish mess now. She couldn't lay more problems onto her brother, who still hadn't recovered from whatever it was she wouldn't tell him. Finally, Darcy would pick up the phone—she needed to tell him something. Something important.

"Are you sure?" he asked her.

"Yes, I've just done a test. It's positive."

"Don't tell anyone."

"I had to tell, I had to. You were not picking up. I told some friends."

"You have to get an abortion."

"Abortion? You are absurd!"

"Does Giovanni know?"

"I am going to tell him tonight."

"No, you mustn't."

"I must!"

But Bron was losing focus. Who was the villain here? Everybody, nobody . . . What of the motive for arson? For murder? Love, hate, greed? None of his stories made any sense.

But he continued to play along. What happened then? Did Giovanni, in a rage after learning of the pregnancy, finally out Darcy to his sister, and then reveal all to his father? Would Mr. Edwards have gone on to pressure them into a marriage neither of them wanted? It was likely: the Vespas, religious and Italian—with a baby outside of wedlock?—and the Edwardses, an upper-class family with a reputation to maintain. Could Darcy see that too, see that he needed to take responsibility for what he'd done, only to abandon them thereafter and resent his father for forcing his hand? Or had he done it of his own accord?

The wedding would have been quick. Quiet. A small guest list. They'd go away for a week and then return to England as proper newlyweds, the facade of two people with all the potential in the world, but really it had already been decided for them: their connection was bound in law as well as the eyes of God. But they didn't have to live as man and wife. On the same night of their return, would Giovanni have visited Darcy? Alone? Would a fight have broken out, or something more like heated passion? What had made Darcy finally leave his family? Was a broken heart too much to bear?

Okay, Bron was onto something, but what? Bron knew what a broken heart felt like. He knew *very* well what that felt like. How it could drive someone to do things, see things they didn't think possible. How deep the wound could cut.

The thought of seeing Harry in Cambridge only weeks ago had left him feeling suspended through air. He was used to envisioning things that only existed in his mind, but now he was seeing them right there in front of him. This thing rolling within him was bursting to come out, and he struggled to contain it, was impelled to displace it.

All at once he relived the most frightening memory: the day that Harry left. The day his parents had taken him away.

The suitcases had been packed in a hurry. Bron had tried to help, but Mr. Blackwater's tapping foot and Mrs. Blackwater's intermittent glance at her watch made him feel useless. He didn't want him to go, after all, and was still processing that he *was* going as he helped Harry to fold his shirts into neat little squares. Harry, who was careless with his folding. Harry, who struggled to meet his gaze and shied away from him whenever he got too near. Bron pulled the misshapen bundles out from the case and began the process again. An attempt at slowing things down in the hope that maybe, just maybe, he'd change his mind. Wouldn't leave. Because it wasn't so bad here, not when they were together. But Harry only hurried the process along, threw things into the bag as he found them, and Bron focused instead on his handling of the little parcels of clothing, how they would make their way from his hands into the suitcase and onto the conveyor belt. Then onto the airplane and over to New York, past customs and into a taxi, until finally they were brought up to Harry's Manhattan apartment. How Harry would find these little bundles on the other side of the world, carefully folded by Bron. Harry would touch them—a tangible connection between their bodies—unpack them into a dresser in a uniformed row, and every time the drawer was opened, he'd be reminded of Bron, the folder, before slipping on a T-shirt and going about his day. Bron's little gift to Harry each and every morning until he'd made his way through them.

"Gotta speed up the folding there, Bron. My parents are waiting."

He couldn't quite believe it: Mrs. Blackwater's pinched and disapproving face, the bleached blond hair tied high into a ponytail. She didn't look anything like what he imagined a mother to be. And Mr. Blackwater, tall and large and Black, in a well-tailored suit and cuff links that glinted brighter than anything Bron had ever seen. They were barely through the front doors before they started pointing out the leaking ceiling, the cracked stairs, the dead rat in one corner, the dimness of the overhead lights that caused strain to their eyes.

"*What sort of establishment is this?*" he remembered Mrs. Blackwater shouting. "*You call this a school?*"

One look at their dorm rooms, and the row of iron beds and mattresses stained with yellow clouds was enough to have him pulled. "*We're leaving this place at once. Harry, go and pack your things. Now.*"

And the thing Harry said to Bron before he left: "*You've got to be stronger, now that I'll be gone. You've gotta be tough.*" He remembered Harry taking him into a hug, how he felt completely like driftwood, like his entire being had been washed away and here his body was to remain, rigid and unmoving. "*Start sticking up for yourself.*"

But what about us? he wanted to say. *What about us?*

"*Please don't leave me here*" is what he said.

"*I have to go, Bron.*"

"*Please, please take me with you. You know what'll happen if you leave me here. I can't be without you.*"

"*Bron, come on, you have to stop this. Not in front of my parents—*"

"*Please, please.*" He remembered grabbing him. By the arm. Pulling into him. Holding him so tightly he couldn't escape. Another hug. Just one more hug.

"*Bron, stop!*" Harry had said, panicked. "*Bron, my parents are coming. You have to get off me. Get off me!*"

"*You're leaving because I kissed you, aren't you? You're leaving because of me?*"

"*Bron, I said shut up!*" Harry pushed him away.

Harry's parents had walked in. "*What are you boys blabbering about? Harry, we've got to go or Daddy's going to be late for his appointment.*"

Bron stood marooned on an island, the raft being pulled from its string without his clinging to safety. Harry who took his eyes off him and looked at his parents, at his suitcase, and then one last glance at him.

"*Don't worry, Mom. I'm ready.*"

"*Is your friend okay?*"

The way their eyes bore into him, like he was wrong, like he was filthy.

"*Yes, he's fine.*"

Harry who shoved the remainder of his things into the suitcase, messing up all Bron's carefully folded clothes as though he didn't exist. Like he was nothing. No look had hurt more than Harry's last look, a quick glance back and a shy little wave that together with "*Bye, Bron*" would be the last he'd see or hear from him.

At some point, he'd fallen asleep. Awoken by Captain's barking down the hall, he raised his head. The alarm clock read three thirty in a reddish glow. His first instinct was to ignore it, but then he heard the quick footsteps that accompanied the bark, and already he was pulling on his dressing gown.

When he opened the door, the knob jammed in his hands. He tried to pull it open, but still it wouldn't budge. Had he been locked in? He felt a sudden rise of panic. Who would've done that? Would it help for him to scream or to bang on the door and demand to be let out? He rattled it again, suddenly sweaty, and beat on the door with his palms. He stepped back when the brass knob twisted of its own accord, and the door swung open. Darcy stood behind it.

"What in God's name are you doing?" he said. "You'll wake the whole house."

"I—I thought I'd been locked in."

"It was the mechanism sticking. It helps to push against the frame when that happens. I'm surprised it hasn't happened before." Darcy shook his head. "Locked in by whom?"

He swallowed. "Nobody."

Darcy grunted before spinning around and continuing left, down the landing and toward the stairs.

"Where are you going?" Bron asked, following behind him.

"Out. I don't have time to talk."

"Are you just going to pawn me off like you do Ada? I think you should find the time to talk, Darcy. There are things that need attention here."

At the bottom of the stairs, Darcy pulled his jacket off the coat stand, quickly shrugged into it. "Whatever do you mean?"

Bron paused on the bottommost step. "Ada needs you—she's not coping," he said. "She's worried—about everything. She thinks you'll send her away to some school."

"And what if I must? I don't see how any of this concerns you."

"How it concerns me? I care for her, Darcy, above other things. And what about me, huh? I depend on your family for money. It's my *job*. Have you ever thought of that? And what about us, what's happened to—"

"Us?" Darcy spat, turning to him. "Bron, do you think for one second I've had time to think about us? There are much bigger things happening here that I need to take care of."

Bron felt this like a punch to his stomach. "What, so you're just going to up and leave?" He felt the swell of anger inside of him. Not this again. Not this. There were always much bigger things, more important things than he. And he felt it, Darcy slipping away between his fingers. What would happen to him then? He'd be left to fend for himself. Again. And Ada, what would happen to her? Would she end up at a place like St. Mary's just as he had done? He couldn't allow it.

When the words slipped out of him, so sharply, it was a surprise even to himself: "Is your daughter not considered a big enough thing in need of care?" His heart jumped in his chest.

Darcy staggered back, his face struck as though it had been slapped. He glanced at the door, then stared at Bron again. At first he looked almost elated, like a weight had been lifted from his shoulders. He stepped forward, climbed the stairs, and reached out for him. "You know? But how?" he asked. Bron remained silent. There was no time to answer. As soon as the question had left Darcy's mouth, his face hardened. "Giovanni?"

"You could've told me. Why all the lies? You left Giovanni for his sister, and thought not to tell me. Fine. Whatever. But Ada—she deserves to know the truth, to hear it from you," he said. He reached out to touch Darcy, a gravitational pull, but whatever it was that drew him forward repelled Darcy away, his jaw flexed, tendons extending his chin sideways. "You are her father, after all."

"I beg you now to stop clutching at things that do not concern you." Darcy pulled open the door, and Bron heard the rain before he saw it, the pelting loud in his ears.

A lightning strike lit Darcy's outline, and Bron slammed the door shut. He could taste blood in his mouth from biting the insides of his cheeks. He rushed back to his room, bounded onto the bed, and clamped a pillow to his chest. Then there was scratching at his door, Captain wanting to be let in. When he was, the dog leaped straight onto his bed and circled his tail before settling himself in the middle of the mattress.

Stupid dog. He couldn't climb back into bed. He stared him down, noticing the silver marks that flecked his coat, the two white patches that spotted above his eyes and into his head like eyebrows. Bron sat in his chair, resting his head in his arms and knocking himself against the desk until he'd calmed his breathing. He knew what needed to be done, and before it could be done to him. Before he was left alone. *I need to leave, get out of here. I won't let this happen again.* But who would put him up? *Where do I go? I can't leave Ada.* Would they ask him to stay if he tried to leave? Ada would, but would Darcy? People left, moved on—it's what they did. Why couldn't he? He'd asked Harry to stay—begged him to—and Harry, what had he done? He'd left him, ignored him for years.

The dog barked, a little sound that made him turn his head. Bleary eyed, he looked at Captain, who stood on his legs and stared at him quizzically. He rose to touch the dog, to scratch his head. Captain sniffed into his open palm and nuzzled his head against his stomach. He kissed his head, an affection he'd never shown an animal before, and rubbed his floppy ears, which made Captain's tongue stick out like the nub of an eraser. "Good boy," he said and scratched some more, the collar rattling against his thin neck as he did. He held it to stop the noise, brushed a finger over the silver tag, a burnished swirl that read "**CAPTAIN**."

He opened his drawer and took out a bundle of letters, the ones he'd stashed at the bottom, beneath a collection of things, and untied the string that secured them. He brushed a light finger over one of the postcards, a picture of white-capped mountains and a Swiss stamp in the corner. Harry's messy scrawl. This had been the last one he'd received, before three of his letters had gone unanswered. And then all the texts. It read:

> Greetings from the Alps!
>
> Having so much fun up here in the mountains. It's always great when Mom and Dad find the time to go skiing. They're still incredibly busy. Dad's phone is always going off—he's practically working through the trip—and Mom's planning all that charity work (which I'm totally bored with hearing about), so I get the log cabin pretty much to myself. Nothing's changed though—they still argue all the time, and I have to pretend I haven't heard. They've even dropped the D word a couple of times recently, which, to be quite honest with you, might do us all some good.
>
> (That's divorce, you sicko!)
>
> I'm sorry to hear that things are hard. But hang in there, Bron. You'll be out of there in no time. I'm sure of it.
>
> Hazz

And that was the last of them. Bron had imagined all sorts of reasons behind the unanswered letters. First, he'd blamed the weather, which had been incredibly windy and overcast those last few months—there were probably tornadoes and hurricanes happening in America—and then the Royal Mail, who could've changed their prices without his knowing it. For his last letter he glued a few extra stamps, just in case. He blamed his school-teachers, who were conspiring against him, hijacking the letters that would have surely arrived. Or perhaps Harry's parents did get a divorce, and the separation had taken its toll on him. Was he okay? Was it time he needed? Yes, that was it. Time. And so he'd given him time. Of course Harry couldn't write to his friend overseas when there was so much going on right there on his doorstep.

But time was not his friend. Harry continued to play on his mind. All smiling and happy and never thinking of him. Bron couldn't name the feeling that constantly seized his chest. Betrayal? For leaving him? For never coming back? No, it was more than that. It was the feeling of years, a culmination of time, seeing not words with every book he read, but only Harry's name, and then hearing only Harry's voice in every character's dialogue, and seeing only his body lingering in the shadows at his bedside. It was the feeling of living every day knowing that at any moment the thought could spark: *Where is he? Why has he left me? I fucked up. I fucked up. I fucked up.* Appearing like a ghost guised in flesh if Bron would let it, the years of practice to silence these thoughts unraveling now, a mechanism breaking.

He thought of his name—Harry, Harry, Harry—and applied the tourniquet, cutting off the phantom before it appeared in the dark. Harry—Harry—Har—Ha—white blurs swirling behind his tight eyelids, and nothing but the sharpness of his jaw as he bit down, down, his teeth grinding and the heaviness of his water-ing eyes to remind him that he was ever there. Still it seeped through, bled into more thoughts, into reasons why Harry had done what he'd done: *You're a loser. You're not good enough. What is wrong with you? He was just being a good person. It was all pretend. He felt it was his duty to look after you, to be your friend.* And these letters were further proof of his being let go. *What were you thinking? You'll always be left behind. Always. Always.*

And he could see it happening again here with Darcy. Darcy, who ebbed like a wave, coming and going, disapproving of him too. Criticizing everything and everyone, always keeping his distance from his family and now, again, from him. He'd been tricked into believing that Darcy was some romantic hero, someone he could rely on, but instead he'd been keeping secrets from him—from everyone—the entire time. What had he to hide now? What could be more important than his family at this time? There was something much darker happening in the house, and Bron would not be blind to it. Harry had already taken over his life. He would not let the same happen again with Darcy. He needed to know the truth before leaving.

He pulled together the true facts he had, starting with what Ada had told him: that Darcy had been, according to her witness, the last person to leave the library. *"He was so angry,"* she'd said. What *was* it that had caused him to react this way? *The photo album* . . . Ada said he'd walked away with the photo album.

Suddenly, there it was. The step he'd force himself to take. He needed to see the evidence for himself. Tangible evidence: a material record or relic that would reveal the truth and shatter his fantasies of who he thought Darcy to be. No more flights of fancy, no more tendency to make things up in his head or pretend that people needed him when they didn't. That they wanted him. What he wanted to see was proof, actual proof of Darcy's marriage. Of the wrong he had done Giovanni and to his own daughter. The answers were there in the photo album. And he was determined to see them for himself.

16

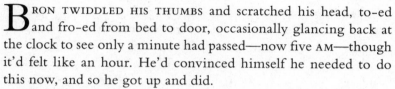

Bron TWIDDLED HIS THUMBS and scratched his head, to-ed and fro-ed from bed to door, occasionally glancing back at the clock to see only a minute had passed—now five AM—though it'd felt like an hour. He'd convinced himself he needed to do this now, and so he got up and did.

He peered through the keyhole to ensure Ada was still asleep, and passed through the gallery without turning on any of the lights. He could navigate parts of the house blindfolded. How might it seem to be caught in Darcy's bedroom? His nerves, always visible on his face, would give him away. He could spin something to satisfy Ada's interrogations if she were to catch him, tell her that he was sleepwalking and found himself there. It was Clarence, always walking about the house, and popping up in unexpected places, who'd be more trouble to him.

He pulled on the door handle at the end of the way and caught his breath. It was heavier than he'd expected—locked. But there was a key left in the hole, which unlocked with an easy twist. He wedged open the door and closed it softly behind him.

He felt the wrongness of his trespassing, like a smog in the air he would choke on. The room itself was large: the entrance was spacious, carpeted, and mostly bare, excluding the great ebony cabinet tucked into the side. On the left was another door, which, when propped open, led to an en-suite bathroom, modern in its glossy white, with a floor-to-ceiling shower in the corner. The sink's wide basin flecked with the clippings of Darcy's dark stubble. Water marks stained the silver tap and the mirror that hung above it. He brushed a finger over the shelf that held Darcy's toothbrush, his moisturizer, the expensive-looking perfume bottle with its brownish liquid and golden cap that took the shape of what looked like a rhinoceros.

He went up a step into the main area of the bedroom, where the carpet cut off to wooden flooring and the wall curved to the fitted window seat; a freestanding bathtub with silver legs was centered beneath the oriel window overlooking the gardens and fields. So silent was the room that, even barefoot, each step sounded like a stomp. To the left, the four-poster bed had one side of its curtains closed. He caught his breath, mistaking the unmade bed and discarded pillows for a body, at first Darcy's, then a corpse, lying still behind the crimson drapes. On the floor beside the bed, and half tucked behind another wardrobe, was a large portrait, an oil painting of a man who resembled Mr. Edwards but whose face was slimmer, with harsher features and brooding brown eyes. As Bron passed and opened the doors and drawers to things in search of clues, the eyes followed him about, as much a presence as any knowing ghost would be.

He found them quickly on the bookcase: two great leather-bound volumes at the end of a row of orange Penguin Paperback Classics. He plucked them off the shelf and relieved the weight in his hands by dropping them onto the bedspread. He flicked one open to pictures he'd seen before—of Darcy as a baby, Mr. and Mrs. Edwards, the photographs of Darcy and Giovanni at the riverside. He leafed to the end, but it was all more of the same: family photographs, holiday, snapshots, Darcy and Giovanni, and then Darcy as a child again. He swapped it for the second volume, skimming through the scenic photographs of mountains and seascapes, a place that looked like Rome. Then, just like that, he stopped skimming.

There was no denying that Toni Vespa made a beautiful bride, standing as she did upon the stone steps leading up to the manor. Her white train ran the length of the stairs that spilled down to the gardens; her neck was erect and tilted, and her manicured hands clasped a bouquet of flowers. She appeared at once camera shy and yet destined to appear before it. Bron couldn't see any bump; if she was pregnant, it didn't show. A second photograph had her standing with a straight-necked and much thinner Mr. Edwards, pulling at his collar, lips tipped upward into an almost forced-looking smile as he held her arm in his. Another photograph of bride and father-in-law, and then Mr. Edwards and Darcy. The two men stood beside each other like two polished columns, identical in their choice of formal wear, though where Darcy wore a neckerchief, Mr. Edwards wore a tie; where one had chosen a gray top hat, the other wore it black. Finally, one of the bride and groom: both man and woman beautiful in their own right, a couple who contrasted with and yet complemented each other so well. Anyone who looked at them would immediately recognize the suitability, the inevitability, of their pairing.

But what about Ada? Had she come across this photograph when flicking through these pages? Was she old enough to understand the true meaning of what was being captured? That would mean she knew about Darcy being married, and that he was her father. No, she couldn't know. He looked at them again. To a less comprehensive eye, Darcy could have been just anyone standing beside this bride. A friend of the family. He felt a prick, then, a tugging at his heart. For bride and groom looked not at each other, but into the lens with lifeless eyes. They stood apart, appearing as though the photograph had captured the in-between moment of the photographer directing the proxemics of his models. Bron examined the slight extension of Darcy's arm toward the outskirt of the composition, animating the image into life. He couldn't quite explain it, the way Darcy's hand reached out for something outside the edge of the frame, his pinkie stuck in an inconspicuous movement. Was it a twinge of the wrist? Or something more?

Was he reaching out for someone else? And then, on the next page, the photograph Ada had described to him.

Here was a photograph of a woman propped up by pillows in a hospital gown, hair matted, eyes sunken, a woman who held onto her baby. Toni looked different from the woman she was today, more youthful and glowing. A different nose altogether, much like Ada's nose. She smiled into the camera.

A&A, newborn, 2:15 pm, 7.6 lbs

And then, in a picture right beside it, one of Mr. Edwards holding the same little bundle in his arms and another of Giovanni holding the baby, and finally several of Ada with Mr. Edwards in the living room, in the garden. Older and older as he turned the pages. Bron might have sifted through for longer if something hadn't fallen out of the book and into his lap. A brown envelope, the seal to which had already been broken, and a letter, dated this year, which read as follows:

My dearest son,

If you are reading this, my words are coming to you from beyond the grave. You always maintained my theatrical ways to be somewhat vexing, and this is my last chance of being so. I hope you'll oblige me and that this letter causes as little pain to you as possible.

I won't dwell upon the words we said to one another in the past, nor can I take back the horrendous things that left my own mouth when I learned about everything that happened. We all made so many mistakes. You must forgive the choices I made in writing you out of your inheritance, and furthermore the gravely mistaken encouragement I gave by forcing you and Toni into a marriage that didn't bring either of you happiness. But it all felt right, at the time, to ensure mother's and daughter's futures were taken care of. You must understand that, like you, Toni was barely an adult herself, and there was a time I couldn't trust in you to commit to your responsibilities as you ought.

When you left us all those years ago, it was such a difficult thing to live through. Suddenly, I lost my son—my most wonderful boy—and just as suddenly I was a father again, to the beautiful girl you left behind.

It was my biggest fear that I would never see or hear from you again, and suddenly I had an infant on my hands, mere years after losing your mother, a grief I was still battling through. How could I cope, a father again and wifeless?

I wished so much for your return, and when I saw you on my doorstep, it was not only shock I felt, but utter disbelief. There are a number of things I should have said to you, back then, and even now. But that day haunts me still. You, approaching me and apologizing for all the wrong you had done . . . Son, it was I who should have asked for your forgiveness. I who should have been there for you, supported you, and understood your needs. I couldn't understand your pain. I shouldn't have criticized your mistakes—we are all guilty of them, and for our broken intimacy I take responsibility. I am your father, and it is my job to do right by you no matter what. And I failed in that. So as my parting words to you, I wish to impart the best advice I can, which I hope you'll take in good faith.

The first thing I wish to say is that to be a grandfather is gift enough. To be more than a grandfather to our little Ada has been one of the most rewarding and invaluable gifts of my life. She is a gem, son, and I beg you give her the attention she deserves. Darcy, that little girl is in need of a friend, a companion, a father—not just another book to race through, and in boarding school she will crumble. She will not be sent there, that is my strictest demand. You know how much I love her, and my only wish now is that you share with her the truth of her parentage. She should not be kept in the dark.

Now I will not pretend that learning you were a gay man didn't come as quite the shock—but I should not have reacted the way I did when Giovanni told me what he did, and the way it all happened. Perhaps if your dear mother had stayed with us longer, she might have realized sooner, provided the comfort that I couldn't in the way only she knew how. And I have seen firsthand what the loss of your intimacy with Giovanni has done—to him, to us as a family, to you whenever he walks into the room.

Darcy, your right to love the one you love is more important than ever. I am sorry for my part in allowing you to grow up thinking you couldn't be anyone but the person you were supposed to be. The loving man I know you are. The only thing you can do now is reconcile your differences, move forward as the best version of yourself, and be true to who you are. Giovanni has been there for me through these trying times, as a friend and as a shoulder to lean on; please put your differences aside. I am sure in time you can put things right.

Now—I can't proclaim to having known how well engaging our dear Bron into the household would suit us. Not only has he brought the best out in Ada, but on you he has worked his magic. Bron is here for you as much as he is for Ada, and to you I hope he brings some aspect of yourself that I know you have struggled to share with the rest of us. And I must say that I, too, have worked some kind of matchmaking magic, because watching the signs of your growing closeness has made me sure of what had only been, till this point of writing, mere suspicions. (Clarence and I have found it very entertaining peeking at you two through the curtains. I finally understand Mrs. Hanson's thrill for such twitching by the window.) From the moment of my interviewing him I knew he would suit us all. Bron has somehow brought you back to me, the boy you always were. Don't keep yourself locked away for anybody's sake. I am proud of you, no matter what. The best thing you can do in this world is to be kind and to love. I love you, my son. I will always look out for you, even from afar.

Your father

Bron gave himself a minute to digest the contents of the letter, then searched the inside of the envelope again, for it was full of yet more paper. Another letter? Before him lay what he understood to be an original copy of the last will and testament of Mr. Richard Edwards, which on inspection specified that Mr. Roger Branson, of Branson & Briggs, acting as executor of the will on behalf of the Testator, Mr. Richard Edwards of Greenwood

Manor, in the county of Cambridgeshire, and witnessed by Ms. Mathilde Clarence of 5 Elderberry Place, and Theobald Hanson, of 2 Greenwood Way, detailed the leaving of all possessions and monies in the care of Ms. Antoinette Maria Vespa, as beneficiary, to be held in trust until Ada Cecilia Victoria Edwards should come of age, dated and signed.

"What?" Bron said aloud, despite understanding it perfectly well. It was here, clear as anything: Mr. Edwards had written his son out of his will. Darcy had been left with nothing. They were equals now. There was another document of similar likeness within the envelope, a second copy of a second will, but this one dated and signed more recently. He moved to scan the particulars, but then there was a noise, sudden movement at the door.

His first instinct was to climb behind the curtains and throw himself out the window. To hide under the sheets. There was no time for it. He quickly shut the album, flinging the sheets of paper into its pages, and threw everything back onto the shelf.

He heard the footsteps stop in their tracks.

"Ada," Darcy said, an angry lilt to his voice. But then, something resembling kindness, melodic, a singing of his words. The door opened and shut behind him. "Is that you?" The ceiling light flickered on. Darcy stood in the doorframe, hovering between the inside and the outside, committing to neither. "You know you shouldn't be in here, oh—" He staggered back when turning into the room. "Bron? What are you doing?"

He was standing at the edge of his bed, waiting to disappear. "N-nothing."

Darcy searched his face for an answer. He reached out to him. "Bron?"

"I can explain."

"Explain?" Darcy said, confused, but a harshness soon inflected his voice again. His words slurred. "Explain what? Are you okay? What is there to explain?"

Bron felt there to be a wildness about him, a fiendishness that made Bron back up into a corner when Darcy moved closer. Suddenly he stood as an entirely different person, his physiognomy altered: rolling eyes, a tense face. Bron could smell the acrid waft of alcohol, not so much on his breath but on his clothes, his hair, everywhere. Cigarette smoke clinging alongside it and clogging up the room. He was missing a button on his collar.

Words didn't come to him, and the closer Darcy pressed, the farther Bron sank into the corner. Darcy extended his arms to either side of his face, fists to the walls. "Well?" he repeated, the smell of him pungent, reaching out to grip Bron's shoulders, collapsing into him. Faces smacking together. Darcy kissed him, his lips, his cheeks, his eyelids, biting at his neck. He pulled at Bron's hands, forced them into the gaps between the buttons of his shirt, ordered him to undo them. The heat coming off him, the alcohol-laden sweat, repelled Bron.

"I want you, Bron," Darcy slurred. "God, I want you right now."

Bron turned his face away, the roughness of Darcy's stubble scraping against his cheeks. "You're drunk." He pushed the bigger man away, a feeble shove with his hands. There was a part of him that didn't want Darcy to stop, but at the thrust he did so immediately, drawing away and wiping his mouth with his sleeve. His shirt undone, his chest heaving, the hair shaved down to stubble.

"You don't want me anymore," he said, grinding his teeth. Sniffed to survey the floor, searching for something in the dark. "Is that it?" His voice rose up the tonal scale as he repeated: "You don't want me anymore."

Bron relaxed his shoulders. Darcy's gestures loosened. *No, no,* Bron wanted to say, because he did—he did want him. "Don't say that."

"Why not?" Darcy shouted, muffling tears. "Now that I've given in to you, I'm no longer of use? I can see it in your eyes, your fear."

Darcy groaned and fell to his knees, his shoulders heaving little convulsions that grew more violent as he cried. Bron thought he was retching, the sounds coming from his throat. He was wailing now. Creating a moment between them they couldn't take back, which for all the years to come would lay claim to them. Bron let him cry, keeping one eye on the door. He could leave now, and that would be the end of it. He could be the one with agency. Be the one to come back when he was ready. Or he could stay, hold up a mirror to this man, and force him to reveal everything to him.

"How could he do this to us?" Darcy said at last, his voice hoarse, broken. His breath staggered. "Not tell me anything. He was preparing me for this—see, don't you see? I'm his prodigal fucking son. All this time I thought he wanted me close by, fearful of my leaving again, and yet he was preparing me. Warning me. I just never saw it."

"What are you talking about?"

"Haven't you guessed it already, going about my things? The will—he knew he was dying. All this time, he knew."

The will. Bron focused on that. On the importance of that.

"The will?" Bron said, and when he didn't get any explanation. "Darcy?"

"He—he had me written out of it—his own son. For so long I resented him leaving everything to Ada, trusting Toni with it, but all these months he's been trying to fix what had been broken between us."

Bron couldn't understand any of it. He repeated what he knew. "Your father, he left everything to Ada—to Toni?"

"Yes, yes," Darcy sobbed. "I treated my father t-terribly, and Ada too. I can't be a father. I'm a monster."

Bron took a step back, his legs trembling. Darcy looked up, his gaze fixed on him, and wiped his eyes, his nose, on his sleeve.

"Why do you shrink away from me like that?" He settled his breathing, rose tall again when he stood. "Please, I know I have made mistakes."

Darcy written out of the will. Ada finding something in the photo album she shouldn't have. The fire. The locket. All these things swirled around in his head.

"Why are you silent, Bron? Talk to me."

The air was whipped from his lungs. Accusations lay on the tip of his tongue. But nothing made any sense. Did the pieces fit together? Photo album. Fire. Locket. Death.

"I—I cannot," he said.

The seconds ticked by, suspended in air, a moment that would never end. But this was what it had come to, so where was the answer? Mr. Edwards had kept the will in the photo album. The photo album that lived in the library. Darcy had already known he'd lost everything. So what did it matter to him? Had Darcy started the fire? But why—what had he to gain? To get rid of the evidence of the will? But here it was now. And the locket with Ada's name . . .

What did it all mean?

"You aren't going to leave me too, Bron, are you?"

Bron took a step back. "I must go—"

"You are going?" A whimper emanated from Darcy's throat. "I will tell you everything. Everything—I swear it. No more secrets. If you'll just stay." He took his arm and held it taut. "I couldn't tell you the truth about Ada, I just couldn't. And then the fire . . ."

Bron swallowed the lump that was hard in his throat. "What about the fire?"

Darcy took a moment to scrutinize his face, then released his tight hold on him to knock him twice on the head. "What's going on in that head of yours? Nothing good, I'm sure of it."

"You're scaring me," Bron said.

"That is why you recoil? What is it you think I've done?"

"The fire," Bron repeated.

"In the library?" He jabbed his fingers at Bron's chest, a curl of his lips.

Was Darcy here admitting it to him, that he had done it?

"Ada saw you leave the room. She saw how angry you were and told me what she'd seen. Pictures of Toni." Darcy's eyes flicked to the bookshelf behind him. "Ada thinks it was she who set the room on fire, thinks she left a candle burning as she ran out. But . . ."

"But?" Darcy's face changed as understanding hit him. "Oh, but you think *I* did it? Have you solved it, Sherlock?"

And then something unlocked in Bron's mind. Something which seemed to slot everything into place.

"It was *you*. Ada—your locket—"

"My locket?" he said, more seriously, without derision.

"The one that Clarence gave you, the one you handed to me. You thought it was Ada's but it couldn't have been. She still has hers; she wears it around her neck." Darcy's eyes settled, latching on to every word. "And then she told me you had one of the exact same likeness. And it . . . it had a ring inside, with Ada's name on it. It didn't make any sense to me at the time. But of course you'd keep it, you're her . . . her father," he choked out.

Darcy nodded his head, letting his words sink in. "Bron, you suspect me in this plot of yours? What else have I done? Go on—tell me."

Something still didn't make sense, of course. The motive. What of the motive.

"The will . . ."

"Aha—there it is! You see an inheritance, and our life becomes an Agatha Christie novel! Tell me, what do you think you know about the bloody will?" Darcy's voice was a guttural snarl.

"I know that you are a poor man, that you have nothing."

Darcy nodded along with Bron's revelations. "And so I am guilty of what? Arson? But then what of these papers?" Darcy stumbled over to the bookshelf, where he pulled the album off the shelf. He dropped it to the floor, scooped up the pages that escaped. The will, the proof of Darcy's lack of inheritance. "Why would I burn the library, supposedly to dispose of the evidence, but *remove* that very evidence from the room prior to setting the fire?"

Bron stumbled. "I don't know . . ."

Darcy pressed on. "And what of the lawyers' copies, the will filed away online for safekeeping? This is the twenty-first century, Bron—there are safeguards for these things."

Nerves weighed heavy on Bron's belly. He had nothing left to say.

Darcy moved suddenly to the writing desk, pulled out a drawer in such a fit that it came away from the mechanism in his hands. He slammed it on the desk, a loud bang, and the bottom gave upward. Darcy picked at it, tossed the wooden layer aside. Below it was another small box. A box which Darcy brought out, shoved into Bron's hands.

"Go on, Poirot, open it."

"What's this?"

"Now," he ordered.

Bron lifted the lid, which opened with a little pressure. Inside it was a locket. A locket resembling the one Ada wore around her neck. The one Bron had stashed in his own bedroom.

"I don't understand." He looked up at him.

Darcy snatched it from his hands, clicked the sides to open it, and placed a ring into his hands. "Look," he said, and when he did he saw the letter inscribed there: D.

"You are quite the tale teller, Bron, and me? Taunting and sardonic. In your story I have claimed the character of villain. I do not live up to my name, but I suppose neither do you. I pray you never take on the role of writer, for there are several holes in this plot of yours. Let's start with the fire, which seems to me the originator of these fantasies—well, we know it might have been a fault with the electricity, although I suspect it to have been Ada's carelessness, and I, blinded in my rage at her snooping, was the fool who left the candle burning. Now the lockets, you see? They carry our wedding rings. Mine and Toni's."

"But there are . . . three?"

"Ada wears her mother's ring—she's had it ever since she was born. It has an *A* on it, does it not? *A* for Antoinette. This one here that I have placed in your hands is my own. And finally, the one you have yet to place in your plot? Well, it must be Toni's."

But how could it be Toni's? And as though Darcy could read the question in his eyes—

"Toni had one made for herself as a token, in remembrance of the daughter she had given up. It has Ada's name imprinted there, does it not?"

Everything crumbled before him—his thoughts, his accusations. Shame hung over him like a cloud. It was Toni's locket?

"That can't be true. Why would it have been in the house? And on that night?"

"What had you down as my movement prior to meeting you in the library? Was I plotting, indeed? Waiting for our guests to leave so that I could set the place on fire? Christ, Bron. It was Gio and Toni who so provoked me. Why I was in such a foul spirit. The both of them, and Father—they all thought it was time to tell Ada the truth, now that I was home. But I just couldn't. Maybe Toni left it in the library for Ada to find, in the hope she'd start to ask questions—I don't know."

Bron shook his head. Everything was unraveling. He'd been led by ghouls and plots and running thoughts. Darcy had made a mockery of him.

He wished the Edwardses had just told him—and everybody else—the truth. "But Mr. Edwards, how did he die?"

"Cancer, so they tell me. He was suffering for a long time. He hid it well."

Darcy looked at him with a penetrating gaze. What must Bron have looked like then? Eyes rimmed and wet, his throat tense; a flailing creature who brought his hands to his face and wished to evaporate. To disappear. He couldn't look at Darcy.

Darcy's fingers were coarse as he pulled Bron's hands away from his face, gripped him by the chin, and forced him to face him. *I'm sorry.* The words spiraled around in his head. *I'm so, so sorry. I'm so foolish, I—*

Darcy wound his arms around him, crushing him into an embrace. Two flat tree trunks, bending together, but not quite fitting. Darcy kissed him again, a slow, soft kiss that felt strange after the hardness of before. Bron kissed him back, more ferociously, still needing him and yet still repelled by him. But he knew the gulf between them was larger than the small distance that opened up between their bodies as Darcy pulled away. He would have grabbed for him if there hadn't been a small knock on the door, then Ada's quiet voice on the other side of it.

"Darcy? Are you awake? I heard a noise."

Darcy pivoted toward the door. "Go back to bed at once, Ada," he commanded. "I will come to you in a moment." He turned back to Bron. "You are a strange thing, Brontë Ellis. Your follies may get you into trouble one day. I must go, as you now know, to my daughter. We will talk about this properly later."

Bron's heart would have ripped in two if he'd spoken another word. They shared a companionable silence before Darcy turned out of the room, leaving him there in the dark. He could chase after him, throw open the door and call out his name, beg again for his understanding. But he felt fully the separation from this man, even from this house.

This house. He felt it so assuredly now that he couldn't understand why he hadn't seen it before: it hadn't been built for someone like him, the vastness of its rooms begging to be filled with all sorts of visions and apparitions, where he had allowed himself to believe, to conjure up something sinister. This house that allowed his already existing follies to manifest themselves more fruitfully into serious delusions. Where he'd sunk further into the reliance of books and movies. *This will happen, and then this will happen . . . and then this . . .* again and again and again, reading and watching like a menace, cementing his experiences.

Every time dependable. Every time knowing the route the story would take. His questions answered.

But Greenwood was a house, just a house. It didn't symbolize anything. It wasn't the set piece to a multimillion-dollar film, hired out for actors and a camera crew to shoot in. It didn't harbor ghosts or feature as the backdrop to his own bildungsroman.

Who was he, standing there rooted to the spot and holding in his need to cry? Was he the same Bron he'd been a few minutes ago, or someone else entirely? He was no longer Lily James, reciting words that, at a stumble, could be repeated for as many takes as it would to get right; he wasn't Keira Knightley, one moment a scandalous lover, the next Elizabeth Bennett. He was someone without an anchor, without a story.

All he could think was: *What should I do? What should I do now?* And the answer, he knew, was clear: *I should go—I need to leave.* Because his infatuation had reached a breaking point, and he knew Darcy would never look at him the same way again. This was his mistake with Harry, repeating itself all over again. Soon Darcy and Greenwood would all be a distant memory, something he would cling to and yearn for and no longer be a part of. He couldn't—wouldn't—have his heart broken again. If it was to be broken, it would be at his own hand. He would be the one to do it. Take himself out of the story he'd created here. The one who got to leave this time. So he did what needed to be done.

It wasn't to be the grand, covert escape in the middle of the night that unrealities depicted it to be. He went slowly into his bedroom, meeting Clarence along the way. She had just come in to start the day. Accepting the gentle hand she left on his shoulder, he thanked her and locked his bedroom door once he'd reached it. He pulled the little kettle from its nook, clicking it on to boil. The whirring noise brought some comfort. He waited for the chamomile tea to brew. This would warm him from the inside. He packed his bag, the essentials of his things, readying himself for the long day ahead. There was no point arguing against it. It was time for him to leave.

PART IV

17

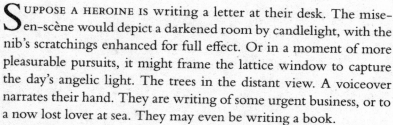

Suppose a heroine is writing a letter at their desk. The mise-en-scène would depict a darkened room by candlelight, with the nib's scratchings enhanced for full effect. Or in a moment of more pleasurable pursuits, it might frame the lattice window to capture the day's angelic light. The trees in the distant view. A voiceover narrates their hand. They are writing of some urgent business, or to a now lost lover at sea. They may even be writing a book.

But Bron is not at his writing desk, for the room isn't large enough to contain one.

He is propped up on a single bed, the rungs of its metal frame digging into his shoulder. He writes not for any specific reason; it is only that he finds the process of writing cleansing, an unlocking that allows his thoughts to freely flow.

Now he finds himself here. He is content with the room as it is, and grateful to Mrs. Flanders for welcoming him in. He hasn't told her much, only that his living situation had turned suddenly sour, and he could no longer stay with the Edwardses. That he needed to get out that very morning.

"And the little one, she is okay?"

"She is okay," he'd said.

She'd ushered him and his bags into the narrow hallway, pulled him into a hug when he broke down in tears. Offered him

a cup of tea, demanded he make himself at home. Took him up
the stairs and into a room. This used to be Ellie's room, she said,
but now she mostly refers to it as the "blue room," adequately
named after its sky-blue walls lined with damask silver wallpaper merging into dusty, royal-blue carpet. The carpet is fraying,
reveals floorboards at the edges, and the wallpaper peels away, is
splotched yellow in places, but Bron's possessions make the room
feel more comfortable and lived in, more like his lodgings used to
be at St. Mary's. He has stuck one of Ada's drawings of him to the
wall beside his bed and has laid out some clothes on the surface
of a trunk.

When he is called down for tea, he steps onto the landing
with its semicircular table affixed to the wall, a crocheted white
tablecloth and a porcelain figure upon it, and moves down the
stairs with shoes in his hands. He asks, "What am I to do with
these, Mrs. Flanders?" holding out a pair of red heels. She meets
him with a puzzled look, claiming to have never seen them before
in her life, and asks him to leave them exactly where he has found
them—that is, tucked away under the left side of the bed. He
places them away into the cupboard instead, underneath a green
parka jacket that also isn't his. All the while he is thinking about
the life that once lived in this room, and the lives of fictitious
characters that take up residence in his head.

For they have bloomed there ever since his earlier years, when
at first he begged his aunt for answers, some to do with matters
of his origins, if his parents loved him, and later, how they died;
and then again questions he asked at school, simply about the way
the world worked. He was always met with a suffocating silence
and learned to discover facts for himself, how to make up his
own mind—the Big Bang versus God's seven-day creation; Sur-
vival of the Fittest versus Man in God's image—or else remain in
the dark. In the in-between space of novels he found solace, his
own boarding school life reflected in one particular work. He'd
followed their trajectories with a prophetic eagerness, the works
of great writers a crystal ball through which his own future was

revealed, with its big country houses and the always brooding men. England and its green. Then came the movies, and his visual senses attuned to them, a strong receptor that blended life with stylized sequences, embedded fiction into memory.

Somewhere down the line he took things too far, twisted facts at liberty, a self-created delusion. With each circumstance that he'd fixed upon—the fire, the locket, the will—these props were there to guide him. No, not guide—mislead and bend him—into an already established framework. He remembered how he felt when first stepping into the manor, how the house, though large, was not foreboding. How his infatuation with what was to play out through his stay could be traced to the influence of Miss Charlotte Brontë, and maybe even Jane Austen too. Countless novels and movies overindulged in. Netflix, and its readily available content, there to throw him into some modern-day Regency or Victoriana at the click of a button, so easy was it to focus the eye upon the screen, and then again at the rooms below him. Slip on the headphones, enact the mundanity of everyday activities to a piano composition by Vlad and Capponi, all the while closing his eyes to reality.

Of course England is still green, and things happen as they happen, but away from a certain setting, on the other side of Greenwood, he reevaluates his persona. The void he had filled in himself is still a void, only it had been plastered over with paper and celluloid.

When he *really* looks back, he finds no queer love, no queer cross-dressers, no representation at all that makes it out alive or unscathed. Maybe he was never meant to see himself in these stories. And still in the world of today he is vilified. Still he is a point of contention. The way of the world then, the way of the world now: it is the same. Of similar shape. He stands at the margins.

Two weeks into his stay, he is sitting at the coffee table and mulling over an unfinished puzzle with Mrs. Flanders. He hears the clang of the letter box, a whisper of a thud in the hallway, and watches through the window as the postman rolls away with his cart. He takes a sip of his tea and rises to collect the mail when Mrs. Flanders stirs. He insists she stay seated; he can get it. Four white envelopes and a takeaway leaflet wait for him at the base of the door. He reads The Dragon City's Chinese menu and salivates over the picture-perfect dishes that adorn it, then hands over the remaining papers to their recipient.

"Tonight might be the night for that sweet and sour you've been wanting," he says, waving the leaflet in the air. "My treat." He has very little money left but will dip into his savings. It is the least he can do. Mrs. Flanders hasn't taken a penny off him for room and board.

"This is one for you dear," she says, leaning out to hand over one of the larger envelopes.

"For me?" He turns it over in his hands, sees at once the crest on the wax seal, the small scrawl of his name above the address, written at the top left. "Would you excuse me for a moment?"

He takes the stairs up to his room and rushes to break the seal. Unfurling the folded pages, he pursues the written words with a sudden shortness of breath. Here it is, the sheet of creamy letter paper, penned in that very small hand he instantly recognizes. He sits on the bed, clutches at a pillow to moor himself, and slowly, with his heartbeat pulsing in his throat, begins to take it in:

Bron,

I appreciate that the facts you've learned will have come as quite a shock. The first fact being that I was wed to Ms. Antoinette Vespa, a circumstance that has caused great distress to me and many in my life. The second, that the little girl you have been teaching is in fact my daughter. It has been my desire to hide this from the world, as well as many other things. You and I agree on one thing at least: I would make a terrible father.

As you know, Giovanni and I were lovers—if a total giving of one's self to another can be considered love. It was messy, dangerous, in that way that love can sometimes go, and we'll never truly put it behind us. There are some people in our lives who will never leave us, despite how hard we try.

The truth, as you know, is that I left him. I couldn't face being out to my friends and peers, and when he started telling people about us, and the interrogations started, I just had to end it. I was afraid of what everyone thought of me. But still I continued to do wrong. Somehow I found myself in a secret affair with Antoinette in an attempt to prove to the world that I could be what it wanted. Then she fell suddenly pregnant. We were so young—she in her second year at Newnham, and Giovanni and I on the cusp of graduating. It was the worst thing that could've happened to either of us. Suddenly I had wronged them both, and yet neither knew of my dealings with the other.

When Giovanni found out about Toni, he spilled every last secret there was to spill. My father was repulsed by everything I'd done, and Giovanni demanded I stay away from both him and his sister, and why wouldn't he? Antoinette wanted nothing to do with me either. Nor did she plan on keeping the baby. An abortion wasn't an option for her, but she also wouldn't parent alone. She would go back to Italy and place the baby up for adoption there. Why should one mistake stop her from getting an education, have her lose her career? She had dreams of being an actress, and I suppose she has fulfilled those dreams. But my father wanted nothing more than to be in that child's life, and convinced her that the right thing to do was not only to keep the baby in the family but to allow him to bring that child up as his own. The child would be well provided for and deeply, deeply loved. He also felt it right that she secure her own future, and that the best way for that to happen was for Antoinette and me to be lawfully bound in matrimony. So we agreed to a marriage neither of us wanted, one destined to be loveless.

I tried my best to do the right thing. But at times it all got to be too much. I felt a stranger in my own home and that my life was going nowhere. I dropped out of university without graduating and fled to wherever it was I could. France, Germany, Morocco,

America—anywhere but England. This was a double-edged sword. During this time I saw the world and things I never thought I'd see, but still I was sickened by the things I'd done to have led me there, and I was lonelier than ever.

When Ada was born, Father begged me to come back. Believed she deserved one of her parents in her life. I, stubborn to the core, stayed away. His disapproval only heightened over time, and he wrote me out of my inheritance. Then one day I returned, hoping—but not knowing how—to care for the daughter I once abandoned.

What I have recently come to learn is that in the years following the early diagnosis of his terminal illness, my father chose to rewrite his will to secure my future once again. The copy you had seen in the album by my bedside is outdated, signed in the years I had left after Ada's birth.

And another fact I should disclose to you, Bron. I told you that Antoinette and I were divorced, but by that I meant that we have lived our separate lives. I apologize here for my deceit. Now that my father has secured her with a comfortable sum of money, we have come to the shared conclusion that a divorce would indeed best suit us all. But we will never truly be separated from one another. We have also told Ada the truth of her parentage. This is what Giovanni, Toni, Father and I have been discussing over the last few months, and though it has pained me having them around, it was all ultimately for the best. As I am sure you are wondering, she is taking it as well as you'd expect of her, with a multitude of questions. She is always asking after you.

This, Bron, is as much as I can admit to you. I hope you will understand my motives up to now were not merely to be secretive to you, nor to push you away, but those of an undeserving father struggling with how to best admit to and live through the wrongs he has caused his family.

I hope you will think of me with less derision. I cannot lie and say that I didn't feel hurt by your poorly plotted accusations, but I am sorry to have made a mockery of you if it played a hand in your decision to leave. You were ignorant of everything concerning our family setup, and it is only now that I can bring myself to reveal the truth behind it. I will continue to insist you think twice before accusing someone of committing a crime, but it is your charm and flights of fancy that so draw me to you, and I would not change you for the world. There is a spark in you that makes me feel things I haven't felt in years.

Do come back to us when you are ready. We miss you very much. Ada wants her governess back. But above all, she misses her friend.

Yours faithfully, and ever true (that I promise, from this moment on),

Darcy

P.S. Please find enclosed herein the remainder of your wages, and a gift left to you by my father in his last will and testament. Do with it what you will. It shall not disappoint.

Attached to the letter is a check addressed to Bron, a check of a considerable amount of money, enough to rent a room for years, and more besides.

He spends several days with the letter tucked under his pillow, trying to read between the lines of what is there and what is not. He thinks about Giovanni and his broken heart, about Ada and her mother, about Toni's decision to entrust her child with the father of a man who had wronged her. He thinks about Darcy's path to committing so many wrongs, wrongs that harden so many people along the way and cause so much destruction in their wake.

Still, he doesn't understand what really happened between them all. There are gaps in his knowledge, in the unfolding of events. But as part of his commitment to being less of a dreamer, and realizing he is tired, he stops. Puts it to rest. This isn't his story to tell, nor his mystery to solve. Things are as they are, they happen as they happen, and one can only move on when given the chance. *Do better.* Mr. Edwards used the last years of his life trying to rectify his wrongs. To do right by his son and understand who he really was. For no matter who

Darcy said his father used to be, Mr. Edwards was to Bron an entirely different man, a man who welcomed him, embraced people's differences.

He thinks then of his keeper, who has not been as successful at rectifying wrongs—a woman changed by the loss of her child, who is wanting of forgiveness but who hasn't been given the chance to ask for it. Some questions may very well remain unanswered, but the last of his meddling is finally looking to be fruitful.

He receives an email from an admissions coordinator at the University of Oxford and is forwarded to Keble College's alumni office, who explain that because of General Data Protection Regulation they are unable to share any personal data or information about any of their former students. However, attached to the email is a link that shares archived material of former year groups, should it be of use, and he finds Keble College's graduating class. He trawls through the names to find the one he is looking for, but still there is no sign of anything more. He uses other students' names to search for any mutuals, any other lead onto which he can jump. Combing through their friends' lists and sliding into their DMs, he explains his reasons for reaching out.

At some point, he receives a reply that says,

> Yeah, I know Ellie.

With messages sent back and forth and contact details shared, he has finally reached the person he has hoped to. An inspiring conversation ensues, one that ends with:

> Thx for reaching out, Bron. Let me think on it? I need some time to digest.

Bron has the sudden urge to add another text message to Harry's blank profile, to the wall of blue messages he has crafted over years. What if, on that day in Cambridge, it really had been Harry he'd seen?

> Hey. I know this is a long shot, but I think I might have seen you the other day?? Outside King's College. It was really weird. But I could've sworn it was you.

And somehow, by some miracle, after a lethargic week of inactivity, his phone buzzes. It had been left on his bed; he is downstairs with Mrs. Flanders, losing a game of Connect Four. When he comes up to his bedroom, he finds that the blank profile is no longer blank. His last message signals "Read" and he is, for a long while, stunned. Crying. The wall of text is miraculously broken by a single reply:

> OMG! How random. Yes, it was probably me?.

He is sitting inside a café off the King's Parade, his eye flitting between the large glass window and the door. To his left, the window allows him a view of the busy weekend bustle: King's College ahead of him, the cyclists whizzing past, the tourists with their shopping bags, and the students doing who knows what they do with their free-from-their-studies Saturdays. There is a woman doing tai chi in the street.

He has scrubbed himself well: figuratively, in the sense that his nails have been buffed, his face serumed; literally, in the way he has loofahed away all the dead skin through his hot shower, and perhaps a layer or more so than that too. He fidgets with the bell sleeves of his blouse, tucks a stray hair behind his ear, and sips at the tea that's been freshly brewed, though it is a little stronger than he usually takes it, glancing down at his phone screen, the message that simply reads,

See you at 1 pm!

But he has been waiting here for thirty minutes, having arrived twenty minutes early. The breath catches in his throat and he is thinking, again, *I'm such an idiot. He's not coming.* He catches a glimpse of himself in the window; the way his hair is tied gives him an elfin appearance, and he scans the streetwalkers' faces as they stroll past, smiles at a few of them. One even smiles back. He feels the nerves of his being seen.

And then he sees him, bobbing along with a backpack slung on one shoulder and headphones slipping from his ears and down to his neck. He turns his head to follow, but hears the ring of the café's door opening, and rights his head again, sits up straighter. He fiddles with his thumbs and stares down at the table before glancing up again. He feels the heat at his side like a pressure.

"Hey, is that you, Bron?"

"Hi," is about all he can manage. It gets stuck in his throat, and he thinks about standing up for a hug, but the backpack is dropped and the chair opposite scraped back, so he stays where he is, a table islanding between them. "It's really me."

Harry is taller than when he'd last seen him, though no higher than six feet, and fuller too. In the cheeks, but also in the way his muscle sculpts his clothes. He is wearing a hoodie, casual jogging bottoms, and Converse sneakers. Bron suddenly feels himself overdressed, like he has made too much effort with his appearance.

"Dang, dude, I almost wouldn't recognize you. You look . . . amazing." Harry is smiling at him, from ear to ear, and Bron can't help but smile back.

"Thank you."

"Oh shit, sorry. I didn't mean to say—I just assumed—do you prefer—"

"It's fine. Don't worry about it. It's nice to see you, Harry."

And it is. For all those sleepless nights at school thinking of Harry and how he'd been forgotten, for all those times he cried himself to sleep and screamed his name in his dreams, shrieking, *Harry! Harry! How could you have left me here alone? You promised me. You promised!* Seeing him now has its own sort of pleasure, tinged with nerves, irrevocably—but still pleasant, like a mass has been lifted off his lungs, allowing him to finally breathe, inhale in the subtlety of the Earl Grey's bergamot. Really taste its flowery perfume.

"It's nice to see you too! How long has it been? Three, maybe four—"

"Five years," Bron corrects. "And a bit."

"Wow. That long, huh?"

"That long," he says. "So, I see you finally made it to Cambridge?"

"Yeah, I'm reading computer science. Turns out it's not so bad here after all. And you! What a small world. Don't tell me you're a student here too?"

"No, I'm not. But I'd like to be." Bron sits forward in his chair, takes another sip of tea. "I'm actually thinking of applying again."

"Good luck . . . It's just so good to see you. I can't quite believe it."

"It's not like I didn't try to make contact." *I wrote to you, every day I wrote to you. Every spare moment I had.*

"Hey, do you want anything to drink?"

Bron shakes his head no, gestures to his tea, but Harry signals for the waitress anyway, orders a lemonade and slice of cake, whatever she recommends. The waitress smiles, says the red velvet cake is very good, and hurries away when another table signals for the bill.

"Why did you, then? Ignore all my messages, my letters."

Harry can't quite meet his eye. Is distracted by a sugar packet on the table. "Yeah, I'm sorry about that."

"It's like you'd died or something. And now the sudden response?"

"I like to stay offline as much as I can."

Bron raised his eyebrows, said with his face, *"You, the tech whiz?"* which only made Harry smile.

"Okay, okay. Maybe I was avoiding you *just* a little. But then I saw it and thought what the heck! Though I did have a look through some of the messages we used to send before coming here, and God, I don't know how you put up with me."

He is unsure how to take this. "Put up with you? You were a big part of my life."

"I know. You were of mine too. Obviously. But when I left St. Mary's I thought . . . I thought it probably best to avoid contact with everyone there. Have you heard O'Brian has got a kid now?"

"I wouldn't know." He hadn't stayed in touch with any of the boys there, though he'd looked up Bertie Barrett's social's a couple of times a year. But he wouldn't let Harry steer them away from the subject. "So you thought it best to just . . . disappear?"

Harry shrugs it off. "Pretty much." And Bron is bothered by this level of indifference. Hopes without faith that his companion has mastered the art of deflection.

The waitress returns to bring Harry his lemonade, which he sips at once, and a thick wedge of red velvet. He digs instantly into it.

"I always thought it was much deeper than that, that I'd done something wrong and that you hated me for some reason. That when I—" It's on the tip of his tongue. He doesn't want to say it, but he cannot avoid it any longer. "That when I kissed you, you hated me. That I violated you in some way. I don't know."

Harry continues chewing his cake. "Yeah." He swallows, focusing down on his plate and looking at anywhere but at him. "You did seem to really like me, huh?"

"I did. And I thought—I know it sounds silly, but I thought you did too. That you wanted me to kiss you."

Harry lets the pause swell into something uncomfortable. But Bron is determined to wait it out, to demand an answer.

"Maybe I did, I don't know . . . You were pretty full on sometimes, ya know. It was so hard to be with you in a way that wouldn't hurt you. And I guess I didn't know what would or wouldn't have happened between us until it did. And then I left, and I thought pulling away would be easier than telling you the truth. I knew you were all alone there, and I guess I just felt bad."

Bron nods to Harry's words, but still there is something left unsaid. "Tell me what truth?"

"That I didn't feel the same way for you as you did for me." There is another pause between them. Several of them, broken by sips of tea, lemonade, and a bite of cake. Harry looks out the window at a girl taking a selfie outside the College. He swipes a finger to his mouth, then folds his hands neatly on the table. "I think I wanted it to be that way with you, and of course I was still in denial about so many things . . . about who I was. But it just wasn't like that between us, and it was just hard for me to admit that to you," says Harry.

"I wish you'd just told me."

"I know. And I should have. But it was so hard. You made it so hard. I felt responsible somehow. Everything you'd say, the way you were around me—it was like you were seeing things through some rose-tinted lens, that I was some big hero in one of your silly stories that I just couldn't live up to. I never would have. You lived your life like it was some kind of movie."

It's not as though these words don't sting, but Bron wants Harry to understand one thing, and one thing only. "You were my best friend. That's all."

"I know. But that's not how it always felt, and I didn't want to hurt you."

He lets it all sink in. He doesn't know how his expression reads, but he hopes to cover at least some of the hurt. Harry offers him a reassuring smile, and he forces himself to offer one back.

"Well, thank you for telling me now."

"S'alright," he says, clocking the waitress to order another lemonade.

Bron wants to hear more from his friend, wants to know who he is as an adult, and all the things that happened in the intervening years. He anchors onto what he thinks he knows. "So you have a boyfriend now?"

"Oh, well . . ." Harry reaches up to scratch at his back. There is a definite grin about his face. Something of a blush. "Just some guy I'm seeing. We aren't official or anything. How did you know?"

He explains what he saw from the side street. The two of them. It feels uncomfortable to say *kissing*.

"Oh yeah . . ."

"And how did you two meet?"

"We're at Corpus together," he says simply.

Bron recognizes the similitude in all of this. How Harry is experiencing the very thing Bron so pined for with him at school. "So when did you know you were . . . like, when did you realize . . ."

"I guess I still don't, in a way. I identify as bi, but I'm never really sure what term to use. I'm just attracted to whoever I'm attracted to. I'm trying to be less definitive about it all and more someone who just goes with the flow."

"And your parents? They took it well? Or do they not know?"

"Yeah, yeah, they know. They took it swimmingly, actually. Dad's my biggest supporter, which was a surprise to, like, everyone."

"That's wonderful," Bron said, and meant it.

"Yeah, I guess I'm lucky, but what are you up to nowadays? Tell me about you."

He tells him. He tells him about Greenwood, about Ada who he's come to love like a sister and of Mr. Edwards's sudden loss. He tells him about Darcy ("Wait, Darcy? As in the *Pride and Prejudice* guy? How random!") and how he's come to have feelings for this man, only to have gone and fucked it up, leaving out the particular details of what he'd said and done. About how he left so suddenly and that he was currently living with an old woman who'd agreed to put him up. He wouldn't overstay his welcome.

"Sounds pretty tough, but not without its good points. This Darcy fella, he sounds like a pretty good thing? I'm sure things will sort themselves out between you. You just gotta give it time."

Time. Yes, he would give it time. He would give himself time. Time to create moments to look back on and see them for what they really are. Time to explore the things he has heard other people talk about, but never seen for himself.

At some point through their conversation, Bron realizes he's slouching. He's relaxed around Harry. That their hands reach out for each other when Bron lobs out a joke, and soon Harry is loading up pictures of O'Brian holding his baby on his motorbike, of O'Brian's girlfriend, who fancies herself an influencer and makeup artist.

He's enjoying the rekindled camaraderie and is hopeful they'll stay in touch after this. Maybe we can hang out again sometime soon?

"That'd be fab! I'm traveling Asia for a few weeks through the summer, but maybe we could link up when I'm back?"

Bron says yes, he'd like that very much; he's convinced they might consider themselves friends again soon enough. Who knows . . .

"So what are your plans over the summer? What's next for you?" Harry asks.

And Bron isn't entirely sure what comes next, but he thinks broadening his horizons might be one place to start. "I'm actually planning to travel myself."

A week after the check has cleared, he sees the figure in his online account, and he feels rich. He thanks Mrs. Flanders for her generous hospitality but announces that he will be leaving her soon.

"Are you sure? You don't have to. Wherever will you go?"

"Thank you, Mrs. Flanders, but I cannot stay here forever. I think I should like to see some places. Travel abroad!"

"Abroad?" she said. "Where to?"

"France, maybe Rome? America? A friend's given me a few tips on where to go and where to stay. I think I should like to see it all for myself, learn what it means to be out there in the real world. To drink coffee on a promenade or eat patisserie on the cobbled stones of Paris. To experience life."

"America," she said. "That's where Ellie went."

Before he leaves, he purchases her an iPad and sets her up with a social media account. He takes a photo of her on the HD camera and sets it as her profile picture. At first, he is her only contact, and he promises to stay in touch through his travels. But soon the requests come flooding in: from her childhood friends in Ghana, from cousins and aunties and their children, and soon she discovers a request from a certain someone that has her in floods of tears.

18

WHERE BETTER PLACE TO become enlightened than Italy?
His flight lands in Fiumicino, and he rides the train
into Termini station, where the Roman streets are plastered in
graffiti and the buildings and ruins crumble around him. The
sky is cloudless, the sun hot, and he takes a taxi to the boutique
B&B with its three-star rating in Trastevere. He checks into his
room overlooking the Tiber River, where he eats complementary
citrus fruit at breakfast and fills a vase with long-stemmed lilies,
which he buys from a market stall one street along.

Riding the tram to the Colosseum is easy, and he walks north
past the Foro Romano and throws a coin into the Trevi Fountain. He eats cacio e pepe for lunch in a restaurant with red paper
tablecloths on Piazza Navona, followed by real limoncello gelato
from one of the ice-cream parlors, before trudging on to Vatican
City. Here the dome of St. Peter's looms mightily, but the Castel
St. Angelo pales in comparison. For days the Eternal City is his
world; he discovers things he didn't know were there, like the
poet John Keats's gravestone in the Cimitero Acattolico, where-
upon it is written: *"Here lies One Whose Name was writ in Water"*;
Percy Shelley's too, though later that night he reads that although
Shelley died in Italy, his heart lay out in Dorset, in the St. Peter's
Churchyard, alongside his wife, Mary.

In an instant his time in Rome is over, and he is back at Termini station at six thirty AM, waiting for the notice board to tell him the platform for his Venice-bound train. He spends only one week here and is expecting something of a fishy smell and sewage. In reality, it is an otherworldly place of winding streets and narrow bridges, of shops selling designer clothing, expensive jewelry, carnival masks, and postcards with cats on them. He buys a tiramisu cannoli despite the taste of coffee, and walks through the Renaissance architecture, the colonnades which remind him, for a moment, of Trinity. From the expansive square he scrutinizes the gold zodiac signs in St. Mark's clock tower in Piazza San Marco. He enjoys watching the boats as they cruise along the seascape, but hates how many tourists clog up the spaces, and he one of them. From Venice he flies on to Prague, where he walks the Charles Bridge up to the castle and plods along the Old Town to hear the chime of the Astronomical Clock Tower at night. He is disappointed not to snag a ticket to the Klementinum library before moving onto Berlin, which on the whole he finds uninspiring. Too much of a modern city, though with lots of people he reads as queer in the edgiest sense.

Exhausted from his travels, he takes a day for himself, to do nothing. Lying naked in crisp white sheets, he has food delivered to the door from an app on his phone, and is glued to another app which has him connecting with male strangers. He changes his bio to "alone and palely loitering," which gains him little interest. One man, Luca, only half a mile away, sends him a headless torso and asks him for pics, then persuades him to meet up that Friday night. He agrees, though it is his penultimate night here, and three cocktails later, a band is tied to his wrist, gaining him entry into a grotty club where he snorts cocaine for the first time in his life—just because it's there and he's under the influence of alcohol—and says no to giving this man a hand job in one of the bathroom stalls. In the morning he finds he has been blocked on the app. *When in Rome*, he asserts to himself, though he still feels disgusting and sad, as though it is he who has done something wrong. He sobers up, remembers he's in Germany.

In Bruges he pursues more innocent affairs. He sees the blood of Christ at the Basilica of the Holy Blood, a Romanesque building tucked away in the corner of the square in the heart of the city, beside a restaurant and a chocolatier (from which he purchases a hot chocolate and then two waffles from an outside food truck). If he hadn't been looking out for it, he would have missed it completely, so indistinct it was to the surrounding buildings. He enters through the triple archway, where, he's read online, the relic will be shown to the public every Friday before and after mass. Visitors gather beneath the pulpit, and from the left chamber the priest ascends holding a glass cylinder, crowned on either side with jeweled coronets, which is said to hold a cloth with the blood of Jesus Christ. The priest places it down for all to see and it looks, to Bron, like a glorified perfume bottle. Not at all worth the wait. He buys himself another waffle. Finally, he lands back into Heathrow Airport, where after a three-hour layover he begins his greatest venture and longest flight yet.

And in truth, America is everything he's imagined it to be and more.

In New York City he witnesses more homelessness than he'd ever thought possible. He gives a man some spare change and fills his own backpack with sandwiches from a 7-Eleven, which he distributes out as he walks the city. When he asks for a bottle of water from a stand outside the Empire State Building, the server struggles to understand him. "Water," he says. "Waw-tuh." He tries again in an American accent, and his purchase is successful.

He comes to the place where it all began, where a brick was thrown by two trans women of color in the West Village, and is proud to see this part of history. He is bumped into by a sinewy man who, on impact, flings his plastic bag onto the pavement. Bron hears the glass shatter and apologizes profusely outside the inn.

"That was my wife's anniversary present, goddamn it," the man says. "It cost me twenty bucks."

Bron immediately fishes out his wallet and offers him twenty dollars for replacement wine.

"Best make it forty for the inconvenience," the man says, and when Bron hands over forty, the man snatches the wallet from his hand, having seen the wad of notes, and runs off, calling him a faggot. Bron crosses the street and hurries in the opposite direction, increasing the distance between them. He didn't expect to be called that here—not in the Big Apple, New York City, where dreams are made. It is almost a mile away on the corner of the street that he understands there'd been no spillage, no liquid puddle emanating from the bag. Just the broken glass of an empty bottle. The remaining hours of his day are dampened, and he returns to his hotel room and shelves today's misfortune in the corner of his mind under "Life Lessons." This is why he is here, after all. To experience more of the world, however terrible it might be. To learn.

The next morning he gets lost in Central Park for hours, finds the Flatiron Building, which Harry said he ought to see, and revisits the streets all through lower Manhattan until he stumbles onto the Staten Island Ferry, which is free to use, only to turn right back around. Passing the Statue of Liberty by boat, he thinks what a sight it must have been for those who'd left their homes across the ocean and traveled for weeks to get here. What a sight.

His phone pings in his pocket. When he pulls it out, the screen alerts him to a message from Ndidi Flanders, with an attachment sent as a message. He opens up the snapshot: she is beaming with joy in her cramped, cluttered living room, and there is a woman beside her who is also smiling, and leaning out with one arm to capture the two-person selfie. Ellie is sitting on the side of the sofa in the place Bron would have normally sat. They are wrapped in a light embrace.

He sees the three dots wriggling away beneath the image, which indicate she is typing.

Thank u xxx

His heart lurches in his chest, and now he is smiling too. He is thinking, *What a sight, what a sight.* And then thinks something more: that there are things in the world worth living for, taking risks for, and there are things in the world that aren't. This is still what he is thinking when he exits the revolving doors of his hotel on his last day here and says goodbye to the concierge, stepping out into New York—where the sun is baking the street's many bags of garbage, and the air is blaring with car horns—on his way to Los Angeles, his final destination.

The end of his travels has come upon him fast, but he is ready to return to England a more well-rounded person. Or so he'd like to think. Sitting on the beach at Santa Monica Pier, he is secure in his location, in this populated place at the edge of the city, where the Ferris wheel shines neon blue and dyes the dark sea purple; the night sky is sharp with the smell of the ocean and potential. Here the whole of the world surrounds him.

What he knows about America is no longer what he imagined of Harry's life, the smell of him at school, or what he's heard from Darcy's time in the California hills. This is America to him: the open expanse of nature, the city sprawl in the palm of his hand, the bending of the marsh plants in the wind and a place where green trees engulf him and all birds sing. New York had given him a sense of the real, buzzing world, and when he walked the streets of Manhattan and Brooklyn, he was a different person altogether. More confident in the way he moved, the stomp of his foot. Might even take to wearing higher heels. But he was also more fearful, of the invisibility that city life brings, of the dangers that surround us all. But either way, more of life.

He now believes what Darcy told him about America to be true: there is so much more possibility outside the realms of England. But he also acknowledges a feeling that Darcy did not express, a connection he knows Darcy will have missed.

At Santa Monica, at the edge of the world, he feels something nostalgic, something outside himself. The palm trees surrounding him are California trees—that much remains true. And yet when he closes his eyes, the wind is English wind. He looks up at the pier, the peaks of the wheel, the knowing crests of the Hollywood hills a taxi ride away. Those hilly paths of Hollywood are the same as those of the Yorkshire Moors or the surrounding fields of Cambridgeshire. The dip of his toes in the water is all at once the flow of the Pacific on the shores of Venice Beach and the oared-through waters of the River Cam.

At the edge of one ocean, he closes his eyes, hears Darcy's voice whistling on the wind, through the reeds of the marshes. He can feel Darcy across the stretch of water and sends kisses through the air, hums notes of song and speaks words of endearment, knowing that the breeze will take them across the world and back to Greenwood Manor, where he hopes Darcy is waiting for him.

At Heathrow he carries his suitcase through the maze of aisles to the underground and onto the Piccadilly line, where he swaps off at King's Cross Station for the next departing train to Cambridge. For the first half of his train journey, he is typing away on his laptop, flitting between tabs where he is fixing sentences, deleting typos, and uploading attachments to a website's interface. When it signals that his application to the University of Cambridge has been successfully sent, he shuts the lid, crosses his fingers, and thinks, *Maybe third time lucky?* He is also thinking through ways in which he can turn an old hobby into a successful side hustle, by building an online store where he could sell T-shirts and mugs with phrases like "Queer Literari" or puns like "I am queer, no box ensnares me." So far, he likes this idea. Then he turns his attention to the dust-speckled window, through which he sees the world for what it is.

The hedges are in leaf, and he is surrounded by English countryside; there lies the parish spire, the monopoly-sized houses, and the old village. He sees an isolated manor house and a lake, and over there a chestnut tree that looks miniature from such a distance, but he imagines a woman walking past it: Jane Eyre, carrying her letter all the way to Hay, or Keira Knightley as Lizzie

Bennet, and the effective way she could walk and read simultaneously. The cows are eating the meadow flowers, and the lambs are bleating and leaping on the lea. Speeding over a viaduct and through a tunnel, the fields and farmland disappear into thickening foliage and crumbling walls, emerging to bleak high-rise buildings, scaffolding, and cranes. The factories are camouflaged blue, gray, white, disappearing into the fading sky as though they were never there. And he feels, with a jolt, a homesickness for what is no longer here and probably never was. This sceptered isle, this pleasant land, has come a lengthy way.

But looking beyond the past at the here and now, he thinks that maybe, just maybe, England is not such a terrible place after all. He doesn't know how he will feel next year or what turmoil may come to rid him of this sense of calm. But today he is at ease. Because clambering through the wooden gate, he approaches another expanse of green, sets down his bags.

He is unsurprised to find Darcy there, who, clad in cricket whites, is crouching in a way that flatters his physique, especially his behind. He is about to throw a ball to his daughter, who is gripping her bat and practicing her swing on a sunny afternoon in September. The gray dog, who is remarkably sitting idle at their side, has his eye marked on the ball, but barks at Bron's approach.

The little girl drops her bat and screams, runs to him, and jumps into his open arms. The dog is frantic now and barking. Bron squeezes her tightly and admits how much he's missed her. She pulls away and says how glad she is to see him, how very glad.

Yanking at his hand she leads him onward to a man who has lifted the discarded bat from the grass, holds it to his chest. He is looking toward them, smiling, and shielding his eyes from the sun.

ACKNOWLEDGMENTS

THE ACT OF WRITING is solitary, but nothing is written in seclusion. The words strung together to form sentences to form paragraphs to form scenes to form chapters to form this book, is an amalgamation of many influences; the books, movies and songs I have consumed over the years and made into my entire personality at one point or another; the cities I have lived in; the joyful and painful conversations I have had with ex-lovers / those who I hoped would, maybe, be interested in me. It is more often than one might think in this day and age that I've had to defend myself as someone who outwardly expresses themself in ways that fit outside the gender binary. And it is these moments that I wanted to give voice to, through a character who knows themself so fully, and who I hope sparkles with confidence even when wading through the doubt.

And like my character Bron, scraps of moments from the Bronte sisters, Austen, Forster, Woolf and more have seeped into me and the person I am today. When I least expect it, and sometimes when I probe, these influences shape a turn of phrase; guide my sense of fashion; my taste in home decor. The seed which was to become *The Manor House Governess* came to me not simply as an idea or a scene, but as an accrual of things: of moments threaded together, characters from one influence talking to those in another. And how did my queer identity mesh with these Classics? Well, *The Manor House Governess* is my attempt at answering this very question, and I am indebted to the influences that have inspired me along the way, and hope my own "adaptation" will in turn inspire another.

But the book as a product is the result of many efforts, not only from those who write them, but those who champion them, edit them, design them, market and sell them, etc. And stories stay alive, ultimately, by those who are willing to give them their time. So thank you, first and foremost, to you, dear reader. I appreciate you.

Thank you to my agent, Caroline Eisenmann, who championed Bron's story from the beginning and got me through the door; you made this all possible. Thank you also to Abi Fellows and Callen Martin, for helping Bron to find a home in the place I call home. Thank you, endlessly, to Jess Verdi, who understood exactly what I wanted to do with this book, and who helped me achieve it in the best possible way. And to Clem Flanagan, for championing Bron's story in the UK. Bron and I are lucky to have you both! To everyone at Alcove Press and Black and White; to Madeline, Rebecca, Dulce, Melissa, Doug, Thai, Stephanie, Matthew, Campbell, Ali, Thomas, Tonje, Rachel, Hannah, Abigail—some of you I have never met, and yet I know how much effort you have put into the making of this book. Thank you, thank you, thank you. Also my thanks to Jaya Miceli, for the gorgeous US cover design, and Sarah Whittaker, for the equally stunning UK cover.

To those nearest and dearest: to mum and dad for your unwavering (and sometimes borderline obsessive) support, and specifically to mum, for watching movies with me as a child and introducing all the governesses I'd come to cherish: Jane Eyre, Maria von Trapp, Anna Leonownens, et al. To Dan, just because. To Fiona Castelletti-Adams, for taking me in when it mattered the most; your selflessness made possible the path that has become my life. I wouldn't be here without you. To Tiny, for reading this book so many times in its earliest iteration. You're the best. To Lily Shahmoon, the most perfect friend, and Suzie Shahmoon, for coming to my rescue more than once—I will never forget it. To Aisha, for helping me wade through all the doubt in the early days of submission. To Nicole, for your unwavering loyalty, and Rita, for being my biggest fan for absolutely no reason whatsoever. To Sonia Graham, for your openness, support, and photography along the way. To Max Edwards, for continuing to help me even when you didn't have to, and for providing me with a game Ada and Mr. Edwards could play—(oh, and for the surname. A coincidence, I promise . . . maybe!) To Tiff Lai, for creating such gorgeous illustrations for the US edition! They are, simply, breathtaking. To Professor Sonia Massai, Professor John David Rhodes, Dr Sarah Lewis, Sarah Crofton—and all my teachers along the way, I couldn't possibly name you all—thank you for inspiring and leaving your mark on me. Lastly, to Christopher Waters, for loving me as I am, and for taking on more than your fair share of housework to allow me time to write these stories that sustain me. I appreciate you, and more.